Cryptic Spaces

Book One:

Foresight

Deen Ferrell

Curio Creative

American Fork, UT   USA

Cryptic Spaces
Book One: Foresight
by Deen Ferrell

First Printing – May 2013
ISBN: 978-1-60047-864-2
Library of Congress Control Number: 2013938392

Printed in the U.S.A.

0   1   2   3   4   5   6   7

As with most journeys, there are many I wish to thank for their invaluable help along the way. From English teachers who told me words were my friends, to parents who, while they may not have always understood my need to write, were always there to support and encourage, I have been richly blessed. My wife was my springboard and steadying rock. My children listened, read, gave suggestions, and put up with endless hours of writing and rewriting, always cheering me on. Without the on-going support of my brother and creative partner, Jon, this book would never have been possible. My agent, Whitney Lee (Fielding Agency), was my first advocate to the publishing world at large. My editor, Sherry Wilson, became a professional partner and a friend. Numerous other friends and family took the time to read, edit, give suggestions, and share encouragement. Each, in their way, added a piece of themselves to the work, making the story richer. I offer to all a sincere thanks.

FRIDAY, OCTOBER 19th: Sydney Senoya, one of the finest concert violinists in the world, lit up the London stage last night with an eclectic mix of haunting music and theatrical bravado. Verging on cult status, the young virtuoso left a spellbound audience in Paris for a midnight flight to Heathrow Airport. After a short morning's rest, she was on the move again, winding her way to a sold-out performance at the London Palladium. Hidden behind the tinted windows of a black hearse, she reportedly ignored the frenzied crowd, who followed her to the Palladium steps chanting "Sydney! Sydney! Sydney!" A dozen or so hooded monks waited at the base of the steps in silence.

The monks surrounded the hearse as it slowed. They held the passenger door open, forcing the crowd back with gently swaying incense burners. Miss Senoya emerged sporting a stunning maroon and black evening gown. The crowd erupted. She let her shimmering cloak fall back and smiled as the burly monks whisked her away. In one hand she held an odd, wooden staff. In the other, she cradled her precious *Stradivarius*.

Once inside the concert hall, the mood changed to one of intense anticipation. Sydney strode purposefully down the main aisle, her concentration riveted on the stage. Within inches of the orchestra pit, she spun, facing the packed house with eyes crackling. One thing was perfectly clear— this girl enjoys keeping her fans off balance. A hush fell over the audience. With calm, deliberate gestures, Sydney unclasped her cloak, pushed back her silver hood, and twirled the garment like a matador, letting it flutter to the floor. She shook loose her silken hair, raised the wooden staff high above her head, and slammed it down. The hall plunged into blackness. Drums rang out. Copper braziers to either side of the stage burst into flame. A ghostly, uneven light grew, finding Sydney poised, staring out from center stage. The whites of a dozen eyes flicked in the dimness around her. She stooped to place her staff on a low, polished pedestal, raised her *Stradivarius*, and cried in perfect Gaelic, "Sisters! We take the night!"

In a flurry of movement, her violin began to sing. The bow strings seemed almost possessed. Music, the likes of which this reviewer has never heard, crashed over the audience like a tidal wave. The violin cried like a bird, then called like a wolf, sending dancing sprites scattering like a cloud of locusts. Sydney commanded the stage, her shining hair a river of black amid the twitter of fluttering fairy wings. Pools of white light filtered like moonlight onto the meticulously crafted set. The dark forest was alive with creatures of night and beings of pure imagination. The young prodigy wove a melody that seemed to question the raw mystery of nature itself.

The audience barely breathed, stunned by the spectacle.

Outside, remnants of the earlier crowd jockeyed for position. They fought for glimpses inside the dark windows of Sydney's hearse. Rumor has it that the tinted windows hide skeletal remains—human remains dating to the early 16th century. Two young hikers are said to have located the bones in a cave near the township of Oban, Scotland. They brought them to the attention of the town mayor. No sooner had the find hit the press than Ms. Senoya was in contact with Oban. She bought the bones, along with an ancient wooden staff and a rusted gold chain, also found in the cave. The sum was purportedly large enough to set the town mayor dancing a Scottish jig.

What next, Ms. Senoya? Will gold doubloons mark the magic of your Dublin debut?

1

Frozen in Time

Winter trees, framed against cold glass, hold more than emptiness in their dark-fingered branches. They hold precise geometry—angles not always easy to calculate or to see. Willoughby Von Brahmer liked observing the trees, rooted in lonely clumps along the boulevard. Looking from each branch to its reflection in the wide-paned windows of local shops kept him thinking.

His interest was not in the branches. It was in the spaces between them. Empty spaces, you see, fascinated him. You can't study empty space by just staring at it. You have to observe the details around the space. You observe the footprint of its reflection. You study the visible edges that frame it. Supposed emptiness has substance even if it can't be seen clearly. It has weight, even if its heaviness is felt only within the depths of the soul. He sniffed, walking on more crisply. He did not accept the existence of real emptiness. Every supposedly empty space had to hold something. It was merely a matter of discovering what this *something* was.

Pursing his lips, he scanned the street. Something was different about the day. He couldn't put his finger on it exactly. The closest he could come to describing how he felt was to say that something or someone was watching him. Watching him from where? The street was empty.

He stopped, turning slowly with a nervous eye.

Was something watching from the emptiness?

He began down the sidewalk again, almost at a run. The street he was following was known by the locals as the Sixteenth Street Corridor. It was an odd street, busy at some parts of the day and quiet at others. He could easily imagine early mornings on the corridor beginning with the tap-tap-tapping of joggers. Soon, a sprinkle of shopkeepers mixed in, each protecting a private coffee steam, or a bagel bagged in the crook of a clenched arm. An hour or so later, the first of the nameless pedestrians appeared. Some came in search of the grand buildings, such as the Foundry Methodist Church, host to U.S. Presidents like Abraham Lincoln, Rutherford Hayes, and more recently, Bill Clinton, and the infamous Ford's Theater on 10th street, the very theater where Lincoln was shot. Others came for the eclectic shops.

Willoughby had interest in one particular shop. It rested on a corner. It had a single large window and an angled, green door, which these days stood resolute and quiet against the deepening blues of an October sky. Printed in gold letters across the large front window were the words, *"Antonio's Corner Barber."* He loved to hear the rhythm in the words as they rolled off the tongue.

The shop proprietor, one Antonio Santanos Eldoro Chavez, was no mere acquaintance. This tall, unusual man, who seemed so well suited to the Corridor, was Willoughby's personal barber and friend. His voice was heavily accented and words flowed from him in a constant, almost unbroken stream, punctuated only by the snip, snip of his scissors.

"See how the shop anchors the intersection of Sixteenth Street and Gales?" he asked Willoughby when they had last met. "Sixteen is a lucky number, I tell you. Think, too, on the name *Gales*. Does it not remind you of the great sea winds ancient mariners would ride to discover adventure, love, and good fortune?" He had given Willoughby a sly wink. "You turn sixteen in only a few months, my friend. Perhaps it is time to think of unfurling your own sails. You are about to embark on the greatest adventure of all time—the discovery of who you are, and what is your place in this most humble world."

What was his place in the world? Willoughby had no clue.

He breezed past Delia's Book Emporium, where "Cupcakes and Crumpets" still held the coveted front window spot and gave a quick glance at The Merry Mystic. Its curtained window sported a slow-blinking neon sign that flashed, "*Open*," and a weather-worn slate with chalked words that read, "*To unlock your heart, I need only to hold your hand*." Tucked around a shallow alcove, a wooden sign in the shape of bent salami proclaimed, "*Wiengart's Meats: We make a leaner Wiener!*"

Willoughby crossed the intersection to Antonio's shop. He stopped in front of the door, turning to look behind him. Once again, he had that feeling—that someone was watching. A tingle began at the back of his neck. It wasn't uncommon for the corridor to have moments of quiet, but *this* quiet? It wasn't even five o'clock and the sidewalks were vacant. There wasn't a soul in sight in either direction. It felt like the world had become suddenly abandoned, and he, alone, had been left to watch the heartbeat of traffic lights as they pulsed in slow progression, first red, then green, then yellow.

He was about to turn back to the door when something caused him to stop. His eye had caught a brief glimmer. He stared. At the corner of Antonio's large window, he could swear that he saw a glowing string of numbers. For the briefest of moments, it appeared as if the numbers were running along the upper edge of the shop window. *Were they forming equations?* One blink and the numbers were gone. Had they really been there at all— flaring in a ghostly glow out of mid-air? Had he imagined it? He stared at the large window for a long time. When the numbers did not reappear, he turned back to the door, spun the brass knob, and pushed the door open.

A brief wind scuttled dry leaves along the sidewalk. Before stepping into the shop, Willoughby let his eyes drift up to the flat stone that hung directly over the barbershop door. They locked on a sequence of markings across the stone. Antonio called it his "calling card." He seemed quite proud of the symbol. Carved into a slab of rough limestone, it had been the first thing to attract Willoughby to the shop. Now, there was the glowing numbers at the edge of the window. Had they been a reflection from some other shop?

He shook his head and stepped into the shop, making sure to jangle the service bell. He always jangled the service bell, but his wiry barber friend seldom noticed. As usual, the man's eyes were riveted to the pages of an old *Architectural Digest* magazine. Willoughby stood, twitching the bell in the doorway. His eyebrows projected impatience. When there was still no response, he cleared his throat. At this, the man looked up.

"Saints and Angels!" he declared, dropping the magazine to the floor. "You are a man who has come on time!" He swung up out of the barber chair and slapped its cracked leather. "Heavens forbid that I should impede the process of teen vanity—please!" He held out an arm as if to steady a teetering toddler.

Willoughby rolled his eyes, staying well clear of the arm. "Yeah, teen vanity that keeps you in business. By the way, I'm always on time. Not that it does me any good, because *you* usually have your nose in a magazine. If you glanced at that oh-so-fancy Rolex Mariner I bought you last year, you would see that, as usual, I'm *exactly* on time. It is precisely 4:45 pm. I pride myself on punctuality."

"Ah," Antonio shrugged, glancing at his watch. "It's good you pride yourself on something!" He spoke in a heavy Hispanic accent. "This copy of a Rolex keeps very good time. A real Rolex, of course, would be far too generous a gift for so humble a barber as me! We have discussed this before."

Willoughby sighed. "Whatever," he mumbled. He bit back a frown and dropped his backpack. Antonio had been more than happy to take the watch when he had given it as a Christmas gift, but now, he seemed embarrassed by it. His friend knew that money was no issue. Why did he have to act this way? Glancing down at the magazine still on the floor, Willoughby decided to let the issue go. Understanding people was not a particular specialty of his.

"So where was the great barber-architect wandering tonight?"

Antonio followed his gaze to the magazine. His face lit up. "India! Tonight I was exploring the Coco Palace Resort in Rawai to be exact. Ah, you should have been there! It had beautiful curling tipped gables with distinctive Asian highlights. The guest rooms, adorned with fall foliage, elephant heads, and Bombay-style wood highlights are accented by the most unique triangular windows. The place is absolutely magnificent!"

"You're sure of that?"

Antonio paused to take a breath. "No, of course not. I just said that to waste my breath." He surveyed Willoughby's wild hair. "You ask me to brave this Medusa of matted curls?" He turned Willoughby's head this way, and then that. "You are a cruel man, Master Willoughby!" With a sudden spin, the tall barber stepped back and slapped the leather of his barber chair; "but, my friend, I am up to the challenge tonight! As Mr. Holmes would say, the game is not to cut a foot!"

"I don't think that's what Mr. Holmes said," Willoughby countered, picking up the dropped magazine with a grin. He handed it to Antonio, who simply tossed it toward a small stack of similar magazines on the counter behind the chair.

"Well, he might have," Antonio mused, "if he was a barber and the hair on your toes is as matted as the hair on your head."

"You cut toe hairs?" Willoughby gave a mock gag.

"No," Antonio sighed. "I do not cut toe hairs. I was only speaking hypothetically."

"Okay, so, hypothetically, do you cut nose hairs?"

"Yes—hypothetically. It would depend on the state of the nose. And where is this leading?"

"Some old men even have long hairs sticking out of their ears—hypothetically, of course."

"This may be true. You seem to know a lot about hypothetical hairs."

Willoughby threw down his backpack and slid into the chair. "From now on," he mumbled, "I think I want you using a new pair of scissors each time you cut my hair."

Antonio barked a laugh. "And, hypothetically, you will pay for all these new scissors?" The barber twirled a crisp cloth around Willoughby's neck with a flourish and clipped it.

Willoughby smiled. "Deal," he mumbled, and then sank back into the chair, letting his barber turn the conversation back to the Coco Palace. Antonio was particularly fascinated with the use of bamboo in the works of Asian architects. As his bony fingers clipped merrily with the well-oiled scissors, Willoughby stared at the gleaming silver and the red of Antonio's prized barber chair. Despite his friend's up-beat mood, he couldn't shake this feeling of unease. What had he seen outside? This wasn't the first time he thought he had glimpsed numbers floating on air. He had witnessed a similar flash of equation once before—the morning after his dream about The Riemann Hypothesis. The dream had helped him solve the mathematical puzzle, one that had stumped mathematicians for hundreds of years. The dream changed his young life forever. Now, he had seen the floating numbers again. Would his life change yet again?

He fidgeted, looking away impatiently. Antonio turned his chatter to a recent soccer match. The local team he supported did, indeed, mount a valiant effort, but (he put great emphasis on the word *but*), in the end, they lost. Of course, it was the fault of a *devastatingly* incorrect call by the officials.

Willoughby half listened. His eyes were roaming the interior of the narrow shop, calculating the empty spaces. As usual, he was Antonio's only customer. He couldn't remember ever having to wait while Antonio finished another client's hair. This led him to wonder how Antonio stayed in business. His eyes flicked to the small TV against the far wall. It was turned off. That was unusual. Antonio almost always had the picture running, though he would turn down the sound or drown it out with his favorite music. He loved to torture Willoughby with opera or mariachi music, mixing in a little classical and even hip-hop or folk to add contrast. In truth, Willoughby's own musical tastes were rather varied, so he didn't really mind. Today, however, no music was playing.

Had Antonio, too, sensed the unusual silence of the early evening? Perhaps it was why he jabbered on so desperately, without even taking a pause. When he finished the soccer game report, he was off to a bit of gossip about the Palm Reader. He had heard the woman would begin reading the paws of canine clients She had approached the butcher, trying to get him to combine forces. He could provide treat-sized doggie wieners for a paw-reading package. "They will call it, '*Meat after de Feet!*'" he snorted, trying to keep a serious face. "Yes, my friend, the neighborhood is indeed going to the dogs."

Willoughby noted that the soft click of the scissors had fallen into a strange harmony with the drone of the barber's deep voice. He turned his eyes toward the shop window to watch the darkening sky. The sun had set and the shadows had lengthened across the ghostly still street. He tried to calculate the subtle rate of this lengthening over the late afternoon.

He liked numbers and their ability to package wonder, to capture the world around him in defined expressions. It was his way of saving the moments of his life, of keeping them from slipping away. When a moment is measured, calculated, and catalogued, it becomes accessible. The sum of life is caught in its patterns, and its patterns are defined by the geometry of its moments. Without stepping back and analyzing these patterns, these moments, it was easy to miss things.

Take for instance Antonio's shop. A quick look around would give one the impression that the building is old. When each bit of observation is analyzed, however, one discovers that green chips of paint hide new wood. Antique fittings have been carefully rusted. The pattern leads to a startling realization—this shop, which appears to be ancient, is actually *new*.

Of course, Willoughby hadn't needed observation skills to lead him to this realization. Easing his head forward so Antonio could trim his neck line, he thought of the day when he first noticed this space that was to become Antonio's Corner Barber. He had been aimlessly exploring the Corridor. He did this often while he was waiting for his step-father to finish work. Klaas, his step-father, worked at a large engineering firm a few miles away. They commuted together on a train that serviced D.C.'s many bedroom communities. He had stopped in front of a crumbling building whose windows had been boarded-up. The floors above the shop appeared to have fire damage. He had sensed something about the building—no, not the building, but the *space* it occupied. He stood there, staring at it for a long moment. The feeling didn't go away, so he decided to keep an eye on this building, this *space*.

Barely a month later, a strange group of workers appeared on the scene and began demolishing the building. The process fascinated him. In less than a week, all three floors of the building had been reduced to rubble and a new building was already taking shape. The ground floor that eventually became Antonio's Corner Barber was completed last. Willoughby paid particular attention as the workers painstakingly aged the shop to give it a carefully-crafted nostalgic feel. The work was so skillfully completed that an average on-looker would never know that the building did not actually belong with the older shops around it. He remembered thinking that the color, the style, everything about the shop felt *right*. It felt to him like these strange builders had calculated the appropriate solution to some odd equation.

His interest became further piqued when the workers, all dressed in matching coveralls with an "O" on the front breast pocket, put Antonio's stone symbol in place. The symbol was carved about an inch deep into the thin limestone. It combined both numbers and shapes. The numbers had no relevance to the building's address, and the shapes had nothing to do with the stated function of the shop. It seemed almost a brazen mathematical puzzle, placed there just to tantalize and tease the casual observer. Tantalize it did. Willoughby made it a point to visit the shop the moment it opened its doors (which, by the way, occurred on a Thursday afternoon and not the typical Saturday or Sunday). From the beginning, nothing about Antonio and his shop were ordinary.

Willoughby eased forward in the barber chair, causing Antonio to grunt. Had that really been almost two years ago? He frowned as a clump of hair rolled off his left cheek. There was sometimes a musicality to the clip, clip, clip of Antonio's scissors, a comfortable precision. Not tonight. Antonio paused for a breath. His friend had to be fast approaching thirty, but he had a vigor that made him seem perpetually young. His thin, bony frame was off-set by jet black hair and a broad moustache. Dark chocolate eyes and a chiseled chin enhanced his movie-star quality.

Sometimes, Antonio, too, would become thoughtful, staring out the grand window to comment on the changing light. Tonight, however, he seemed desperate for mindless conversation. Willoughby listened. There weren't many people in his young life that he liked to talk to. This made Antonio unique.

The barber stopped clipping. "Hello? Is anyone stirring down there? I would certainly not want to wake you, my most mathematical friend. Is there a problem you wish to speak about? Does the proud rooster have trouble with his flock?"

Willoughby barked an unintentional laugh. "Flock?"

Antonio paused a moment, considering. "You know, how do you say—with his chicks?"

Willoughby peered up at Antonio through parted bangs. "*Chicks?*"

"I give. What do they call the young ladies in your world?"

"Let's see—techno-glams, vampire slayers, warrior queens, tree-huggers…"

"Ah!" Antonio smiled. "I do understand tree-hugger!"

Willoughby cracked a smile. "In my day, Antonio, there's no connection between poultry and romance."

"Lovers no longer 'fly the coop?' What a shame, oh, illustrious one. I have always felt that, when dogs and wieners fall flat, one can *always* rely on poultry!" Antonio raised an eyebrow. He often referred to Willoughby as *illustrious*. The word was defined as: *highly distinguished; renowned; famous; glorious; bright.* While the barber was a bit odd at times, he was a good judge of character.

Willoughby glanced around the shop. "So, why am I always the only one in your shop, Antonio? Over the last three months, I've seen a total of, well, let me see… There was me, and, oh yeah, me! Do you actually have other customers?"

Antonio launched into a series of grumbles about the challenges of attracting a good clientele. Willoughby let his eyes wander toward the shop window. *What had those floating numbers meant?* Was it his mind trying to help him uncover the secret of the shop, of the symbol? He thought of one of his personal heroes, James Glaisher. Antonio told him once that this mathematician, famous for founding the Royal Aeronautical Society and riding weather balloons to chart the troposphere, had reported that the sky was filled with numbers, floating equations and answers. He said people just have to learn how to see them.

At that very moment, while thinking of James Glaisher, with Antonio going on about clientele, and the light outside deepening to a dark blue, Willoughby's life, once again, changed.

The incessant buzzing of a fly had caught his attention. His eyes located the pest, flitting from the window and dropping low. He lost sight of it against the black and white checked floor, and then saw it again as it turned abruptly and angled back toward the dusty sill. It careened through a forest of old coffee cups and lit, at last, on the highest stack of wrinkled magazines. Willoughby had the strangest impression that the fly was trying to tell him something. He squinted, staring harder at the spot where the fly had landed. He was staring at a carefully cut-out bit of newsprint that had been angled over the edge of the stack as if to highlight the photograph in a particular article. The picture was of a girl, holding a violin and staring out from a medieval cloak. There was something purposely precarious about the placement of the article. It called to him, like a broken equation—like a shingle hanging to the edge of a rickety roof. He couldn't help being riveted. He was hopelessly drawn to things out of sync—out of order or alignment.

Antonio blocked his gaze momentarily, moving slowly around the side of the barber chair. Willoughby strained, determined to discern some of the text of the article. The girl mesmerized him. She had captivating, dark eyes, and shimmering, black hair. *Who was she?*

Antonio twisted the chair around, but Willoughby was undeterred, continuing to strain toward the article. The glare from the shop's overhead lights made it hard to even make out the title of the article, much less the fine print. The title was two words; he couldn't make out the first, but the second was "*Shines.*" A tuft of dark hair dropped unceremoniously to his cheek. He puffed it away, distracted for a moment.

"I don't usually see such big globs of hair. What are you doing up there?"

"Oh, you noticed! It feels as if I am trying to tame a restless bull, attempting to excavate wild tangles while my client twists like a monkey on a hot roof! On the bright side, I think you will have no problems getting into the Navy." Antonio held scissors in one hand and a thin comb in the other. His words spilled out rapidly, laced with a lilting Spanish accent. "By the way, if you move just as I cut, the cut goes badly. The cut tonight is going very badly, my friend. At the moment, you have a hole the size of a walnut over your most illustrious ear. If you can stay *still*, perhaps I can fix it. If not, I take no responsibility. You may yet walk out of here as a genuine, hack-headed zombie."

"*Cool!*" Willoughby grinned.

"'*Cool?*'"

"Yeah—zombies are in."

"In *what?*"

"In, you know—*in!* It's as if zombies have taken the place of princes in the mind of modern females. Girls drool over *hot* vampires, roaring beasts, or kind-hearted zombies. The bloodthirsty alien with overactive hormones takes fourth place. As near as I can tell, girls today want to be frightened, bitten, and in some cases, possessed. It doesn't matter what creepy thing is after them as long as *they* are the object of the chase."

The barber shrugged. "Well, some things don't change."

Willoughby nodded. "I'm telling you, it's not a world for the faint-hearted out there, Antonio. Maybe you should lock the shop door when I'm not around."

"Ah. Yes, I'll keep that in mind."

Willoughby tried to cheat a glance over at the article again. "It could even be a niche for you, though. Think of all the potential customers on Capitol Hill alone. Much of the Press is brainless and operating on Espresso or Red Bull, and then you have the unending pool of bloodthirsty politicians…"

"I am awed at your insight," Antonio said, narrowing his eyebrows. Willoughby tried again to angle his head to look at the newspaper clipping.

"So, what can you tell me about the girl?"

Antonio looked up. "What girl?"

"The article! You left it there for me, didn't you?" Willoughby nodded toward the magazine stack. "We've already established that you're the only one in here besides me, so there aren't a lot of other choices."

"Who said I left it for you?" Antonio fought a grin. "Forget about her. She's out of your league." He let

Willoughby fume a moment before he continued. "All right, I will humor you. As you can tell from the article, her name is Ms. Senoya."

"And?"

"She is close to your age. Her father is Japanese and her mother is Polynesian." His long fingers worked the well-oiled scissors, click, click, clicking them like dragon teeth. "She is actually a friend of mine. I like that picture. It captures her, how to say—*haunting look*, would you not say?" He sent another coil of dark hair cascading to the floor.

"You're joking, right? You don't really know her?"

"Oh, I know her very well. I am a great fan of her music." The barber straightened. His dark eyes sparkled as he brushed back his own slightly damp black hair. "I am also a fan of her…style."

"So, her name is Senoya? Is that her first name?" Willoughby pursed his lips.

Antonio cocked his head. "Is it my imagination, or is your interest slightly more than academic? Perhaps you want to know the numbers of her measurements?"

"Come on, Antonio—I asked for her name, not for the keys to her apartment."

"So, now you want keys to her apartment?"

Willoughby groaned. "Okay," he sighed, "just forget it." Of course, his body language (especially the fact that kept twisting in the chair trying to get a better view of the article) made it obvious that he *did not* want to forget it.

Antonio chuckled softly. "Her name is Sydney, my friend—Sydney Senoya. Like you, she is, hmm, gifted. No one in the world plays the violin like Ms. Senoya. She can make the Stradivarius sing like the heavens in chorus! Ah, you should see her, with her shiny, black hair flying, and her deep, penetrating eyes…She is famous, you know. I clipped the article from the *London Times.*"

"You were in London?"

Antonio guffawed; "In London? No, I was not in London. This time, you are kidding, right? The *London Times* is read all over the world—"

"I don't care about the publication!" Willoughby barked; "I want to know about the girl."

Antonio savored the silence for a moment. "As I was saying, the *London Times* is read all over the world, which tells you, my friend, that the girl is known all over the world. Many say they hear music just by looking at her face."

Willoughby turned away. "Okay, I can see that getting anything out of you is going to be hopeless tonight." He turned back toward the photo. "She looks like a cross between Goth and anime."

Antonio raised an eyebrow; "*Goth and anime?* I will have to tell—"

The barber's voice was clipped off in mid-word. Willoughby's senses immediately heightened. He felt more than saw a disturbance near the top left corner of the window. He thought of the glowing numbers he thought he had seen earlier. Something was happening—something that had to do with this place, with this night. *Was the girl part of it?* He spun, his senses seeking for the heart of the disturbance. Glowing numbers greeted him, highly visible this time, floating on nothing but air. The numbers strung together into equations, crawling slowly down from the top left corner of the window. The glowing strings were also reflected in a car window across the street. As Willoughby watched, he noted that the ghostly numbers seemed to be following an invisible line, spilling from the direction of the symbol to a point near the center of Antonio's large window. The strings began to divide, seeming to spawn multiple smaller strings. They seemed to be growing brighter. He glanced up at Antonio.

"Hey? Are you seeing this?"

The barber stood frozen. His frame was perfectly still. His mouth hung open, poised in the act of forming a word. His eyes, his chest—nothing moved! It was as if he wasn't even breathing. Willoughby felt a chill run down his spine. He jerked his eyes around the shop. *Everything* was frozen. There was no sense of sound, no buzz from the lights, nothing living in the room at all.

"*Antonio?*" he whispered again. No answer.

With alarm, he caught sight of the pesky fly he had watched earlier. It hung suspended and lifeless in the air only a few inches from his face. He turned back to the window. The blue lines of floating numbers had grown brighter, highlighting a jagged edge of light maybe ten feet from one end to the other. The line pulsed with bright fluctuation. The pulsing line seemed to suck the crawling number strings inward, and then in a single blinding flash, the air ripped down, letting light spill through. Willoughby shielded his eyes from the brilliance. *What was he seeing? A different dimension?* The light dimmed slightly and a gaunt face peered out of the jagged tear. As his eyes adjusted, he could see it was the face of a man, an older man with dark eyes and thin, wispy hair. The man wore what looked like a trench-coat, pulled tight around his shoulders and buttoned fully to his neck. At first, he peered up at the symbol, and then, as if sensing Willoughby's gaze, his eyes slowly lowered to the shop. The dark, penetrating gaze locked on him, and Willoughby found the brilliant light suddenly less blinding. The man seemed surprised, or at least confused. He nodded at Willoughby.

Willoughby blinked and nodded back. He glanced up to see if Antonio and the fly were still frozen. In that instant, everything reverted to normal. The bluish light, the numbers, the man's face—they all vanished in the blink of an eye. Antonio was speaking again and the ambiance of the room returned. The fly banged against the front glass of the window before buzzing back past Willoughby's head.

"—her. She would be amused. *Anime?* She might well turn it into a whole new show—"

Willoughby tuned out Antonio's words. *What had just happened?* He grasped for an explanation. Had he hallucinated the whole thing? Had he fallen into a trance and had some sort of daydream? Had the face been a ghost, a projection of some kind? Who had the man been? Why had he been wearing a trench coat, buttoned all the way to the neck?

The image had vanished as mysteriously as it had appeared. Willoughby started to say something, but stopped. Again, it was something out that window that attracted his attention—a quick movement from the shadows. Someone was watching the shop from an alley across the street. Willoughby narrowed his eyes. A huge bruiser of a man stepped out of the alley and walked to the dim glow of the book emporium. His bulging arms were heavily tattooed. In one hand, he carried a camera with a zoom lens. His eyes were transfixed on the carved symbol outside the shop. He raised the camera to his cheek and began to click. After a few pictures, he lowered the camera and seemed to focus on Antonio.

"Hey," Willoughby said, trying to steady his voice. He saw the iris in the zoom lens click. The man lowered the camera again. *He was focusing right at him.*

Antonio stopped talking and glanced in the direction of Willoughby's stare. He stepped protectively in front of the barber chair, moving toward the window. The man slipped back into the shadows. Willoughby watched for a moment and then spoke.

"He photographed us—well, the symbol first, and then us. Is that normal for this time of night?"

Antonio turned back toward the barber chair. His countenance had darkened. "A strange time to be photographing—it is after dark."

Willoughby could no longer see the bulky man. He had probably slipped away down the alley and disappeared. Antonio, too, was searching the shadows. Though he shuffled back to the barber chair and returned to the haircut, he seemed to have difficulty pulling his attention away from the incident. "You say he photographed the symbol?"

"Yes; and that's not all. A moment ago—it was like everything froze for a few seconds."

He decided not to go into details about the floating numbers or the man's face that appeared and then vanished.

"*Froze?*"

"Yeah," Willoughby said thoughtfully. "There was no sound, no motion—well, almost no motion. Just for a few seconds. It was weird."

Antonio bit his lower lip. He raised the scissors. "I did not notice anything."

"You were frozen," Willoughby said, almost under his breath.

Antonio didn't respond. He resumed his steady clipping. Willoughby went over the experience in his mind again. *Had it been real?* He thought about the symbol and how the bluish flares seemed to be coming from it. He knew very little about Antonio's strange symbol, even though it had been the source of many of his questions to his barber friend. He knew it had been mounted two days before the shop opened. It was formed by the numbers "313", with the last 3 carved into the stone facing backwards. A spiral of right triangles swirled just above the numbers. Antonio had said it was his *calling card*—his declaration to the world that this shop would not be just a humble barbershop, but a place of adventure, of mystery. Now, the sense of mystery had become real. He claimed to have forgotten where he got it from, joking that he may well have bought it on eBay. Willoughby became suddenly convinced that there were things about this symbol that his friend was *not* telling him.

What?

2

Wasted Space

The hum of electric clippers interrupted Willoughby's thoughts. Antonio trimmed his sideburns, then gave the antique barber chair a quick swivel and pushed down his head, shaving the fuzz on his neck and touching up his neckline. After a long moment, he flicked the clippers off. With a wild flourish of clicks and a few whisks of his soft brush, the cut was finished. Antonio lowered the barber chair, unclipped the white barber smock, and whirled it away, glaring with pride as clumps of stray hair flew in every direction. He took a bow.

"It is finished—a masterpiece, if I must say so!" He seemed to have suddenly regained his bravado. "You will be happy to know that I have swept precisely 910,656 hairs from my checkerboard floor this very year—that is an average of roughly 100,000 hairs per haircut, but tonight I cut at least 200,000—"

Willoughby frowned. "101,184."

"What?"

"Your average is 101,184, and I doubt I have 200,000 hairs on my head."

Antonio stared at him, pursing his lip. He raised a single finger. "Alright, great hair counter, but tonight, I

21

have a most curious proposition for you. Tonight, I ask you to use that magnificent gift, the one that helped you solve the most magnificent Riemann Hypothesis."

Willoughby cocked an eye. His friend knew better than to speak openly of his solving the famous puzzle. Only a handful of people knew about it. The world in general wouldn't know until he turned 21. That's when his solution to the Riemann Hypothesis would be released. It was the "*deal*" his parents had brokered with the academic community. Academia was anxious to laud the young man's achievement for their own purposes, but wasn't overjoyed by the prospect of admitting that a twelve-year-old boy had solved a puzzle that hundreds of famous mathematicians had spent their lives chasing. His mom and step-father also got what they wanted. They believed they were protecting their son, allowing him a "normal" childhood, whatever that was. Willoughby, alone, despised the deal.

He sucked in a quick breath. How had the psychologist described him? She had said he was brilliant and restless, and the *deal* didn't do much to help him on either account. He got a mere pittance in allowance, skimmed off the top of the million dollars in prize money he had won by solving the famous puzzle. He also got free tuition at a fancy private school, an *investment* from the academic community. He hated the school. The only positive thing about the snooty school was that he got a personal limousine and driver to ferry him between the school and his father's office every day—a gift from the website that had sponsored the million dollar contest.

On a day when he felt he couldn't hold it in anymore, that he might jump off a cliff if he didn't tell someone, he had told Antonio. The barber had merely taken the revelation in stride. Other than a bit of teasing about being a mathematical genius, his friend knew better than to speak of it. Now, he was not only referencing the Riemann solution, but he was asking for some sort of assistance. Could this night get any stranger?

The barber finished folding his cloth smock and headed toward the small entry that led to a back room. "I have need for the observations of your most extraordinary mind. Wait—I will return shortly." He held up his finger again, letting it trail through the air as he disappeared into the darkness.

Willoughby slid down from the barber chair, shaking hair from beneath his collar. The street outside was deathly quiet. He stepped over and picked up the article about the girl. She was pretty, he had to admit that, but there was something more. *What was it?* He felt a pang of irritation that he hadn't gotten more information from Antonio. Glancing quickly over the article, he carefully folded the clipping and crammed it into his pocket. Glaring up at the window, he had a vivid memory of the man he had seen wink in and out of existence. Could he have imagined such a face?

Antonio swept back into the room holding a long paper tube. He screwed off the end and tapped out a bundle of rolled papers. "I need your help with a most curious puzzle, my friend."

Willoughby watched him carry the papers over to an open bit of counter and begin spreading them out flat. He moved closer. They seemed to be architectural designs of some kind.

"I must let you in on a most private secret. I do not earn my living cutting hair."

Willoughby felt a grin flash across his face. "*Really?* I would never have guessed."

Antonio barely seemed to be listening. "I am what you might call a chaser of mystery."

"What kind of mystery?"

"I chase mysteries that need to be solved. I am paid great sums of money to see things that others cannot see. This brings me to the curious symbol outside my door. You have seen first-hand that others have begun to take an interest in it. I need to find out why, my friend. Will you help me?"

"How?"

"That does not matter. Look at these drawings. They are architectural blueprints of another building designed by the same man who designed the Corner Barber. The initial construction was by the same construction company who built the shop."

"'O' something? They were the guys with the white coveralls."

"You saw them?"

Willoughby nodded. Antonio nodded as if digesting this bit of information before pulling attention back to the blueprints. "Do you notice anything odd about this building?"

Willoughby studied the drawings. "This looks like the Certus Grove building." He remembered the name because his step-father, Klaas, had been called in to do some final engineering work on the building. Klaas worked as a civil engineer for a large firm. He had pointed the building out to Willoughby when they passed it on their commute home from work. The Certus Grove was one of the tallest buildings in a newly renovated section of Georgetown.

Willoughby noticed that Antonio seemed to be studying him as he looked over the blueprints. He glanced back down at the plans. "Is there something I'm supposed to be looking for?"

Antonio tapped his finger on the counter. "To the casual observer, these are just building plans. If you look closer, though, you may find that there are links between the symbol, the building, and even the mysterious girl with the violin." He ran a finger along the blueprints. "Listen to me, Willoughby. You must concentrate. You must focus. The architect who designed the Corner Barber and the Certus Grove is a reclusive man rumored to know secrets of great worth. Do you note any...peculiarities in the plans?"

Willoughby's eyes narrowed. He scoured the pages for a long moment until his eyes fell onto the street view of the building's front. "Well," he began; "this top row of windows appear to be designed as a series of golden rectangles."

"Yes," encouraged Antonio, "the same as the window of my humble shop."

Willoughby looked. He hadn't noticed before, but Antonio's front window was in the dimensions of a golden rectangle. A *golden rectangle* had side-lengths that follow the golden ratio (one-to-phi, or 1 to 1.618). The Greeks often worked the rectangles into their architecture. They believed that the *golden ratio* was divine. Willoughby thought of the spiral of *golden triangles* carved above Antonio's door.

"What else?" Antonio encouraged.

"Well," Willoughby looked back over the blueprints, "each floor is consistent in height except the top floor. As you can see, the windows on the top floor are taller by at least three feet than the lower floor windows—a fact obscured by the elongated window trim and these decorative window shades." His finger came to rest on a scribbled number that measured the space between the sill and the scalloped edges of the shade. His eyes narrowed on the number.

"Look at the number scribbled here. 1.618 is the numeric representation of *Phi*. The ancient Greeks were crazy about it. It forms the basis of the golden ratio. Some Greek architects believed that shapes and angles based on the golden ratio could create doorways, inviting the Gods from their places beyond time."

Antonio smiled, nodding. "Yes. I, too, noted the space between the top of the windows and the edge of the roof. I visited the building, thinking the space might be explained by a sunken roof, or high ceilings. That is not the case. What's more, I could find no access to the space above the ceiling of the top floor. I stopped a janitor, and he assured me there was no storage space above the ceiling. He showed me the one access, which led to the roof. It is in the top of the stairwell next to a blank wall the size of a whole floor."

Willoughby squinted at the drawing. "What are you getting at?"

"Don't you see? This is an architect who decries wasted space! Look for yourself…every inch of space in the building is utilized in some way. Except here." Antonio pointed back to the space above the top floor. "Here, we seem to be missing an entire floor. So, tell me—why the wasted space?"

Willoughby cocked his head and looked back down at the papers. He curiously thumbed from one page to the next. Antonio was right. There seemed to be at least 10, maybe12, feet of unused space at the top of the building. "I don't know," he finally shrugged. "Maybe it's for insulation or heating and air ducts."

"Ten feet of insulation? The air ducts are in the floor—I checked. You do not find this odd?"

Willoughby shrugged. "Well, yeah, but, he seems to be enamored with the golden ratio. Maybe the ratio of wasted space ties in somehow. The symbol above your door also has a spiral of golden or right triangles."

"Yes, speaking of the symbol..." Antonio pulled out a black and white photograph of a section of decorative stonework. At its center, Willoughby noted the same symbol as the one over the door to the Corner Barber.

"I photographed this with a high zoom lens. It is a section of stonework along the roof, invisible to the naked eye from the ground. So I ask you; why waste the space in the building? And why the same symbol, with the numbers 313, and the last 3 turned backward, just like the symbol outside my door?"

Willoughby's face clouded. It was true that the architect was obviously fascinated with Greek tradition, but he couldn't think of anything in Greek tradition that could explain the number 313, or the backward 3, or the choice to leave an entire floor of wasted space.

Antonio carefully rolled the blueprints back up. "There is a logical answer, my friend, I am sure of it. Perhaps a mathematical mind such as yours could see things that I could not. I wonder—could there be a secret entrance to the hidden space? If there is, the clues would most likely be mathematical. I want you to go to the Certus Grove building for yourself."

"Myself? My parents would—"

"Find a way to convince them, my friend. I need your help." Antonio seemed earnest. He handed Willoughby the blueprints and then glanced at the magazine stack. "We did not finish our conversation about Ms. Senoya." A smile cracked his face. "She is close friends with the architect of my shop and the Certus Grove building."

Willoughby nodded vaguely, feeling a bit guilty about grabbing the clipping. His eyes focused on the shop's single wall clock and he panicked: "Ah! I'm late—Mom's picking me up tonight—Klaas has to work late again." He grabbed the blueprints and shoved them into his backpack. "I'll do my best. If I find out anything, I'll let you know." He flung his backpack over his shoulder. He was halfway to the door when he realized he had not even thanked his friend for the haircut. "Thanks for the buzz—don't work too hard!" he shouted over his shoulder.

"*Buzz?* Out with you!" Antonio boomed; "I have other clients fighting to get in!" He made a shooing motion with his arm and then moved toward the window.

Willoughby slammed through the door, once again rolling his eyes. He waved once more before hurrying away, down the sidewalk. At the end of the block, he glanced back. His barber friend was still there, still watching him intently, silhouetted in the glow of the barbershop window with the strange symbol brightly lit overhead.

3

Streetlight Meeting

Willoughby frowned as he turned down Lamont Street. The air had gotten colder and the slap of his sneakers against the sidewalk was deafening in the quiet. As a young boy, he had dreamed of becoming a Shaolin Priest, able to walk on rice paper without leaving a trail. Right now, he felt like a rhinoceros, sure that his footfalls were betraying him for blocks in every direction. He slowed, straining to pull his muscles back under control. He wasn't exactly Olympic material, but he could hold his own in soccer and basketball. He hated the stereotype of the skinny math whiz with zits and thick glasses. He liked to push the envelope. He liked to think of himself as a renaissance man, able to dodge any stereotype.

He smiled sheepishly. He had a clear picture of what he was *not*. It was the image of what he *was* that remained a bit fuzzy in his mind. He looked down at his watch and quickened his pace. His thoughts returned to Antonio. What was his friend really after? He had implied that a mystery in the Certus Grove building *might* be connected to the mystery of the symbol over his door because both buildings were designed by the same architect, but hadn't he claimed earlier that *he* had bought the symbol on eBay?

So, which version of the story was true? Why was he so interested in the seemingly hidden space above the Certus Grove? There had to be more than just hidden space in that attic. What?

He felt a pang of caution. He also felt something else: *adrenaline, exhilaration.* His pulse always quickened when there was a puzzle that needed solving. He wasn't about to walk away.

He moved into a slow jog. Mom would probably be drumming her fingers on the steering wheel by now. On a good day, he might slide by with only an irritated look. On a bad day—well, just suffice it to say he would feel lucky to sleep out in the yard with his pure-bred Husky, Snowball.

As he sucked in another breath, about to push into a leisurely sprint, he noted someone standing under a streetlight ahead. He froze. The figure seemed somehow familiar. He had that strange feeling in the pit of his stomach again. He ducked behind the metal backing of a covered bus stop. Why had the feeling returned—the sense of something being out of place, or not right? He sneaked a quick glance around the corner of the bus stop. *It was him—the man with the trench coat buttoned up to his neck!* He recognized the thin, gaunt face and dark eyes. The man appeared to be actually flesh and blood. He stood tall, like a sentinel under the streetlight. Willoughby eased away from the corner, trying to calm the sudden panic that welled up inside him. He stared at the man's reflection in a shop window. *Could the man see him as well?* He didn't think so. He noted a cab parked in a no-parking zone a few feet away, its engine idling quietly. Though it was parked expertly against the curb, he could see no driver. *Had the tall man driven the taxi?* Why would he leave the motor running?

Willoughby squinted to make out a red glow through the rolled-down window of the taxi. It was the fare meter. It took a long, straight glimpse at the taxi to read the current fare—$6.65. As Willoughby watched, the meter clicked to $6.66. For the third time that day, a shiver tingled up his spine. What an odd number sequence to see at that moment, one that was often associated with evil. He glanced up at the reflection of the man again. The tall figure stood unnaturally still. He seemed to be focused on something further down the street.

Willoughby pushed up against the cold steel of the stop, trying to meld with the shadows. This *was* the man he had seen earlier. It was the same eyes, the same wispy hair, the same trench-coat buttoned up to the neck. That could mean only one thing—*his experience at the Corner Barber earlier had been real!* He *had* seen a tear open out of thin air and then disappear again. What was it? Some sort of high-tech transport device? What had it been looking for at Antonio's shop? Perhaps his perceptions had been somehow manipulated. *Why?* What were the glowing number strings about?

A car approached from further down the road. The tall man moved, craning his neck like a praying mantis. He raised a hand to his chin, frowning. The car pulled over to the curb and the back door opened. Willoughby slid to the other side of the metal stop and shot a quick glance around the corner. A short, stocky man climbed out of the back of the car and lumbered toward the taller man. The man wore only a thin muscle shirt in the chill air. He had tattoos running up both bulky arms. *Was it the same man he and Antonio had seen taking pictures of the symbol and of them?* The man was the right height and build and he had the tattoos. Willoughby hadn't seen him clearly in the dim light across from the Corner Barber, but he could see the man clearly now. It wasn't a pretty sight. Even from a distance, it was obvious that every inch of this man's visible skin was covered by long, twisting tattoos. They seemed to crawl up his arms and neck as the man flexed and relaxed his muscles. The twisting tattoos seemed to come to an elaborately detailed head that hooded the man's bald scalp. Willoughby could make out few details, but even from a distance, the seeming crawl of the tattoos was both disconcerting and mesmerizing.

"I suppose you find it humorous to keep me waiting?" the tall man snapped in crisp, European-sounding syllables.

"I suppose you find it humorous to call me out of the blue and demand a meeting," the tattooed man countered in a deep, gravelly croak. He had the stance of a middle linebacker and the voice of a chain-smoking whaler from New England. The burly man stopped at the edge of the light and grinned, his tight-fitting t-shirt barely muting the undulation of his painted demons. "I'm not one of yours, Mr. B. In fact, you can keep those, those fly-boy things away from me, you hear that? Far away! My driver didn't even want to come tonight."

"I'll see that you get a new driver," Mr. B said coolly. His smile was pure ice. "You amuse me Reese. That's lucky for you that you do."

"I'm sorry," Reese grinned. "I meant to insult you."

"Always pushing, aren't you, Reese? You know I'll only put up with so much."

"Ah. So, I should be shaking in my boots? Last time I looked, I wasn't on your payroll."

The tall man gave a tight smile. "You know of me, and yet you are alive. I would say that trumps your *payroll*."

Reese raised an eyebrow. "Do you want something from me, Mr. B? If you don't, I've no time for this—not if we're to stay on schedule. In fact, that's what you're all about, isn't it? You're the man with the schedule."

Again, the man flashed a tight smile. "I was attracted tonight by an unusual junction, Mr. Reese. Care to venture a guess as to what that is?"

"Your...pleasures are not my concern."

The tall man ignored the jibe. "An unusual junction is a rip in the natural seam. These rips are hard to find and even harder to exploit. It formed quite near here. You wouldn't, perhaps, be aware of the location?"

"Enlighten me." The stocky man stuck his hands into his pockets.

"Of course," the tall man said, pursing his lips. "It formed right in front of your eyes, Reese. It effectively drew attention to you, but you...were not able to identify the junction." The man's mouth widened into a broad smile, showcasing a row of yellowed, pointy teeth. "Someone else did, though."

The tattooed man frowned. "Who?"

"It was the boy."

"The boy...? You mean the kid in the shop, the one getting his hair cut? Impossible!" The man spat on the ground. "Where was his technology? You trying to tell me he has voodoo power like you—that he can just see the seams? I watched the whole time. There was nothing to indicate this kid has any special talent. He was just a kid who needed a haircut. He happened to look out and see me. So what? It was coincidence."

"I don't believe in coincidence, Reese. He may be just a boy, but he seems to have abilities we didn't anticipate. I'm beginning to wonder what else you and your…patron didn't anticipate. If this group proves to be more advanced than your team has surmised, our entire plan could be compromised."

"We've done our due diligence." Reese said. "We aren't worried about the plan." He scratched at his face, making what appeared to be thin fangs, tattooed above his ears, wriggle like those of a striking snake.

"I'm glad to hear you're so confident. I don't like failure." Mr. B walked to the edge of the light's glow. "The boy saw me, Reese. No one should be able to see me unless I choose to let them."

Reese raised his eyebrows, dumbfounded. "That's what you got all in a fit about? Some kid may or may not have seen your ugly mug and you think the sky is falling?"

"I find your stupidity shocking. I have no interest in what someone thinks of my 'mug'. I do find it disturbing when a boy is able to see into one of *my* junctions. Current time stands still in a junction, which is why you did not see me. A boy who can find and step into a junction would be a formidable enemy, don't you think?"

"What's the kid's name?"

Mr. B shrugged. "I thought you were in charge of surveillance." His smile seemed plastic. "You were at the shop tonight. Why don't you illuminate me?"

"He's just a friend of the barber guy. He always seemed like an ordinary kid to me. He gets his hair cut there every other week. In fact, he's one of the few regulars that frequent the shop."

"He comes there regularly and you know so little about him?"

Reese shrugged.

The tall man frowned. "I thought you were a professional, Reese. You certainly tell me that enough. What have you been doing this past month, playing games on your cell phone? What do the barber and the boy discuss? Do they trade papers or disks? Go on, tell me. I won't bite. Not yet..." Mr. B flashed what was more a leer than a smile, designed to show again his sharp, yellowish teeth.

"Listen," Reese said impatiently. His eyes narrowed to strained slits. "I was there to watch the shop and the barber. This kid comes in for a haircut every couple of weeks. How would I know what they talk about? They shared iPods a few times, like they were listening to music. That's all."

Willoughby pushed away from the corner into the shadows.

Reese squared his shoulders. "I'll tell you what else—I think the whole shop is a sham. So the place has a copy of the symbol over its door, so what? That don't mean they got the mechanism there. In that place in St. Petersburg, there was a whole segment of underground subway re-routed, even though the full mechanism was buried hundreds of feet below the subway level. The building at ground-level was in constant use too. It was some sort of office building. People came and went all the time. Not this barbershop. The place is like a tomb. There's nothing under it, or beside it. Cheap apartments fill the three floors above it. I see lights go on and off. The place sits empty most of the time. The barber only shows up a couple of days a week. He has maybe six or eight regular customers. He leaves and locks up soon after dark. Some days, he just sits there reading magazines. The kid is his most consistent regular. The barber seems chummy with him, like the boy is a nephew or brother or something."

Brother? Willoughby raised an eyebrow at that one, but he did find it interesting that other customers did, occasionally, venture into the shop. This didn't, however, give him any clue as to how Antonio stayed in business. The tattooed man looked over toward the bus stop.

The tall man hissed, almost imperceptibly. "Keep an eye on this 'kid', Mr. Reese. He is…an item of interest to me."

"You want more surveillance? That will impact the time-table."

"Hmm. No, keep to the plan. We're too far vested. But if you do see the kid, see where he comes from. Where does he go after he leaves the shop? Does he live around here? I'll watch as well."

Reese gave a curt nod.

"One bit of advice, Mr. Reese," the man narrowed his dark eyes. "You're a middle man dealing with danger on both sides of the knife. You would do well to remind Belzar of that, too."

Not turning from Reese, he held up a thin, bony hand, and motioned at the still idling cab. The cab glided slowly toward the lamp-lit side of the street. Willoughby saw with astonishment that there was a driver in the cab now—a stiff, unmoving figure. *Where had the figure come from?* No one had gotten in or out of the cab as he had been watching, he was sure of it. Had the man been hiding in the seat, or napping, or something?

The tall man walked to the cab and opened the back door.

"We're not your lackeys, Mr. B," Reese muttered, partially under his breath.

The tall man glanced over his shoulder. "Not yet, Mr. Reese...It will go badly for you when you are."

Reese spit at the ground. He forced a grin. "I'd like to see if it's true that you can't die."

"Oh, we all die, Mr. Reese." The tall man said, climbing into the cab. Once seated, he rolled down the window. "Some of us just know how to come back." He gave another flash of yellow teeth. "Tell Belzar it won't be long."

The cab glided away.

Reese looked after it. He spat on the ground again, spun on one heel, and jabbed a hand into his pocket. He pulled out his cell phone. As he walked back to his car, he stabbed furiously at the keys on the phone. He opened his door, threw himself into the back seat, and screamed, "Move!" The car squealed away from the curb.

Willoughby waited until it was a good block down the street before he came out from behind the bus stop. *What had that been all about?* Why couldn't people see this Mr. B unless he wanted them to? What was their little "enterprise," and why was the tattooed man watching Antonio's shop? The man called Reese had said something about a building in St. Petersburg. St. Petersburg, Russia?

With questions racing through his mind, Willoughby started moving down the sidewalk, pushing again into a jog. Why had *he* been able to see this Mr. B guy anyway, and why did this make him an "item of interest," or a boy they "can't afford to ignore?" He knew he was bright and unusually gifted in mathematics. Was there something else? He picked up the pace as he rounded a corner. "*Don't be paranoid,*" he mumbled to himself. He hadn't seen any guns. There had been no talk of violence. The tall man had made a reference to coming back from the dead, and the whole exchange had been creepy, that's all.

He forced his thoughts to shift. He tried to think of his mom and his sisters, waiting for him in the car at his step-dad's work. A thought of his birth father, Gustav, popped into his head. *Why was he thinking about Gustav suddenly?* Was it this sudden sense of mystery he found himself embroiled in? Up until tonight, Gustav's disappearance had been the biggest mystery in his life. No one knew what happened to him. No one had heard from him since he disappeared almost twelve years ago. No trace had ever been found of a struggle, or motive for a crime. He had just left and never returned.

Willoughby puffed out his cheeks. Gustav was gone and his disappearance had nothing to do with this new mystery in his life. Still, he felt a pang of longing. He had tried to bury the hurt away, but somehow it was always there, mingling with the faintest wisp of hope. *Was it possible that his real father could someday come home?*

The cold air turned his warm breath into mist. He forced his mind back to the conversation he had overheard. This Reese guy didn't know his name. He was just a kid who came to the shop for a haircut. He didn't want to put his family or anyone in danger, so he would take precautions. He would let Antonio know that, since the shop was being watched, he wanted to mix up their schedule a bit. Maybe come on random weeks, or on Saturdays when Klaas had to come in to work in the morning, which was a fairly often occurrence. and they would have to meet somewhere else for a haircut for a while. If he ever caught the tattooed man following him directly, he could call the police.

A memory burst suddenly upon his mind. He could see his father, Gustav, patiently arranging blocks on the floor. Willoughby watched him stacking distinct piles. There was a pile of three blocks, a pile of five blocks, a pile of seven. Gustav pushed the unarranged blocks toward him, not saying a word. As Willoughby looked at the piles, he felt he knew how many blocks should be in the next pile. He set up the next pile to contain nine blocks. His father laughed, delighted. "You can't help it, can you?" he said. "Mathematics is in your blood."

Mathematics was in his blood? Willoughby stopped abruptly. He had been told that Gustav was a highly sought-after structural engineer. Could his father have had a similar gift with numbers? Could this gift have led *him* to a puzzle too—one so intriguing that he couldn't turn away? Had he followed the mystery until it was too late to turn back?

He looked down, surprised to see his feet pumping away in a slow jog. His mind was so preoccupied that he hadn't even realized he had pushed again into a run. He rounded the corner and saw the family Nissan in the distance. Mom had parked under a streetlight. Klaas was on a new project that required him to work long hours and Mom had brought him dinner. Besides, she didn't like the idea of Willoughby riding the commuter train home alone. So, for now, she picked him up here at Klaas's office after school. Usually, it was earlier, but on Tuesdays and Thursdays, Densi, the older of his two half-sisters, had violin lessons. So, he had time to squeeze in a haircut.

He could see her frown through the driver-side window. She had probably been waiting for a good 20 minutes. He should have called. He could see her drumming her fingers on the steering wheel. He slowed to a walk, gulping air, and tried for a casual smile, rounding the front of the car and jumping into the passenger's side. Sweat trickled down his face and his breathing was still in ragged gasps.

"Sorry," he mumbled. "I thought I could squeeze in a haircut today, and Antonio was…slow."

"Why didn't you call?"

Willoughby shrugged. "I didn't think of it."

"You *didn't think* of it?" Mom's eyes were spitting fire. "So, what if I just happen to not *think* of cooking dinner, or coming to pick you up? You have a cell phone. You pay good money for it. You seem able to call Klaas, your barber, your friends, but you can't *think* to call your Mom?"

Willoughby frowned. "Okay, what do you want me to say? I was an idiot. Antonio and I got to talking and I didn't realize the time. I won't let it happen again, so can we just drop it?" He couldn't help but wonder what "friends" his mom thought he was calling.

"'That's the point, Willoughby; you're not an idiot. But you faithfully tell me every time we have this discussion that it won't happen again."

"Do we get a vote?" Densi, Willoughby's half-sister, piped up from the back seat.

Mom glanced up at the rearview mirror; "A vote on what?"

"On whether Willoughby's an idiot," the seven-year old said innocently. Mom's frown was enough to silence her. She turned back to Willoughby.

"I expect to be compensated for the 20 minutes of my time you've wasted," Mom added.

"Yes!!!" his younger half-sister, Cali, shouted. Cali was five. "Can he empty the dishwasher for a year?"

"No, he can scoop the dog poop for the rest of his life!" Densi sang out.

Willoughby sighed, turning to glare at his sisters. "Thanks guys. You give me the golden chores, what a surprise! For your information, a year of dishwasher duty is roughly 5500 minutes, not 20. Nor do I believe that 20 minutes of poop scooping will extend to the end of my life."

Densi stuck out her tongue. "You don't impress *us* with that numbers talk!"

"Yeah," Cali said. "Don't impress *us!*"

Mom started the car and put it into drive. The Pathfinder accelerated into the empty street. Willoughby took a deep breath. He was always the one who had to say something to break an uncomfortable silence. "So," he finally said, looking into the rear-view mirror at Densi. "How was violin lessons today? Kill any cats today?"

"MOM!" Densi squealed. General mayhem broke out. Willoughby tried to amend his question while Densi loudly proclaimed that she had NEVER actually killed a cat, maybe annoyed a few, but that wasn't the same as *killing* it! Mom tried to stop the argument, but Densi just yelled louder, saying that she didn't know why cats screamed when she played—maybe they just didn't like Mozart—and she had every right to *not* like cats if she wanted to because this was a *free* country, and she was a *free* citizen!

Mom finally got her voice to be heard shouting; "*Enough!*" There was a brief silence, punctuated by Cali adding softly, "A-A-Amen!" The two girls fell into flutters of giggles.

Mom took a long breath throwing a sideways glance at Willoughby. He tried to ignore the fact that he had started the exchange and bent quickly down to fumble in his pack. Truth was, he liked his half-sisters, though they could be trying and annoying at times. He waited until Mom had settled into a lane on the freeway.

"Klaas's firm worked on the Grove Street renovation, right? It included the Certus Grove building." He opened the roll of blueprints he had pulled from his pack. "Antonio got these for me. He's...he wants me to help him with a project. He's studying the architecture of the building."

Mom glanced over. "Well, I can't rattle off every project Klaas works on, but the name Certus Grove sounds familiar."

"Klaas pointed the building out to me a few times on the ride home," Willoughby said. "I think he worked on it three or four years ago. Look here—" He pointed to the bank of upper floor windows. "If you look closely, there's space up at the top of the building that doesn't seem to be used."

Mom glanced over but kept her eyes on the road. "What does Antonio want you to do?"

Willoughby's eyes never left the plans. "Well, it's the same architect that designed his shop—Antonio's Corner Barber." He finally tore his eyes away from the plans and began to re-roll them and stick them back into his pack. "They've used some interesting angles. They also use the golden mean in a number of sub-structures. I was thinking of going tomorrow to take a few measurements. Sam could drop me off there after school."

"You didn't answer my question, Willoughby. What does Antonio want you to do? Why is he suddenly interested in architecture?"

"He's always been interested in architecture. It's one of his hobbies."

"And he needs *you* to take the measurements?"

"He wants me to...uh, to verify some things that he discovered."

Mom furrowed her brow. Her face darkened as she restated the question. "You want me to give you permission to spend a whole afternoon alone in the middle of Georgetown?"

"It's not in the middle of Georgetown, Mom. The Certus Grove is like a block from the metro station. Sam can drop me off around 3:30, and I'll be waiting to catch the 5:20 commuter home with Klaas. He told me this morning that he's not working late tomorrow, and he could save me a seat."

"You're talking about downtown D.C., Willoughby."

"So? I'm not a kid anymore, Mom. I'm 16—"

"You're 15," Mom corrected, "and while I agree that you are decidedly mature in many areas, I may prefer you to wait until you're really ancient—like maybe, 17—before I let you go traipsing around downtown D.C. alone."

"So, I'll be careful! I need to do this, Mom. Antonio's a good friend."

Mom looked over at him. "So, I'm your Mom. You can't even remember to call me to tell me you're over getting your hair cut. How can I trust you to make sure and get to the station on time?"

"You just do it," Willoughby said. "You just trust me."

At length, Mom sighed. "You promise you'll call me as soon as you finish your measurements?"

"I'll talk to you the whole walk to the subway station."

She raised her eyebrows; "A whole eight-minute conversation! I'd die of shock…I *will* expect a glowing report from the rabble tonight. You remember that planning meeting for the home association is tonight, don't you?"

Willoughby gave a quick nod. The *rabble* was Mom's pet name for Densi and Cali. Both girls had Mom's blue eyes, but Klaas' white-blonde hair. Willoughby had neither. His eyes were a sort of hazel and his hair was dark brown. He raked a hand through the newly clipped bush, noting that his hand still trembled. "Do I get brownie points if they're both still alive when you get home?"

Mom ignored the jab, though the girls in back had plenty to say about *who* would be still alive at the end of the evening. Densi shoved a dirty sock toward Willoughby, dangling it from the end of a straw. He pushed it away, giving her *the look*, the one that says *"don't push it!"* She pulled the sock back, snickering and pushed it over toward Cali, who was much more vocal in her displeasure. With a sigh, Willoughby turned to look out the window. They were almost to the point where you could see the Certus Grove building from the freeway. Staring out at the city lights, he couldn't help but let his mind drift back to the mysterious space at the top of the building, of the glowing number strings he had seen seeping out from the symbol, and of the number sequence on the taxi meter: 6, 6, 6…

4

Secrets of the Certus Grove

The next school day seemed almost endless. When sixth period finally came, Willoughby tried to appear attentive, but Professor Dobson made it difficult. He made the inflationary pressures in pre-war Germany sound as exciting as watching a snail cross a sidewalk in misty rain. The man's voice could put an insomniac to sleep. Unlike typical high schools, Worthington Hills had no mere *teachers*. It staffed all classes with fully-accredited university-level professors. Everything about the school was stuffy and high-brow, which was one of the things Willoughby detested about it.

His chin slipped suddenly from the palm that had been propping it up. He jerked upright causing a ripple of giggles. Professor Dobson didn't even seem to notice. He simply forged ahead; "...and one must remember that the German Democratic Socialists were more of a splinter group at this time. Now, let's compare this time period with the anchors of German wealth immediately before the first world war..."

Willoughby leaned back, trying to will his eyes to stay open. The fact that he had laid awake most of the night didn't help his situation. He had gone over and over his experience at the Corner Barber. He had dissected and considered every word of conversation he had overheard between the tattooed man and the mysterious tall man. He had thought of the space at the top of the Certus Grove building. Though he probably wouldn't admit it to anyone, he had also thought about the gothic-looking violinist with the silky-black hair. Actually, he had thought about her quite a bit—thought about her and looked her up online and watched hours of YouTube videos of her concerts...

He wiped at his brow, feeling suddenly a little hot under the collar. He needed to focus. Going over the Certus Grove plans again in his mind, he tried to recall every detail Antonio had shown him. What could connect the symbol over Antonio's shop with the cleverly hidden space atop the Certus Grove building?

An image of the muscle-bound man with tattoos crawling down his arms and up his neck flashed across his memory. Was there a chance the man could show up at the Certus Grove building? It was unlikely. After all, Antonio hadn't shown him the plans until after the man had sped away, but still, the thought of the huge man made him nervous.

A tall girl with wavy, auburn hair looked over as if daring him to nod off. He winked at her and she raised a questioning eyebrow just as the bell rang. In seconds, he was up from his chair and out the door, racing through the quickly crowded hall to a less-used side door. He sprinted across the front quad and down to the pick-up lane where his limousine was third in line. *Good old Sam!* He was someone who could be counted on. The chauffeur gave a curt hello as he swung open the passenger door. Willoughby nodded and dove in.

"You think you can squeeze out of line?" he asked when the driver had situated himself in the driver's seat.

"I shall do my best, Master Willoughby," Sam hummed as he snapped his seat belt. He glanced into the rearview mirror. "Was it that tough of a day?"

Willoughby shrugged. "I had to endure another lecture on inflationary pressures in pre-war Germany. I survived, but only just. I'll have to buckle down and read the material this weekend, though. Last year, anyone who failed the chapter test was forced to read *Mein Kampf.*"

Sam gave a low chuckle as he threw the car into gear, backed up slightly, and swung the large car into the passing lane. He smoothly accelerated away from the line of other limousines. Willoughby peered at his chauffeur for a moment in the mirror. *Sam may be quiet, but he's basically a good guy*, he thought as he pushed his backpack over and snapped into his seatbelt. He felt a little guilty pulling his iPod out and sticking in his earphones. Experience had taught him, though, that Sam was somewhat uncomfortable with conversation. He tended to give one word answers, like "yes," "no," "sometimes," etc. The two had been driving together for over two years now—from the very day he started at Worthington Hills—and he still didn't know if the man had any hobbies or side jobs.

He turned to look out the window. Weird that he should be thinking of Sam's communication skills when he had so many other thoughts to occupy his mind. He began, once again, to go over the building blueprints in his mind.

True to form, forty minutes and a grand total of ten words later, the limousine pulled up to the front of the Certus Grove building. Willoughby stepped out, smiled, and waved Sam away.

Once the car disappeared into traffic, he turned to take in his destination. The building was stunning—even more impressive up close than it had been from the freeway. He shouldered his pack and stumbled across the width of its front facade.

The building was unusually wide, taking up almost a full block, and was about half again as deep. Everything about it seemed designed to mask the height of its upper floor. A decorative ridge just below the top row of windows hid the fact that the top of the building angled in slightly. Dark shades were pulled to the same point in each of the windows, obscuring the floor's actual height. Decorative soffits framed each window, angling opposite the inward tilt of the wall. The effect was an illusion that the distance between floors was more or less consistent.

The whole building was like a painting by the famous illusionist Escher. Willoughby thought of Escher's work— the way he created endless looping stairways where figures were forever climbing or descending, and structures that bent perspective so that, no matter how you turned the picture, there was always some alcove or doorway grounded in your point of view. The Certus Grove was just this sort of structure. Someone had specifically designed it to trick the eye. The question that burned in Willoughby's mind, though, was *why?* Was the architect just having a bit of fun? Was it his unique signature, so to speak, or was there a more practical reason? Was he trying to hide something?

Willoughby pulled out a scratchpad and a pen. He set off at a brisk clip, exploring the sides and back of the building. He mumbled to himself, as he often did when he was alone. "No interesting markings on the building exterior, and nothing visible on the roof." He noted that the period-specific style of the architecture carried the same sort of nostalgic elegance that gave Antonio's Corner Barber its quaint feel. Walking completely around the building, he filled about half a page on his notepad with estimated measurements and observations.

When he finally entered through the building's tall glass doors, he found the reception hall tastefully functional. The floor was tiled. Marbled columns and crystal light fixtures extended down short corridors to either side of the entry doors. Willoughby carefully examined the decor. He was fascinated by the carefully-aged details that gave the building a sense of grand history. In the end, however, he found nothing particularly unusual about the ground floor. He strolled to one of the central elevators. There was no basement option, so he decided to go straight to the top of the building. He pushed the number 12. If there was a hidden floor, he thought, it would be the 13th. He grinned at the realization. Knowing the mythical bad luck associated with the number 13, it was no wonder that no one had gone looking for it. Or had they? He wasn't frightened of 13. To him, 13 was just a number, and that was that.

The high-speed elevator abruptly decelerated, reminding him that, despite the building's carefully-aged appearance, the building's infrastructure was new. Within seconds, the elevator doors dinged open. He stepped out onto a tile floor consistent with the one he had just left. A large number 12 hung in gilded gold letters in front of him. He stepped out and began his careful inspection, checking the entire floor for anything out of the ordinary. He found nothing.

He walked the floor again, this time checking for loose ceiling tiles, or some other way to get access to the space that should be above. The floor was quiet and partially empty. No one challenged him as he poked around. The few people he did pass in the hallways only nodded politely and hurried on. He had a short speech prepared if someone asked what he was doing, but he never had to use it.

He turned a corner and caught the eye of a receptionist as she looked up from her desk in a glass-walled reception area. The business was called Skylark Annuities. He smiled and nodded pleasantly, but she only stared, unblinking. Her cold, stone-like face reminded him of something from atop a cathedral—a human gargoyle of some kind. He decided not to pass this particular reception area again.

Once he had covered the entire floor a second time and found no loose ceiling tiles, no open closets, and no way to get into the space above, he turned to the bathrooms. Both bathroom doors were locked. He took one last measurement toward the stairway door. Just as Antonio had said, the ceilings were ordinary height. He glanced back the way he had come and then slipped through the heavy stairway door marked "EXIT." Maybe he could find a maintenance access at the top of the stairs.

The stairwell was gray, cold, and deserted. Willoughby peered down. Each floor had a landing with stairs leading both up and down, continuing around in a tight square. A hollow space in the center extended all the way to the ground floor. The view, looking down, was geometric—a square, repeating itself 12 times. It reminded him again of the artist Escher.

Curiously, though, a bank of steps led up from the 12th floor. His eye followed them to a railed ledge about halfway between where he stood and the stairwell's high ceiling. On the left side of the ledge, a metal ladder extended up another 10 or so feet to a padlocked hatch in the ceiling. The ledge itself seemed to be 5 or 6 feet wide and extended the entire width of the stairwell. It seemed to dead-end into a smooth wall.

Willoughby began to climb. "Well, there is extra space between the 12th floor ceiling and the roof," he mumbled to himself. "There has to be some way to access it." As he came to the ledge, his mind raced and his heartbeat quickened. *Maybe there was an access from the roof.* He climbed slowly up the metal ladder, but the roof hatch was padlocked shut. He inspected it. No one had opened this hatch for a long time. Spider webs were strewn across the corners and the lock was visibly rusted. He climbed back down and turned his attention to the ledge.

Walking the length of the empty ledge, he sighed. To one side was a railing and everywhere else was blank walls. He ran a hand over the large expanse of blank wall. No matter how he looked at it, the blank walls were just that—smooth, featureless walls. If he couldn't come up with something fast, he had to face the fact that he might come away from his exploration empty-handed. He turned to start back toward the stairway, and then stopped. Something wasn't right. Why build a section of ledge only to dead-end into bare wall? He moved back along the seemingly pointless ledge to the segment of wall. Along its lower-left side, he thought he saw something out of the corner of his eye--a glow, or a glint, that flared only for a fraction of a second, but long enough to pique his curiosity. He bent to study the area of interest and noted a slight dimpling.

As he carefully explored the rest of the smooth wall, keeping at roughly the same level from the floor, his hand found a second imperfection on the lower-right side of the wall. He took out his tape measure. Both imperfections were roughly 18" from the floor and about 24" from the edges of the wall. This was too mathematically exact to be coincidence.

He began to probe the imperfections closely. They were formed by small groups of dots arranged across a barely perceptible plate of some kind, very flat and thin, attached to the wall and painted over. What interested him most was the shape of the plate. The left plate came to a point on the outside, like a triangle that had been tipped onto its left side. The right-side plate came to a point on the outside like a triangle tipped onto its right side, pointing in the opposite direction. It was as if the two plates were actually indicating lines of a larger triangle.

Willoughby stepped back. He lifted his eyes slowly up the wall, but there were no other visible imperfections, even if he put his eye right up to the wall and squinted at where he thought the top of the triangle should be. He wished he had a ladder so he could climb up and physically run his hand over the spot, but he did not. The upper wall appeared to be unbroken and completely smooth. He knelt at one of the plates and ran his fingers over the dots again. They seemed to be ordered, not random. His mind seized upon the answer: *Braille!* He had studied Braille once on the internet. The logic behind creating a series of dots that could translate language into a touch-based system had intrigued him. He pulled out his cell phone and connected to the internet. Also pulling out his notepad, he began to slowly interpret the letters: *T, A, N, G, E, N, T.* He stepped back. The letters spelled the word *"TANGENT."*

He moved to the second plate and ran his fingers over the dots; *T, N, E, G, N, A, T.* He stared at the letters, trying to make sense of them, before suddenly recognizing that they represented the same word spelled backwards.

"Odd," he mumbled aloud. What was the purpose of the two plates and the larger triangle they seemed to indicate? Why was the word *tangent* spelled forward on one plaque and backwards on the other?

He frowned, stepping away from the wall to lean against the railing. He thought about what he knew of the word *tangent*. In trigonometry, it's the ratio between the leg opposite an acute angle and the leg adjacent to it. That seemed to fit, but if the line between the plates was supposed to indicate the base of a right triangle, where was the point to indicate the tip of it? He moved up to the wall again, placing his eye close and carefully scanning the wall above, paying particular attention to the area where the point, or tip of the triangle, should be. Again, he saw nothing but smooth wall.

In geometry, a tangent line, or tangent, is the point at which the line touches a curve. *A curve...* The thought gave him an idea.

Willoughby pulled his tape measure from his pocket and began to carefully measure the distance between the two plates. He made a small pencil mark on the wall at the exact center between the imperfections. "This is the pivot axis," he mumbled aloud. "A right triangle has vertical and horizontal lines that are equal, so, if I consider the horizontal distance here, and turn the tape measure up," he held the tape measure against the wall so that its tip pointed up from the small pencil mark he had made. He mentally drew the back to back right triangles on the wall. He paused, staring at the wall.

"Okay. If the right triangle is pivoted 180 degrees, it will mirror itself on the other side. That would account for the word being frontward on one side and backward on the other. In the process of pivoting, it would also create a curve across the floor. If this is some kind of *three-dimensional* puzzle, perhaps it's the curve that's key."

He looked down. By taking the tape measure and drawing a thin line along the floor, stretching from his axis line the distance of the right triangle's horizontal side, he was able to calculate the apex of the curve. He marked this point on the floor, carefully studying the smooth cement for any hint or clue. Again, there was nothing. Then, he caught something out of the corner of his eye. It was a brief, bluish glow, the same sort of glow he had seen when time froze in Antonio's shop. It appeared near the ceiling, exactly above the point he had been scouring for clues on the floor. He had barely seen the numbers wink in and out of the glow, but they had been there. His senses heightened as he studied the ceiling where the glow had been.

At first, all he saw was a sprinkler head, one that looked like any of the dozen or so other sprinkler heads that covered the stairwell ceiling. Its position was perfectly placed—directly over the point he had marked on the floor—but otherwise, it didn't seem to be anything special. As he looked closer, however, he saw that there *were* differences to the make-up of this one particular head. Its nozzle was slightly different from the others. It was maybe a half inch wider, and hung down at least an inch or so lower. The nozzle itself was shielded by a metal disk that was darker in tint than the metal on the other sprinkler heads. The more he studied it, the more Willoughby became convinced that this was not part of the building's fire protection system, but, in fact, a *button* of some kind. He impulsively snatched his backpack, stood directly under the odd sprinkler head, and threw the pack up, directly at the metal disk.

The pack connected with the sprinkler head. There was an audible *snap* and then a *tick, tick, tick, tick*—as if a bank of switches was kicking in. The top stairwell lights clicked off, plunging the ledge into semi-darkness. The exit door on the floor below bolted shut with a deafening clang.

Groping for the rail, Willoughby bent over, staring down toward the bottom of the stairwell. Lights on the 12th floor went black, followed by the sound of its door bolting shut. Then lights on the 11th floor, the 10th floor, the 9th floor, all went dark. Lights continued to wink off on every floor all the way down to the ground floor. The doors on each floor locked. When the stairwell was at last in total darkness, Willoughby noticed a soft glow from the wall behind him. The glow was faint at first, but it brightened in intensity. He moved away from the rail, his heart pounding, and groped for his pack. When he nearly tripped on it, he snatched it up.

The floor began to rumble, almost inaudibly. A rush of cool air brushed against his face. He squinted in the dim light, watching. First, a smooth crack appeared, expanding until it outlined the shape of the two right triangles that shared a central axis—the very shape he had mentally sketched out on the wall. Next, the edges of the crack began to shimmer. Before Willoughby even realized it, the wall actually began to move. It pivoted slowly, the right tip of the triangle pushing inward while the left tip pushed soundlessly out. Finally, the triangle came to rest precisely on the line he had sketched onto the floor. The left tip of the triangle rested directly below the fake ceiling sprinkler Willoughby had identified and triggered with his backpack. *He had done it! He had solved this three-dimensional puzzle!* Sizzles of electricity zapped all around, tracing the edges of the open wall and the triangle. Willoughby moved cautiously, making for the opening to the left. Excitement surged in him. *He had now found his way into Antonio's secret space!*

5

Hidden Space

Willoughby stared. How could he have not seen, or at least *felt*, the seams of the hidden door? He had stood only inches away, running his hand in wide arches to make sure the wall was perfectly smooth. It was as if the triangular door had just materialized—as if the atoms in the wall had cut themselves free and pulled away. He approached the opening slowly. Around its edges, the neatly severed wall seemed to bend slightly, as if it had become soft rubber and was now being sucked inward. He touched the edge, feeling a strange pull that nearly jerked him off his feet. He ripped his hand away and took a step backward, startled. A voice echoed from inside the room. The accent was unmistakably British.

"Seventeen minutes from entry to solution. You are impressive, Willoughby."

Willoughby peered into the strange room. The voice came from near the center of the room, but he could see no one there. The air in the center of the room seemed to distort, the voice undulating with a strange pulse, as if it were being carried wirelessly over a great distance. "You've gone to a lot of trouble to find this door," the voice continued. "Were you just wasting time, or do you wish to

57

step in? We can't keep the stairwell locked all day. I don't think James Glaisher would have hesitated. Do you have what it takes to be a true explorer? Do you have the courage to step through the door?"

Willoughby had not moved. "Who are you? *How do you know my name?*"

There was a long silence and Willoughby once again got the feeling that the voice was traversing a great distance. "Once inside, you will feel a tug. *Don't fight it!* It will only make the journey more difficult. There are answers to your questions, but pointless is the answer without the proper question. If you are the boy we think you are, you feel drawn to the puzzle, the paradox of this room. You haven't time to reason it out, Willoughby. There is only time to act, or to lose forever the chance. This doorway closes forever for you in 14 seconds; 13; 12…"

Willoughby tried to take in the faintly buzzing dimness. He could still feel the pull from the room. He heard a soft clicking from overhead, and felt a rush of cool air. The floor rumbled again. He bolted forward without thinking. The door was closing!

Angling his shoulder so that he just slid through the narrowing gap, he rolled onto his back and yanked at his backpack. He pulled his feet clear just as the wall sealed behind him. Panting for a moment, he slowly pushed to his feet. The floor in the room felt oddly rubbery. The tug on his body was more intense. It pulled toward the dim center of the room. He resisted, inching his way back toward the smooth wall. Pushing up against it, he ran a hand over where the edge of the doorway had been. It appeared as smooth and unbroken as it had been when he first approached the other side. There wasn't the slightest hint of a crease or seam. *What was this place?*

He turned again to face the center of the room. The force pulling at him seemed to ebb and flow, like the pull of an ocean current, and the room was filled with spidery, luminescent lines. He breathed in deeply, trying to calm the rapid beat of his heart.

"Okay!" he called into the room. "I'm here. Show yourself." No answer.

What he saw made no sense. At first glance, the room appeared empty except for the glowing lines. Upon closer inspection, he could make out a swirling mass near its center, a place where all the spider lines seemed to converge to form a miniature dust-devil or a funnel cloud. The dull glow in the room was provided solely by the glowing, spidery lines. There was no visible light source at all. What's more, the spidery lines *were moving.*

He leaned close to the nearest one and could see it was formed by streaming lines of glowing number combinations. The combinations gapped, but the movement of the strings was fast enough to make the lines appear unbroken. Bolts of electricity crackled between these lines. The whole room seemed to pulse slightly, in harmony with the ebb and flow of the light. Suddenly, the funnel, or dust-devil, or whatever it was in the center of the room sprang outward, exploding in a bright flash. Willoughby saw that the floor near the base of the funnel had begun to ripple, as if it had liquefied. The pull in the room increased and light dimmed. Willoughby remembered the strange, undulating voice: "*Don't fight it! It will only make the journey more difficult.*" But he couldn't help himself. He pushed harder against the wall.

Every muscle in his body strained as he fought against the invisible force of the pull. He tried to push to his feet, but found that he couldn't move at all. While the room itself was growing steadily cooler, sweat poured down his face. *What had he done? How could he get himself out of here?*

He slid sideways. His eyes had adjusted somewhat so that he saw the room more clearly. It was huge, probably extending the whole length and width of the building. Large, steel braces anchored the walls about every 10 to 15 yards. They angled in slightly. Arcs of electricity shot out from them every time a glowing line got near, and then the electricity seemed to ping-pong its way around, zapping other lines and braces. The vortex in the center of the room swirled faster. Flashes of bright light shot out from it like solar flares. Each time one of these flares contracted, the pull drew him closer to the vortex. The floor began to vibrate hard and then seemed to liquefy. He felt a yank and was flying through the air.

"*Hey!*" he started, but a bolt of electricity zapped him before he could say more. He felt his muscles involuntarily seize up. The room exploded in a blinding kaleidoscope of sparks. He spun like a weed in a wind funnel. Folds of glowing, chaotic number strings boiled around him on all sides. A second bolt of electricity zapped, spinning him toward a crack of bright spark.

He tried to scream as he hit the crack, but no sound escaped his throat. He tensed, gritting his teeth. The air around him grew heavy, like molasses. He couldn't breathe—*he was suffocating!* His eyes blurred. He felt pain in his chest and then an intense cold, as if he were freezing to death from the inside. He wanted to shout, scream, kick, but a feeling of intense speed was crushing the life from his body.

Cold gave way to a sensation of burning heat. He felt as if he were being literally ripped apart by some force, his skin and muscle and bone being stretched to their limit. Then, suddenly, his body snapped back together. He could suck in breath. It was as if he had been pulled through a tiny hole and his whole being had turned to rubber for a split-second. His knee bounced against something, and then his hands hit it. It was hard, damp, and smooth. It didn't move, though the room still seemed to be spinning around him. *Was it the floor?* Gasping for breath, he opened his mouth to scream, and promptly retched, though there was little in his stomach to come out. After several moments of dry heaves, he realized he was shaking uncontrollably.

He became aware suddenly that this was no longer the room he had stepped into atop the Certus Grove building. The floor no longer glowed, and though it was mostly smooth, it was cold and had occasional dips and rises. *It felt like rock!* He slowly felt around in the dark, probing his body. He seemed to be in one piece. He couldn't feel any blood anywhere, and everything seemed to work. As soon as the white spots quit dancing before his eyes, he pushed to a sitting position. He became aware of a dim light somewhere ahead. He panted, letting his eyes further adjust.

The place felt like some kind of cave.

6

Window of Wonder

Willoughby didn't move again for a long moment. The space directly in front of him seemed dimly lit by a distant light, and roughly hewn. It felt like a tunnel of some sort. He cautiously grabbed at the rough wall a foot or two to his right and inched his way up to a standing position. His muscles trembled, jerking in brief spasms. He felt dizzy and had to lean back against the wall to keep from falling, taking in deep, even breaths until his heartbeat calmed and he felt some semblance of strength returning to his limbs. He wiped sweat from his forehead.

"Where am I?" he yelled. "That was just loads of fun! *Show yourself!* Where have you taken me? How did I get here?"

After a short pause, a voice spoke. It seemed to come from all around him at once. "There's no need to shout, Willoughby." It was the voice with the British accent, but crystal clear this time. "When you're out of the tunnel, we'll talk."

Willoughby noted for the first time a dim glow flickering behind him. He turned. A shrinking version of the swirling vortex, intersected by crimson arcs, dissipated slowly into a cloud of lazily rolling mist. The mist lit up occasionally with crackling arcs as it melted slowly into the rock floor and was gone. Willoughby stared after it for a long moment, then turned and peered down the tunnel in the opposite direction. *Where was he?*

"Any more surprises?" he called out. "If I walk forward, I won't fall through to some other weird place, will I? I've had my fill of surprises today."

"You'll be amazed," the voice said, and then went silent.

Breathing deeply and swallowing hard to try to dislodge the lump in his throat, Willoughby stepped cautiously forward, dragging a hand over the side of the tunnel. He rounded a narrow bend and noted that the walls had smoothed. He was walking down what now seemed to be a polished corridor. The light brightened a little, but seemed to flicker as though through heavy foliage, or underwater.

Willoughby felt shaky and confused, but there was also another feeling: *excitement.* He was intrigued. How had he gotten here? What had they used to transport him? This couldn't be the Certus Grove anymore. Would there be marvels or dangers at the end of this corridor?

He steadied himself as he reached the end of the polished corridor and stepped out onto a steel platform of some sort. He was in an enormous cavern. It was easily as large as an airplane hangar. His feet clinked on the platform, and he noted a metal staircase winding away to the left as he pushed cautiously to the platform's thin railing. He looked down. The space below seemed to be part natural and part man-made. Walls on three sides were formed by alternately smooth or roughly-hewn rock. The fourth side of the expanse, however, was what took his breath away. It consisted of a massive window. The three-story high wall of glass was broken into oblong squares by thin strips of metal webbing and bowed out gently, curving maybe 15 degrees from center to edges. The size of the window was easily 120 feet in width by 40 feet in height. The view behind the glass, however, was almost beyond his ability to take in. Undulating colors and hues filtered through a great expanse of water. Willoughby stared in awe. Framed in the squares of glass was what appeared to be a thriving coral reef—though unlike any reef that he had ever seen—unlike any reef that existed in *his* world.

The seascape stretched on for what seemed miles. Thick pockets of seaweed covered low coral mounds that were both odd and vaguely familiar. The scene, illuminated by hazy streaks of sunlight, was dotted with bizarre plants and teemed with odd, darting creatures. His mind recognized some of the strange shapes from books he had devoured as a child—books on prehistoric plants and primordial seas. But this wasn't the page of a book. *This seascape was alive!*

He forced his eyes away from the panoramic window and took in the rest of the room. Its smooth metal floor was divided into neat cubicles to the left, and opened into a sort of reception space to the right. In addition to soft lights over a smattering of small desks, orb lights lit a number of sitting areas. A sort of twinkling glow from the seascape also bathed the room. Willoughby's eyes focused on a rather portly man who glanced up from a particularly central overstuffed chair.

"Ah! You've navigated the way at last!" He finished draining his teacup before pushing promptly to his feet. Bending over, he dropped the teacup and saucer onto a low table. With hands clasped behind his back, he straightened and peered up again. His smile was good-natured and genuine. "It *is* a pleasure to meet you in person, Willoughby. Sorry for the rough transport. There's no easy way through the conduit. I do have advice to help you relax for the trip back, but the initial trip is, by necessity, a bit of a baptism by fire. You did land in one piece, I hope. You might want to double check. Sometimes things don't come properly together. We wouldn't want a toe, or ear, or some other critical part poking out where it shouldn't be, would we?" He seemed to be enjoying Willoughby's discomfort. After a short laugh, he continued; "But where are my manners... Come on; come down. Let's sit and chat a bit. That's why we brought you here. You did, by the way, endure the trip admirably for a first timer. Your vital signs never stayed in the red for more than one or two seconds. It probably seemed a bit longer than that to you, but I assure you that your fate was never in question—speaking of which, I'm sure you have a few."

Willoughby stared at the man. "A few what?"

"Questions, of course." The man continued smiling.

"Uh, yeah...you can start by telling me where I am and how I got here."

"Where do you think you are?" The man seemed to be enjoying himself.

Willoughby was too shell-shocked to react. He simply glared. The man didn't seem to mind in the slightest. He was tall, with a large frame—considerably larger, in fact, than Willoughby had imagined from the voice. With his crisp accent and size, one could easily imagine a walrus moustache, a hunting rifle tucked under one arm, and a dog the size of a small donkey panting at the man's knee. The man pulled his smile inward as he studied Willoughby with a bright, curious eye.

"Which do you find most overwhelming—the mystery of who I am, the mode of your transport, or the wonders you see before you? It has been a while since we've had such a young perspective."

"What *do* I see before me?" Willoughby pointed to the water scene outside the glass wall. "It can't be real."

The man's eyes literally danced. "Oh, but it is! I guessed that this view would carry particular fascination for a man of your age. Please, come down for a closer look. It gets even more fascinating."

"What happened to the Certus Grove building?"

"It's right where it should be, Willoughby. It hasn't moved an inch." The man's eyes twinkled.

"That's another thing—how do you know my name?"

"I know everything about you, my friend. I've been watching you for almost three years. I funded the contest that offered a million dollar prize for the solution to the Riemann Hypothesis. I funded the construction of Antonio's Corner Barber on the 16th Street Corridor. You're younger than our average recruit. We had to watch you for a while. We had to be sure."

"Sure about what? Sure I wouldn't think you're a raving lunatic? Is Antonio part of this?"

"Of course, on both accounts."

"How did you do this? How did you bring me here—and where am I?"

"Fair questions," the man nodded. "I intend to answer all questions in due time, but we are not on due time at the moment, so I go back to my original question to you, Willoughby; where do you think you are? Think, my boy… Look around you. Dare to dream."

Willoughby edged toward the stairs. He calculated that the man below must stand at least 6 feet tall from bedroom slippers to the shine on his bald head. He wore what looked like a silky bathrobe over his slacks and shirt. He looked from the man to the expansive window covering the far wall.

"That is either the most realistic 3-D image I've ever seen, or we're looking out on some huge, weird aquarium."

"No, not an aquarium," the man grinned. "Take your time. It is a lot to take in. Meanwhile, I'm off for a quick nip to the kitchen. Hot cocoa and another pot of steaming tea are just the ticket! Caves always seem a bit drafty to me, no matter how you set the temperature..." The man ambled along toward a lit alcove beneath the stairs. He called out as he walked; "By the way, good work on the Riemann Hypothesis. I found it most impressive for your age. We checked it against the original solution, of course. It's a pity that your parents won't let you take advantage of the money, but then they are looking out for your interests, you know. It's good to have the right sort on your team."

"Who are you?" Willoughby called down, barely listening to the man's rambling. The man stopped, backed up a step, and glared up, blinking.

"Who am *I?*"

"Yes," Willoughby repeated. "Who are *you?*"

"Why, I'm H.S. of course. The gadget man, the mad scientist, the—"

"Listen, if you solved the Riemann years ago, why fund the contest? Why not take the credit for solving it yourself? The puzzle has baffled mathematicians since 1859. This doesn't make sense."

"Of course it doesn't make sense! Look out that window, my boy! Does *that* make sense? You've been brought here to learn to see beyond what '*makes sense.*'

Once you understand where you are and how you got here, the purposes and goals of our organization will make perfect *sense*. Until then, you are woefully in the dark. Throw out ill-conceived assumptions without understanding and you appear juvenile and foolish. My word, Willoughby, we've been around for a long time. To stay atop our game, we have no time for defining the mistaken obvious."

Willoughby chose to ignore the tirade rather than try to puzzle it through, but he did cling to the man's reference to goals of an organization. "So, you admit to being part of an organization. Have I heard of the organization?"

The man barked a laugh. "I sincerely doubt it. I'll fall to my grave if you dare accuse us of being CIA or British Intelligence! *Please!*"

"How long have been around?"

The man cocked an eyebrow. "Let's see…Plato was one of us. He didn't comprehend all of what we're about, of course, but he was certainly part of the team."

"Right…and Socrates taught you how to answer questions, I suppose." It was Willoughby's turn to raise an eyebrow.

The man laughed again and began to amble away. "You *are* entertaining, I'll give you that! I'm beginning to understand why we invited you for this visit."

"You mean, shanghaied me," Willoughby mumbled.

"I heard that!" the man responded from somewhere under the stairway. Willoughby heard what sounded like rummaging through a stack of dinnerware, punctuated by the clang of what sounded like pots or tins, and a sound of water running. "I suppose, in a way, we did shanghai you," H.S. continued. "Of course, you would really have to see the origins of Shanghai to appreciate the finer points of the analogy, but all in due time..." The man rummaged around for another four or five minutes, giving Willoughby time to better take in the scene of the room and the strange seascape. At last, the portly man lumbered back into the room with a small tray. He stopped below the stairs and looked up.

"Why on earth are you still up there? Are your feet fully operational? Come on down, my boy! I don't bite—unless, perhaps, you're a crumpet! I've a cup of steaming cocoa prepared here, or perhaps you'd prefer a spot of Earl Grey tea? You need to get some liquid and sugar into you to counteract the effects of the transport."

Willoughby watched the man again and then gazed out the window. "Why would I want to come down and drink tea? You haven't answered my questions."

"Not so! I've answered some," the man stared up, eyes still sparking. "If you're going to stand there and throw out generalities, we'll never get anywhere, now, will we? I'll tell you what, let's do an experiment! You like experiments I believe. This experiment will help you answer your own question, since you don't seem to appreciate the way I answer them. Do you happen to have a pencil?"

Willoughby rummaged in his pack and pulled out a number 2, Ticonderoga pencil. "Which question did you say this would answer?" he asked as he flung the pencil down. The man deftly caught the projectile and took it to the right side of the window. Smiling, he ran his hand over an area that appeared to be smooth glass. An odd, narrow drawer popped out. It was covered by a thin slab of sliding glass. He opened the glass window and placed the pencil in it. The window closed, and the narrow drawer seemed to meld back into the wall.

A moment later, the man pointed: "Look!" he said softly. A sliver of glass on the other side of the window seemed to be moving. The long, narrow drawer slid a full meter outward, into the shadowy waters of what appeared to be sea. The glass over the drawer slid back a crack. Willoughby could barely make out the yellow of the pencil, bobbing to the surface of the box as it filled with sea water. Moments later, the glass lid closed and the drawer slid back into the glass of the window. A soft chime sounded and the narrow box slid back out of the wall on the inside of the room. The man lifted out the drawer. After pausing a moment to pull back the lid, he took out the pencil, replaced the drawer (which slid back into the window) and brought the pencil over to the small table in the center of the huge room. He laid it down next to his tea tray.

"If you ever come down here, you'll see this *is* your pencil, teeth marks and all, waterlogged and smelling of briny sea. Not so easy to pull salt water out of a holographic image, or a video representation, is it now? The smell of sea water also differs sharply from the smell of aquarium water, though this may not be conclusive enough for you just yet. This is no new movie technology or aquarium, Willoughby. If you come down, you'll see that the water goes on for as far as our sight can follow. I dare say you are gazing upon what history calls a '*primordial sea*.'"

Willoughby coughed. "That's—"

"Impossible?"

No. Willoughby had choked the comment because impossible was too limiting a word. He fought for a better way to express his doubt; "*H-how?*"

"*When* would be the precise question. This particular bit of watery real estate is middle to late Jurassic. I've always found the period fascinating from an underwater perspective. How about you?"

The man arranged himself in his chair and then bent over to pour himself another cup of steaming tea. He had spoken as if to himself—as if he didn't really expect a response. He raised his bushy eyebrows, looking back to Willoughby with a wry smile. Leaning back into his cushioned armchair, he gestured toward the overstuffed couch just across from him. Willoughby began to creep down the long, meandering staircase. He was lost for words. The site of the huge window looking out on what appeared to be a Jurassic sea made him completely forget the fear and discomfort of his transport.

"Ah, the biscuits!" the large man shouted, jumping to his feet again. He placed down his cup and saucer. "We can't have tea without biscuits! What *would* Poppins say?" He berated himself sternly as if this were the stupidest mistake anyone could ever make.

Willoughby shook his head. *It was impossible!* That's what it was—utterly and completely impossible. He couldn't be looking at a Jurassic sea! What was he looking at, then? Could the man's experiment be some kind of digital trick? But then, he was *somewhere*—somewhere other than the top of the Certus Grove building. Could they be altering his mind in some way? If so, this was quite a trip. If it was real, the transport mechanism alone proved that these people had serious technology at their disposal. *Could they have conquered time?* He looked out of the glass wall. The depth of perception and the color qualities he could see were so real, and the random movement of plants and creature were so lifelike—*too* lifelike. What was it that the man had said? "*Dare to dream...*"

Thin rays of sunlight danced through the underwater forest of the ocean world, throwing kaleidoscopic patterns across the coral shelf. A quick flurry of movement caught Willoughby's eye. Something bigger than your ordinary fish was swimming in the greenish waters behind the glass—a *lot* bigger! It streaked toward the window, moving fast. The odd, black shape swam with the agility of a seal, changing direction abruptly before diving out of sight. Willoughby's face paled. *He had recognized the shape, but it had been extinct for millions of years!*

The beast darted up again, swimming in a rippling motion, its mouth slightly ajar. Rows of yellow-white serrated teeth grinned below eyes so vibrantly yellow that they seemed to glow. The beast had four broad flippers, a long, snakelike neck, and a flat, pointed head. Its total length had to be at least *45 to 50 feet!* It circled, keeping its distance, then spun suddenly and rushed the window. The glass dimmed. An alarm sounded, and the thin, metal webbing that held the glass in place pulsed stark red. Willoughby could barely make out that the beast had veered away, sinking from view. As the windows again became transparent, he caught a glimpse of the beast darting toward the underside of the coral shelf.

The whole encounter had lasted barely a minute, but Willoughby was spellbound. He stared beyond the distant thicket of weeds where the beast had vanished. His palms were sweating and his breathing was irregular. He pushed the rest of the way down the stairs and crossed to the couch. He needed to sit down.

Within moments, the shuffling, bald man had reappeared. His vibrant blue eyes and smooth face made it hard for Willoughby to judge how old he was. In his hands, he carried a plate of what looked like assorted cookies. He set the cookies down on the coffee table beside the cups and teapots. He then sat on the edge of his overstuffed chair. He picked up the empty teacup and lifted the larger of the teapots.

"Cocoa?"

Willoughby nodded, absently. He was staring down at the pencil on the table. It was his pencil. He could tell by the teeth marks, even without picking it up, and he could smell the briny sea water. The man poured a rich, brown liquid from the larger teapot. He handed the steaming cup over, then picked up his own saucer again and sank back into the comfort of his chair.

Willoughby glanced at the window, stammering; "You, you got a *p-plesiosaurus…*"

The man lowered his cup, raising both eyebrows. "Yes! I thought you might like that. It's why I chose this window." He turned and narrowed his eyes, studying the window before looking back.

"You have other windows?"

"Oh, yes. Dozens. But not in this time period…" The man seemed distracted, peering out into the murky depths of what appeared to be a coral shelf. "Ah!" he said, his face brightening; "We're in luck! The show is only beginning. See that eel fish darting around the edges? See if they don't feed on that—see if they don't!" He placed his teacup down and rubbed his hands together with the excitement of a child. "I never tire of observing the brutes, though they are a bit of a challenge. They're determined to smash through our observation window, you know. I sometimes get four or five alarms in one day."

Willoughby sat near the edge of the couch, peering out at the incredible sight. A massive eel-like fish swam lazily into view. It seemed only twenty or so yards away, wriggling up over the coral shelf. Its teeth were long, pointed and fanged. It had interest in a particularly thick clump of what looked to be sea cucumbers on steroids. The plesiosaurus floated silently up from its hiding place. It inched up behind the eel, barely stirring the water until it was in striking distance. Then, in a sudden blur of motion, it spun, sinking its teeth into the eel-fish just behind the eyes. The fish jerked violently, coiling itself around the plesiosaurus's neck. A second plesiosaurus appeared, darting in from the right side of the glass. It zoomed in on the kill. Blood inked the water. Willoughby turned away.

The large man's eyes twinkled as he picked back up his cup of tea.

"We've an entire pack of the beasties living along our ridge...so graceful, and yet, so *deadly*." He studied Willoughby. "I've named five of them. They hunt all along the rock shelf. In time, I'll introduce you. That one that just attacked—I call him Brutus. He is a cold hunter."

"*What is this place?*" Willoughby whispered, entranced.

The man gave another quick grin. "I've already told you, Willoughby. This is exactly what it appears. You are gazing at a slice of Jurassic Era sea."

"*How?*"

"You tell me."

"You recreated it somehow—cloned it, like in *Jurassic Park*."

"Right—we've found an abandoned cave somewhere and built a Jurassic Era eco-system that stretches on for miles, complete with carnivorous predators such as the plesiosaurus and we keep that secret from the rest of the world. You find that plausible, do you?"

"No."

"Is there a different alternative?"

"You've found a way to travel backward in time."

"Bravo! The first leap of faith! It is hard to accept at first, but yes, you're hundreds of thousands of years from Georgetown, or the Certus Grove building, Willoughby. You won't find any cell reception here."

Willoughby didn't know what to say. He half expected someone to jump out with a camera and explain that this was some sort of hi-tech show for the Sci-Fi channel. But this was real. He looked out the window and saw with his own eyes an unpredictable rawness, one that only nature could create.

The man leaned forward. "For us, my boy, time travel is no longer a movie plot or a theme park ride. It is pure mathematics put in motion. We've unraveled the nature of time, I dare say." He leaned back. "I knew you would need to see it for yourself or you wouldn't believe me. It is grand, isn't it?" He waved a hand absently toward the window. "What do you think? Is it a worthy prize—the chance to cheat time itself, to see a plesiosaurus in the wild? You see now why I had to pull you through, don't you?"

Willoughby gulped. He closed his eyes trying to grasp the concept. When he opened them again, his face was ashen. "Through what? You mentioned a name—the NT or something. What is it? And who are 'we'? Is this some sort of secret multi-government project or agency? Who do you represent?"

The man laughed again. "We are talented at hiding things, but hiding brilliance behind a government agency is beyond even our skill." He lowered his teacup, turning it exactly a quarter turn on the saucer. "Can you imagine a government agency efficient enough to achieve something of this magnitude? We're not political, Willoughby. We're a clandestine group of like-minded scientists and financiers. Fringes of us have been around in some form or other for thousands of years. Here," He handed Willoughby a business card. "The name is Hathaway Simon. My friends, who I hope will soon include you, call me H.S. Think of me as a visionary. I have…brought enhancements to the historic organization. We are completely independent of all military agendas or politics. What we do could save or destroy mankind. Only a handful of unique individuals can be trusted with that kind of responsibility."

"But you're able to be trusted with this kind of responsibility?" Willoughby gestured toward the window.

H.S. smiled. "Again, you pose a fair question. Perhaps I'm not to be trusted. The best defense I can provide is that I surround myself with checks and balances. I have also learned enough about God to know He has checks and balances of His own."

"What do you want from me?"

H.S. lifted his teacup and took another slow sip. "We've been watching you. We think you may be interested in working with us. You solved a puzzle that has stumped the world's greatest mathematical minds for centuries and you allowed your parents to hush it up. That's hard for a boy still young enough to fall prey to the mirage of world fame. I have a proposition for you,

Willoughby, a way for you to use that mathematical gift that you possess in ways you can't imagine."

"To map time?"

H.S. smiled. "Perhaps... A more accurate description would be to explore time; to learn from it."

Willoughby wiped a hand across his eyes. "I feel like I'm hallucinating—like this is some sort of dream. It's too incredible to be believed. I keep looking for some sign of Disney Imagineering or Lucas's Industrial Light and Magic. I saw a solid wall melt open and a floor turn to liquid. I was pulled through something and felt like my body was torn to shreds, then pieced back together. I've watched a plesiosaurus feed in the wild. I can't seem to get my mind around it."

"You will. When one's reality shifts, it takes a while to adjust. But it always does. Besides, this may yet become little more than a dream to you. You have not accepted our offer."

"What offer?"

H.S. ignored the question. "You will not get a second chance. If you turn us down, we disappear from your life forever. You will wake up, dazed and confused, in the stairwell of the Certus Grove and will be left to wonder if you ever really time-traveled at all." H.S. gave a wry smile and took another sip of tea. "Drink your cocoa, try a biscuit. I find myself partial to the chocolate-tipped crescent moons."

As Willoughby took a cookie, he looked at the business card in his hand. He read; "H.S., Executive Director, Observations, Inc." At the bottom of the card, in slanted italics, was a short catchphrase: *Cryptic Spaces, Doorways to Distant Places.*

"Cryptic spaces... what's that supposed to mean."

"Can't you guess? Encryption is a way of hiding information in plain sight. In our lives, we perceive only those patterns around us our brains identify as important. The average brain perceives less than 10% of what exists. Part of the issue is distraction. Text messages, iPhone libraries, fashion choices—there are so many patterns easily accessible to occupy our time. Part of the issue is the chaotic nature of time itself. A fleeting thing in an all-too-finite world, we cling to the comfort of routine. Whatever the reason, Observations, Inc. was created to operate in the other 90 percent—the places the average mind does not see and could not comprehend. How many people, for example, enter and exit the Certus Grove building each day, having no idea that there is hidden or unused space in the building? How many have climbed the very stairwell you climbed, wondered about why the top ledge extends the entire length of the wall, well past the ladder to the roof, but stopped there, never guessing that a hidden door was there for the discovering? We are an elite group, Willoughby. You should feel honored."

Willoughby listened, but gave no response. He flipped the card in his hand over. On the back of the card was the symbol 313, with the last 3 backward. Just above the numbers, a faint spiral of golden triangles drifted into infinity. He thought of how he had sensed that something was different about the space that became the Corner Barber. He then remembered how he had sensed more than seen the hidden door in the Certus Grove. He thought of the flares of light he glimpsed around this same symbol that was on the back of this business card. *Everything seemed to be tied to this symbol!* He placed the card slowly into his shirt pocket and pushed back into the couch. "What was that thing that brought me here? You called it a conduit. Does it sometimes appear as more a rip or tear?"

H.S. gave him a curious glance. "The conduit, or Negative Density Tunnel if you want a more scientific description, is a sort of punctured hole that momentarily creates a conduit by equalizing the density between points on a continuum, creating negative suction," H.S. answered. "Of course, that means little to you. Further explanation would only confuse you at this point. It will take years for you to figure it all out, Willoughby. Could we get back to our...proposition for you?"

"You can propose what you like, but until I know more—until I have some idea how all this works—I'm not saying yes to anything."

H.S. smiled. "Okay. I expected as much. I'll give you the 10,000 foot view."

Willoughby waited as the large man sipped at his tea. He decided to take a sip of his own hot chocolate. It was warm and rich. A thought occurred to him. He looked up; "What is Antonio's connection with you? The symbol on the back of your card is over his door."

H.S.'s eyes twinkle. "Antonio may not be what he seems." He leaned forward in his chair. "I trust his opinion. He's been observing you for almost two years now. He is part of my team. His whole shop was built primarily to attract you. Sam, your chauffeur, is also a part of our organization. Not every barber, or mundane worker, is what they may appear. When Sam isn't driving you to and from that dreadful private academy, he coordinates multi-dimensional transportation for our organization and pilots my yacht. Antonio has even richer skills as a structural architect and a first rate inter-dimensional engineer."

"Multi-dimensional transportation? Inter-dimensional engineer?" Willoughby shook his head. "You sound like a character from some Sci-Fi Channel movie. Antonio is a barber! He's good at cracking a joke and he may be smart and adventurous, but he sure doesn't appear to me to be some kind of engineering genius. He was born in East Los Angeles. He received his training from his father, who was also a barber."

"True. Would you describe yourself, then, as a typical teenager? That's how you probably appear to those who don't really know you." H.S. pursed his lips; "You won't be long with us, Willoughby, if you don't learn to look beyond initial appearances. Did you know that, typically, less than ten percent of an iceberg is visible above the water? When you learn to truly observe, you'll find life to be more fascinating than you ever imagined. Antonio designed the Certus Grove building and Antonio's Corner Barber. A Hispanic barber like his father? Yes…but I think you suspected there was more to him than that."

Willoughby was quiet for a long moment. Suddenly, H.S. didn't seem as much like a dotty old Englishman. He seemed very bright, very alert, and very much in control of this conversation. "So, what has Antonio told you about me?"

"He thinks you have potential. He wants to personally supervise you on the team."

"Antonio cuts my hair every other week. I solved a famous mathematical puzzle. How could he possibly know enough about me to suggest me for something like…this?"

"He has uncanny abilities of observation."

"You rely solely on his observations? How do you know I won't go straight to the police? Or the military, or something?"

H.S. raised an eyebrow. "You'd have a hard time finding them here. Besides, I do rely on my team, and Antonio is a key member. I trust his instincts. And, I...knew your father."

Willoughby felt as if he had been punched. "*Knew?*" he mumbled numbly.

"Yes. He worked for me for a while. Then, he left us. I am speaking of your birth father, Willoughby, of Gustav."

Gustav? He fought to keep the strange mix of anger, hurt, and hope out of his face. "My father knew about...about this?" Willoughby gestured toward the window where a pair of plesiosaurs darted past.

H. S. paused, considering the question. "Oddly enough, no. He worked for us as a civilian engineer, though I immediately saw in him great talent. I had planned to offer him the position that eventually went to Antonio."

"Why didn't you?"

H.S. shrugged. "I couldn't. One day, he disappeared. We were never able to find him."

Willoughby looked away. "He was good at disappearing."

"I'm sorry, Willoughby. I know it's been hard."

Willoughby gritted his teeth. No, the man did *not know* what it was like to have your father walk away and never come back. Still, he wanted to somehow find Gustav. Could this man help? Controlling his expression, he managed a casual question: "So, you felt he was right for your team?"

"Yes. He had many of the same traits we observed in you—mathematical brilliance, modesty, an ability to look beyond the superficial, a wry sarcasm, a sense of humor, a stubborn resourcefulness, a guarded optimism—"

Willoughby cut H.S. off. "Yeah, but I wouldn't just walk away from my family."

H.S. peered at him curiously. "Remember what I said earlier about assumptions, Willoughby. I don't know why your father left you and your mother, but I do know that things are not always what they may seem."

Willoughby sighed, blowing out a long breath. It was time to change the topic of conversation. "Did you recruit Antonio as a kid, too?"

"No." H.S. said after a pause. He took another sip of tea. "We don't usually recruit this young, Willoughby. You're a special case. There has only been one other."

"Who?"

"A girl. She's brilliant with languages and is a world-renowned violinist."

"Sydney?"

"Yes. So, Antonio told you about her?"

"Not much." Willoughby couldn't help thinking of her shiny black hair and haunting eyes. He looked down at his hands. "So, is your interest in *me*, in *my* mathematical skill, or am I here because I'm Gustav's son?"

"All of the above. Gustav had an uncanny ability with infrastructure algorithms, but he did not solve the Riemann Hypothesis."

"*Infrastructure algorithms?* …this is a lot to take in."

"Yes. It is. And I'm afraid it's only the beginning. Time seems to have a sense of humor, I dare say, a sense of balance. The more you delve in, the less you're inclined to believe that chance is ever purely random. We believe we were meant to find you, Willoughby. Perhaps you were meant to find us, too. Perhaps there are questions in time that you are meant to answer."

Like why Gustav left, Willoughby thought. He felt suddenly edgy. He didn't like discussing his birth father, especially when his mind was so confused and he was speaking with a man he barely knew. *Antonio a brilliant architect and engineer? Time travel to a Jurassic era sea? The chance to find out what really happened to his father?* The possibilities collided and competed in his mind.

"Antonio and Sam are not the only people you've seen from our organization. Remember the men with the coveralls that sported the 'O' for '*Observations Inc.?*' You've also mentioned Sydney Senoya. What is your impression from what Antonio has told you of her?"

"She's beautiful. She's creative. She likes surprising people. She doesn't like to be thought of as ordinary."

H.S. pursed his lips. "I would have said she likes *shocking* people, but you have the gist. Now, I suppose I should start explaining how we do what we do." He stood, pausing a long moment to stare out the window toward the undulating sea. When he looked back, his eyes nearly glowed. "We are capable of wonderful things, Willoughby. We offer adventures beyond your wildest imaginations... We help connect the present with the past in ways that can safeguard the future." The man carefully gauged Willoughby's reactions. "You're curious, but you're cautious. Good."

At that very moment, shadows darkened the window. A siren sounded as a plesiosaurus slammed what was left of the eel fish against the window. The panes of the enormous window not only pulsed red this time, but crackled with electricity. The beast jerked, sliding off the window to pull its prey away, over the edge of the coral reef. H.S. nodded toward the pulsing window. "That jolt of electricity was enough to kill a fair-sized elephant. There *is* danger involved in what we do, Willoughby. You need to know that. After all, we travel in time, we visit hostile environments. The decision to join us is not one to be taken lightly. But, there are compensations. We offer you a home among peers, challenges that will daily test your ability, and a place where your mind can grow without limits."

Willoughby thought about something Antonio had said to him once. They had been chatting about James Glaisher, fantasizing about what it would be like to soar alone into the troposphere with nothing but a single weather balloon to hold you in the sky. Antonio had stopped clipping hair and looked at him wistfully. *"Sometimes, my friend, the greatest adventure is the one right in front of your nose."*

Was this what he meant? With a single word, could his whole life really transform into a landscape of wonder and intrigue? He tried to hide the rush of exhilaration that tickled at the back of his mind. Leaning forward to pick up the steaming cocoa from the coffee table, he took a sip. "Okay," he said, wiping chocolate from his lip, "you've got my attention."

7

Nessie

H.S. placed his teacup down and gave a curt nod. "I should hope we have your attention." He stood, fishing for something in his pocket. "So, let's make the best use of it." He turned his head slightly to the breathtaking view of the window. The battle in the water was over. The eel fish had gone limp as the beasts dragged it to a flat section of coral. One beast began to devour the carcass while the other bobbed toward the surface. It shot back moments later, bulleting straight down. It tore a huge chunk from the fish, leaving a new stain of dark blood diffusing into the water. The scene provided a dramatic backdrop to H.S.'s large profile. The large man turned to him.

"Should we discuss the how and the why behind our technology first?"

Willoughby pushed to the edge of the couch. He stood and moved toward the window, running a hand over its smooth, glassy surface. It was warm to the touch. "Why here? What do you do besides just observe? Did you plan this, this predator battle? Did you somehow know it would happen the moment you pulled me here?"

H.S. pursed his lips. "We observe, Willoughby. We learn. Timing is not always a happy accident. The Jurassic is raw and untamed. I could not predict the exact show you would be witness to in our great, natural theater, but I knew nature wouldn't disappoint."

"You can't predict time with mathematics?"

"Mathematics is at the core of everything we do, but nature is mostly beautiful because it defies absolute predictability. We observe. We speculate. We laugh when nature proves us wrong. "

Willoughby considered. "But why? What do you want from time? Money? Power? Treasure? What do you want from me?"

H.S. tapped his lip, leaning down conspiratorially. "Adventure," he whispered, "a hunger to know simply because it challenges life's limits. Treasure, money, power—these are hollow solutions in and of themselves. The real prize is the quest, the journey. What do we want from you? Eyes, capable of helping us see in the dark."

"*What?*" Willoughby didn't give H.S. time to answer. "Maybe I'm comfortable with my life as it is."

"Then, by all means, go back to it. Our organization is not for everybody. If you worked with us, you would not be able to share what you discover with your family, with those who are close to you, Willoughby. The life we will ask you to lead as a member of Observations, Inc. will, at times, seem lonely. You'll be asked to lead a double life— one as an ordinary person in a typical span of life, and another as an adventurer across multiple time spans. Is this a sacrifice you could make?"

Willoughby ran his hand over to the metal webbing that separated the glassy panes of the window. It had the same smooth, cool feel as the walls inside the hidden room at the Certus Grove building. "This isn't an ordinary metal, is it?"

H.S. shook his head.

Willoughby turned. "Okay, let's talk about the technology. I have to have some idea of how all this works. I also want more specifics about what you do."

H.S. stared down at him thoughtfully. "The passages of time are full of wonders, Willoughby, but you don't have to travel outside of time to find adventure. You may be destined to accomplish much in your life even without us."

"What about *with* you?"

"With us, you will gain perspectives that change you in unpredictable ways. You will be like a rat that has escaped time's clever maze. We observe patterns in the parade of life, patterns that written history and conjecture lack the perspective to see. We extract from those patterns understanding, to shape for life a brighter future."

"Then you are trying to shape the future?"

"Of course I am. Men of destiny have always tried to shape the future, my boy."

"With very questionable success."

H.S. gave a good-natured shrug. "Agreed."

"How do you know that your '*observations*' won't somehow darken the future of mankind?"

"How do any of us know that our footprints won't have effects that are unintended?"

"Yeah, but your footprints, from what I see, are enormous."

H.S. grinned. "Quite so... Which is why our '*observations*' must be so keen. There is power in careful observation. Secrets are hidden all around us. For one with eyes that truly see, the world can be a most fascinating place. Just think of the top of the Certus Grove building."

Willoughby did. He also thought of the Corner Barber and the glowing number strings he had seen. *Should he mention this to H.S.?* The man continued to talk with animated enthusiasm.

"Even our name, *Observations, Inc.*, was not randomly chosen. A willingness to open eyes and mind to new potential realities is essential to everything we do. In fact, the clues that allowed us to develop our time-travel technology have been in front of us since life on this planet began. We just had to learn to see them."

"Some of those clues are hidden in the symbol, aren't they? The symbol marks both the door to Antonio's shop and the door at the top of the Certus Grove."

"Yes, but the symbol is just a start."

"A start…You mean a launch point for time travel? Does that mean we could somehow travel from Antonio's Corner Barber as well as from the Certus Grove?"

"Not exactly—" H.S. started, but Willoughby cut him off. His mind was racing now.

"Are there number strings associated with the travel—strings you can see? Was Antonio planning some kind of travel last night?"

H.S. stopped cold. He was quiet for a long moment and then gave Willoughby a curious look. "Those are interesting questions. Antonio's shop rests on a natural hole, a weakness in our present time/space that we have not yet exploited. What brought up your question about number strings?"

Willoughby stared at the man for a long moment, afraid that he had already said too much. "In that room at the top of the Certus Grove," he finally said. "I thought I saw flickering lines of numbers. They lit the whole room."

The man's eyes narrowed. "Transport generally provides quite a light show—or, at least, the perception of one—but to see number strings...Extraordinary."

H.S. was quiet for a long moment. "What you could not have known is that there are devices that help us translate gravitational potentialities into equations. They scroll very quickly, so it takes a brilliant mathematician to be able to follow and understand the number strings that branch from and to various time corridors. Perhaps you have some sort of innate sense of these corridors. You begin to see why we are interested in you. The theory is that these equations can help one navigate a natural hole successfully to unsecured points in time. We surmise, though, that this sort of navigation will only be effective in a natural hole, where travel is based on timing rather than on the enhancement benefits of technology anchoring both ends."

"Technology?" Willoughby frowned. "I don't understand."

H.S.'s bushy eyebrows lifted. "Of course you don't." He paused a moment, then let his face break into a wide grin. He held up what looked like an old fountain pen. "What do you know, Willoughby, about the circumpolar stars?" He slid a finger over the pen and a holographic image bloomed out. It seemed to be a star field.

Willoughby blinked. "*Circumpolar stars?*"

"Centuries ago," H.S. continued, "Egyptians embraced the idea that time and space could be warped by arranging mass into shapes with exacting mathematical properties. They believed that the pyramid, with its perfect right triangles, could bridge our fragile mortality with the eternity of the Gods. A secret pyramid tunnel, designed to anchor this bridge, pointed to a place of fixed darkness in the night sky, a hub around which all stars seemed to rotate. We know this hub today as the center of our universe. The two bright stars rotating closest to the hub are called the circumpolar stars. "

Two stars in the hologram glowed blue. Willoughby sat back, stealing a nibble on his chocolate tipped crescent moon. H.S. brushed his finger back over the pen. The hologram disappeared.

"The Egyptians weren't far off. There is indeed power in the heavens and exacting mathematics *can* tame it. When properly harnessed, gateways can be created that intersect various cracks in time's plodding corridors—rips in the unraveling ribbon that connects present and past. But how do we harness a power so vast that it can penetrate the walls of time? Fast forward to the time of the ancient Greeks…They discovered a ratio that is repeated in nature over and over and over."

H.S. touched the pen and holograms of various images populated the air; a nautilus, a leaf, a human face, a sunflower…

"The *golden mean*," Willoughby noted.

"Yes." H.S. started toward the back of the cavern, motioning Willoughby to follow. He walked directly at a section of smooth wall. When he was within two feet, a flash of light engulfed him and he was gone. Willoughby hesitated before walking cautiously toward the section of unmarred wall. Light flashed, and he found himself standing beside H.S. in a brightly lit corridor. He glanced back. Unmarred wall was only about two feet away, this time, *behind* him. H.S. only smiled.

"I trust you're familiar with M theory?" he said, conversationally. Willoughby looked up, his jaw hanging open. "Oh, come now," H.S. continued; "What self-respecting Ninja couldn't walk through walls." With a wry grin, he set off again at a brisk pace. Willoughby had to almost run to catch up with him.

"Einstein theorized that time was the fourth dimension," he lectured as Willoughby caught up. "M theory concludes that dimensions form as membranes or '*branes*,' and that there are an infinite number of them."

Willoughby had to fight the urge to pant as he matched the big man's stride. He offered what little he knew of the topic. "M Theory is a spin-off of string theory, isn't it? While string theory allows the concept of gravity to work within the framework of quantum mechanics, M theory pushes it out over the dimensional *branes*."

H.S. ducked into a dim archway to his left. As Willoughby followed, he found himself in a circular room with a high, domed ceiling. He paused a moment, letting his eyes adjust. H.S. had already taken his pen out again and was pointing it toward a low console. The light dimmed further, allowing the ceiling to become alive with millions of stars. They seemed to have stepped into a planetarium of sorts.

H.S. gazed up. "Actually, the two theories are connected. Time, you see, is not a single dimension, but an infinity of dimensions. Individual *branes* flow over us like a vast tide flowing over an isolated coral reef." He pointed his pen at the star-bedazzled dome. The dome darkened, throwing the room into a deep, penetrating blackness. Only H.S.'s voice filled the void. He spoke in a heightened, excited tone, as if he were a child showing off a prized possession.

"In the visual spectrum, when the various colors of light combine, they form a pure, blindingly white light. Try to imagine, Willoughby, an intersection of all mass, and space, and time. We will call this point of intersection *infinity*. It is a point that has no beginning and no end—a perpetual dynamo of ceaseless potentialities, manifest by *ceaseless, seething motion*." Swirls appeared across the dome, slowly caressing the darkness.

"The speed of motion is called *velocity*. What is the velocity of infinity? Einstein speculated that a velocity at or above the speed of light would be the point at which time stands still—the point of breakthrough between the finite, governed by time, and the infinite, where time ceases to exist, or '*stands still*.' Now, let's turn the equation around. What could make a velocity at or above the speed of light slow down? Imagine in this infinity of ceaseless potentialities two diametrically opposed velocities colliding… "

A massive explosion shattered the dome with blinding light, forcing Willoughby to look away. As he finally turned back, gas and matter began to appear near the center of the explosion, spreading out in a sort of inky soup.

"The Big Bang," Willoughby murmured.

"Yes," H.S. agreed. "The speed of motion is slowed below the threshold of infinity and a hemorrhage ensues. The hemorrhage spreads, and time is born. I don't expect you to fully grasp the concept, but you may get a sense of it. What your science describes as a single, colossal event is actually the result of an ongoing event, an infinite event occurring *outside* of time.

Willoughby raised his eyebrows, but H.S. didn't seem to notice, caught up in his explanation.

"We may not see the active rift, but we are aware of the ripples or pulses emanating from it. The measure of these pulses is the basis of finite time. Now, back to M

Theory; imagine each pulse from this hemorrhage as a *brane* or a dimension of time. Remember our discussion on velocity, and consider how many of these branes are created each moment—rippling outward like waves on a pond. They are the heartbeat of our finite universe. Everything we know, everything we can surmise of our physical universe is shaped by how we move within the field of these pulses. The push of this flow is outward toward an expanding horizon we call the future."

The star scene above disappeared as a series of white-lined sketches populated the blackness, intersecting the stars to portray familiar angles and point out ratios. "Which brings us," H.S. continued, "back to the golden mean. As velocity slows, movement becomes more organized. Patterns of movement develop that are able to anchor themselves within the flow of time/space. The golden ratio is one of nature's most effective patterns. It helps stabilize us in place, allowing time to flow through us."

Willoughby spoke into the darkness. "You're saying the *golden mean,* as a pattern, holds matter steady in a point of space—and that allows it to resist the push of time?"

H.S. patted his shoulder and gave a quick nod. "You're getting it. This pattern is built into us at the atomic level where the line between motion and matter blurs to extinction. Our world is not as solid as we suppose. We are beings created entirely from *patterned* velocity, from organized motion. A train moving at a high enough speed will seem to be solid, despite the fact that there are wide gaps between cars. A movie seems to be fluid, though it is made from hundreds of still images.

"M Theory, as you rightly observed, was developed to account for the weakness of gravity—the weakest of the four known forces we study in standard physics. It suggests that this weakness exists because gravity acts across multiple *branes* simultaneously. Physicists have long stated that there's no such thing as *empty space*. Even in the remotest corners of our universe, what appears to be nothingness is, in fact, teeming with particles and antiparticles appearing and disappearing in subatomic foam. M theory attempts to explain how these particles wink in and out of existence. It gives us our first clue into the enormous role gravity plays in creating our finite world."

"You're losing me. What does this have to do with time travel?" Willoughby felt his mind spinning. He had expected H.S. to show him some sort of fancy machine or point him to some simple, mathematical equation that could act as a framework for him to build on. Maybe H.S. was purposely trying to confuse him so that, if he didn't agree to be part of the organization, he would have no clue how the technology worked.

"Think about it, Willoughby," H.S. said patiently. "You are losing particles and antiparticles from finite space—you have a tire that is losing air. You believe the tire has a slow leak, so what do you do?" H.S. waited a moment, and then answered his own question. "You find the hole."

The man drew in a sharp breath. "That's what we've done. We've followed the map of nature and found the hole. The *golden mean* is, as the Greeks asserted, *God's own ratio*. It's the 'X' that marks the spot, so to speak. You see, *shape* is critical to penetrating individual *branes*, allowing one to tunnel backward through the pulses of on-coming dimensions—to travel backward in physical time."

"Only backward?"

H.S. gave him an approving nod. "That's a perceptive question. To go forward in time, one must have a target point to anchor the travel. We cannot anchor travel to a future we do not know, though we can travel back to the present from the past."

Willoughby tilted his head. This seemed to make sense. H.S. continued on.

"Geometric shapes adhering to the *golden ratio*, you see, forever repeat within themselves. They collapse and expand in perfect *golden spirals*. This is critical to understanding time travel."

H.S. clicked the pen instrument again, creating another hologram that illustrated the collapsing of matter to move through a sub-atomic hole, then the matter reforming on the other side.

"These golden spirals allow pulses of infinity to pass through us so that we're not washed away. The process includes a collapsing, a reverse of polarity, and then an expanding again until the pulse passes and polarity once again shifts. The process happens hundreds or possibly thousands of times a second, so we fail to notice. What seems to us solid matter is, in point of fact, a continually collapsing and expanding pattern of motion. But we can't stop here. We started with a discussion of gravity. We would propose that gravity is a by-product of this specific pattern of motion—a sort of cosmic inertia created by the motion." The dome of the room burst into a panoramic view of a wind farm. "To better understand, imagine a wind farm, Willoughby. How is the energy of the wind harnessed?"

"The wind turns propellers, which operate a generator."

"How is the wind able to turn the propellers? The wind interacts with the *shape* of the propeller blade. This shape allows the energy of the wind to create motion, to cause the propeller blade to turn. This motion, then, allows for the harvest of the energy. Certain shapes in matter facilitate the harvest of energy. While propellers are used to harvest energy from the wind, shapes formed to approximate the *golden ratio* harvest energy from the pulsing of time. The by-product of this process is a force capable of anchoring an expanding and collapsing element of motion to a definable point, creating finite space. This by-product acts as a counterforce to the pulsing hemorrhage of infinity. It is the force we call gravity."

H.S. clicked the steel pointer. Star charts appeared, broken into vectors and spirals.

"Here is the key we found to drilling backwards in time. What would happen, Willoughby, if a monster wind hit a certain wind farm, cranking out so much electrical energy that it overwhelmed the grids and containers designed to store and control it?"

"I don't know. It would probably blow up a generator or something."

"Yes. And the same thing can happen with gravity across multiple *branes*; it can arch out, like some great lightning bolt, yanking matter from its resident anchor point in time and jerking it backwards."

"Only to the past?" Willoughby asked.

"Yes, only to the past, counter to the direction of the outward ripples. Gravity gains its energy from working against these ripples. It must be understood, though, that matter jerked away from its resident anchor point maintains a mathematical connection to its resident time—a corridor, so to speak, that will eventually draw the matter back. Every point in time, you see, has a signature. A thing out of its signature time is like a bit of sand in a clam shell. Forces naturally build around the thing, isolating it, smoothing its edges so that, eventually, it is more easily carried back to where it should be. So you see, everything we do with our technology is designed to accelerate a natural process. Look."

Words and images began to appear across the dome. A small picture of an old, army-type airplane appeared over the words: *Flight 441, Navy transport, 42 passengers, disappeared less than 100 miles off the coast of Bermuda, 1954.*

"We've found that some points, some areas, seem more prone to gravity strikes than others. We've found some holes that are, more or less, constant." He clicked his control again and a different configuration of stars appeared. He traced the spiral to its point. New words and a new video enactment appeared: *Entire British battalion disappears into a storm cloud, never found, Suvla Bay, Turkey, 1915.* H.S. turned to Willoughby.

"In a swiftly flowing river, Willoughby, there are places where eddies and whirlpools form. The fabric of time/space is peppered with such anomalies. They are areas where massive gravity storms have struck, weakening resistance against the constant onslaught of new pulses, new waves, new ripples of time. We call them *natural holes.* We have located several across the breadth of our globe and have built structures designed to attract and enhance whatever gravity storms exist at any given moment across our world. In essence, we've built a lightning rod to help us call and then tame the storm."

Willoughby listened, fascinated. "But how can you control where a pulse sends you? How can you return?"

H.S. had started walking toward a segment of dark wall and motioned for Willoughby to follow. A light flashed and they were suddenly on the other side of the wall, walking on a metal catwalk that overlooked a hive of industrial activity. The sound was deafening. Willoughby stared with disbelief at the dimensions of the cavern below him. Carved into the solid rock, the room was five times the size of the observation room. The catwalk extended across the top of the cavern for about 30 yards, then disappeared into billows of black smoke. An intense arc of light zipped and snapped from the center of the smoke, masking the tip of a huge, revolving structure of heavy, well-greased metal. Wrapped in a skin of dark metallic sheeting and pitted with silver piping and bundles of copper wire, the enormous structure was in the shape of a revolving pyramid. The bundles of wire glowed red with heat and the dark metal skin emitted a bluish haze. Electrical arcs crackled and buzzed up the sides of the pyramid toward the crimson gasses at the tip.

Willoughby stared, amazed. The room was functioning like a giant organism. Automated arms swung and reached, heavily-shielded computer screens scrolled lines of telemetry, industrial turbines whined, like some ancient beast's foul breath. Heavy iron braces, similar to the ones Willoughby had seen at the top of the Certus Grove building only immensely larger, clung to the cavern walls like giant ribs. It was like nothing Willoughby had ever seen. *"An electromagnetic pyramid?"* He yelled.

"A very powerful one," H.S. nodded. He pointed to the brilliant arc. "Here, an un-tethered hole exists, raw and unbridled by the safeguards of the door through which *we* travel. By feeding the energy of this hole into a structured corridor, we can create an arc, so to speak, between the two lightning rod points."

"You have similar devices on both sides of the natural hole?" Willoughby asked. "I didn't see anything of this scope at the top of the Certus Grove building."

"Quite right," H.S. shouted. "The Certus Grove is merely a conduction point. The real tip of the corridor in your resident time is hidden thousands of fathoms below the sea off the coast of Bermuda. Remember, time has an order in which everything fits nicely. When something is pulled out of its natural time, its phase is shifted. It creates repulsion to the artificial time it has landed in, and carries attraction to where it should be. Over hundreds, sometimes thousands of years, all things that were pulled out of their natural time are returned. Of course we can't wait that long, so we use the power of the natural hole to quicken the process."

"By how much?" Willoughby yelled back.

"The return trip takes less than two minutes," H.S. smiled. His voice was growing hoarse.

Willoughby blinked. It all seemed like a dream to him. "Okay. Let's say I believe you, you've found a way to hitch a ride through natural holes in time. What keeps you from affecting the past? What if you destroy things?"

"Contrary to popular myth, Willoughby," H.S. began, pausing to cough and then leaning in close, "it isn't possible to travel in time and change things. The past is set; it has a weave, a design, a substance. Though certain elasticity allows for minor deviations, any attempt to alter essential events causes a bulge in time's fabric. Forces you cannot imagine act upon the anomaly until it is forced back into alignment with the natural weave. It would take a great deal more power than we have discovered to make a change that could imprint back through hundreds of millions of unique pulses of time. So time ignores us. We are here, but we are not here. We are solid and real while we stand here, but we are not allowed to stay outside our time for extended periods. When we leave, we become to this time only ghosts—slight blips, buried and forgotten in a weave that heals back into its known form."

"But what about the facility?" Willoughby said.

"That's a little more difficult to explain. In essence, the facility is transported here anew every 48.7 days. The old facility becomes a ghost and never existed."

H.S. was wheezing now, and motioned Willoughby to follow him back. He continued to try to talk as they were walking. They once again passed through the dark wall into the star-studded domed room. They passed out of the archway into the brightly lit corridor. "The jerk you felt when the hole activated was the force of being sucked through the porous skin of multiple branes or dimensions."

"That's a pretty neat trick. I didn't see any machinery or hardware at all in the room atop the Certus Grove." They moved quickly toward the walled dead-end of the hallway. Willoughby felt his eyes watering at the sudden change from the dim, smoke-filled cavern where the electromagnetic pyramid had been, through the dark planetarium, and now into the sudden brightness of the hallway.

H.S. licked his lips. "*Certus* is a Latin word. It means '*certain*' or '*undisputed.*' One of Antonio's great talents is his ability to design great shells to hide our machines. Do you see the hint in the name of the building? A grove is a place that can hide many secrets. You didn't know it, but our technology was all around you in the Certus Grove building." They reached the end of the bright corridor and flashed back into the flickering ambiance of the observation lounge. H.S. sighed with satisfaction at the quiet calm that seemed to permeate the observation room. He stopped beside his chair and picked up his tea. He took a deep drink, smiled, and placed the teacup back down, rotating the cup slightly. The hot liquid obviously worked wonders for his dry throat. He clasped his hands behind his back with a grin. "Well, young Willoughby, there you have the nickel tour. Are you ready to give me a decision?"

Willoughby stared back at the smooth wall they had passed through. "How do you do that door trick? It's like we just reorganized on the other side."

H.S. smiled. "You're looking at the ultimate Sholin priest. I can teach you to walk through walls. But not today—today I think I've given you plenty to think about. So, how about it? Are you in?"

Willoughby didn't answer immediately. He wandered over to the great, curved observation window. Just beyond, he saw dark creatures, like nervous minnows, darting back and forth between odd-looking underwater plants. Streams of sunlight penetrated down through the greenish blue water, forming a patchwork mosaic across the ancient ocean view. It was unbelievable, incomprehensible, *and yet it was there!*

A third, much smaller plesiosaurus swooped down, poking at the shredded remains of the giant eel-like fish, determined to devour every last morsel from the skeleton.

H.S. came up behind him. "There we are...Nessie," he whispered.

Willoughby turned. "*Nessie?*"

H.S. explained. "Yes. I named her in honor of her many cousins who have died formulating the myth of Loch Ness. Links between two natural holes do exist, though they are rare. We call them *time bridges*. One such link connects our sister cave, about 200 yards around the back of this same rock structure, to a dark, narrow chasm that opens into the thick murky depths of that particular Scottish lake."

"The Loch Ness monster..." Willoughby mumbled.

H.S.'s voice became soft, almost affectionate. "It's a cruel trick of time. When both ends of the link become active, the hole itself glows. The beasts, attracted by the light, swim into the glow. Invariably, one gets too close, and is jerked forward to be spit out into an icy sediment soup. With the frigid water temperatures and lack of available prey, the creature will last less than a week in the Loch before sinking to the deep bottom and disappearing, like countless others of its kind, buried under blankets of silt."

Willoughby imagined the hulk of a beast sinking into darkness and oblivion.

"So," H.S. said, shifting gears, "do we count you in?"

Willoughby was caught off guard. "You haven't told me about my assignment. What, exactly, are you recruiting me to do?"

H.S. replied carefully. "We're interested in a self-proclaimed seer named Nostradamus. He predicted many future events with uncanny accuracy. We want to know what makes him tick. We've assembled a team to travel to medieval France. That's all I can tell you for now."

"There are a lot of unknowns," Willoughby said.

"We are explorers, Willoughby. Probing the unknown is what we do. Life, raw and uncharted, is the grand adventure. Look out at that primordial sea. Don't you feel it in your blood? You can't get that kind of feeling staring at a book or lecturing for the accolades of academia. What does your current path offer—a bench on the sidelines where you push chalk? With us, you push *boundaries*. With us, you enter the unknown, the indefinable game."

Willoughby breathed in deeply. He looked out again at the view from the observation window. Three squid-like creatures darted by the glass. *Belemnites*. It surprised him that he remembered the name, but then prehistoric creatures had always fascinated him. He glimpsed an eel-like fish in the distance. *An ichthyosaur, here to feed on the belemnites*. He had done a report in school on Belemnites, a primary food source of the Ichthyosaur during the Jurassic. He looked to H.S.

"I tell it like I see it and expect others to do the same."

"Understood."

"If I'm to be a member of the team, I want to be treated as an equal."

"Done."

Willoughby turned back to the window. He felt a shiver of excitement tingle down his spine. He exhaled loudly. "All right," he said. "Count me in."

"Excellent," H.S. responded, letting the thinnest shred of a grin spread across his lips. He reached into his jacket pocket and pulled out a fold of papers. "There are those who would give anything to know how we do what we do," he said. "Don't abuse the privilege we are affording you, Willoughby. One misstep and you shall never find us again." He threw Willoughby a severe glance.

Willoughby took the papers from H.S. He thought about the things he had overheard from the two men who had been photographing the symbol over Antonio's shop. Should he tell H.S.? He dismissed the idea. He didn't know the man well enough yet, and the idea, well, just felt wrong. He glanced over the papers and looked up as H.S. continued.

"We're sponsoring a contest about the mathematics of medieval France. It is being legitimized by an affiliate organization called the *Society of Historic Artifacts*. You are to write an essay. The winner will be treated to a three-week cruise aboard our Windjammer 'Aperio Absconditus'."

"*Windjammer?*"

H.S. let the grin return. "It's a beautiful vessel. I rigged her out myself. The name is Latin again. It refers to one who can '*uncover the hidden*'. You will supposedly be cruising to France, Spain, and Britain. The cruise, however, is merely a cover for your real assignment, which begins in a unique cave in France. You'll meet your five-person team on the ship. Your contact person is Antonio. Any questions?"

Willoughby looked down at the papers and caught sight of his watch. "*The time!*" He looked up in a panic. "I'm half an hour late! My stepfather'll—"

"*Willoughby!*" H.S. said forcefully. "We have no desire to call attention to ourselves. You will arrive back at the Certus Grove less than five minutes from the time you left it." His tone softened. "It's one of the additional perks of time travel. Time passes at the rate of one hour in our dimension for every 31 or so hours in a time hole. There's an entire equation, but suffice it to say that the barrier pulses at a ratio of one to .313 cubed."

Willoughby's eyes widened. "*.313 cubed?*" He thought of the symbol above Antonio's door, the '313' under a spiral of right triangles. The last piece to the puzzle had finally clicked into place.

"Good to have you on board, Willoughby," H.S. said with a warm handshake. "On the way back through the time hole, jump in feet first and hold your arms close to your chest. Don't fight against the force. Just try to clear your head and flow with it. With practice, the discomfort seems little more than the sensation of hitting an air-pocket during a plane ride."

"A very *large* air pocket," Willoughby mumbled. He took one last look at the window. "After I finish this assignment," he said, "I want to spend some time studying the plesiosaurus."

H.S. nodded. "Then study them you shall, Willoughby," he said. "Study them you shall…"

Willoughby began to clank his way up the metal staircase. He ducked into the tunnel that led away from H.S. and his fascinating observation room. He pushed himself into a slow jog. It took every bit of courage he could muster to force himself to jog faster, and at last, leap, feet first, into the dark surface that had earlier spewed him out. The jerk back to the *Certus Grove* was less terrifying but still awkward. Within moments, though, it was over. Once back in the dim, buzzing room, hidden atop the Certus Grove, Willoughby fell to the floor, hugging the cool firmness for a long moment. The flow of force in the room was pushing out now, like a tide that had turned. At length, he pushed to his feet and stumbled forward, slinging his backpack over his shoulder.

He felt a rush of cool air and saw the half triangle doorway swing open at the far end of the room. Seconds later, he was out, watching the lights in the empty stairwell click back on. He heard the door latches unlocking floor by floor. He watched the seamless wall seal behind him. The railing he leaned against was solid and stationary…

He was home, in *his* time, in *his* space!

A wide grin crossed his face. The whole experience seemed in retrospect like some crazy hallucination or wild daydream. He turned and made his way down to the 12th floor landing, bursting out from the stairwell with a sigh of relief. He was still trembling as he hurried down the empty hall toward the elevator. He glanced up at the wall clock as he turned the corner and tapped the *down* arrow: *4:51!* He had been gone for less than 5 minutes!

He pulled the business card H.S. had given him from his shirt pocket and read it aloud. "*Empty Spaces to Distant Places.*" A ding sounded and the elevator door opened. He pressed "L" for the lobby.

It was real! It had happened. The elevator ride down seemed to take forever.

8

Havana at the Hills

The halls of *Worthington Hills Academy* were ancient and narrow. Willoughby felt as if he would suffocate trying to navigate the crowds between classes. He tugged at his collar, determined to loosen the mandatory uniform tie that constricted his breathing like a noose. He found it funny that kids paid tens of thousands of dollars for the "privilege" of wearing this uniform strait-jacket when he would pay equal amounts for the privilege of being rid of the thing. He ducked around a group of tough-talking pretty-boys and flew out the hall door.

His demanding schedule required him to literally trot between the dozen or so ancient buildings that served as lecture halls, labs, and classes. He wove around an ivy-covered corner and under one of several red-brick arches, side-swiping a thin, cheerleader type. He glanced back to apologize, but he had inadvertently caused her to dribble Coke on her pristine sneakers. She looked up, eyes full of venom.

"*What's your problem?*" she gasped.

He turned back around and sighed. People didn't seem to want to hear "sorry" here. If you offend them, they would rather you dropped dead. He set out again in a slow jog. At least he was seeing Antonio tonight. Conversations had been kind of weird at the barbershop since he met H.S. At first, his friend wanted to know all about it—how long had it taken him to find the clues? What did he think about the three-dimensional puzzle that safe-guarded entry to the hidden room? Willoughby had described every aspect of his visit with H.S., spending considerable time describing the plesiosaurus. They talked briefly about the upcoming assignment to find Nostradamus. Antonio told him he didn't have many details.

"H.S. only shares what you need to know, when you need to know it. There is much about the coming mission that I have yet to be told."

Conversation had returned to the normal banter, though they had both decided to mix the haircut schedule up a bit in case someone was still watching the shop. Willoughby had been particularly careful to never go to the shop the same way twice. He rounded another corner, his mind returning to thoughts of the regional soccer game Antonio was taking him to. He had dropped hints for almost a month before actually extending an invitation. Willoughby had turned sixteen earlier in the month, and this was the barber's big birthday surprise for him.

He missed the regular visits to his friend. He had only returned to The Corner Barber three times since returning from the Certus Grove building. They had talked by cell phone a few times as well, but their conversations had been short and oddly strained. Willoughby wondered if he should tell his friend about the tall man in the buttoned-up trench coat and how he had appeared out of nowhere, or about the nonsensical conversation he had overheard, but for some reason, he never did.

As time passed with no signs of the strange duo, Willoughby began to wonder if he had only imagined a sinister intent from the two. Maybe he had misheard some of the conversation. Maybe the two were just ordinary thugs on some wild treasure hunt, or corporate spies trying to steal secrets from the reclusive Observations, Inc. Antonio assured him that the corporation had the best security money could buy. Maybe the creepy old man with the buttoned-up trench-coat had learned more about him and discovered that he wasn't the "person of interest" he initially seemed to be. Still, caution was called for.

Willoughby had slowed to a fast walk. It had taken some work, but with his step-dad's help, Mom had finally given permission for him to go with Antonio. The game was supposed to be a good one. It was an important regional game for their semi-pro team and Antonio had gotten them killer mid-field, second-row tickets. Most important, though, this would give him time to just hang out with his good friend. Antonio hadn't changed at all, but *he* had. Knowing that Antonio was a world-famous architect, not to mention part of a secret scientific organization, left him feeling awed and intimidated. This made for awkward moments when neither of them knew what to say. Perhaps getting away for a little fun together would help bring back the old feelings of camaraderie.

He rounded another corner and began to beeline for the library, spinning out of the way of a group of jeering boys who often played haki-sak in the center courtyard. He no longer tried to join the various school cliques. He found it easier to steer clear of them rather than invite pain by trying to fit in. After all, these groups typically fell into two categories; brain-challenged jocks or social-climbers. He knew how both groups viewed him. He didn't come from money, he had no claim to fame, and he had no patience for the daily dramas of high school social structures. He spent his time evaluating problems and seeking viable solutions. He had no time to think up retorts to shout into a cell phone and had no desire to hone his talents at texting so he could become a twitter junkie. Let them view him as laughable. The loudest laugh seldom survives to be the last.

Jogging up uneven steps, he finally reached the high, brass doors of the Daniel S. Davenport Library and slipped inside, wrinkling his nose at the familiar smell. Despite countless renovations, the library had never lost its distinctive aroma—that faint odor of wood stain, carpet solvent, and mold. Only amid the clean shelves, where book titles staked out their thousands of sentinel kingdoms, did the library scent give way to a more pleasant smell of aging bindings, cut paper, and ink. Willoughby had always loved libraries, and the Daniel S. Davenport had its charms. Its high ceilings and highly polished wood panels and desks were reminiscent of Oxford or Notre Dame. It was the tall, stone windows, however, that Willoughby liked best. They gave the quaint library a sense of class and a feeling of elegance.

He glanced around looking for a free chair. Spotting one by an east window, he claimed it. Ten minutes later, he put his biology notes away and took out his American history book. He opened the book, not really looking at it. His eyes were focused out the window on the budding shades of green and gold around campus. It was hard to believe that spring was fast approaching. Though he had no great love for students or professors at the school, he did have to admit that the grounds and architecture were breathtaking. He tapped a pencil absently on the desktop.

It had been almost five months since his experience at the Certus Grove building. *Had he really traveled back in time?* With every passing week, the experience seemed more incredible and more remote. He pulled out the card H.S. had given him and looked at it for the hundredth time. *Cryptic spaces to distant places...*

In the brief time he and Antonio had spent together since his joining Observations, Inc., Antonio had seemed compelled to tell him more about his own life. He spoke about his dream as a young college student—the first in his family—to build his gifts into something special. He told of how he was close to giving up at one point, but decided to rest all his hopes on an unusual contest, sponsored by a British magazine. A professor had brought the contest to his attention. He was to create a design that utilized the *fourth* dimension. At first, he thought the contest was a joke. The more he thought about it, though, the more the challenge intrigued him. He ended up winning, and was recruited by H.S. five weeks later.

As always, his barber friend continued to be free with his advice: "Learn to observe with more than just the eyes, Willoughby! The eyes can be self-serving. They will see only what you want them to see if you let them. They will betray you if you truly wish to learn and grow. You must come to *sense* the world around you. Learn to truly listen, to note patterns, to observe the texture of time and how it changes with each moment well-spent. Live for the quiet moments when you come to know your true voice."

*You must come to sense the world around you...*Did Antonio know? Willoughby had become gradually aware of constant flares of bluish light that seemed to indicate some weakness in the time continuum around him. Usually the flares were only out of the corner of his eye and disappeared almost as quickly as they flashed, but they were there. He had considered telling Antonio more detail about the night in Antonio's Corner Barber when he had seen the old man's face peering through a rip in time, and about the conversation he overheard afterwards. But there had been no more incidents with number strings and he had not seen either the tattooed man or the tall, dark-eyed man since that night, so he kept silent. He wasn't sure how Observations, Inc. would react. Did they know they were being watched?

Willoughby leaned back in his chair. If Antonio or H.S. knew he was a "person of interest" to the ones watching them, would they still want him to be part of their team? Leaving the team now wasn't an option. Willoughby knew too much. His could never walk away from the possibilities Observations, Inc. presented. Observing the past, not through the filters of a book, but by actually being there to watch it unfold, was the sort of thing the true adventurer only dreams of! There was also the connection with his father to work out. He still found it odd and a little too coincidental that he should have stumbled upon the same clandestine organization that had once been observing his father.

Willoughby's thoughts were a million miles away when he heard a soft voice call out his name.

"Willoughby?"

He looked up to see a slender blonde peering down at him. He straightened, running a hand through his hair. "Yeah," he choked, recognizing her as one of the Junior Varsity cheerleaders from his chemistry class.

"Sorry to interrupt, you seem lost in such, such *concentration*, but I was wondering if you wrote down the last formula from class today? I think I must have lost it."

Willoughby fumbled to pick up his pen. "Uh, yeah, sure."

Of course you lost it, he thought as he wrote the formula down; *you were texting on your cell phone*. While handing her the jotted formula, his sleeve caught on the spiral of one of his notebooks. The book flipped to the ground, causing a group of girls at the next table to giggle. He bent clumsily to pick it up. It wasn't fair. He could travel through time, solve the Riemann Hypothesis, but put him in front of a pretty girl, and he always managed to choke. He sat up, irritated. "Uh, here…"

"Thanks," the girl said, placing a hand on his shoulder. "By the way, do you know your book is upside-down?" Willoughby noted with horror that he had propped his book up against his backpack upside-down. "Did you know that, or is this, like, some sort of meditation thing?" The girl bit her lip, trying to keep a straight face as her friends at the next table burst again into snickers and laughs. She turned, at last unable to contain her own laughter, and hurried over to rejoin them. Willoughby knew that his face was probably pretty red, but he pursed his lips and tried to make the best of things. He looked over at the girls with a mischievous smile, picked up the book, and began moving his mouth silently, as if chanting in a trance. The girls laughed even louder.

Another girl called out his name. He glanced over his shoulder. Seldom did two girls speak to him on the same day. He saw a rather odd girl leaning her chair back and resting worn hiking boots on the corner of a table one row back. She had a mountain of books stacked to one side. With brown skin and ankle length fatigues, she seemed like some kind of guerrilla for an underground war. He recognized her as a relatively new girl from his American history class. She transferred in from out of the country only two or so months ago. She tugged at the sleeve of her tattered army jacket and pulled it tighter around her sunshine yellow t-shirt. A red dot adorned the center of her forehead. She was rather attractive, actually, but also sort of weird. Once, during a particularly boring lecture on Elias Boudinot, framer of the Bill of Rights and the first president of congress, she had caught his attention by holding a bulls-eye up to her forehead. It was like the red bulls-eyes you see in an ad for Target stores. She pointed to the bulls-eye and then to him, raising her eyebrows. *What was that supposed to mean?*

She called his name again, black hair exploding in smooth waves down her back. Perhaps attractive wasn't the right word for her. The better word was *exotic*.

"I didn't know you were a fan of John Kushnell," she called over in a loud whisper. "You must have read his infamous 1970's doctoral thesis on memorization: 'Turn your book upside down and read right to left. Forcing yourself to read this way will burn critical information into the semi-conscious resources of your brain.' Good method, I think!"

Willoughby gave the girl a hesitant wave, smiled, then nodded. He had no idea who John Kushnell was. Laughter from the Barbie girls died down. After some mumbling and a few shrugs, two of them turned their books upside down and started trying to read. Willoughby glanced back at the dark- haired girl. She winked and tapped her forehead. *Too weird*, he thought. He gave her a quick nod, closed his book, and slung his pack over his shoulder.

He still had ten minutes before his appointment with Dean Hollifield, so he took a few minutes to browse a book aisle. Books were a thing he loved. He loved the smell of them, the feel of them in the hand. There was something magical about words on paper to him. He wondered if electronic technology would ever be able to replicate the experience. A moment later, he pushed through the tall, brass door. Hurrying across the quad, he found himself thinking of the Dean.

Dean Hollifield was a stern, no-nonsense sort of guy. He usually only summoned Willoughby if he felt there were issues with his academic progress or to lecture him on his lack of social development. *So, what was it this time?* Willoughby hoped he wasn't in for another lecture on school spirit.

Approaching the administration building, he sighed. For all its plusses and minuses, Worthington Hills was just a place. It wasn't the place he hated so much. It was just that there was no-one *in* this place whom he really cared about.

His mind drifted to the soccer game. Antonio was supposed to pick him up in just over half an hour. He hoped the Dean's speech would be short. The game was an exhibition match between D.C. United, their local team and the reigning division champs, and a new contender for the MLS Cup, the San Jose Earthquakes. Antonio had promised to "*take them to the game in style,*" whatever that was supposed to mean. "You will be amazed!" he told Willoughby. "It will be a most excellent surprise!" Willoughby envisioned a stretched Hummer limo, stocked with snacks and fruit drinks. It *could* be interesting…

Just as he reached the door to the administration building, his cell phone rang. It was Klaas. "Hey…yeah… No, I haven't seen him yet. My appointment is at 4:00… Right. We're going straight to the game after that… Girls? Are you kidding? I had a rather interesting exchange at the library, but it was more the 'what planet are you from' type of conversation…Of course not! If I was sneaking time with my dream girl, do you think I'd take a 30-year-old Hispanic barber along? I promise, Klaas—when there's something to tell, you'll be the first to know… Yeah. I'll call you from the stadium… I don't know, he didn't say…Okay, I'll call. See ya."

Willoughby frowned. He didn't like keeping Klaas in the dark. His step-father was one of his best friends. Even though it had seemed odd when he told them his 30-year-old barber had invited him to the soccer game, he had been the one who convinced Mom to let him go. Despite his age, Antonio was one of Willoughby's few friends, and Klaas thought it was healthy for Willoughby to take a break from the books. Klaas also promised to square it with Mom if he won the *Society of Historic Artifacts* contest. He seemed genuinely excited that Willoughby might win a chance to be on a real sailing ship—especially a *windjammer*.

Willoughby crammed the cell phone into his pocket and raked his fingers through his hair. He knew it was best that Klaas didn't know Observations, Inc., but what H.S. said about it being lonely holding on to such a secret was true. He just wished the days would move faster. He could taste the adventure of the summer to come.

As he stepped into the building lobby, the receptionist grinned and waved him past. The door to the dean's office was open.

"Willoughby, come in," Dean Hollifield said, motioning toward a seat. "You're not in any trouble, though I might welcome that development as a sign that you do have a life beyond your studies." He barely glanced up from the neat stack of printed documents he was scouring. Willoughby stepped into the office and seated himself in one of the stiff, uncomfortable chairs facing the dean's desk. Dean Hollifield glanced up. He smiled, folding his hands together and resting them on the paper he was currently reviewing. "You seem to have rather important friends. I've been asked to inform you that your essay has won the annual *Society of Historic Artifacts* competition, a competition not usually open to students below graduate level studies."

Willoughby smiled. "*Great!*"

He tried to seem surprised and elated, but the dean didn't buy it. He looked Willoughby up and down, pursing his lips.

"What intrigues me, Willoughby, is how you knew of the contest and why an exception has been made regarding your age. Not to discount the brilliance of your thesis." He looked down. "I find the essay most stimulating." The dour man narrowed his eyes and set his chin. "Did they know of your age? You haven't by chance mentioned our little, uh, secret to anyone, have you?"

The dean was well aware of Willoughby's solution to the Riemann Hypothesis and the "deal" he had made with the heads of the mathematics community and the sponsor of the million-dollar prize. All of the Academy's staff had been briefed. Willoughby's eyes darted around the room. "No. That was the deal...I put my age on the cover bio sheet."

"Explain to me how you learned about a contest that is generally only open to college graduates?"

Willoughby shrugged. "I, uh, I saw it listed in a magazine," he said, trying to think of a publication that might run an ad for this type of contest.

"Magazine?"

"Yes," Willoughby continued, swallowing hard. His brain worked fast. "I saw the ad in a publication from MENSA."

The dean raised his eyebrows. He seemed almost amused. "You want me to believe that you are a member of MENSA? Since when did the organization start recruiting young boys?"

"I've already turned 16."

Dean Hollifield cracked a smile; "Your point?"

Willoughby hesitated. "Listen, sir," he gulped, searching for words. He had heard of MENSA by name, but knew little about the organization's rules or structure. If the dean chose to question him closely, he was in hot water. "MENSA is a private organization for people with high IQs, right? I consider myself in that category, so I applied. I guess if you're paying, they're accepting, and I, uh, I included a little donation." He forced a smile and held his breath.

The dean rocked back in his chair, letting go a loud laugh. Willoughby exhaled, feeling the tension ebb. "MENSA does collect dues, Mr. Von Brahmer, but the caliber of people in this particular organization is rarely at a loss for funds. Perhaps your '*donation*' helped buy them a tasty lunch, but I don't think it got you in the door." He leaned forward again onto his desk. "I would agree, however, that you do fit the MENSA profile intellectually, and it is an honor for the school that you won this competition. I must say I envy you. You will be spending three weeks aboard the windjammer Aperio Absconditus in the company of some of the most brilliant minds of our day. Dr. Davis O'Grady is one of the foremost astronomers on the planet. Dr. Hathaway Simon is a master physicist and Eldoro Chavez is a uniquely talented architect."

The dean looked down at his paper. "The other winner is a young psychologist with strong academic credentials—a Dr. James Arthur Washington." He looked up with a twinkle in his eye. "Of course, Dr. Washington is not as young as you." He looked back down at the paper. "You will also have the chance to meet Sydney Senoya, the world-renowned violinist. She'll be performing on the cruise. At 16, she's a true genius. I've seen her play."

As if H.S. would recruit anything else, Willoughby thought. He imagined the picture of the girl (which he had pinned to his bulletin board at home). *Why a violinist?* Why would they need a musician on the team? Was she just part of the smoke-screen to make this appear to be a genuine academic cruise? Willoughby shook the thoughts from his mind, turning his attention back to the dean's words.

"...unbelievable exposure for a girl of her age. It should be a most fascinating voyage, provided your parents approve. They do know about the contest, don't they?" He threw a stern glance toward Willoughby.

"Absolutely," Willoughby answered. "Klaas is a big supporter."

"And your mother?"

Willoughby didn't answer. The dean grinned. "Mothers sometimes take a little work. Now—"

His words were interrupted by a loud commotion outside. Willoughby glanced out the window. A huge boat of a car had pulled up. It was gold, something like a Lincoln Continental, with crisp, white-wall tires and shiny, silver spoke rims. It waited at the curb, idling between two black limousines. Its horn sounded like the trill of an ice-cream truck. The dean cleared his throat. "Your boarding papers and your cash prize," he nodded, handing Willoughby an envelope. "You're scheduled to leave from Boston Harbor a week from Thursday."

"*A week from Thursday!*" Willoughby's mouth dropped open. "My classes…" He was distracted again. The car outside the dean's window was fast attracting a crowd. It had begun to pitch and lurch, hydraulics bumping the front end up, then the back end, then dropping the right side, and then the left. *A low-rider?* Willoughby thought. *Who would dare bring a low-rider to a place like Worthington Hills?* A knot formed in the pit of his stomach. Antonio had promised a "surprise."

Dean Hollifield ignored the commotion, pulling his lips into a tight grin.

"You'll miss three weeks of school, but I've arranged make-up courses. I believe it's manageable."

"Of course, sir. Thank you, sir."

Willoughby took the papers the dean was holding out. "Have fun, Willoughby," Dean Hollifield said. He took a document from a neat stack to one side of his desk and began scanning it. Outside, the strange horn sounded again. Willoughby mumbled his thanks and then hurried toward the front door. *Was this Antonio's idea of a joke?*

"Willoughby!" a familiar voice shouted as he exited the administration building. The side of the car lunged up and Antonio leaned out the window. "Hurry! A fine plate of piping hot enchiladas awaits us!" The side of the car slammed down. Willoughby's ears burned as he felt the collective eyes of everyone within a hundred yards look his way.

"*Love* your new chauffeur, Willoughby!" a girl chirped, causing peals of laughter from her friends. It was the cheerleader from the library. "Hey, a Havana limousine!" another boy joked. Antonio laid on the horn. Out of the corner of his eye, Willoughby could see even more kids heading over. He pushed through the growing crowd and quickly grabbed the handle of the passenger door. As soon as he slid onto the seat and slammed the door, the passenger side of the car rose about three feet off the ground and dropped. He fought to keep from being tossed into Antonio, or onto the dashboard, as the back end of the car shot up.

"Would you stop that?" he shouted at Antonio as the car leveled out again. "And please, quit honking that ridiculous horn!"

"So you like my most fantastical car?" Antonio beamed. He turned the key in the ignition and revved the engine. "Don't hold back—what do you think of her?" He hit a button on the dash and the front-end of the car hiccupped, throwing Willoughby against the head rest.

"I think she should come with a warning label!" Willoughby yelled. He grabbed his seat belt as the car lurched yet again. "Antonio! What are you doing—just get us out of here!"

Antonio threw the car into gear and swung it into the street, seemingly oblivious to Willoughby's embarrassment. "It has 549.37 horses," he shouted; "and the radio—much bass!" The sound rattled the windows as Antonio turned up the volume and punched the accelerator.

Willoughby fought the g-forces as he reached toward the dash to flip the radio off. Antonio laughed and began to slow the car. They were approaching a traffic light. "I told you! I told you!" he bubbled. "She is magnificent, no?"

"Antonio," Willoughby said, wiping beads of sweat from his brow, "come on! Where is the *real* car?"

"*Real* car?" Antonio looked suddenly wounded. "*You insult my Lola?*" He bent forward, caressing the fur dash. "Don't listen to him, Lola! He's a *gringo*, he knows nothing about the beauty of a fine, precision machine."

"*Lola?*" Willoughby's eyes narrowed. "Lola, as in '*...her name is Lola. She is a showgirl'?*"

"Barry Manilow! A most excellent song!" Antonio smiled. He began crooning, sounding like a hyena sitting on a jack-hammer. "*...with those feathers in her hair, and the dress cut down to there...*"

Willoughby slapped his forehead. "Antonio! You're brilliant and unbelievably wealthy! Why are you acting like, like—"

"Like a humble Hispanic barber who respects his people and his culture? Why do people like you believe a man cannot be humble and respectful of his people despite wealth or achievement? Tell me this, my friend; would you have been willing to confide in a snobbish and conceited architect?"

Willoughby leaned back heavily in the seat. After a moment of silence, he sighed. "There has been so much, I don't know—hidden stuff. I meant no disrespect for Hispanic culture. I only thought—"

"You only thought I was pretending. You thought that I would change who I am because someone noted that I have brains and gave me the chance to have wealth. I would never do that, my friend. I am the same person I have always been. My shop may offer a different setting from my buildings, but it is a setting I relish and genuinely love. The hind quarters of a burro may be more muscled than you suppose, but how does that make the face less friendly?"

Willoughby knitted his eyebrows. The beginning of a smile spread across his face. "Did you just compare yourself to the butt of a burro?"

"I did not compare myself to anything," Antonio declared stoically. "I was merely being, uh…" His voice softened, "philosophical. Now, shall we go straight to the soccer game, or would you like to explore the wonders of the back-roads with my many horses?" His voice was rising again. "We will get to the game eventually, but for now, we thrust ourselves into the great unknown! There are castles to conquer in this city, my friend; windmills to defeat!" He punctuated this last comment with a wild, hydraulic hiccup that caused the rear of the car to spring up, then fall sharply, leaving the whole frame of the vehicle bouncing off the asphalt as it sped along.

"Does H.S. know about Lola?" Willoughby shouted over the revving engine He couldn't help himself—he was smiling. He felt his stomach lurch and let go a spontaneous laugh. It was like riding a kiddies' roller coaster. With his hand gripping tight to the armrest and his teeth gritted, he peered hard past the carpeted dash and the furry dice dangling from the rear-view mirror.

"H.S. believes my Lola is a warm and sensitive creature. He has no knowledge of her, shall we say, other talents, though I did tell him that she could be dangerous."

"What did he say?"

Antonio let he back tires hiccup slightly. "He said, 'Yes, aren't they all.'"

Willoughby's smile broadened. He shouted as the front of the car shot up and almost immediately dropped. "*Once more into the breach!*" he cried. Antonio wheeled right, the left side of the car flying into the air, leaving him pinned against the door rest. He managed to point a finger off into the distance, at somewhere beyond the horizon. *"Once more into the breach!"*

Antonio said nothing. He just punched the gas.

9

Sydney

Ten days later, on a sunny Thursday afternoon, Willoughby and his family pulled to a stop near a rickety pier in Boston Harbor. They were awed by the sight of the Aperio Absconditus. Tall masts of polished wood and shiny brass trim made the majestic ship glimmer in the sun.

"A true *Windjammer!*" Klaas cried as he climbed out of the car. "Look at her—such a beauty! Did I tell you that the name was created by steamship crews?" Even though Klaas had lived in America for years, he still had trouble pronouncing words that started with "w." Usually, they came out sounding more like a "v." Willoughby had grown used to the slight accent.

"Steamship crews?"

"Yes. It was a taunt. They thought the square-rigged vessels were too big and clumsy and had to be *jammed* into the wind." Klaas had been reading up on windjammers.

Willoughby opened the back of the Nissan and let an enthusiastic pair of white-jacketed porters push past him. They struggled to yank his luggage trunk out of the Nissan, and then lugged it over to a waiting dolly. He had to grin. He and Klaas had almost gotten hernias from hefting the thing into the vehicle back home. Mom walked up behind them.

"This is an awfully rickety pier. You sure that boat is safe? I shouldn't have let you two talk me into this."

Willoughby looked her in the eyes. "Mom, it's a sea cruise. Not a trek into uninhabited jungle. What could happen?"

He regretted the questions just as soon as he spoke it. His mother raised a serious eyebrow. "You don't know what you're sailing into. The sea is nothing to be trifled with. I bet more sailors have been lost over time than were lost in the First World War!"

"Mom, this isn't the Navy—"

"I'd feel safer if it was!" Mom's tone was sharp. She eyed him warily for a moment and then the tone softened. "I've packed two of everything you might need. You've got your traveler's checks too—in case I forgot something, right?" Willoughby nodded. He felt a tug on his shirt. "Willby," his sister Cali said, "here." She handed him a small box. "So you won't forget us on your way to Europa."

"Europe," Mom corrected. "Europa is one of the moons of Jupiter."

"I like the Europa idea," Willoughby, added as he struggled to open the well-wrapped box. "It would be fun to sail through space." At length, he pulled out a gold pocket watch with a picture of his family inside. He loved precision instruments, especially old Swiss watches and pocket watches. He could tell this was no department store knock-off. On the back was an inscription, engraved in a tight, spiraling circle: "*Chasing the moment, someday you'll find, you yearn for a place where the memories bind.*"

"Are you sure you're ready for this?" Mom mumbled. "You never even went to summer camp, and now you're off to play Captain Ahab."

"Mom—it's an educational voyage, not a death sentence. I absolutely promise I won't harpoon a single whale." He was hoping to lighten the mood, but Mom didn't seem to appreciate use of the word "death." Densi jumped to his rescue. "Hey," she said, "maybe they'll let you try to drive the boat. That would scare away every whale within a hundred miles."

Willoughby grinned at her as he began to put the pocket watch back into its box. "Thanks for this," he said, looking up at his mom. He glanced back to Densi and Cali. "I'll bring you back something." He bent closer to their level. "But you've got to promise that you'll stay out of my stuff, deal?"

Cali spoke up with brazen honesty. "We'll *try*."

"I set booby traps," Willoughby added.

"Fun!" Cali clapped. "That makes it sort of a game! So, what are you going to bring us? Mine should be sunny yellow."

"Lavender and crimson," Densi added, as if ordering fries at McDonalds.

Willoughby straightened, ruffling Cali's hair. "We'll see," he said looking down sternly. "I better not find anything *missing*." Before he had a chance to turn and walk away, his mom grabbed him by the shoulder. "Uh-uh. You're not leaving without *physical* contact with your mother."

Willoughby sighed. "Sure, but …can we leave it at just a hug?"

"As opposed to a blubbering sob fest?" Mom held him in a quick embrace and then pushed him away. "Was that really that bad?"

"I'll be back in a couple of weeks," Willoughby offered weakly.

"Get going!" Mom said, trying to fake a smile. "You have a ship to catch. They're waiting."

"Yeah," Willoughby said, sucking in a deep breath. His thoughts turned to the trip ahead, and the things that could be *waiting*. He tried to push his steps into long, confident strides as he moved away from his family toward the gang-plank, but his legs felt like jelly. He bit his lip as questions surfaced in his mind: *How many years could pass in the time grid while I age only three weeks? What if he never came back?* Mom was right; a lot *could* happen. He gave her one last look over his shoulder and smiled. She smiled back, offering a hesitant wave.

Klaas was waiting for him at the bottom of the boarding ramp. "Looks solid and fit to sail," he pronounced, testing the ramp.

"Uh, thanks, Klaas. Thanks for everything."

Klaas was quiet for a moment, beaming at him. "A sailor off to the sea …"

There was another beat of silence.

"My father was in the Navy, you know," he said. "He told me once, 'I felt so big to go off to sea. But then there were nights so dark, and waters so deep, and this big sailor felt sometimes very small.' Remember, big or small does not always matter. It is what is in here that counts." He patted Willoughby's chest. "Be careful, Willoughby."

"I'll be fine, really," Willoughby said, rather unconvincingly.

"I know," Klaas said. "I know you will."

Willoughby gave him a nod, and then stepped past, starting up the ramp. He slowed only once, when Klaas called after him, "Godspeed, Willoughby! Godspeed!" He felt an odd tightening in the pit of his stomach. *Was he doing the right thing? Would he really be fine?* He was heading into the unknown, into possible dangers. What if he never came back? What if he came back somehow changed or wounded? There had to be a million ways something could go wrong. He turned and gave Klaas another wave. He stood there, staring back for a long moment, until a tinkling from above caught his attention. He looked up. A girl was peering down from the ship.

"It's Willoughby, right?" She lowered her voice to a strong whisper. "Don't look like such a lost puppy! Be excited! *Smile wider!* Wave again…good! Now, turn. Breathe in, step; breathe out, step. Breathe in, step; breathe out, step. That's the way! Let the oxygen *flow* through your body."

Willoughby felt stupid being instructed on how to— to *what?* Play his part better? He studied the girl. She was beautiful. She had the darkest, most captivating eyes he had ever seen. They crackled with inner intensity, drawing one in. These were the kind of eyes a guy could get lost in. He stumbled upward, all possible dangers of the cruise forgotten.

A gust of wind made the boat and the ramp sway. Willoughby caught himself, throwing his arms out for balance. "Whoa!"

"Scintillating, isn't it?" The girl exhaled. She had a casual self-assured stance, one that he recognized from the newspaper clipping he had pinned to his wall. He had studied the clipping over and over in the past few months, tracing the lines of the girl's face—a face that exhibited both the poise of a monarch and the smile of a fairy queen. The girl leaned over the rail, lowering her voice conspiratorially.

"I could breathe in the romance of the sea forever. Smell it? Here, a hint of India; there, a whiff of the Congo. Breathe in deep enough and you feel the chill of Tibet, winds blowing from the high, forgotten peaks..."

She seemed to lean out over the water as she said this—or was it just the gentle rocking of the ship? He tried not to think about it, feeling as though a thousand eyes were watching him as the girl raised an eyebrow and stared. She rolled a hand delicately along the rail, moving slowly toward the top of the ramp. He wasn't sure if the hand was mimicking the wind, or a wave, or just dancing to a melody she alone could hear. He watched the hand come closer. Stepping awkwardly off the ramp, he grabbed the rail, almost tripping.

"It keeps *moving*," he complained.

The girl laughed. "It's a ship! Haven't you ever been on a ship before?" Now, her eyes danced about him. He flinched from their full gaze. She was waiting for him to say something. He felt sweat trickle down his neck. *What was he supposed to say?*

"I, uh, I—I'm Willoughby," he started, pleased that he remembered his name, then recalled that the girl already knew his full name. "I guess you know that," he said, taking a wobbly step toward her. She had not moved, staring at him. He made a short bow. She responded with a flowing curtsey that caused her many bracelets to jingle. She looked slightly older than she had in the news article Antonio gave him. She was dressed in silky, oddly-matched layers of clothing that were definitely *not* Worthington Hills fare.

"So," she said, "we meet at last, Willoughby Von Brahmer." She held out her hand, filling the air with pings and tinkles—soft, like the random melodies of a wind chime. "I'm Sydney Senoya." Her voice was both musical and amused. "I've been waiting for you to make your *grand* appearance. By the way, you don't look anything like your picture."

"My picture?" Willoughby wondered if she was making fun of how he stumbled up the ramp and nearly tripped stepping onto the ship.

"Yes," Sydney went on. "I looked up your school photo. I have done my homework. I understand you have a picture of me on your wall?"

"I—uh, no, not exactly—I, I was interested in the—it's a…news clipping."

The girl smiled, her eyes still dancing. "Not one of my best pictures. I'll see that you get a better one."

Willoughby had barely opened his mouth when Sydney turned, yammering on. "I had you pegged as taller." She grabbed his arm, lightly, her touch like the flutter of a butterfly. "Did they make you sit on thick, old books—encyclopedias or something?"

She stopped, looking at him. The delicate fingers of her free hand toyed with silky strands of hair. She pulled a few across her face and laughed. Willoughby wasn't sure if he should try to answer her earlier question, or just close his mouth before the flies flew in.

"It's their trick, you know," she continued, prodding him on again but keeping to the rail. She seemed to revel in keeping him off-balance. The wind tugged at her jacket. "They use it at those expensive private schools. You sit on a stack of books and it's supposed to make you look stately or something. I've heard it's quite common at those ritzy all-boy schools. Tall and stately—it's so important for you boys to hold up appearances, isn't it?"

Willoughby stared, oblivious to what she was saying. Ripples of ebony hair flowed across her shoulders like a mysterious, shining river. She eyed him squarely.

"Surely, you don't believe that appearances are everything, do you? I mean, really, if people feel that it's so imperative that they *look* tall in some ridiculous photo—imperative enough that they'll sit on a stack of books—well, I say to them, '*Congratulations!*' You've just proved yourself to have the brains of a peacock."

Sydney grinned wickedly, glancing away. "Von Brahmer, Von Brahmer..." She looked back at him. "We'll have to do something about the name. Von Brahmer simply won't do."

Willoughby struggled to decide if the girl really thought he had the brains of a peacock, or if she had just been making a general statement. The ship rolled slightly, as if coming alive. He steadied himself again, placing both hands on the rail this time.

"It takes some getting used to," the girl offered, still smiling.

"Going back to your original question," he said shyly, "school photos aren't usually very accurate. I mean, granted, some books might be put to better use by sitting on them, but I have no desire to appear as something I'm not."

"Bravo!" Sydney clapped, "Humor in a mathematician!"

Willoughby wasn't sure how to react to the outburst. He decided to ignore it and just plow on. "If I looked taller, it was probably the starch in my shirt. Mom picked the shirt out just for my pictures and that was the only time I ever wore it."

Sydney paused. Her mood darkened a little, like a wind, changing direction.

"You're close to your mother, aren't you?" she asked, her eyes drifting to somewhere far away. Willoughby wasn't sure how to respond. He said nothing, letting the silence drag. She quickly noted the silence and pulled her thoughts back to the present. "So, what should we do with your name?"

Willoughby shrugged. "I think Senoya is a beautiful name. You're a violinist, right? Antonio said you are very talented."

Sydney reacted with cautious delight. She nodded and leaned onto the rail, her delicate features lit by the fireworks in her eyes. "Yes. They call me a consummate *virtuosa*. That's a female type who comes out of the womb humming Brahms' lullabies. It says right on my birth certificate that I arrived carrying a tiny violin in one hand, my thin legs curled around a bow." She peeked over, flashing a smile as hair whipped in her face. "But enough about me. What's it like, leading the life of a dashing young mathematician? Will I have to dress in boring academic fashions or is there space in your world for elegance and style? I'll give you a year to grow taller, but don't ask for two, that's pushing it."

Willoughby had never met anyone like Sydney, nor had he heard the words "dashing" and "mathematician" in the same sentence before. He felt oddly outnumbered standing beside her. He glanced away, surveying the rest of the ship. Why hadn't he looked up information on the other team members as she had obviously done? Outside of a few conversations with Antonio, he only knew what H.S. and Dean Hollifield had told him, which wasn't much.

Sydney pulled his attention back to the rail. Her smile had melted into melancholy again. "Those people down there—that's your family, right?" She pointed dramatically across the pier.

Willoughby looked and waved. Mom and Klaas had corralled the two girls near the car. They chatted and watched. When they saw him look their way and wave, they waved back. Klaas gave him a thumbs-up sign, making him blush and hope that Sydney hadn't seen. "Yeah," he said, trying to mask a slight tremor in his voice. "That's the gang." He looked back at Sydney. "So, what do I do now? Is someone supposed to show me the ship?"

Sydney stared at the family a moment longer and then motioned Willoughby forward. "Yes. Me." Her silk hair swished and her bracelets tinkled.

As they walked toward the bow, Willoughby looked out again over the pier. "Hey, where's your family?"

Darkness returned to the girl's face. "Where, indeed," she said, not looking back. "There's a topic for the morning inspirational." She avoided his gaze, catching an unruly strand of hair and slipping it back behind her ear. "My dad," she finally explained, "is a senior executive in one of the largest firms on the Tokyo exchange." There was an edge of bitterness to her tone. "While technically I live with my mother in Honolulu—she's Polynesian—I don't see her much. She works as a professional dancer and is rarely at home. Actually, I like it that way. We don't exactly get along."

She raised her hand and shook it, checking the lay of her bracelets. Her fingers were thin and carefully manicured. "Dad is seldom around, but he pays the bills, and takes pride in my achievements, which is more than my mother can manage. I'm usually off somewhere in the world touring, or auditioning, or something like that. This cruise is really no different so why should they be here to send me off?"

She turned to look at Willoughby, daring him to speak. They had stopped near the front mast. Willoughby looked away from her gaze, unwilling to make any comment that might upset her. The ship looked even more majestic from the deck than it had from the pier. After a moment of gazing around, he realized that Sydney expected a response.

"I was just curious," he said. "I thought maybe *you* would want to see them here. I'm sorry." He couldn't help but think of *Gustav*. He did have some sense of how she felt.

Sydney narrowed her eyes, then turned and started walking again.

Had he said something wrong? He fought to change the subject; "Uh, what's your expertise for the team? Music?"

Sydney looked over with a sad grin. "I'm Sydney Senoya, Willoughby. I'm the resident expert on *empty spaces.*"

For a moment, there was no sound but the wind, and the water lapping at the side of the boat. Sydney seemed to be searching for something. Willoughby had no idea what to do. Just as he was ready to launch into an apology, the girl spun, pirouetting on her toes. There was a renewed energy in her voice.

"Music and languages are my specialties, if you must know. Sometimes the two are one thing," her eyes became misty for a moment. "Music is a language, you know. To my people, it was a sacred language—the language of the

Gods..." She looked off toward the sea, then gave her head a slight shake and turned back to Willoughby. "My, but you are curious! You should be ashamed of yourself, prying into a girl's private life. I can only overlook your deplorable lack of sensibility if you lean over, right now, and kiss me."

She raised an eyebrow. Fear and panic gripped Willoughby. *Was she serious?*

Sydney burst into laughter. "I'll give you time to warm up to the idea, Mr. Von Brahmer—one day, maybe two—but your carefree days *are* numbered." Without warning, she twirled again, watching the layers of her dress flair and swirl. "Tell me," she called back, "where did you get the recruiting speech?"

"The what?"

"The recruiting speech! It's where H.S. babbles on about infinities, and potentials, and the shape of windmills. He made me think of Don Quixote. I can see him now, on his white steed, barreling forward, bent lance in hand, anxious to engage the monstrous forces that make time's windmill move. Of course, you probably lapped it up. It's the sort of thing you mathematicians dream about, isn't it?" Her voice dropped to a whisper. "Or do you have other, more interesting dreams?"

She waited, eyes wide, as the wind tussled her hair.

"Uh...Jurassic period," Willoughby stammered. "I watched a plesiosaurus attack a fanged eel. It was raw and...fascinating."

"*Raw?*" Sydney raised an eyebrow, then spun and continued forward. "It was probably a prehistoric shark, actually. They look a lot like eels. One was found, alive, near Japan a few years ago. I saw the video on YouTube. Anyway, my speech came in ancient China. It was somewhere around the 6th century B.C. Our observation window overlooks the Yangtze. I glimpsed Loa Tsu, and lotus blooms, and all around us, the hint of young love..."

She stopped, spinning in a full circle before becoming perfectly still. "Okay, forgive me. I *am* supposed to be the welcoming committee, not the afternoon entertainment." She offered an elegant bow, her bracelets jangling. "Consider this your official welcome, Sir Willoughby. Would you like to meet the other members of the team?"

"Yes," Willoughby replied, trying to keep his balance as deck hands began pulling up the ramp. He felt about as graceful as a stuffed avocado on this ship. Sydney turned abruptly and motioned him forward again. With a slight spring in her step, she wound her way through the rigging toward the cabin of the ship.

Willoughby had never seen such grace and poise in a girl. When she wasn't talking, it was easy to think of her as some sort of Asian princess, captured, perhaps, by Moroccan pirates in the China Sea. When she was talking, it was hard to think of anything. You were too busy trying to keep up.

10

Shipmates

Sydney stopped beside the center mast, giving him a chance to catch up. "Antonio was the first to arrive. He's below deck somewhere, studying the design of the ship. Dr. O'Grady is holed up in his cabin, as usual, and James Arthur..."

She scanned a narrow corridor on the seaward side of the ship and pointed, flashing a smile. "There! On the starboard rigging, ladies and gentlemen, meet the reincarnated Errol Flynn!"

Willoughby followed Sydney's finger and caught sight of a lean, muscled black man who seemed to be swinging from the ropes.

"Errol Flynn?" He watched the man's exaggerated antics. "Movies in black and white leave little confusion about skin color."

Sydney laughed. "I'm impressed! You actually know Errol Flynn?"

Willoughby offered a grin. "Well, I don't know him. I have watched a few of his swashbuckler films. My mom secretly adored *Captain Blood*. Before she remarried, she used to bribe me every time the colorized version came on. Then, of course, there was *The Sea Hawk*, *The Adventures of Robin Hood,* and the infamous *Don Juan.* I think she was in love with him."

"I want to know more about the *infamous* part."

Willoughby stared blankly at her, perplexed.

She sighed. "Ah, well. Maybe someday *Don Juan* will ride again." She watched the lean, black man scale the main mast.

Willoughby followed her gaze.

"Hey, Errol!" The girl suddenly called out; "Come meet Willoughby!"

The man gave a hurried wave and then leaped from the rigging. He swung gracefully, holding tight to a thick bit of rigging. The arc of his swing brought him down only a few feet from them, hitting the deck lightly. He straightened, breathing easily, and held out a hand.

"Willoughby, is it? The name is James Arthur—Dr. James Arthur Washington to be more precise. My friends call me Dr. J"

Willoughby smiled. "Julius Erving—an early NBA king of finger rolls and slam dunks. If you handle a ball as deftly as that rope, I understand the reference."

"I like to think I do. We'll have to spend some time on the court and you can let me know if you agree."

"This ship has a basketball court?"

James Arthur smiled conspiratorially. "Yes—of a sort."

Though soccer was more his sport, Willoughby had forced himself to memorize key basketball and football trivia so that he could be more conversant with the sporting crowd.

"A sports trivia buff!" James Arthur grinned widely. "I think you and I shall get along simply swimmingly!"

Willoughby raised an eyebrow. "Swimmingly?"

Dr. J barked a short laugh just as a squat, rotund seaman rounded the corner. "Hey! Hey! No pull loosely the sail, Mr. Doctor! That rope pull loosey the sail!" His waxed moustache quivered comically.

James Arthur's face twisted in a mischievous smile. He jumped onto the rail, still holding the thick rope in his hand. "Stop there, ye foul sea dog! Be gone, else I spit upon your grave!" He gave Willoughby a quick wink. "You and your villainous scum shall never take me alive!" He began to run along the top of the rail, using the rope to steady himself, and once clear of the seaman, swooped across to the center mast. He then used the rope to pull himself up the mast. The squat seaman was now joined by two others, and within moments, half a dozen bony, thin fellows with jagged beards had joined the chase.

"I'll say this for the man," Willoughby nodded. "He's got strong arms."

"And a strong neck—to carry that fat head!" Sydney added.

Willoughby laughed, turning to follow her into a dim doorway. They entered a low structure that housed a small sleeping berth, a few counters with dials and instruments, and a huge, wooden wheel. He gaped at the wheel. It was easily as tall as he was. A loud, whooping commotion outside the wheel room caused him to step back to the doorway and look out. Dr. J had scurried down the narrow breadth of a yardarm and threw himself into a swan dive, plummeting past the railing of the ship. There was a sound of him smacking into the water with a thunderous splash. The crewmen panicked, scrambling to throw out lifelines. After a tense moment of silence, an unmistakable sound gurgled up from the waters below—*uproarious laughter.*

Sydney pulled Willoughby's arm, jerking him toward a flight of wooden stairs.

"He jumped!" Willoughby exclaimed, as they clamored down the stairs, finding themselves in a brightly-lit, narrow hallway. "He ran right off the edge of the yardarm and jumped!"

Sydney was not amused. "Good. He probably needs a bath after playing pirate for two hours. Hopefully, he'll find the sharks equally amusing."

"Sharks?" Willoughby looked down, seeing that Sydney had just linked her arm around his elbow. "In Boston harbor?"

"Quite so," Sydney smiled, mimicking a British accent. "What lies beneath, what hides before you in plain sight—here is where the treasure lay. Observation is the key. Truly *look* and you shall discover."

The sparkle in her eyes was alluring. Willoughby found himself needing to blink. "Huh... Is the team always this academic?"

Sydney whipped her hair around. "Brilliant minds have a stimulating capacity for play," she winked, and then widened one eye. "Just wait until it's our turn." Her smile spelled triumph as she pointed out a large, dim room to the left. "Chartroom," she sang out. "Wardroom..." They passed a completely darkened room to the right. Reaching the individual cabins, she waved her arm in an all-encompassing sweep. "Here we have the officers and us!"

Each door had a small engraved name-plate which identified the occupants. Willoughby read them aloud as they passed; "Captain's Quarters, Officers' Cabin, Dr. Hathaway Simon ..." He stopped at the next name plate.

It read *Sydney Senoya,* then immediately below, *T.K. (Cabin Girl).*

"*Cabin girl?*"

"That's what it says," Sydney said with a hint of disdain. She pouted. "I get to room with the hired help. It's my reward for being the only girl on the team."

Willoughby was intrigued. "Old ships used to have cabin boys."

Sydney's eyes twinkled. "Ah, but this is *not* an old ship, my boy! I've met her, by the way—a little self-absorbed, but adorable in her own way. She's sort of *Barbie* meets *Attila the Hun.*"

Willoughby raised his eyebrows, trying to picture the girl. Sydney ignored him, pointing to the cabin across from hers. The top of the gold name plate read *Willoughby Von Brahmer.* Below his name, *Dr. James Arthur Washington* filled up the bottom half of the plate. He stared at Dr. J's name with a look of disappointment.

"What's wrong?" Sydney asked.

"Uh, I thought I'd be rooming with Antonio," he mumbled. "We know each other pretty well."

Sydney winked. "Not anxious to spend the night with Tarzan of the yardarms? Your secret is safe with me." She lowered her voice to a whisper, widening her eyes conspiratorially. "If you're really nice, I might be able to squeeze you onto my bunk. I'll put a sock on your head and pretend you're a teddy bear."

Willoughby felt his face get hot. "You don't let up, do you?"

Sydney pursed her lips, tapping one foot softly in a slow spin. "No, Mr. Von Brahmer, as a matter of fact, I do not." She stopped, daring him to respond.

Willoughby looked away, searching for something, *anything*, to help him change the subject. He cracked the door to his berth. There were two beds in the cabin, one on each side of the room. His trunk had been placed beside a small desk, at the foot of the left-side bed. A pair of low mahogany dressers adorned the far wall and the room was decorated with nautical knick-knacks and paintings. All in all, it seemed cozy and bright, despite the fact that there were no portholes. He thought of the stairway and realized the cabins were below deck. He did not remember seeing any portholes in the polished wood hull of the ship. That seemed a bit odd.

Sydney had wandered over to the final cabin and knocked lightly on the door. She turned. "You'll probably like James Arthur once you get to know him," she said. "He's a bit showy and over-confident, but he wouldn't be here if he wasn't brilliant. His theory of BioMagnetics is already revolutionizing the world of self-healing."

Self-healing? Willoughby tried to think of how self-healing would be important to time-travel. Was it simply that Dr. J was smart, or did his athleticism bring an important element to the team as well? He walked up behind Sydney and read the nameplate on the final door: *Dr. Hal O'Grady, Antonio Santanos Eldoro Chavez.* She knocked again, and the door swooped open. A wiry, balding fellow, with thick glasses and large, bushy sideburns peered out. He held a saucer in one hand and a teacup in the other. His hands were shaking. "Ah, Miss Sydney," the man sputtered with a heavy Irish accent. He seemed embarrassed.

Sydney smiled. "Dr. O'Grady, this is Willoughby. He's just arrived."

Dr. O'Grady looked over, his eyes shifting nervously. He bent clumsily to hold out a hand, realizing too late that it still held his teacup. He pulled the hand back, sheepishly, and motioned the two in, moving back toward his untidy desk. "Afraid I'm apt to get a bit nauseous on voyages—motion sickness, you see."

He seated himself on the wooden desk chair. "I, I must say, it's a pleasure to finally meet you, lad. I was greatly impressed with your treatise and solution for the Riemann. I have some things I'd like to discuss with you when you're settled in. I've a theory you might be able to help me with. Have you read my work on string theory and its applications to present day star-mapping procedures?"

"Uh," Willoughby swallowed, "not yet. It sounds fascinating though."

He watched curiously as Dr. O'Grady fingered his teacup. The man placed the cup on the desk, turning it slightly on its saucer. He looked up, jolting his hand out again to try for a handshake, and knocked the teacup over. Tea, or whatever the brown liquid was, sloshed across the desk and began to drip onto the floor. Willoughby and Sydney both sprung to try to help minimize the damage.

"Ah," Dr. O'Grady fussed, looking for something to mop up the mess. "Clumsy, clumsy—quite clumsy, really." He pulled a handkerchief from his pocket, and dabbed nervously at the pooling liquid.

As soon as the mess was cleaned up, Sydney pulled lightly on Willoughby's arm, pointing him toward the door. "Well, we don't want to take up your time Dr. O'Grady. I just wanted to introduce the two of you. We'll be off."

Dr. O'Grady grunted nervously, still dabbing at the carpet.

"Uh, see you around," Willoughby said as Sydney pulled him out and closed the cabin door. When they had stepped away, back toward his cabin, he whispered. "A bit skittish, isn't he?"

Sydney sighed. "Yes. He's a resident professor at the University of Dublin. He took a sabbatical to be with us, but he is a bit of a challenge for the team. He was all gung-ho for joining us, but it took months to get him away from his job at the university. Now that he's here, I think he feels a bit like a fish out of water. He's brilliant, but also the nervous sort. You're never sure if he's going to break out into a dissertation or start crying."

"You know a lot about everyone."

"I told you, I do my homework," Sydney replied, stepping in closer. She started walking her fingers up his chest. "I complete *all* my assignments."

Willoughby stepped back.

Sydney burst into another round of laughter. "Well, well...you'll have to do better than that, Willoughby!" She tapped his nose and twirled away. "The Absconditus sails at 4:15. That gives you roughly an hour to get settled. You'll want to be topside when we pull out of the harbor. They say it's quite a show. Dinner is at 5:30, and after dinner, there's a brief orientation by H.S."

"He's on the ship?" Willoughby asked.

"Don't know. No one sees him unless he wants to be seen." Sydney rocked back on her heels. "I'm just going by the instructions I received from the ship's Captain. He met me when I first came aboard. He's sort of a tall, silent type. I think he's related to the cabin girl."

Jingling her bracelets, she added, "Now, if you'll forgive me, I need to—*freshen up*." She winked again. For some stupid reason, Willoughby blushed. This girl was a lot to handle. Standing next to her was like standing in the middle of a fireworks display. He watched her gracefully pirouette through her cabin door. Before the door shut, she called over her shoulder. "Oh, and the Captain was hoping you'd take *some* level of responsibility for your roommate. They'd like to keep all those bristling muscles of his still bristling—at least until the end of the voyage." The door whooshed shut.

Willoughby stood staring after the girl. He would have normally been intrigued by the ship, his teammates, and a million other things, but this girl had a way of keeping him strangely off balance. He started to turn and walk back to his cabin, but something out of the corner of his eye made him turn toward H.S.'s cabin door. For a moment, he thought he had seen that same string of ghostly numbers floating out from a section of door a few feet higher than the doorknob. He watched. Nothing—he was just staring at an ordinary door. What was he expecting to see, a man rip open space and peer through? He shook his head. It was probably just this whole weird day. He struggled to pull things into perspective. A shout echoed from the end of the hall. It was Dr. J stepping into the hallway.

"Surf's up!" he yelled with a wide grin. He walked, dripping, down the hall. Barefoot and bare-chested, he had his pant legs rolled up and a lifesaver slung over one shoulder. His soaked shirt was draped over the other shoulder, oozing thin streams down the man's brown skin. The white of his teeth seemed to glow in the dim hall light. As he passed Willoughby, ducking into the cabin, he sang out in a fine baritone voice; "Fine, my boy; oh, oh, *oh*, that water is *fine!*" Willoughby watched as a slippery trail of lifesaver rope snaked into the cabin behind him.

11

Donuts and Diphtheria

Willoughby followed James Arthur into their room. He unlocked his trunk, and threw it open. Dr. J ducked into the bathroom just long enough to drop his shirt into the sink and drape the life preserver over the shower spigot. He grabbed a towel and popped back into the main cabin area, walking to his small dresser to grab a dry outfit. In the process, he peered over at Willoughby's trunk and whistled. "Now that's what I call packing! You could be marooned on a desert island with that trunk!"

Willoughby grinned. "Anything outside of D.C. proper is a desert island to my mom. "

James Arthur rummaged around until he found a slightly wrinkled t-shirt and pair of shorts. "Ah, yes—*Moms!* My mom used to dump my whole drawer onto the middle of the floor and bark, '*Fold!*' I tried to tell her that I had a system. You see, folding everything makes it so I can't find *anything*. Alas, she wouldn't listen."

Willoughby shrugged. "Moms are like that." He glanced over at the clothes sticking out of Dr. J's dresser. "Looks like you got your system back."

James Arthur chuckled. "Yes, I do. I'm able to dig through everything much faster if I'm not worried about protecting hours of hard labor. There are better things to do with your life than folding, you know." He paused, looking over Willoughby's shoulder. "What all have you got in there?"

Willoughby scooted things around, holding up a travel size bottle of seltzer water. "I don't know, but she seems to have covered all the 'D's'—diarrhea, dehydration…"

Dr. J chuckled, reaching down to pick up a pocket-sized bible, "Dracula. How about 'd' as in '*donut*' or '*date-nut bread*' or '*devil's food cake*'?" He asked, hopeful.

"Yeah, I wish," Willoughby moaned. "We weren't allowed to bring perishables. Didn't you read your instruction sheet?"

Dr. J grinned. "Of course… I had it right there in the bathroom next to the 1200-page biography of Thomas Jefferson." He dropped his knee-high shorts into a wet heap on the floor. "Man, I'm hungry. Pirating works up a powerful appetite!" He spun on Willoughby. "Okay, enough with the pleasantries. If we're going to be bunk mates, we need to know each other. So who is Willoughby Von Brahmer and why has a kid been invited to join this type of highly unusual organization?"

Willoughby's eyes darkened. "First, I'm 16. I'm not a kid."

"Wow!" James Arthur barked, his eyes smiling. "All of 16? How did you get selected, win a soprano contest?" He fell into laughter.

Willoughby ignored the outburst. For the first time, he was beginning to question his decision to join Observations, Inc. *Where was Antonio?* The group he had met so far seemed more like a collection of eclectic nut jobs than a brilliant scientific team. Had he made a mistake?

"Of course, playing pirates to annoy the crew does show your superior maturity," he shot back.

"Hey!" James Arthur shouted back with a smile. "I wasn't *trying* to annoy the crew. That was sort of a by-product. Anyway, good to see there is a little spunk behind that sheepish grin! I think we we'll get along fine." He held out a soppy hand. "Now, let's try again. I'm James Arthur: brilliant, fun loving, and built like an Amazonian God. I always get the girl, win the game, and vanquish the villains. I'm a wholly likable guy and loyal to those I deem my brothers, whatever their skin color. I'm here because I designed a way to observe vital signs in a person's aura. H.S. has helped me fine-tune my science to become somewhat of a spiritual healer—one who can mend physical concerns by invisibly manipulating the magnetic force that surrounds a life form. Besides, H.S. realized he needed my charisma on his team. Tell me of your specialty. Do you play sports?"

"Well, there's playing, and, well, *playing*…I doubt I'm being scouted for the Olympics, but I did play two years of community soccer. I usually follow the MLS Cup."

"Soccer! Love the game! Took pointers from Beckam once. He was awesome at driving, but I was positively punishing on defense!"

"*Beckam?*" Willoughby rolled his eyes. "I suppose you also played tennis with the Williams sisters."

"I've talked net strategy with them, but most of it had nothing to do with tennis," he winked and smiled. "Thrown the pigskin with my man Culpepper. Did handstands with Peter Vidmar. Sports, in my house, was pretty much everything. They had a hoop hanging over the edge of the crib and no babies got fed until they could slam-dunk! So what about your specialty?"

Willoughby shrugged. "I'm good at mathematics."

James Arthur stared at him. "That's it? You're good at mathematics?"

"Well," Willoughby shrugged, "really good. Tell me more about this, this thing you do with people's auras. I think Sydney called it BioMagnetics?"

Dr. J pulled on his shirt and a pair of khaki shorts, failing to remove his wet underwear. "Ah, good ol' Sydney! The theory is called BioMagnetics. It measures the causal relationships between our internal life force and the magnetic flux at the place we position ourselves in the time stream. You've never heard of the theory?"

"Only from Sydney," Willoughby confessed. He added a bit sarcastically, "She does her homework."

"Yes," Dr. J chuckled, "that she does. Well, anyway, that's my problem in nutshell. Too few people have heard of the theory outside of a handful of psychology professors. That's why I'm writing a book. It's the sort of idea that people should know about." He slipped into a pair of deck shoes. "Now, back to Ms. Senoya; didn't I see you tagging along behind our resident debutante, looking for all the world like a love-sick, wide-eyed puppy?" He flashed a snide grin. "She's about your age, if I remember right. I could have sworn that those eyes of yours were doing a little *calculating* of their own when it comes to our resident violinist."

Willoughby felt his cheeks flush a little. He tried to stay nonchalant as he reached into his trunk and took out a handful of clothes. He slipped them into the top dresser drawer neatly and looked up. "She is interesting. She's also out of my league."

"I don't know about that," Dr. J mused. "I don't know if they have a league for Sydney yet. Don't get me wrong, she's a looker, but after an hour of keeping up with her, you start to sweating, and your tongue hangs out like a dog that's been chasing its tail." He did a quick imitation that made Willoughby laugh. "So, do you surf?"

Willoughby shrugged. "I wouldn't mind learning to surf, but waves are a bit scarce in D.C."

"D.C. as in *District of Columbia*?"

Willoughby nodded.

"No wonder you're pale! We've got to get you down to California and I'll show you some *real* sun. That's how I got recruited. I was soaking it in one day, sitting on my board, and lo and behold, I spied a low-tide cave. I decided to investigate. Next thing I know, *bam!* I'm jerked to some strange window and H.S. is standing there with a cup of tea. *It was, like, ancient Egypt, man!* I'm watching them reface the Sphinx."

"Reface it?"

"Yeah. It was originally a lion's head before they changed it into a human face. You didn't know that?"

Willoughby shrugged again. "So tell me more about BioMagnetics," he said, careful to step around the puddle of water his new roommate had left in the center of the floor.

Dr. J took a deep breath and plopped onto the bed. "Okay. I believe there's a certain path in time and space that has your individual name carved on it. To stray from it weakens your aura and makes you more susceptible to illness and disease. To be at the peak of health and vitality, you've got to find and follow your true path." Dr. J stood. "I have a whole process outlined for helping people find their true path. I call it *time-streaming*. Every activity we choose, every choice we make, causes minute changes to our *aura* or magnetic signature. By mapping these changes, we can begin to see patterns that lead us toward a healthier life."

"Very Californian." Willoughby grinned. "You said you could 'heal' people by manipulating the magnetic forces around them?"

"Not around them—inside them. I can help people learn to adapt their aura to the environment they find themselves in for short periods of time. Over the long-haul, true health and happiness come from finding and following your true path."

"So, what led you to this study of magnetic auras?"

It was Dr. J's turn to shrug. "I wasn't chosen for the Olympic team either...In truth, the study of consciousness, of life-force, is what really excites me. My family will always be about sports, so I've worked hard to fit in, but it's not really what I do. I was born smart. At two days old, I built a crane out of a stuffed giraffe so I wouldn't have to know how to slam-dunk. My folks saw this was where my real talent lay and worked their tails off to get me the best education money can buy. My dad coaches football and teaches high school. My mom works as an office manager at a law firm. Still, they found a way to put me through college and help with graduate school. I was one of the youngest doctors ever to graduate from USC's Keck School of Medicine."

There was a knock on the cabin door. Dr. J swung it open to reveal a slender figure in a crewman's uniform. Willoughby stared. The white dungarees of the uniform were obviously too large and bulky for the figure, and long strands of blond hair spilled out from beneath the cap. In fact, it wasn't a crew*man* at all, but rather, a crew-*girl*. She was a bit older than Sydney, possibly 18, and her face had a certain porcelain quality to it, perfect and shiny, like a china doll. Her smile was warm and genuine and her eyes were the brightest blue he had ever seen.

"Might want to get topside," she said with a slight accent. It wasn't British, but she was possibly from Australia or New Zealand. "Ship casts off in ten minutes. Captain thought you might like to know."

Sydney had hinted that the cabin girl had a tougher edge, but this girl seemed dainty and delicate. She was definitely not what he had expected. "T.K.?" he asked, confused.

The girl stared at him. "Have we met?"

"Uh, no," he answered, quickly. "I met your nameplate. You're the cabin girl, right?"

The girl looked puzzled. Dr. J jumped in.

"Yeah, Willoughby here likes being acquainted with *things*. He says '*Hello*' to chairs, talks strategy with bedclothes, even occasionally scolds the light switch—"

Willoughby cut him off. "I mean, I read your nameplate. You room with Sydney, right?"

"Ah," T.K. said, "you've met Sydney, the one who does her homework. Sinks her teeth in rather quickly, doesn't she? Has she drawn blood yet?" Seeing Willoughby's blank stare, she laughed. "I'm only joking! You must be Willoughby." She leaned forward conspiratorially. "She imagined you taller." Her blue eyes sparkled in the cabin light. "I've been looking forward to meeting you, actually, but I'm on my rounds. Maybe we could catch up a little later?" She winked and was gone.

James Arthur raised an eyebrow. "Well, well," he chided. "Little junior has a way with the ladies. I'm reading in your aura right now an awful lot of hormone activity.

That one must be at least two or three years older than you and she wants to '*catch up later*'? What did you do, slip her a twenty?"

Willoughby shrugged. *What had happened?* He was the same awkward teen. He had the same wild hair, the same baggy pull-over and jeans. *What had gotten into these girls?*

He didn't know, but he liked it. A smile twitched at the corners of his face. "I guess, when you got it, you got it," he mumbled.

James Arthur's laugh could be heard all the way up on deck.

12

Setting Sail

The sun blazed crimson as it sank toward the horizon. A small tugboat led the Absconditus out of the harbor toward the open sea. Willoughby huddled on deck with Sydney, Dr. J, and Dr. O'Grady, trying to stay clear of the crew, who scurried about hoisting sails and checking riggings with aloof precision.

"I miss home already," Dr. J sighed. "Where I live, the sun goes down painting fire in jagged lines across the sea. An explosion of shimmering color, that's a sunset done right, done *California style*. Watching the day sink behind cold, dark buildings seems to me solemn and sad, like some kind of presidential funeral. Maybe that's why this whole coast, to me, feels, I don't know—colder."

"Well, the *water* is certainly colder," Sydney said. "I'm sure you discovered that for yourself earlier today. We're hundreds of miles further north."

Antonio watched from the bridge. "Willoughby!" he called out with a smile and a wave. "Your hair is most unfortunate to be matched with your head. You must visit me soon in my shop! It may be difficult to find scissors sharp enough to tackle those Medusa curls, but we shall try! Hello, James Arthur! No, I do not want you visiting

155

my shop. I do not cut hair while a man is doing gymnastics!" The man's eyes darted to Sydney. He made a slight bow. "Greetings, Ms. Senoya, my most beauteous friend! Hello, also, to you, Dr. O'Grady! Please, visit me in my shop at any time! It is on deck three, next to the quartermaster's store."

"Who gave you a license?" James Arthur yelled back. "You're nothing but a kamikaze with scissors." He leveled his gaze at Willoughby. "You let him cut your hair? I thought you were supposed to be smart."

Willoughby shrugged. "He's not a bad barber, actually. I thought that was all he was for almost two years. He opened a shop a few blocks from my Dad's office. I only found out that cutting hair isn't his main profession when, when I was invited on this cruise."

"You're telling me he has a shop and a clientele?"

"Well, not exactly a clientele. He's been working on it."

"Yeah, and he'll keep working on it." James Arthur snorted. "So, tell me, did he come up with that, uh, current hair style?"

Sydney glanced over with a grin. "Hair style?"

"My point exactly."

Willoughby ran a hand through his tangles, which were worse than usual due to the sea and the stiffening wind. "Okay, so I look a little rugged today. I think it's the sea air."

James Arthur guffawed. "The *sea* air?"

Sydney gave Willoughby a pat on the shoulder. "Don't mind him, Willoughby. I like Antonio. He *is* a good barber. His grandfather ran a neighborhood barbershop for 37 years, working long hours to help his dad get through college. The family was very close. He has a special love for his heritage, which I think is a good thing."

Dr. J snorted. Willoughby considered the words. He wondered if Sydney had ever been given a ride in Antonio's *Havana Limo*. He had to smile thinking of how reporters would describe her arriving for a concert with its silly horn blaring and the body of the car bucking up and down until it literally threw Sydney and her violin out the passenger door and into the waiting throng.

Sydney had turned her eyes back to the coastline. "Heritage can be a good thing. It can help us feel connected, even if our immediate links to the chain are weak ones."

Willoughby wasn't sure what she was trying to say, but there was a sort of sadness in her voice. She threw a quick glance at Willoughby. He grinned.

"Just do me a favor," he said. "Don't let him drive you anywhere important in his car."

The tug boat, at last, detached from the ship and turned back toward the harbor. For a moment, the creaking ship slowed and languished. Then it caught the breeze. Its sails rippled, snapping taut, and they were underway.

Watching the land grow smaller with distance, Willoughby drank in the taste of adventure—the curious exhilaration of a ship leaving for a voyage. There was a sense of the raw, the unscripted. The tedium of Worthington Hills slipped away. The burden of being *secretly famous*, a burden he had rarely even thought about over the past few months, shrank away like the final views of shore. Ahead were new horizons. He was part of a team now. Maybe they were a bit odd in one sense or another, but they were, nonetheless, a *team*.

"It's quite grand, isn't it?" whispered Dr. O'Grady, squinting at the red and gold wash on the waters behind them.

Willoughby nodded. He didn't say anything. It wasn't a moment to be talked to death. It was the kind you savor, like a favorite candy or a drink of ice-water on a hot day. He breathed in, tasting the proud ship—the tang of its polished wood floor, the bitter hemp of the ropes. He heard the timbers of the ship creek, the ropes straining to hold barrels and cargo in place. The rigging groaned with the roll of the waves. Folds of white mist sprayed over the bow of the ship. Water slapped rhythmically against the ship's hull, tainting everything with its salty brine.

From the corner of his eye, he saw Sydney side-step discreetly to sidle up to him. "You've grown quiet," she said. While he had been unpacking and getting acquainted with Dr. J, she had completely changed her outfit. She now wore an ankle-length vintage dress, complete with silver-inset pearls and a dark blue shawl. Black, lace-up boots highlighted her thin ankles. Her bangles and bracelets, though more subdued than earlier, still had no trouble announcing her presence. She bumped shoulders with him. He tried to avoid her eyes. They had a depth to them. If he ever let himself fall into them, he wasn't sure he could come back.

"I'm just enjoying the view. It's all…new—the way the sails snap, the feel of spray as the ship cuts into the swells … By the way, I like that dress. It, uh, it suits you."

"What, this old thing?" Sydney smiled. "I had the hardest time figuring out how to match bangles to the print and my ankle bracelets did *not* want to go over the boots."

Her voice softened as gold light from the sinking sun lit her face. She sighed. "I love the sea. I've always loved the sea. Perhaps it's my Polynesian blood." She held her chin high into the wind. It was a moment when the mask slipped and Willoughby could see past Sydney's flamboyance and showmanship. There was a longing in her eyes, a feeling of loneliness. She was quick to recover, however, beaming over at Willoughby with a mischievous grin.

"Later tonight, I might come up here—barefoot, with the moon cresting over the brooding waves. I'll dance for you, Willoughby. I'll surround myself with my ancient sisters of the sea, singing with the wind at my back and the mists as a veil...That's when you'll kiss me. You'll have no choice. You'll be mine."

James Arthur, who had been standing behind her, gave a laugh. "Whoa! Pull those claws back in and behave, child! Willoughby's barely wet behind the ears and you're already introducing him to your *ancient sisters of the sea?*"

Willoughby wasn't sure what was going on with this conversation, but he wasn't totally averse to the kissing under the moonlight idea at some point in the cruise. He decided to remain quiet and see where the conversation ended up.

Sydney kept her eyes trained on Willoughby. "Of course," she said, holding her hands up to the strengthening breeze, her voice elevating slightly. "When I call, they'll come from the depths. They sing a song, millions of years old, high-pitched and lonely. They'll beg you to dance, dance, dance, until there's no more ship and there's no more ocean, and you'll be completely under my spell, Willoughby Von Brahmer." Her eyes pierced him, glinting with wicked fire. She held out a slender hand, one finger curling in a slow, beckoning gesture.

Willoughby felt himself starting to move. He had forgotten to breathe. Suddenly, the hand dropped. Sydney flicked her hair and leaned back over the rail, as if engaged in a completely ordinary afternoon chit-chat. The spell was broken. "With ordinary sailors," she confided, pleased with the effect she seemed to be having, "I simply turn their hearts to stone."

Willoughby forced himself to exhale. "I, I think I'll pass," was the best he could manage.

Dr. J busted up with laughter. "You think you'll pass! That was classic, Willoughby. And Ms. Senoya—girl, *where* is your Mama? Didn't she warn you against terrifying young intellectuals?"

Sydney glared at the doctor. "Stone it is for *you*," she said. She pirouetted in a precise semi-circle and strode gracefully toward the cabins.

Dr. J watched her leave. "Well, well, Mr. Willoughby, old roommate, old pal," he said with a raspy chuckle, "*you* seem to be the object of considerable attention on our little cruise. I'm beginning to wonder if you'll make it home alive."

Willoughby felt a grin tugging at the edges of his mouth again. "I can think of worse ways to go," he said coolly. "She's a bit of an electric personality, isn't she?"

"*Electric?*" James Arthur hooted. "Boy, *that* woman could power the city of Cleveland and still keep Chicago warm! I'd keep a healthy distance from her if I were you."

Dr. O'Grady interrupted their conversation with an excited shout. "There! Whales!" Willoughby and Dr. J glimpsed dark grey shapes, disappearing quickly under the waves.

"Probably just a school of black sea-bass," James Arthur remarked, but Willoughby watched with interest, determined to see where the humps surfaced again. He stayed on deck with Dr. O'Grady until it was time for dinner. Twice, he thought he glimpsed something. It was only a speck on the horizon, bobbing up and down, but it didn't seem to move like a whale or a fish. The truth was, he sensed something. Though he found it odd, he had glimpsed flares of bluish light several times since boarding the ship—complete with number strings. Did that mean there was a time door on board? How could there be on a moving ship? He tried to calm his apprehension, to steel his nerves. They were barely away from harbor and already he had a bad feeling about this voyage.

13

Mark of the Menace

Willoughby sat next to Antonio at dinner.

"You like my ship, amigo?" Antonio winked, slapping him on the back.

"*Your* ship?" Willoughby eyed the plate of greens in front of him warily.

Sydney had just taken a seat opposite them at the table. "Yes, everything first belongs to Antonio. Then, if we're good little children, Papa Chavez will come to visit us in his wondrous barking car—"

"Ah, you've met Lola!" Willoughby grinned.

"Ah, I'd like to *forget* Lola," Sydney rolled her eyes as she continued. "As I was saying, he will visit in his infamous machine and distribute to the peasantry those things he deems insignificant. This ship, for example, built and commissioned by the Corporation years before Mr. Chavez joined us, has been fortunate enough to be designated as significant, and, as such, has become *his* property."

"Dearest Sydney!" Antonio beamed, "Such a beauteous vision, with the tongue wagging and the words as sharp as a barracuda's fin!" He turned back to Willoughby. "Isn't she something? Look at that practiced pout and the scorching black eyes! I recall when you first laid eyes upon her in that most interesting *Times* article. What was it you called her—a wild, Japanese anime?"

Willoughby choked on his sip of water as Sydney cocked her head and raised an eyebrow. "Uh, well, I, uh, meant—I, I don't remember using the word '*wild*'."

"But it fits—a wild, caged animal, so tragic in her beauty!" Antonio continued.

Willoughby made swift cutting motions across his throat trying to tell his friend to shut up. Sydney tilted her nose up. "As I remember, Mr. Chavez, last time I visited, you were managing an incredibly *empty* barbershop; a place where you spent most of your time dusting chairs and polishing ancient hair-tonic bottles. Did you ever actually find a customer—I mean, one you weren't sent to observe."

"Charming! Simply charming," Antonio sang. "Such wondrous foresight in bringing up the very topic I was wishing to discuss! I am most happy to report that I, Antonio Santanos Eldoro Chavez, will be opening a most amazing haircut establishment on this very boat!"

Before either Sydney or Willoughby could respond, James Arthur curtly motioned at a waiter, pointing emphatically at his plate. "What's with this house plant stuff? We came here to eat *food*."

"Your wheat bread and onion soup are on their way," the waiter said with a smile.

Dr. J winced. "Wheat bread and *what?*"

T.K., the cabin girl, stepped hurriedly into the room. "Please eat quickly. The captain tells me that Dr. Simon is already waiting for you in the chartroom and is on a tight schedule. I'm sorry, but we will have to postpone your dessert of chilled pummelos until later tonight."

"Chilled *what?*" Dr. J moaned. "How about something cooked on a George Foreman grill? That's healthy."

"Pummelos are a type of fruit," T.K. offered indulgently, "and I'm afraid our chef does not cook with a George Foreman grill."

Dr. J sighed. "Okay. Chilled pummelos it is. Do I get eggs with my wheat grass in the morning?"

"You could have pummelos with the wheat grass. They are a citrus fruit native to Southeast Asia. They taste a lot like a sweet, mild grapefruit."

"Sweet, mild, grapefruit? That's what you call dessert?"

T.K. didn't answer. She just stood quietly by the door as the soup and bread were brought in. James Arthur grunted and stared down at his plate. Everyone seemed intent on finishing the meal as quickly as possible. When Dr. J, with great ceremony, devoured the final crust of bread, T.K. smiled. "If you'll follow, the room is this way."

Willoughby rose and pulled H.S.'s card out of his wallet. He glanced at it quickly. *Hathaway Simon*, the card read, *Cryptic Spaces to Distant Places*. He jammed it back into the wallet as the others started moving toward the dining room door. James Arthur led the way. "There's tea and crumpets in the chartroom, right? Please tell me there's more food *somewhere!*"

T.K. laughed. "The sparse diet is only temporary, Dr. Washington. It's best to eat lightly your first few days aboard. The Absconditus rolls more than your typical cruise liner. Meals for the first two days will consist mainly of grains, fruits, and vegetables—very little in the way of greasy foods or rich sweets."

"Just kill me now," Dr. J groaned.

The chartroom was easily one of the most elegant rooms on the ship. It featured a library, nautical paraphernalia, and a dozen over-stuffed chairs arranged in a semi-circle around an ornate gas fireplace. A small fire flickered in the hearth, giving the room a cozy feel. Willoughby could easily make out the bald, imposing figure of H.S., seated to the left of the fire, a teacup and saucer in his hands. He wondered when the large man had boarded. Sydney had said H.S. was not on the ship initially. The man looked up.

"Nice of you to join me," he said cheerily, nodding at them as they filed in and took their seats. He signaled to T.K. and then waited while she exited the room and the chartroom door swung shut. A series of loud clicks indicated that the door had locked tightly. Willoughby was a bit perplexed. He had assumed that T.K. was part of the Observations Inc. team, but maybe not. Maybe the others on the windjammer were simply hired workers for the organization and were not fully aware of what it did or the technology it controlled. H.S. confirmed his suspicions.

"Before we begin, a quick housekeeping issue: what is discussed in this room is not discussed anywhere else on this ship, is that understood?" H.S. took another sip of tea. "While we take care to recruit our staff, they are under the impression that we are a scientific think-tank collecting data for a series of studies on ancient cultures. Everything we say outside this room should support that." He lowered his teacup and saucer to his lap. "I regret I was not able to be topside to welcome each of you aboard, or to participate with you in your first sumptuous meal aboard the Absconditus." He leaned forward to place his tea onto a low coffee table. Willoughby saw James Arthur raise his eyebrows at the word "*sumptuous*." It was Sydney who spoke, however.

"The cabin girl said you weren't on the ship."

H.S.'s eyes twinkled mischievously. "Things hidden, things in plain view but unseen, are what we seek most of all. What is your opinion about my present location, Ms. Senoya?"

Willoughby noted a faint glow at the edges of H.S.'s substantial bulk. When he had reached forward to put his teacup down, there had also been a momentary flash of transparency—as if his fingers had softened for a moment, letting flickers of fire through. Something about what his eyes told him didn't feel right. He watched closely as H.S. reached up to nibble at a chocolate-covered biscuit. For the briefest second, the biscuit swirled like a cloud before settling into the solid shape of a cookie with a bite taken out of it. H.S. chewed, and then smiled. He looked over the group with twinkling eyes.

"Well," Sydney began, "it's obvious that you're—"

"*Not really here!*" Willoughby shouted. Everyone turned toward him, stunned by the outburst. H.S. cocked his head.

"Would you care to explain that deduction, Willoughby?"

Willoughby smiled. "You're speaking to us from somewhere off the ship. You created here a, a," Willoughby thought how to put into words what he had noted. He felt sweat break out on his forehead. He gulped and continued, "a very life-like 3-D conferencing image of some sort. It's all an elaborate trick…" His voice trailed off. He knew that last part was guessing, but every instinct told him that H.S. was not really in the room.

Everyone looked back at H.S., who brooded, as if outraged at the accusation. Then, with a twinkle, he raised his hands and with his fingers drew lines of faintly glowing light around his head until it seemed to be encased in a sort of translucent cube. He then lifted the head from his shoulders. He turned the head 180 degrees so that it, while held at arm's length, could scrutinize the body with a critical eye. "Well, I haven't the foggiest how you came to such a conclusion. That body looks frightfully solid to me. Perhaps the sea air and the rich meal have left your mind rather…detached." He flashed a quick grin at Willoughby, his eyes sparkling.

Willoughby gave a short laugh, joined by the others.

"Bravo, Willoughby," H.S. smiled, reattaching his head to his body and with a snap of his fingers, losing the translucent cube. "What gave me away?"

Willoughby shrugged. "Bits of you seemed to swirl—as if you weren't quiet solid. Once, I saw flickers of the fire right through your hand."

H.S. stared forward. "Astute observations," he said. He leaned toward the oblong coffee table and sunk his hand into the wood. A swirl of shimmering dust seemed to pool where his hand disappeared. When he raised it again, the dust seemed to reattach itself. "It is a projection, of course. I am sitting in an exact replica of this room in one of our facilities thousands of leagues below the surface of the sea, near one of the strongest natural holes on the planet. The facility is located off the coast of Bermuda. It is equipped with a dozen or more specially designed cameras and this chair," he motioned at the chair he sat in. "The replica chairs facing me in my facility are identical to the ones you are sitting in. They are equipped with some of the most sophisticated 3-D projection arrays the world has ever known. Both the cameras and the projection arrays are cleverly hidden in the furniture, walls, and ceiling around you.

"Of course, you may wonder how my image could appear to have bulk and form. The projection looks so lifelike due to a special grid-screen we have created. My every move is sourced by high-definition video and beamed to a live feed on the Absconditus. The image is then broken down over a three dimensional pixel grid. The key is a microscopic glitter we've developed. When secreted from the chair, the glitter, made from a slightly metallic synthesis, settles onto the magnetic grid lines of the three dimensional image. My form is thus projected—or perhaps recreated is a better word—to mirror my every move using an enhanced hybrid of current flat screen technology.

"We call the special pixel dust *projection soup*. Quite a neat trick, is it not?"

Everyone agreed. Willoughby let his eyes scour the room for cameras. He found one or two hidden in the ornate décor of the room, but H.S. said there were a dozen or so. He again marveled at the company's ability to mask its secrets.

"Well," H.S. said, finishing his biscuit, "now, on to weightier matters." He took another sip of tea. Willoughby stared at the cup. Were the teacup and saucer a projection too? They looked solid and real on the coffee table, but a little less so when he picked them up. Could H.S. have planted a replica set here and precisely lined them up? The possibilities made his head spin. The technology was amazing. Antonio broke the silence.

"I thought you were to join us. What has happened, my friend?"

H.S. sighed. He looked directly at Antonio. "St. Petersburg," he said softly.

Antonio's eyes narrowed. "What has happened?"

"A full break-in," H.S. said gravely. "One guard was killed, one was seriously wounded. We're not sure what they were after, but they did probe the computer for information on the Aperio Absconditus."

"Did they find the door?"

"No. But they came close. Our response team scattered them as they were trying to break our code."

"Someone has found us?" Dr. J mumbled; "How? I mean, what are the ramifications?"

H.S. gave a slight shrug. "It is difficult to know. Our interest in the famous 16th century seer Nostradamus seems to have hit a raw nerve with someone, which makes me all the more certain that we must learn more about this individual. Our security technology should have been enough to thwart any normal thugs. We are looking at something different here."

"You think it is the sign?" Antonio said softly.

H.S. pursed his lips. "I'm afraid so. We may no longer be the hunters in this game. We are beginning to look like the hunted, and those hunting us seem to know more about our operation than we ever imagined."

Willoughby cocked his head. "What sign? Are you referring to the symbol over Antonio's shop?" He couldn't help thinking about the tall stranger who called himself "Mr. B" and the tattooed man who had carefully photographed the carved stone before their notice scared him away.

H.S. gave a curt shake of his head. "No, we are speaking of a different sign, Willoughby. The sign Antonio refers to is contained in a warning letter from our infamous seer. We'll discuss that in more detail in a moment, but I wanted all of you to be aware that our mission is no longer strictly academic. We've stumbled into something, meaning our work has become riskier than we ever imagined. The St. Petersburg break-in is not an isolated incident. It may have been simply a distraction in a much larger operation. We are also aware that other supposedly '*hidden*' facilities have been cased. Willoughby and Antonio spotted a man photographing Antonio's barbershop last November, and there have been other incidents. Yesterday, I spent the better part of the day with internal security. They feel we need to scrub the mission until we have more concrete information about who or what we're dealing with. I'm not sure that I agree."

"*Scrub the mission?*" Sydney barked. "Our interest in Nostradamus may or may not have put these goons on our tail. We've done a lot of different kinds of research over the past few years. Who knows what has caused this group to take note? The fact is, they've taken note—*they're on our tail.* If it's a race to some sort of critical information, or if we're close to uncovering some ancient secret, how does disappearing really help us? I think we need to be discussing how we can stay a step ahead of these guys, not how to hide, shivering, in the basement."

H.S. frowned. "No-one here wants to '*hide*' in a basement, Sydney. I do take your point that we may well be getting close to something. I also agree that we need to find out what that '*something*' is."

Dr. O'Grady had taken his glasses off and began to polish them. "Is it a wee handful of men or a much larger organization we're up against? You make it sound a bit like a monster."

H.S. widened his eyes. "*Monster* may be a very apt word, Dr. O'Grady. This brings us back to Willoughby's question about the sign. Some of you already know the information I'm about to share. For some of you, this will be new. In the early eighteen-hundreds, our organization came across what they believe to be evidence of something unfriendly in the time corridors. The evidence was never conclusive. Generations passed without direct threat or incident, so the suspicions were eventually filed away and the issue closed. About ten years ago, however, further evidence came to light. We re-opened the files. What began as academic curiosity around Nostradamus and medieval France has spiraled into a trail of danger and intrigue. Before I ask a final decision of the group, I will share with you what we know."

H.S. took a thin pointer out and, without leaving his chair, began to draw in the air. He completed the image of a pyramid with a line and curl.

"Antonio mentioned a sign. We have found that breaking the sign down into individual components is instructive. Dr. O'Grady, would you be so kind? I know you've taught summer lectures on the history of alchemy. Can you identify this recognizable alchemical symbol?"

Willoughby could see bright flicks of firelight reflected on the surface of Dr. O'Grady's glasses. The man shifted in his chair. "It is the alchemical symbol for *air*," he responded.

H.S. nodded. "Correct. Now," He drew a curved line over the curl, creating the semblance of an eye. "Does this suggest anything to you?"

James Arthur squinted; "The *All-Seeing Eye?*"

"Go on," H.S. encouraged.

Dr. J blinked. "It, uh, it looks like the Buddhist symbol for the All-Seeing Eye. I'm not sure what tying it to a symbol of *air* means."

H.S. shrugged. "Perhaps it refers to a personage of power who could appear, or materialize, from thin air. Both the pyramid and the all-seeing eye appear on the back of the American dollar bill, but they are not physically connected there."

H.S. began to draw again. Dr. J bent sideways and whispered to Willoughby. "The unfinished nature of the pyramid on the back of US currency is said to mean that the United States will always grow, improve and build, and the "All-Seeing Eye" located above it is said to suggest the importance of divine guidance in favor of the American cause."

H.S. completed the image he was working on. It floated in the air just below the lines of the pyramid. He turned back around. "Does this symbol mean anything to any of you?"

"Aye," Dr. O'Grady wheezed. "It's the alchemical symbol for *ammonia.*"

"True," H.S. nodded. "What else?" After a silent pause, he reached back up to the floating hologram and drew a thick line from the center of the triangle through the center of the symbol below.

"How about now?" he asked.

Willoughby jerked his head backwards. "*313,*" he whispered, "with the last '3' backward."

H.S. nodded gravely. "This is the completed symbol, first noted by our organization over 200 years ago." He leaned back in his chair, peering out at the team with wide, penetrating eyes. "The team who infiltrated our St. Petersburg facility had this symbol tattooed on their necks, just below the left ear. We uncovered this fact when we carefully scrutinized the footage of our security camera feeds, going frame by frame. We can clearly see the tattoo on two of the three infiltrators." H.S. clicked his pointer. A grainy image of the symbol tattooed on the back of a broad neck appeared. "As you can see, there's no mistake. It *is* the very same mark."

H.S. slowly stood and began to pace.

"We were originally introduced to this mark by a Buddhist monk who sought our people out. He worked out of an obscure monastery where he showed our people a rare bit of parchment. The parchment included monastic writings about a mysterious outsider who called himself the '*Fifth Friend*.' He was said to have visited the monasteries in southeast France repeatedly over a 30-year period before seeming to vanish for good. One monk described him as 'the right hand of God, knowing things that have been and will be—*God's answer to Beelzebub and his Cult of the Mark*.'" The parchment included a crude rendition of this very same mark.

"The monks believed that this *Friend* was key to defeating the Cult of the Mark, a cult that was hiding within the folds of time, waiting to begin that final battle referred to in holy-script as *Armageddon*. The monks believed this hero could command more than just the four elements—water, fire, wind, and earth—that he wielded a fifth power, one capable of purging time."

Willoughby stared, spellbound, as H.S. continued.

"Observations, Inc. made a number of efforts to discover the whereabouts of this *Friend* and to probe the origin of the mark. Stories from various cultures tell of a final battle, and many mention a dark mark, but no direct reference to the *Friend* could be found. There was only this Buddhist parchment. The scroll ends with a chilling account of the climactic battle, which begins at a mythical location known as the *Library of Souls*, a place outside of time where all lives are known and catalogued in great, magical books.

"It is important to note that, according to this scroll, the *Friend* is joined in his battle by a group of like-minded heroes called the '*Seekers of the Obvious.*' Together, they defeat Beelzebub.

"Nostradamus refers to the mark in a communication to his son. He, too, refers to "seekers of the obvious," claiming that they will hold power in the *Library of Souls*. Below his scrawled words "demons of the mark," the seer hastily drew a rendition of this same symbol. Beneath the symbol, he underlined five words; *Mathe'maticien, Prenez garde, voici Beelzebub.* Interpreted, it reads: 'Mathematician, beware of the Beelzebub.' The words are followed by a string of numbers—the month, day, and year of the St. Petersburg break-in."

Willoughby felt his face go hot as questioning eyes turned to him.

Was he this mathematician?

How could anyone in ancient France have known he would solve the Riemann Hypothesis? How could they have known he would stumble upon Antonio and Observations Inc.? The whole thing stretched believability. *Was this a set-up?* Was he supposed to break out laughing and say, "Good one!" He signed up for this trip because of a thirst for knowledge, a sense of fun and adventure—a chance to uncover lost mysteries. He hadn't signed up to be part of some save-the-world crusade to be fought in an obscure library of time! He didn't even know how the time corridors worked. *Why was H.S. looking at him?*

H.S. continued, his eyes carefully watching Willoughby.

"I don't mean to frighten you, Willoughby. I also consider myself a mathematician, as does Dr. O'Grady. But you asked me to talk to you straight, as an equal in the group, and so I am. No other mathematician in this room has exhibited such talent so young." He looked up. "We have carefully analyzed the Nostradamus letter. The paper and ink carbon-date to only a few months before the seer's supposed death. We have determined it to be genuine. Hence, our growing interest in the seer. Nostradamus has shown an uncanny ability to accurately predict future events. Could he be a time traveler, like us? Could he be our link to this '*Fifth Friend*,' or, perhaps, even *be* the elusive *Friend*? It certainly seems that he sent us an invitation."

H.S. looked up, his eyes keen. "So, what do you make of it?" he said to the group.

"You mention that you found no other reference to this friend, but have you found anything else about this cult?" Dr. O'Grady said, rather uneasily.

H.S. raised an eyebrow and drew in a quick breath. "We believe it could be related to the snake cults of the Ophites, an obscure Egyptian people who used to lay loaves of bread on the table, then lure cobras out of their baskets to slither around the bread. Only then, kissing the snake's head, would they eat. I tell you this so you have some idea of what we are up against. The cult was considered deadly even then. They boasted links to dark gods with powers over life and death, time and matter.

"Three of the most interesting references to the cult's supposed mark will be downloaded into your individual research dossiers. A tribe of nomadic herdsmen in central Africa spoke of frequent visits from one who they called the *Lonely One*, a healer and prophet who taught them to beware of the mark. They carved close facsimiles to it on their story stones, and used them to mark 'places of devils.' The mark was also found carved into the ebony throwing knives of Vlad III, Prince of Wallachia, also known as Vlad the Impaler. Some believe that this man is responsible for the myth of the blood-sucking vampire. Finally, the mark seemed to have interested the Third Reich. Though it was never proved, some claim to have seen it tattooed on the left hand of elite SS officers to signify a dark fraternity that operated within the larger SS structure.

"Questions? Comments?"

"Beelzebub was some kind of Philistine god, wasn't he?" Dr. J asked.

H.S. nodded. "The Jews referred to Beelzebub as the 'Chief among Demons.' Other cultures referred to him as 'Lord of the Flies.' We may be dealing with a very nasty customer. But I remind you, a pack of hungry plesiosaurs was no walk in the park either." He looked around the room. "What do you say? Do you agree with the security folks? Should we scrap the mission?"

The group considered the questions. Willoughby felt a growing sense of panic. Snatches of the conversation he had overheard from the tattooed man and the taller figure he called "Mr. B." rang in his ears. The tattooed man had made reference to the taller man's "fly-boys." Willoughby thought of the breach in space that had seemed to just materialize outside of Antonio's shop. He thought of the creepy cab driver and 6,6,6 on the cab meter. His face went pale. He looked up. Antonio was watching him. *Should he say something? Should he warn them?* Antonio gave a quick jerk of his head as if reading his thoughts. *Did Antonio know?*

"What would happen if we did scrap the mission?" Antonio asked. "We are already on the Absconditus."

"We would turn around, go back to Boston Harbor, and think of some excuse for cancellation of the voyage."

H.S. frowned. "Of course, that may or may not make a difference. We don't know what this cult wants. We don't know how much they know about us, our families, and our lives. It may actually be safer for us to continue without alerting the hunters that we are on to them."

Willoughby agreed. He was a part of this now—whatever *this* was—and going back home would only involve more people. He didn't want this 'cult' having access to his parents or little sisters. His conversation with H.S. at the observation facility jumped to mind. Referring to Gustav, he had told H.S. that *he* would never run away from those he loved. H.S. cautioned him that sometimes there was little choice. He glanced around. Everyone seemed to be fidgeting, waiting for someone else to speak. He cleared his throat.

"I guess it's like the inventor, Henry Ford, said; '*Obstacles are what you see when you're looking behind you.*' I say the best path is forward."

H.S. smiled, seeing the others give nods of assent. "Well said, young Willoughby. Are there other thoughts? …Good. Each of you, of course, has unique talents to draw upon—I suspect you know that by now. You will need to know each other's abilities much better, however, if you hope to become a cohesive team." His demeanor became suddenly very business-like.

"Willoughby, you are key to this mission. A mathematician is required to understand the complex formulas that control the grid and guide the team. We will not have tethered holes in the places we must go. The skill you showed in solving the Riemann Hypothesis proves that you're more than up to the task. You are the team navigator."

Dr. J coughed, looking down the row at Willoughby. "*Riemann Hypothesis?*"

Willoughby kept his attention focused on H.S. The man's voice continued, "I want you to look at Michel de Nostradame's book of predictions—his quatrains. See if you can find any discernible patterns in the nature of their construction. Do they hide mathematical formulas? I would not be surprised if the real beauty of the text becomes known only when we determine why the quatrains are structured as they are."

"What am I looking for?" Willoughby asked, a puzzled look on his face.

"All I can tell you is that you will know when you find it," H.S. assured him.

He turned to Dr. O'Grady.

"Dr. O'Grady, you are our insurance. Should it become necessary to return by some other time hole than the one used to take you to ancient France, your extensive knowledge of astronomy and astrophysics gives you a keen insight into when and where holes may form. I've stocked your shelves with star charts that mark every time-hole we currently know of. Anticipate variances for earlier centuries, and memorize as many of the holes as you can, especially in areas that Nostradamus was known to frequent."

Dr. O'Grady nodded silently, somewhat uneasily.

"Sydney, your knowledge of languages will be essential to our ability to function in ancient France, and your musical abilities will give credence to our cover. The advance team will consist of Willoughby, Sydney, Dr. J, and Dr. O'Grady. The four of you will pose as a troupe of traveling court musicians."

Willoughby felt a pang of panic. *Court musicians?*

H.S. seemed to sense his concern. "Don't worry. You will be equipped with electronic replicas of instruments from the period. The instruments are designed to play a variety of regional tunes. You will be taught to mimic the movements, speech, and mannerisms of the musicians of the period. Sydney's considerable ability to ad-lib and perform requests should make the illusion complete and credible."

H.S. looked to James Arthur. "James, you're a rather unconventional medic. With your medical background, you will be a valued resource. You have also done groundbreaking work on how to read a person by studying their aura. You help them use their own internal energy to heal. In a time when medical facilities may be sparse or nonexistent, this should prove an invaluable skill. This same ability to read people will help us assess Nostradamus once we locate him.

"We will provide you with detailed records that will help you learn more about the typical conditions your troupe may run into. Take what you feel you may need and may be able to successfully conceal.

"I want all of you to brush up on period manners and styles. All of you speak at least passable French, but let Sydney do most of the conversing as she has been studying dialects and slang from the time period. James Arthur, you need to work on speaking French with a bit of a Middle East accent as the black men of that age typically did. You will be responsible for the group, a traveling troupe under the protection of Lord Francois Degallanie, a French Lord with connection to East African trade. Your troupe is traveling to Paris to perform for the royal court."

"Antonio, you will organize and direct the team from this side of the hole. As chief technical advisor on the project, you are responsible to not only monitor the hole at all times, but to ensure that the timetables are understood and adhered to. You will also handle all logistics, including the timetables of the Absconditus, which will dock in France."

H.S. paused. "That's all I have for you tonight." He leaned back in his chair and smiled, his eyes twinkling. "Now, my friends, you are on one of the most beautiful ships ever to have roamed the seven seas. Let's take advantage of it, though, in your case, Dr. J, I would ask for a little more prudence. Your antics in Boston Harbor have cost me a very fine bottle of sherry, and the Captain still isn't convinced that allowing you to remain with the Absconditus is a wise choice." He gave his head a shake. "Whoever led you to believe you could pull off a believable Errol Flynn? I may give you Zorro, or a modernist interpretation of The Count of Monte Cristo, but Flynn?" He chuckled as he rose to his feet. "Sydney, I believe you are scheduled to provide an evening concert for tomorrow night. I would like all to attend. My yacht will rendezvous with you the following night. That gives you two full days, and I expect you to make good use of them. Oh, yes, and the food does improve, James. To begin the festivities, I offer my own contribution—a vanishing act. Goodnight."

H.S. vanished. After a long moment of silence, the bolts on the door to the hall released and clicked open. Lights in the overhead wood panels brightened, highlighting the shelves that contained books and other materials relevant to the team's assignments. The group sat there for a long moment, slightly stunned. There was little conversation as, one by one, they stood, stretched, and browsed the shelves. Willoughby looked closely at a long row of books against one wall. There were at least two dozen or more titles dedicated to Nostradamus and his book of quatrains. He grabbed a few, vowing to come back in the morning for a more thorough inventory.

"So, how did he know I complained about the food?" James Arthur asked as they moved into the hall. "You think the ship is bugged?"

Willoughby was only half listening. He looked over his shoulder, hoping to corner Antonio, but when there was no sight of the man, he turned back to Dr. J and shrugged. "He probably saw the misery on your face. You pretty much telegraph your feelings, and, of course, you are on his list of infamy."

"Yeah," Dr. J grinned back. "I live on that list."

Ahead of them, Sydney and Dr. O'Grady were deep in conversation. "Languages have been somewhat of a hobby," Sydney explained. "I speak eleven fluently, six of them considered dead or endangered languages, and I have a passable understanding of several others. I'm fluent in French, Japanese (which I learned from my father), Spanish, Quechua (an indigenous Peruvian language), Mandarin, Khitan, an ancient Chinese language, ancient Egyptian—I'm fully conversant in Hieroglyphics as well—Oielo Hawai'i, or native Hawaiian, which I learned from my mother, Mycenaean Greek, Minoan (which H.S. is oddly conversant in), Old Persian, and Phoenician. I have a rudimentary understanding of several Native American dialects, German, Portuguese, and Russian. Of course, my favorite language is music. Music has been the center of communication for many cultures. It is a language that can transcend all barriers, even time."

Willoughby listened, stunned. He had taken two years of French and a year of Spanish, but he didn't feel conversant in either language. He could barely tell Antonio he liked tacos. The thought caused him to look around again. He needed to talk with Antonio—to let him know about the tall, thin man, the tattooed man, and about the conversation he overheard. He was confident his friend would know what to do.

After Sydney said goodnight and whirled into her cabin, footsteps sounded from behind them. Willoughby looked over his shoulder and spotted Antonio about 30 yards back, motioning for him to stop. He waited. James Arthur continued toward the cabin breaking into a mangled refrain of "Midnight Train to Georgia." The hallway became quiet.

"Thank you for waiting, my friend," Antonio whispered, slowing to a stop. "We should talk, no?"

"Yeah, about that…I didn't quite—"

Antonio stopped him, raising a finger to his lips. He glanced around nervously. "Not here. I have my own concerns about the, shall we say, accommodations. I am not comfortable with the security on the Absconditus. I have been concerned, even before the briefing. Some of the crew do not seem fit and have far too little to do."

"Why didn't you bring it up?"

"I have my reasons," Antonio answered frankly. "I have a feeling there are facts you did not exactly volunteer at the briefing as well."

"That's true. Where can we talk?" Willoughby said. He couldn't help thinking of the speck he had seen on the horizon, bobbing up and down, soon after they left Boston harbor. Antonio opened his mouth to answer, but a loud clank from a few hundred yards down the corridor stopped him cold. An oily-looking crewman had slammed a mop bucket into the wall. He swore at it profusely, then tried to steer the wheeled bucket around them using the mop handle. "Evening,'" he said gruffly when he had pulled up beside them. "Anything you gents need?"

"No," Antonio responded, realizing that both he and Willoughby had stopped talking the moment they saw the man with the mop bucket. He turned to Willoughby. "I was just telling my friend that it has been a most excellent day! Tomorrow, we must be early to greet the sun!" His voice hit full volume. "I think, at dawn, we *practice* our rowing, no? Perhaps we may even take a dip in the ocean?"

James Arthur opened the door just as Antonio finished. He seemed to have been wondering what had become of Willoughby. He was stripped to his shorts and had a toothbrush dangling from his lips. "You guys going to brave the Atlantic waters? I'm in!" he sputtered bits of toothpaste across the hall as he spoke. Antonio ignored the distraction, his gaze fixed on Willoughby.

Willoughby shrugged, confused by the suggestion.

With a subtle nod, Antonio smiled. "Yes. A little fresh air will be good in the morning, I think. Until the dawn, my friends!" With a flourish, he spun to his cabin and disappeared.

Dr. J narrowed his eyes, staring after Mr. Chavez. He stepped back and closed the door.

Willoughby had already pushed past the doctor. He turned and collapsed on his bunk. Though he was tired, his mind was whirling a million miles a second. *Morning rowing?* What's that all about?

Dr. J walked into the bathroom and spit in the sink. He ducked his head back around the door frame. "Good at math?" he said sarcastically. "You sort of omitted the little detail about solving the Riemann Hypothesis. That's a little more than just '*good.*'"

Willoughby had a hard time pulling his mind away from Antonio's puzzling behavior and the revelations of the debriefing. "Well, I did say 'really good' at math," he mumbled, fighting a yawn.

Dr. J barked a laugh. "Oh yeah, I forgot. You're the guy that's just '*got it*,' right? It's all in a day's work. So, tell me, did academia foam at the mouth when they learned the Riemann was solved by a teenage boy? They gave me grief for graduating med school five years early."

"Well, I wasn't officially a teenager when I solved it," Willoughby corrected. "I was twelve."

"Twelve what?"

"Twelve years, Dr. J," Willoughby sighed, rolling over. "I was twelve years old when I solved the Riemann."

James Arthur's jaw dropped open. "So, what did you do for an encore, *cold fusion?*"

Willoughby cracked a smile. "Well, I didn't try to pass myself off as Errol Flynn."

Dr. J clicked off the bathroom light and walked over to his bed, plopping down. "Well, you don't have the physique. Me, on the other hand—"

"A regular legend in your own mind, aren't you?" Willoughby was grinning wildly.

"If you got it, flaunt it!" James Arthur said. He clicked the light off over his bed. "And with that, I say, '*lights out and goodbye to the day!*'" Willoughby leaned up and did the same. "Amen, brother," he added, clicking off his own lamp.

Dr. J clicked his light back on. "Brother? Did you just call me '*brother?*'"

Willoughby looked over. "Uh, yeah."

"Is that because you feel a family relationship?"

Willoughby groaned. "It's just an expression—you know, *Amen, brother!*"

Dr. J peered at him a long moment.

Willoughby raised his eyebrows; "What? I'm not allowed to say, '*Amen, brother?*'"

Dr. J lay back down, clicking off the light. "I haven't decided."

"If it makes any difference, I *have* been officially accepted into the African-American brotherhood," Willoughby remarked with another yawn.

"I've got to hear this," Dr. J snorted. There was an edge of amusement in his voice.

Willoughby gave a shrug. "It was in the fifth grade. A girl named Shakrah wanted to go steady. Lewis let me know. He was the best athlete in the class and he liked me."

"Shakrah was black?"

"Yes."

Dr. J was silent for a long moment. "So, how'd it go?"

"How did what go?"

"Your romance with Shakrah."

"Romance?" There was a note of panic in Willoughby's voice. "I was in fifth grade! How do you think it went?"

Dr. J broke into a smile. "A bit much for you, was she?"

Willoughby grinned too. "Shakrah was *more* than a brick house. Just think concrete fortress with twin cannons and a full radar array."

James Arthur burst into laughter. "In fifth grade?"

Willoughby couldn't stop himself. "That's how I remember it. That girl could have roasted me for dinner."

By the time Willoughby finished, Dr. J was moaning and wiping his eyes. It was a good two or three minutes before he settled down and spoke seriously. "Okay, change of subject. What did you make of the briefing? A bit on the weird side, wouldn't you say? You believe all this 'Beelzebub' stuff?"

Willoughby tried to think of how to answer the question. *Did he believe the Beelzebub stuff?* He thought of the face he had seen through a tear in time; of the tall, bony body and gruff voice that went with the face. He found the memory of the man both scary and somehow compelling. He felt himself being drawn in like a moth to a flame.

"I don't know," he finally said. "I'm not sure what to think. What's your take?"

He listened for a response, but none came. A few moments later, James Arthur's breathing became loud and steady. Willoughby looked over at his cabin-mate's bunk and sighed. He punched his own pillow and rolled to his side. Tired as he was, he seemed a long way from falling asleep. After a while, he turned onto his back and stared up at the darkness. The ship rolled with rhythmic regularity. He thought of Antonio's strange invitation to practice rowing and possibly go for a swim. *A swim?* He thought of his family at the pier, waving goodbye. *Should he have hugged them tighter—been more hesitant to leave?* As fatigue finally claimed him, he slipped into a fitful sleep. His dreams were clouded with lilts of song, and the dark form of Sydney, eyes burning, calling again and again to her sisters of the sea.

14

Morning Swim

The voice sounded far away, but Willoughby's mind told him it was important. He struggled to force his eyes open. Dr. J was leaning over, staring down at him. He flashed a wide grin. "There he is! Brother Romeo, the Riemann-slayer, is alive! Come on, get up! I've been pounding the iron for twenty minutes while you've been mumbling, *'coming my Goddess,'* and *'yes, yes, they are so beautiful, such beautiful sisters!'* I'd like a little more information on that dream if you don't mind."

Willoughby sat up, pushing James Arthur away. The clock on the dresser blinked 6:18. He groaned and fell back against the pillow. "It's 6 a.m."

"6:18," Dr. J said between curls. He looked over with a grin. "Ah, now, look what we've done. We've gone and disturbed our playboy's beauty sleep, haven't we?" Dr. J plopped down the weights, stretched, and walked back to the bathroom, grabbing a towel to wipe his face. "Okay, so I'm a softy. I let you sleep in. Antonio knocked almost ten minutes ago, so you better get those swim trunks on, *brother*, or the man might just *throw* you in that cold water butt-naked. Seems that the ship has lowered sail—a few of the crew want to do some fishing. He thinks this may be our best chance to take the boat out."

Willoughby forced himself vertical and swung his legs over the edge of the bed. After a long moment, and a lot of eye-rubbing, he leaned over his drawer and pulled out a pair of swimming trunks. "He really wants to jump in the water this early? Is he crazy?" He padded to the bathroom and splashed water on his face. James Arthur was already at the cabin door. "Hey, I go out surfing in the winter all the time. It'll put some hair on that skinny chest!" He let out what sounded like a wail, followed by butchered song lyrics, "I *feel* good, just like I knew that I would, now—I *feel* good, like a good brother should, now…"

"Lots of brotherly love this morning," Willoughby cringed. "You and Antonio ought to get together. You murder songs with equal intensity."

James Arthur ignored the comment. "You know James Brown?"

"It depends," Willoughby sighed. "What is his stance on 6:00 a.m. screeching?"

James Arthur flashed a smile as he danced down the hallway. Willoughby wiped off his face, threw on his swim trunks and followed, amazed he could stay upright.

On deck, the sun was easing over the horizon—a golden fire, poured out like molten brass. It spread across the gently cresting waves. The brisk sea air raised goose bumps on Willoughby's arms. He rubbed his eyes yet again. Antonio was already sitting in a small boat, helping a wiry crewman lower it over the side. He motioned to James Arthur and Willoughby. "*Buenos Dias!*"

"Morning old A.S.E.C., old buddy, old pal!" James Arthur snapped, poking fun at Antonio's initials. He hopped over into the boat making it sway. Antonio nodded.

"Ah! Good morning to you, Dr. James Arthur Washington, or should I call you J.A.W.s?"

Dr. J laughed. "Not bad for a broken-down old barber!"

Antonio gritted his teeth, forcing a smile, as Willoughby climbed onto the boat. They slowly sank below deck level. A second crewman meandered over and began to help crank. The boat began to lower much faster. Before it could settle onto the bobbing waves, however, Dr. J had pulled off his shirt. With a high yelp, he dove into the choppy water. He came up spitting.

"Now that's …c-c-cold! Have to be a sh-short swim!" He set out on a brisk pace.

Antonio steadied the lifeboat as it hit the water. He disconnected the rigging and picked up the oars, expertly turning the little craft before beginning to row away from James Arthur, directly perpendicular to the ship. When they were maybe 30 yards away, he began to speak in a slow, soft voice.

"I am smiling to pretend this is a quick and pleasant morning exchange. We are being watched, my friend. Listen to what I say—I must speak quickly, and then we must jump in the water for a quick swim."

"What's going on?" Willoughby said through a forced grin.

Antonio held up a hand. He looked over to James Arthur, who was maybe 40 yards away and was already angling in the direction of the boat. "Are you okay, *amigo*?" Dr. J didn't answer, but gave a quick wave of his hand. Antonio looked back to Willoughby.

"Take off your shirt," he instructed, then continued to talk, fast and quietly. "What I tell you I have shared with no one. I think it would have done no good to turn back last night. I think whatever is going to happen on this mission has already begun. I have been to most of the observation platforms, *amigo*. I have even designed two, but H.S. has been very secretive about the purpose of the Absconditus." He splashed water onto his face and bare chest. "Since I arrived, I have been checking out the ship. The hull has been reinforced with solid titanium. The titanium nose, in fact, is 6 to 10 feet thick. It has sophisticated laser weaponry. The sails and riggings are only for show. Hidden in the bowels of the ship is a fully operational nuclear reactor, capable of powering the ship without them. If I were to venture a guess, I would say the ship was built for Arctic exploration."

"Arctic exploration?" Willoughby whispered.

"That's not all," Antonio added. He was speaking so fast that Willoughby could hardly keep up with him. He pulled the oars in and prepared to hop over the side of the boat. "Hidden below this reactor, I found two very small signs. They had the word "Tangent" spelled frontward and backward below the shape of a golden spiral. I found the 313. Though I could not find my way into the chamber, I know it is the sign of a doorway."

Willoughby's eyes narrowed. "Like the one at the top of the Certus Grove building?"

"No," Antonio said; "different. The Certus Grove is a time door, built to access a natural time hole in our physical space and tethered to a specific observation platform like all of our time doors. This is on a moving ship. Think of the implications."

"It could travel to holes—ones that may be difficult to build or hide a facility near," Willoughby said, realization dawning on him. "Why do you think H.S. has an arctic exploration vessel? Is there something in the arctic that he wants to find?"

"I don't know. To say the least, this ship is more *unusual* than I had supposed. I saw numbers appear and fluctuate onto a hidden read-out above the symbol. They seemed to flicker with the pitch and roll of the ship. At times, I thought I saw complex equations with the numbers '313' in them. I think the read-out is measuring the continuum flux, as if the ship itself can sail the folds of time. I think, perhaps, it is the ship the men of the mark are after."

Willoughby looked up with a spark in his eyes. "I, I thought I saw numbers on the ship too. But they weren't on a read-out. They were just hovering by H.S.'s cabin door. When I turned and looked full at the door, they were gone."

Antonio motioned and then jumped into the water. He came up blustering. Willoughby had been lost in thought. "That would make this ship quite a prize—especially if they knew why H.S. built it. What if this cult is after something up there in the polar ice as well? Maybe the break-in at St. Petersburg has nothing to do with our current assignment or Nostradamus. Maybe they want the ship so they can beat us to whatever the Arctic prize is. It must be big." He dropped his shirt onto the bench.

"W-we are trying to s-solve a puzzle with half the pieces m-missing," Antonio added. "H-hurry, jump in! D-don't know h-how long..."

Willoughby dove in. He came up shrieking. "C-can-can't t-take this!" he panted, turning immediately back toward the boat. He managed to grab its side and started pulling himself in. Antonio, too, was anxious to get out of the water. He glanced over and saw that Dr. J was beginning to flounder.

"W-we m-must g-g-get to J-James Arthur!" he hissed. He started toward the boat. It felt as if all the strength had been sapped out of him. Willoughby was gasping and shivering, but he made his way toward the bow of the boat and grabbed Antonio's arm. Together, the two helped each other back into the boat.

"Ch-ch-charlie horse," Antonio spluttered, after seating himself onto the first bench and looking directly into Willoughby's eyes. "T-t-tell them you got a Ch-charlie horse." Willoughby opened his mouth to speak, but Antonio held up a hand. He grabbed the oars. "We only have s-seconds before we p-pick up James Arthur. Tell me what happened at the sh-shop when t-time froze."

"I s-saw numbers," Willoughby said as his friend started rowing. "They f-floated, l-like the ones I saw on the sh-ship, only much c-clearer and b-brighter. Th-they were in strings. They s-seemed to glow, then they p-pooled along a seam and the s-seam ripped open. Light b-blinded me, and then, a face appeared in the b-breach and leaned out from the brightness. It looked over the symbol and the sh-shop. Then looked s-straight at me. It seemed surprised. Then, the breach closed. The face and numbers were gone and everything went back to n-n-ormal except the man photographing the symbol and us."

"Is that all?" Antonio said quickly. They were barely a dozen feet from Dr. J.

"I was heading back to my Dad's office, and stumbled onto a conversation. It was between the man with the camera and a tall thin m-man with the same face I had s-seen in the brightness. They talked about some plan, and how I might have s-seen something and sh-shouldn't have been able to."

"They mentioned you by name?"

"No. They just referred to me as a boy, or kid."

Dr. J threw a shaky hand up to catch the side of the boat. "L-l-little, h-h-help!"

Antonio dropped the oars and he and Willoughby struggled to pull James Arthur into the back of the boat. It wasn't easy as Dr. J was weak and shaking violently. They finally got him on board and seated on the back bench. Antonio moved up to the middle bench and Willoughby took up the bench in the bow.

"Sorry, James Arthur," Antonio called over his shoulder. "This was n-not such a good idea."

James Arthur gave a quick nod, throwing his shirt back on and trying to catch his breath while controlling his shivers. "N-need w-w-warm sh-shower," he managed, forcing a weak smile.

Antonio threw his shirt on as well, picked up the oars, and started rowing back toward the ship. Willoughby pulled his t-shirt on. He sat facing Antonio and Dr. J with his back toward the bow. Antonio bent down so that only Willoughby could hear his whisper.

"I w-want you to make your w-way down to the wall of symbols. Y-you seem to have abilities beyond me— beyond any of us. You c-can s-sense equations, m-maybe even s-see openings in the time flow. We n-need to kn-now how to use that d-doorway if things go badly. If anyone s-sees you, say you are looking f-for my barbershop. Make sure you are alone before you l-look at the wall. Tell me what you m-make of the equations."

"S-s-strange," James Arthur called from the back of the boat. "C-c-can swim a-a good mile at home, in c-cold water. M-m-must be the choppy seas." Antonio looked back. "N-not this cold," he said. Dr. J again gave a curt nod and forced a grin. Antonio's gaze turned toward the Absconditus as he increased the intensity of his rowing. He spoke softly, almost to himself, "Good fishing they told me, yet I see no one catching a fish."

James Arthur and Willoughby both followed his gaze. Dr. J's eyebrows rose slightly. It was true. The few lifeless lines dropped over the boat seemed abandoned.

15

Nostradamus

After a hot shower, Willoughby was finally able to stop shivering. He grabbed a quick breakfast and picked up a couple more books on Nostradamus from the chart room. Finding a small bank of lounge chairs on the starboard side of the ship, he settled in and began to read. Sails had been raised and the speed of the ship had increased to a steady clip. Willoughby breathed in the tangy air. The sunlight and fresh breeze raised his spirits a bit, but only a bit. He thought of Antonio's description of the time door on the ship. He wasn't sure how he felt about the odd revelation. On the one hand, he was glad they were going ahead with the adventure. On the other hand, they faced more intrigue and danger than he had ever imagined. He felt a tense knot at the pit of his stomach—like the feeling you get when you reach the top of a really high rollercoaster. He tried to ignore his stomach and turned back to his reading.

Nostradamus, he found, was a fascinating character. Some scholars called him a crackpot. They claimed that he wrote so obscurely that his writings could mean anything. Others launched into long defenses, trying to prove that the man had an amazing gift. Whatever your opinion, it was hard to escape the uncanny accuracy of some of his predictions.

In one quatrain, for example, he predicted the death of King Henry II of France:

> *The young lion overcomes the older one,*
> *On the field of combat, they fight a single battle;*
> *He will pierce his eyes through a golden cage,*
> *Two wounds are made one; he dies a cruel death.*
> (Century 1, Quatrain 35)

The quatrain, published in 1555, certainly seemed accurate judging from history. King Henry II, of France, died in a jousting accident in June of 1559. He was competing in a tournament against the Comte de Montgomery, who was several years younger. Both men used shields embossed with lions. During the final bout, Montgomery failed to lower his lance in time, and it shattered against the king's helmet, sending a large splinter through King Henry's gilded visor. There were two major wounds, one to the eye, and the other to the temple. Both wounds pierced the brain, leaving Henry II to die a cruel death after ten days of agony.

Other quatrains also seemed to accurately reflect historic events:

The French Revolution:

> *From the enslaved people, songs, chants and demands.*
> *The princes and lords are held captive in prisons.*
> *In the future by such headless idiots,*
> *These will be taken as divine utterances.*
> (Century 1, Quatrain 14)

President Kennedy's assassination:

The ancient work will be accomplished,
And from the roof evil ruin will fall on the great man.
They will accuse an innocent, being dead, of the deed.
The guilty one is hidden in the misty copse.
(Century 6, Quatrain 37)

Willoughby remembered reading a book about the Kennedy assassination. Lee Harvey Oswald had been accused of the murder, but was killed in prison before he could come to trial. Some claim that modern forensics evidence pointed toward two assassins, one on the roof, and the one who fired the fatal bullet in a row of bushes to the side of the Texas School Book Depository.

Willoughby read on. Some quatrains were so vague that people claimed them to foretell everything from space aliens invading the earth, to knowledge of the computer revolution, to the collapse of the Trade Towers on 9/11 and the untimely death of Princess Diana. He was so fascinated with his reading that he almost missed lunch. After a quick sandwich, he grabbed two additional volumes from the chartroom, and went back to his chair on the deck.

In skimming the books, his eye lit upon a fascinating letter that Nostradamus wrote to his son, Caesar, in March of 1555. The letter was different from the one H.S. had referred to that mentioned the *Cult of the Mark* and the *mathematician*, but it was still fascinating. It spoke about how the seer learned his secrets. At one point, Nostradamus states: "...*by means of harmonizing divine and supernatural inspiration with astronomical computations, one can accurately name places and specific times... Through this, the cycles of time (past, present, and future) become incorporated into one eternity.*"

198

Was this a description of using stars to chart the appearance of time holes? What was meant by "harmonize divine and supernatural inspiration with astronomical computations?"

The key to this puzzle seemed to be a line written earlier in the letter: "*For human understanding, being intellectual, cannot see hidden things unless aided by a voice coming from limbo, by means of the slender flame showing what direction future events will incline toward.*"

Voice coming from limbo? The words seemed to indicate that Nostradamus did not act alone. *Slender flame?* Willoughby thought about the brilliant arc, dancing amid the dark gasses above H.S.'s electromagnetic pyramid...

The afternoon passed quietly. Willoughby's eyes drooped. When he awoke, he found Sydney next to him, sunning. He tried not to notice the striking figure beneath her bathing suit.

"So, are you coming to my concert tonight?" she asked.

"I guess so," he replied, sitting up.

"It's at 8:00 sharp—don't be late. I think you'll enjoy it." Sydney rolled onto her stomach and rested her cheek on top of her clasped hands. Willoughby gathered his books and stood to leave. "I've, uh, I've got to stop by the chartroom," he said. "See you at 8:00, then." His eyes lingered a moment on Sydney's taut curves.

"See you," Sydney said, noticing the attention and smiling. "8:00 *sharp*."

16

Golden is the Song of the Sea

The concert was on deck. The night was starlit and cool with only a half-moon. Willoughby saw Dr. J and Dr. O'Grady sitting a little way down from the Captain's officers, forming a wide semi-circle that faced a small band of Polynesian musicians. A brass tub, standing in the center of the musicians, held a fire that flared in the faint sea breeze. The musicians chatted quietly. They had a variety of traditional instruments—gourd drums, hand drums, bamboo sticks, conch shells, and ukuleles. Willoughby wondered when they had come on board. He was sure they hadn't been on board when the ship left Boston Harbor. The mystery was solved when he noticed a medium-sized ship being towed behind the Absconditus. These musicians must be paid a lot to make such a long jaunt for a single performance, he thought. He looked across the rest of the deck, trying to find Antonio.

He had tried to go below like Antonio instructed twice now, determined to find the wall Antonio had told him about. Both times, he had been turned back by beefy sailors with Brooklyn accents. They wanted to know what he was doing roaming around down there. He used the excuse Antonio suggested—that he was looking for Antonio's shop. Both times, he had been directed to the shop, but it was closed. The way the brutish sailors patrolled the floor, and the fact that they were obviously not accustomed to mundane concerns like politeness or customer service worried him. Had H.S. requested extra bodyguards to beef up security, or was Antonio right and someone already infiltrated the Absconditus?

He saw Antonio across the deck of the ship. His friend was talking quietly with the Captain. He started to approach, but Antonio, looking over the Captain's shoulder, purposely caught his eye and motioned him away with a slight flick of his hand. His face looked grave and he did not seem in a mood to talk. The Captain put a hand on his shoulder, leaned forward, and whispered something quickly in his ear. Antonio gave a curt nod of his head. The Captain then turned and strode toward the concert area. Antonio paused a moment, and then slipped away down the darkened stairway that led to the lower decks. For a moment, Willoughby was torn. Should he go after his friend? Then he remembered his promise to Sydney, and how Antonio had motioned him away. He turned back toward the concert group and made his way to a space next to Dr. J. The doctor looked up with a smile and opened his mouth to speak, but his words were drowned out by a loud booming.

All eyes turned toward a massive, bare-chested man who had suddenly jumped to his feet and begun beating on the largest of the drums. A woman wailed and shook a small hand-drum. Willoughby saw Sydney approach from the flickering shadows. A grass skirt adorned her narrow hips, and a delicate, flower-print tank top hung on her lightly-tanned shoulders. Ankle bracelets jangled against her bare feet, and a fresh lei hung loosely around her neck. A delicate ring of flowers crowned her head and wrists. She held up a coconut bowl, her head slightly bowed. She stopped and lifted a radiant, smiling face.

"Greetings, honored guests. Before we begin, I would like to share with you a ceremonial dance of my people. It will invite the spirits to bless our performance. I will ask one of you to drink kava from the ceremonial bowl. It will honor our ancestors." The music grew louder as additional chanters and instruments joined in.

Sydney began to dance. Willoughby was immediately entranced. He knew she was a famous musician, but he hadn't expected such grace as a dancer. He had never seen anything so beautiful as the way she moved—with such precision, her footwork soft and swaying. She switched the bowl from hand to hand, twirling it before the fire. Her delicate frame wove in and out of shadows in a hypnotic spell. At the height of the music, she swooped suddenly to kneel in front of him, her head bowed, her arms extended toward him holding the coconut bowl. His heart raced as he stared at her trembling body, silhouetted by firelight, only an arm's reach away. He suddenly realized that the music had stopped and all eyes were on him. A surge of panic welled in his chest. *What was he supposed to do? Take the bowl and drink the gooey, white stuff inside it?*

"Drink it, please," Sydney whispered. "It's kava. I promise it won't hurt you."

Willoughby took the bowl, closed his eyes, and in one quick motion, gulped down the liquid. It had a heavy, chalky taste, but was warm and felt soothing as it went down. He handed the bowl back to Sydney and wiped his mouth. She flashed a quick smile, then stood, and danced away. The chanters began again. Everyone in the circle clapped politely.

James Arthur leaned over. "It was already worth the whole evening just to see Sydney *bowing* to someone! And did I hear her beg?"

Willoughby didn't say anything. He just gave the good doctor a quirky smile. He was suddenly feeling very relaxed and particularly good about himself. It almost seemed as if he weren't really sitting on the cold deck, but floating. Sydney picked up her violin.

"We would like to thank Willoughby for inviting the spirits of the night and the sea to bless our performance," she began. Everyone clapped again. "Now," she continued, "I will perform an original composition, weaving traditional chants into a classical work titled 'Island Dream.' Of course, the violin is not a traditional island instrument, so this is a bit of a bridge between the world of my island heritage, and the world of my classical training. There will be no breaks in the performance. The concert will last approximately 30 minutes." Sydney raised her instrument and stood poised.

The music began with a long, slow chant from one of the older Polynesian women. Though he could not understand the language, Willoughby heard things in the woman's voice. He heard the voice of the restless wind— whistling over ancient rocks against a far-away island cliff. He could see the cliff clearly in his mind.

Sydney began to play. Her violin melded seamlessly with the cadence of the chant, adding a forlorn wail that was at once sad and hopeful. A soft counter chant began, building slowly, like an approaching storm. The drums rolled. Discord pierced the blackness as Sydney's violin wailed with anger at the thundering drums. She moved around the circle as she played, at one with the music, every particle of her absorbed in the passion of the melody.

Willoughby felt the intensity of the music swirl around him. It seemed to gnaw at his skin. He could see the storm in his mind as if each note carried a piece of the story. The winds raged violently. Sydney's body twisted and spun, jerking in odd contortions. Flames leapt high into the air, eclipsing what was earlier only the flicker of a modest blaze. Blood pounded in his ears. His throat tightened. Suddenly, the air was alive with numbers, with equations. It was as if he were reading the weather, as if the music somehow unlocked his mind to the very essence of the world around him and he could see it now, all in mathematical expression. He jumped to his feet. "Wait!" he cried out. Flames roared higher and some of the numbers turned red, like glowing coals. He felt a pang of fear; *the sails, the wood—they could catch fire!* He had to warn Sydney. He had to slow the growing violence; to silence her violin.

His words were swallowed by the deluge. Waves of number and music crashed over him until he felt as if he were drowning in them. He yelled, but no one heard him. What could they do to help, anyway? The storm raged on, drowning out his protests, the flames from the fire pit grew higher, being shaped and structured by streams of glowing coal equation. It lapped around the sails, the ship, the flow of Sydney's lithe form, like a hungry dog chasing its tail, but never able to catch it.

As he watched, Sydney's feet completely left the deck. She no longer played the music; *she had become the music.* She spilled rivers and bridges of number in cascading waves and climbed atop them. Willoughby followed, rising from the deck as well. His feet swayed to the strange tune, the pulsing equations. Then the sails, the ship were completely gone. There was only the fire, and the storm, and Sydney spinning her web of magic equation. The fire curled before him into a perfect golden spiral. He looked down. He had a bird's eye view of the violent sea.

Sydney's music became high and haunting, transcending the fury of the storm, calling outward. Voices from afar answered and began to take shape in the mathematical mists. People—island people of all sorts—approached. They seemed to represent distant times and distant places. He saw distinctly their different styles of ships: flat boats, outrigger canoes, ocean-going basket-style boats, long barges. They sailed into the maelstrom from a haze of churning equation, each ghost-like craft weaving in and out of the whirlpool tide.

The music faded, replaced by a grand chorus of voices and chants calling up from the ships and bubbling up from the sea. The numbers shrank into mist and sea spray. Still drifting, Willoughby spun to find Sydney swirling in a tight arc above him. She had become the center of the storm, of the slow spiral that drew her people on. She had become translucent, glowing with a luminescence like the full moon.

"Look," her voice echoed in the wind, strong and deep, "blood of the very heart. Here is my life, my line." Her arms spun outward. "I offer it all to you, Willoughby. *Come to know who I am.*"

Her radiance engulfed him, bursting upon him like a downpour. It melted his skin. For a brief moment, he *was* time. He was at one with the voices, his fingertips extending as he spanned the vast eons, as he truly understood the massive infinity of time's equations. When the sensation faded, he was alone, descending, floating light as a feather, floating, floating, like a lone gull, kiting in the breeze …

17

Blonde over Blue

He didn't know how long it had been when he finally opened his eyes. He felt the solid deck beneath him. He heard the soft creak of timbers, the lap of waves. He tried to focus and found himself staring directly into eyes of rich, soft blue. He tried to push away, to speak, but no words came. His head was swimming, and the jumble of images surrounding him made no sense. Then, his brain began to kick in and the fog cleared a little. T.K., the cabin girl, was bending over him. He was laid out on blankets somewhere near the stern of the ship.

"*How,*" he said in a forced mumble. He listened for music. There was none. The breeze had picked up. He could feel the ship rocking in a heavier sea.

"Feeling better?" T.K. grinned.

"H-how did I get here?" Willoughby croaked. "How long have I been here?"

T.K. stood. "Well, let's see... You danced here."

"*Danced?*" Willoughby's voice was thick. He sat up, wishing that the world would stop spinning.

"Danced," T.K. repeated. "You followed Sydney around like she was the pied piper, yelling something at the top of your lungs that was completely unintelligible."

Willoughby tried to stand, but T.K. pushed him back down. "Give it a moment. You've been out for hours."

Willoughby looked up at the stars, bewildered. *Had he really made such a spectacle of himself?* He noted that the moon was gone. He checked his watch. It was well after midnight. "Almost 1:00 a.m.? *What happened to me?*"

"What indeed," T.K. sighed. "When the performance was over, you stumbled into the shadows. Everyone was concerned. Antonio and I found you here, mumbling something about *the heart of time* and Sydney offering—"

"Please," Willoughby cut in, "don't take that any farther."

T.K. smiled. "When you passed out, I called for the ship's physician. He said it was just the kava and that you'd sleep it off. The Captain sent everyone to their cabins, but asked me to bring a few blankets up and keep an eye on you through my watch. He was afraid moving you might make you vomit. How's your head?"

Willoughby leaned forward, placing his forehead between his knees. "I think it's closed for the season," he said quietly. He sat for a moment and then looked up. "I saw a fire grow into a high, golden spiral," he said. "I thought it was going to set the ship on fire. I tried to stop Sydney, and then there were numbers everywhere— running equations—and then faces and ships and I heard voices and saw things from long ago. It was incredible, like I could touch other minds and feel the beat of their hearts. I felt like I could really comprehend the mathematics of time."

T.K. flung back her long, blonde hair. "Wow. Sounds like quite a ride. Kava has an almost narcotic effect. It puts people into trances and causes hallucinations. I was sitting with the crew watching the show. I was worried when you drank it."

"But there was something about the music," Willoughby mumbled. "The notes, the rhythm, the movements—the piece was brilliant, like a musical expression of the golden ratio. It was nearly perfect, mathematically. You didn't feel anything from the performance?"

T.K. stared at him blankly. "I felt that Sydney did a good job of making a fool of you."

Willoughby nodded. "Yeah, she's good at that." He stood slowly, grabbing hold of the ship's rail. The blood rushed to his head. For a moment he thought he would be sick. He sucked in gulps of fresh air.

T.K. moved up beside him. "I have no interest in Sydney's music, Willoughby. I wanted to speak to you. You remind me of someone."

Willoughby breathed deeply, trying to lose the nausea. "Who? From your description of my performance tonight, I would peg myself as a cross between Pinocchio and Clarence the Clown."

T.K. smiled. "This someone is a, a person I lost a long time ago."

"A long time ago?" Willoughby grinned. "What, you're maybe nineteen? You make it sound like it was back in the time of Egypt."

"I don't know. When was Egypt first settled?"

Willoughby stared at her blankly. Finally, she broke into a mischievous smile. "Okay, I'm just kidding. I'm pretty sure Egypt was there, but I am older than you imagine."

"How old?"

The girl shrugged. "Doesn't matter, does it? I mean, we can still be friends. Anyway, you remind me of a person who was very dear to me. He was young and innocent. He never saw danger around us, only adventure." She was quiet for a moment and then sighed. "That's why I'm concerned about you. Something isn't right about this cruise. It feels all wrong."

Willoughby looked away. "Who have you been talking to? Antonio?"

"No." T.K. peered at him with narrowed eyes. "Why? Does he sense it, too?" She turned away. "It's odd. People are on this ship who shouldn't be here, I'm sure of it. The Captain and I have worked with H.S. dozens of times before, but it never felt like this."

"Are you related to the Captain?"

"He's my adopted father."

"Who do you think is on the ship that shouldn't be?"

"I don't know. Some of the crew don't feel right. A month or so before this voyage, a handful of our regulars became suddenly sick or incapacitated. Observations, Inc. cleared their replacements, but the guys that showed up feel wrong. They looked good on paper, but when they arrived...I don't know. I can't put my finger on it. It just feels wrong." She fell silent, looking out over the rolling waves and the starlit sky. Several minutes passed before she spoke again, almost in a whisper. "It's pretty, isn't it?"

Willoughby strained to see what she was looking at. All he could see was ocean, stretching out as far as you could see until dark waters melted into dark, starlit sky.

"Sometimes I forget how beautiful the sea is at night," she continued. "There was a time I knew it well. I'd walk the rock cliffs in the moonlight and watch the breakers roll their strange thunder below a grand chorus of stars."

Willoughby was dizzy and confused. Why would T.K. be so concerned? Was she telling him everything?

"What else feels wrong?" he asked, probing.

"I told you, I don't know," she replied. "The Captain is paid handsomely, and in advance, to pilot this cruise. Dr. Simon acted different this time, though. He's usually pleasant, if a bit business-minded, but this time, he's been AWOL. The few hours he was here, he seemed upset and distracted. He yelled at Sydney, then promptly stomped off to his cabin and disappeared. I went to look for him in his cabin ten minutes later at the Captain's request, but he was gone. He'd just disappeared. If he hadn't sent a message to us over the telex an hour later saying he would still lead your orientation, the Captain would probably have postponed our departure and called the police." She paused. "Maybe it's nothing, but I can't help how I feel." She looked back out to sea.

Willoughby considered what she had told him. "You mean Sydney got here the same time as H.S.?"

"No," T.K. answered. "Sydney was here two days before him. She's been here for almost a week now."

The moon had sunk low in the sky, reflecting off the cresting waves. She slid slender, delicate fingers absently along the smooth wood of the ship's rail. "Ever been off the coast of the Bahamas? There's a phosphorescent algae there that sparks off the waves. They actually twinkle at night."

Willoughby shook his head.

T.K. turned suddenly. "Okay, you don't seem to be buying this. Maybe I know a little more than I'm saying. I've tried to research Observations, Inc. There's no mention of the company on the internet. In fact, there's no mention of it anywhere. I've checked all the major world stock exchanges—nothing. Doesn't that seem odd to you? I mean, they seem to have unlimited supplies of money. What do you know about them?"

"Uh, they do research," Willoughby said nervously.

"What kind?" T.K. asked. "They shipped in Sydney's musicians, and took them back as soon as the concert was over. What kind of research organization does that?"

"Well, they're into antiquities and cultural things," Willoughby said truthfully. "I don't know a whole lot about the organization. I've only met the team here."

T.K. was silent for a moment. She reached forward and touched his shoulder. "Thanks for being honest with me. I know, as Sydney would say, I'm just a cabin girl."

"Hey, don't sell yourself short," Willoughby said, his eyes earnest. Perhaps it was the lingering effect of the kava, but he couldn't stop himself. "Nobody is a *just*. Maybe you don't have as much money as someone else. Maybe you don't wear three outfits in a day, and you don't have a daddy who is a President or King. The way I see it, people who perform, get elected to office, or who throw money around, expecting the world to lap at their feet, usually aren't the greatest people to emulate. People are more than what they do for a living. They're what's inside them. I get treated like a *'just'* all the time at my school—*just* a smart kid; *just* a kid from the suburbs; *just* a kid whose folks must know someone to get into such an 'upscale' academy. Those people don't know me. By the way, the only *'just'* I can think of in connection with you is *'just beautiful.'*"

Did he just say what he thought he said? From the smile on T.K.'s face, he decided he must have. She let out a laugh. "Whoa! Definitely the kava talking."

"No, I mean it," Willoughby said, embarrassed now.

T.K. was silent for a moment. "Well, we best get you back to your quarters." She grabbed his arm and they started walking. After a few steps, she turned suddenly and kissed him on the cheek. A part of him wanted to take her and kiss her full on the mouth. Then, he realized he didn't know how. He had never kissed a girl full on the lips. Wouldn't the noses get in the way? *Boy, am I ever under the effects of this kava!* He grabbed T.K.'s arm tighter to steady himself.

As they approached the cabins, Willoughby noted a dark figure, squatting by a stack of rusted barrels. The figure rose, moving into the moonlight to block their path. He was a bald man with a patch over one eye and tattoos covering his arms and chest. He smiled, the starlight gleaming dimly on his teeth.

"You're up late," T.K. huffed. "I'll have to report you—*Reese*, is it?"

Willoughby froze. *Reese?* He stared harder, finally coming to recognize the dim outlines of a striking snake on the man's bald head.

"Well now," the man grunted. "Ain't we the Captain's pet?"

T.K. glared at the man, who was twirling something in his hand, letting the moonlight glint on its silvery surface. She grabbed Willoughby tightly by the arm and led him away from the man, taking him the long way back toward the cabins.

"See what I mean," she whispered under her breath.

Willoughby was still trying to come to terms with the fact that Reese was on the ship. When they reached the doorway to the lower decks, he glanced back one last time. He shuddered. The man had turned to watch them and smiled. *He was playing with a long, slender knife.*

18

Hickory, Dickory, Dock

Willoughby woke to Dr. J belting out an off-key version of the '80s pop group ABBA's song *Dancing Queen*. While he was only vaguely aware of the song, he was pretty sure that the words were not "… *dancing king, young and spry, I thought I'd bust my spleen!*" Forcing open his eyes, he slowly pushed to a sitting position. His head throbbed as he leaned back against the wall. "That's really funny. What time is it? If it's 6 AM again, I'm telling you right now, I'll kill you."

"Hey—it's my man, Romeo!" James Arthur clucked. "*Late night?* I'd have let you sleep longer, but you were breathing all heavy, calling, 'Sydney, *Sydney*, I open to you all that I am…' I figured I better do something. I couldn't let my '*bro*' make a bigger fool of himself than he already has, now, could I? Why, he might go pirouetting off down the hall."

Willoughby rubbed his eyes hard, trying to chase the fog away. He felt in no mood to deal with the good doctor. "Ha, ha, ha," he managed. "Listen, could you get me an aspirin? My head feels like, like—"

"Like you've gone ten rounds with a hammer and the hammer won? I hear you, but no aspirin. I'll get you ibuprofen. Aspirin is too hard on the empty stomach. Feel up to breakfast? How about some nice, greasy sausage and gooey, sunny-side up eggs?"

Willoughby's face took on a slight twinge of green. James Arthur laughed. "Seriously, here's the ibuprofen and I'll bring you a stiff orange juice and some wheat toast."

"Thanks," Willoughby grunted. He pushed his head back and closed his eyes. The good doctor took to singing again as soon as he left the room. "*You will dance, and you will take the chance, she'll make you dance like a puppet on string; see that girl, watch her finger twirl, she's caught you with her bling...*"

"Real catchy!" Willoughby shouted after him. "Spend all night thinking that one up?"

"Multi-talented, my man," James Arthur barked back. "Some of us just *got it*." He collapsed into a fit of laughter.

Willoughby gave his head a slow shake, wishing he could clear out the cobwebs and forget about dancing at the concert. He stood up, shut the door, and splashed a little water on his face. *What had he said to T.K.?* Ugh! He had almost grabbed her and kissed her! On the one hand, he wondered why he didn't. He'd never kissed a girl before. What a great chance for practice! T.K. *was* beautiful and he could have always claimed he still affected by the Kava. Ah, well.

He climbed back onto his bunk, started to lie back, then shot up again, rigid. He had remembered seeing the tattooed man, Reese. The man had been playing with a knife. Everything in his memory had a foggy quality, as if from a dream. But it hadn't been a dream. He had to try to find Antonio. He eased back onto the bed, trying to think of where his friend could be.

A timid knock at the door made him almost jump. He straightened again and shouted that the door was open. As it swung in, he could see it was Sydney. She came over carrying a tall glass of orange juice and a small plate of toast.

"Hi," she said. She was her usual, radiant self, though a little subdued this morning. Her jeans, sneakers, and t-shirt could almost have passed as normal teenage attire if it hadn't been for the cluster of bangles on one wrist and the tangle of leather cords on the other. He studied the cords for a moment, noting small, silver ornaments woven into them. A necklace of the same type of leather hung around her neck. It held a simple silver cross. "James Arthur said you could use this." She moved her hands gracefully, placing the orange juice and toast onto the stand by his bed. The cross dangled as she pulled containers of butter and jam out of her pocket and deposited them onto the plate. The cross was particularly interesting. Sydney hadn't seemed that religious before.

He caught her eye. "Uh, hi," he said awkwardly. He quickly turned away. Why did he always feel so self-conscious around her? He remembered that he hadn't combed his hair. Putting a hand up to smooth it down, he realized, with horror, that all he wore under the sheet was boxer shorts. He slid down slightly, doubting that the bare chest he sported was the sort of thing teenage girls fantasized about. Another stray thought attacked him— *had T.K. tucked him in?* The thought made him blush. Sydney was eyeing him curiously.

"You're mad at me, aren't you? I heard Dr. J's incredibly inept attempt at, at—well, at what? It certainly *wasn't* music...Humor?"

Willoughby smiled. "From all reports, I had it coming."

Sydney sighed. "That little amount of kava usually doesn't have such a marked effect. I didn't think it would hit you that hard. Honest."

It wasn't just the kava, Willoughby thought, glancing over at her trim frame, but aloud he only said, "Well, sounds like the ancestors got quite a show." He found it difficult to look her in the eye.

Sydney gave a nervous laugh. "I don't think they're ready to write you into the act just yet," she said. Willoughby cocked his head slightly. *What was that supposed to mean?* Sydney went quiet, eyeing him with a strange, tight smile. "Well," she said, lowering her head. "I owe you one." She turned without another word and hurried out of the room, not even closing the door.

Willoughby stared after her. He wasn't at all sure what he thought of this girl. She was brash, feisty, and controlling on the surface, but then, there were depths—unreadable depths. He saw again in his mind the image of her intense eyes as she floated above him in the air. Her voice rang out, soft and strong. "I offer it all to you, Willoughby. Come to know who I am." *Had that only been the kava?* He shuddered, wiping a hand over his face.

Dr. J ducked his head around the corner, holding a basketball under one arm. "*Owe you one?* Now, that's the understatement of the decade. Man, she had you dancing like Pinocchio on a string. I had to roll up my jaw in a carpet bag when you came pirouetting past."

"It's working just fine this morning," Willoughby said with a resigned sigh. He reached down and picked up a piece of toast and took a quick swig of orange juice.

"Well, true enough," James Arthur said with a grin. "So, I'll tell you what I'll do. Eat up. Drink down your orange juice, and I'll give you a chance to get fresh air, a bit of exercise, and to shut this fat mouth up for good! How does that sound? What's it worth to you to know you'll never hear another rendition of *Dancing King?* Believe me—I've got more where that came from."

Willoughby raised his eyebrows. "I need to find Antonio," he said between bites.

Dr. J held up the basketball and spun it, balancing it on a single finger. "The good barber has disappeared. I ran into the First Mate earlier and he said A.S.E.C. is nowhere to be seen. I'll tell you what, though—if you take a few moment to shoot hoops with me, I'll help you find him. Take your worries, your frustrations to the court, my man," he grinned. "You win, my lips are sealed and I am your personal blood-hound for sniffing out incompetent barbers. I win, and you get the extended version of '*I Could Have Danced All Night!*'"

Willoughby rolled his eyes. He finished his toast and drank down the last of the orange juice. "Not a fair bet," he finally said. "Basketball isn't my game, but alright, a few hoops. Then we find Antonio."

"That's the spirit!" Dr. J beamed. He bounced the ball twice against the doorframe. "Okay, let's make it interesting. Game is to five. I'll spot you four to begin with, but I get to take the ball out first. Pretty good odds, huh?" James Arthur broke into singing again: '*If your brood's in the laughing mood, here comes the dancing dude!*'"

Willoughby threw off the sheets and began digging for some gym shorts. "All right, but NO more singing until you earn the right!" He pulled a t-shirt over his head, grabbed a jacket, and exhaled loudly. "Where's the court?"

"Well, it's just a practice board and net tied to the back of the quarterdeck, but it'll do."

Fifteen minutes later, in the middle of a sound drubbing from James Arthur, Willoughby saw T.K. walk by. She gave him a little wave, calling him over. He handed the ball to Dr. J. "I need to quit for a while."

"Quit?" James Arthur panted. "The score is tied 4 to 4! Fans are on their feet! You don't just walk away!"

Willoughby sighed, grabbed the ball back from the good doctor, and with a sudden burst of speed, drove to the basket. He pivoted, feigning a shot, then banked the ball in over Dr. J's outstretched fingers. It snapped cleanly through the net. Dr. J. stared in shock. Willoughby gave him a shrug. "I told you, I needed to quit," he said. James Arthur finally found his tongue.

"What do you mean *quit*? Where are you going? Get back here! You can't just score some miracle basket, and then trot off like you just won an NBA title or something!"

Willoughby ignored him. T.K. had stopped by the rail. She looked worried. He walked over. "Hey," he said. "What's up?" She gave him a shy smile, with her eyes dancing, swimming in their sea of soft blue. "You didn't tell me you're athletic." He blushed. "Well, sort of...pretty average. I do have moments, though."

"Yeah...I bet you do," T.K. smiled, more warmly this time.

"Moments?" James Arthur screeched from the court, still fuming. "Yeah, and that's all they are! Now get that skinny little backside over here and *prove* to me you got something!"

T.K. looked out over the ocean, her look of worry returning. "About our conversation last night," she began.

Willoughby stopped her. "Uh, yeah, about that," he said, wiping sweat from his brow; "I, uh, I wanted to thank you...and to apologize—"

"Apologize for what? For calling me beautiful? For deciding not to kiss me?"

"Well, uh, yes—I mean, no," Willoughby turned away, sure that his face was about the shade of a ripe tomato. "I mean, you are beautiful. I, uh—was it that obvious? The kissing thing, I mean?"

T.K. gave a slight chuckle. "Your face telegraphs everything you're thinking, Willoughby, even before your brain knows it's thinking it!" She looked back over the ocean, her amused smile slowly fading. She gave a sigh. "That's not what I came to talk to you about, though." She turned back to him. "Remember how I told you that I felt like something was wrong, but I didn't have any specifics?"

"Yeah."

"Well, I've got them now." She looked away again, her eyes narrowing.

"Hey!" James Arthur shouted. "Are you listening, Romeo? We got ourselves a game going on over here. Of course some people might not call it that, beings as the score is 87 to 1, but I'll call it a game." Willoughby and T.K. ignored him.

"I haven't seen the Captain since after the concert last night," T.K. said. "We always meet for breakfast, but he didn't show this morning. I tried to contact him. I tried to page him. Nobody has seen him." She dropped her head to the rail.

Willoughby frowned. "I've been looking for Antonio too. The last time I saw him was just before the concert, talking to the Captain. You think it's related?"

T.K. thought a moment, and then lifted her head. "Yeah, I do. Where do you think they could be?"

Willoughby thought of the time door. He remembered how he wasn't allowed to get close to it. He shook his head. "I don't know, but I think we need to find out."

T.K. shook her head. "I want to do some more snooping before sounding any alarms. No need to worry a lot of people if the two are just holed up playing chess somewhere. At the same time, I can't just stand around, waiting."

"Yeah…I agree."

James Arthur swished another basket from 20 feet away. "See that!" he yelled. "See that one? Now that's what I'm talking about! Your life-path isn't looking so good right now, brother!"

Willoughby gave him a quick hand wave, as if to say, "*chill!*" He bent his head down toward T.K. "There are still a few places I could check too. I was going to do that anyway."

T.K. gave a quick nod. "Okay. Let's meet back in about an hour."

"Be careful," Willoughby said, touching her arm. "Where should we meet back?"

"Meet me at the kitchens. I know the head chef. I trust him. We'll be able to talk there." T.K. took a slow breath. "You be careful, too, Willoughby," she said. She leaned over and gave him a quick peck on the cheek. She then spun and was off toward the ship's helm. Willoughby watched her go. *Why had she kissed him?* He finally turned from the rail, shrugged, and grabbed the jacket he had dropped near the edge of the court. He slipped it on, and gave the doctor a quick smile and a wave. Before he could turn and move toward the lower decks, however, Dr. J had closed the distance between them.

The doctor swiftly grabbed his arm. "No, you don't!" He was panting from the quick sprint. "No, no, no. You're going to tell me before you go anywhere what that was all about." He adjusted the basketball under his arm. Willoughby fumbled with his jacket zipper.

"What do you mean?"

Dr. J gave a toothy grin. "Man, what is it with you? You've got girls falling all over you, giving you kava, giving you kisses, and you act like it's just another day at the office! Come on, tell us the secret sauce that makes those of the female persuasion take note of a scrawny thing like you."

Willoughby grinned back. "I guess when you got it—"

"Uh-uh. None of that stuff. This is James Arthur you're talking to. What gives?"

Willoughby sighed. "Listen, that kiss wasn't romantic. She's worried. She can't find the Captain and something feels, well, odd to her. She's right. Something is going on. I can't find Antonio anywhere."

James Arthur paused. "Is that your only concern, or is there something else you haven't told me?"

"Look, remember when H.S. mentioned that Antonio and I had seen someone watching The Corner Barber? Well, I saw the guy last night—I'm sure of it. *He's on this ship!* Every time I try to look around, I'm running into gruff crewmen who seem to be watching my every move. The guy last night was playing with a knife. How could that guy be on the ship?"

James Arthur dropped his voice. "I've noticed plenty, and you and T.K. are right to be concerned. We all are.

You don't get recruited by H.S. by keeping your eyes closed." Dr. J looked up, and then barked a playful laugh, as if they were having a pleasantly competitive exchange. Still smiling, he lowered his voice even further. "What I don't understand is why, with all the technology this organization has at its disposal, we haven't been pulled off this ship. Something must be wrong beyond our little problems here. I didn't bring you up on deck just for the exercise."

Willoughby glanced up, giving Dr. J a bit of a smile. "No, you also brought me up here to kick my butt in basketball."

Dr. J grinned wider. "Well, that too, but I do think we should stick together."

Willoughby considered the words. He was ready to agree when he noted a scraggly crewman approaching from the stern. The man was huge, black, and staring right at them. What had happened to the neat, white uniformed crewmen he had seen in Boston Harbor? "Maybe that isn't such a great idea," he mumbled. "We're being watched. I promised T.K. I'd check out Antonio's shop. I'm supposed to meet her at the kitchens in about an hour. She said there's a place we can talk there."

James Arthur bounced the ball a few times, casually glancing behind him. "Alright, but watch your back. I think I'll go see if I can locate the First Mate. I'll circle around to the kitchen in 20 minutes. We'll compare notes while we wait for T.K."

Willoughby gave a quick nod. He made a grab for the ball and then pushed Dr. J away playfully. "Next time I won't be so forgiving!" he said loudly. He punched the doctor in the arm, turned, and headed down the stairs to the lower decks.

James Arthur looked after him, bouncing the ball for a few minutes. He shook his head as he shoved the ball back under his arm and walked toward the basket. He drew closer to the rough crewman. The man was not only huge and black, but as James Arthur drew close, he could see that the man's giant face was scar-riddled. In his right hand, the man carried a bucket filled with wooden pins. They were the kind of pins used to secure the rigging on the ship. Dr. J forced a smile.

"Morning," he said, nodding. *Why hadn't he seen this man before?* Surely, it would have been hard to hide a crewman that big and ugly. The man grunted as they passed. Two steps later, he heard the bucket clatter to the deck. Dr. J spun to see. Before he was fully turned around, a huge, black arm flung toward him, wrapping around his neck. It tightened as he staggered back. The world began to reel. He tore at the arm. The big, black man only laughed. He started mumbling something. Dr. J tried to drive his elbows into the man, but it was like punching a rhino. The black man laughed harder, slowly increasing the pressure on James Arthur's neck. As everything began to dim around him, the jumble of words the man was repeating echoed in Dr. J's mind; "Hickory, dickory, doc, no man escapes the clock. Except for one, who don't like sun; Hickory..." Bright sparks burst in Dr. J's head. His body went limp even as his mind tried to fight. The arm released, letting him slam hard to the deck. The last thing he remembered seeing before his eyes winked out was a black, scarred face, peering at him with white teeth glowing in a half-moon grin. "Dickory... Doc..."

19

Cabin Fright

Willoughby hurried quietly down the stairs. He hadn't even looked back at James Arthur as he left the deck. There were so many things running through his mind and he was beginning to have a bad feeling about this day. There had been real fear in T.K.'s eyes. Even Dr. J had seemed tense and distracted. Willoughby stopped a moment, listening. He tried to slow the rapid beating of his heart. *There is no reason to panic yet*, he told himself. He looked down. His hands were trembling and his muscles were constricting, pulling his chest tight, as if a heavy force were squeezing him. This wasn't adrenaline, like reaching the top of a rollercoaster and waiting for the wild plunge. It wasn't exciting or fun. It was his first taste of raw fear—*real* fear. He had at least one friend missing, possibly more. As he reached the next deck down, his sense of dread increased. The ship was too quiet. *Where was the crew?*

His initial plan was to go straight to the deck where Antonio's shop was and nose around until it was time to meet up with James Arthur and T.K. With everything being so quiet, though, he wondered if he should turn around and go back to his cabin. He could wait there and try to figure things out. What had Antonio been arguing with the Captain about last night? Had he gone back to the deck his barber stall was on and found the hidden room that appeared to have no entry point? Why had the brutish crewmen been watching them so diligently? Was the mystery room some sort of base of operations for them? Had they found the symbols of the hidden door? Did they know what these symbols meant?

Standing still on the landing, he heard something. It had sounded like a scuffle of some kind, and then a muffled cry. He fought an instinct to flee back up the stairs—to race back to James Arthur and tell him what he heard. *But what had he heard?* He wasn't sure. Slowly, cautiously, he forced himself forward. The sound had seemed to come from somewhere at the far end of the dim hallway. He passed an empty weight room. This deck was mostly recreation facilities and storage. He made his way almost to the end of the hall when a short, wiry figure stepped into his path. The man was dressed in a white crewman's uniform. Willoughby had seen him before. He had been the man with the mop who had seemed to be trying to eavesdrop on his conversation with Antonio after the first-night briefing with H.S. Now, however, the man brandished a high-powered machine pistol. Willoughby tried to duck around a corner and run for it, but the man's gun fired inches from his head. He froze. The man sauntered lazily up, giving a wry chuckle.

"Not fast enough, are you, city boy? Not near fast enough for *Mouse!*" The man pushed the barrel of the gun up to Willoughby's head. He held it there for a long moment. Willoughby stood stock still, thinking, calculating. Now that the moment had come and his life hung in the balance, when the man could pull the trigger or not, he was not aware of a sense of fear or panic. He felt only a detached sense of wonder that this could be it. This could be the end of his life.

The man moved closer. "Well, you stand like a man—that's in your favor. Suppose you tell me where you're sneaking off to, right? Looking for your mates? Or were you running to find something else? Want to fake another morning swim?" The man gave a raspy cough. "Fat chance you'll find your wet-back friend again. Not now. Not ever."

Now Willoughby felt fear—not for himself, for his situation, but for his friends. The feeling came in a sudden sharp pang. Had they killed Antonio? What had they done with Sydney and Dr. O'Grady? He shut his eyes for a moment, taking a long breath. "What have you done to them?" he said, his voice a little shaky. The man shoved the cold steel of the gun into his temple. Willoughby instinctively slapped it away. The man rammed him painfully against the wall, chuckling as if he were having a great time.

"Feisty one, ain't ya?" He slammed Willoughby harder into the wall, stuffing his pistol into the back of his trousers. He pulled off his white, cloth belt. Still pinned to the wall, Willoughby felt the man fling the belt over his chest and cinch it tight. The cloth cut into him. The man pulled slowly back, once again pulling out his pistol.

"Don't get me wrong," the man said, wiping spittle from his mouth. "I like spunk in a boy, but I ain't got no time for this. Pity you happen to be BL's prize. I'd love to teach you manners myself."

BL? Who was BL? *Mr. B?* Were they talking about the man he had seen rip a hole in time? The man he had seen climb into a taxi with a creepy driver and a fare meter that read, *666?* Willoughby tried to rack his brain to come up with an alternative, but nothing else seemed to fit, and he already knew that Reese was here. The wiry man gave Willoughby a short kick, spinning him around.

"Now, you're going to walk where I tell you to, and if you try to run again, you get a bullet in the leg for your trouble. You understand me? I don't like repeating my warnings. The next time you step out of line, you got a hole in your leg. You try anything bigger than running and you get a bullet to your head. As a corpse you ain't gonna be much good to nobody. Now walk."

Willoughby flared his nostrils for a moment, then lifted his chin and began to walk. The man's breath was hot and he had a stink of alcohol about him. He kicked Willoughby again, prodding him toward the main hallway with the barrel of his gun. Willoughby tried to set a pace that would put some space between himself and the wiry man. His mind was whirling. The man was right—getting himself killed wouldn't help Antonio, T.K., or anyone. He had to come up with some way to trick the man, some way to get a warning off to the others without the man realizing it. The man spoke up again, wiping his nose with the back of a filthy hand.

"Now, that girlfriend of yours," he said in a croak that ended in another spasm of coughs. "She's a different story. I might let her live a little longer than the rest. She plays right nice on that violin. I might just choose to make some music of my own with her. "

Willoughby's face went red with rage, but he held his tongue. He could not come up with a plan, an idea of how to escape this madman with a gun. Where were those clever ideas the hero always comes up with? Maybe that was the problem—he wasn't a hero.

The man coughed again, pushing Willoughby against the wall facing the stairwell. They had waited scarcely a minute when a tall man and a beefy man, both dressed in jet black fatigues, dragged a barely-conscious man down the stairs past their landing. "James Arthur!" Willoughby shouted, recognizing the sleek muscular shape of his roommate.

Dr. J didn't budge. He was out cold. The men in fatigues ignored the outburst and continued down the stairs, but the man with the gun didn't. He slapped Willoughby hard in the face. "You speak when I say so, or you die with your mouth open. You understand that, boy?" He pulled a small hand radio out of his pocket and spoke into it. "I got the kid, Gates. I got him by the fourth deck corridor. Advise."

A deep voice bellowed back, "Wolfer and I be on our way."

Less than five minutes later, the stairs groaned under the weight of the biggest man Willoughby had ever seen. The man stepped onto the landing. He was easily seven feet tall and pushing 300 pounds. He was black from head to toe, his flat, bald head shiny in the dim light. The man with the gun looked over at him. "Hullo, Gates. Look what I brung you." The huge, black man pulled himself out of the stairway. He moved closer. His face was the only thing more frightening than his size. It looked like something partly chewed by a meat grinder. The man stood silent for a long moment. The smaller man with the gun fidgeted nervously.

"It's the kid. Saves you the trouble of running him down, don't it? No hide and seek across the decks."

The huge man gave a chuckle, his white teeth and eyeballs almost glowing against the deep black of his skin.

His voice carried the hint of a Jamaican accent. "Yes, Mouse…Good work for you. I no like the games like hide and seek. Go now. You find for me pesky little cabin girl."

Willoughby's eyes flicked up. *Pesky cabin girl?* That meant T.K. hadn't been captured yet. The realization gave him a flicker of hope. He wondered if she had made it to the kitchen area and found a good place to hide. He watched the man with the machine pistol head back down the hallway, visually perturbed at the minimal praise from the big man. He coughed again. "The cough do you no good," the giant called after the man they called *Mouse*. "You have failed to gain the entry for us. Now, we be forced to go pushing the plan. Diablos no like pushing the plan. A cough be no help to you now, I think."

Mouse tried to stifle the next cough, muttering to himself as the big man, the one he had called "Gates," gathered a handful of Willoughby's jacket, pulling the collar tight. He hefted Willoughby up from the ground with little effort. When he held him level with his scarred face, he spoke again.

"So, you think you be the smart one? I don't like people who think they be the smart one. We soon see what that be bringing you." He forced a grin. "I think you no be so smart for too long."

Willoughby wriggled in the man's grasp, fighting to breathe. He choked, his face turning red, but could find no way to wrench free of the man's iron grip. "Now," Gates continued, seeming not to notice Willoughby's struggle. "I be putting you down, you come to breathe, okay? You be trouble, I pick again. You die if you no breathe. That be unfortunate, it be? You no make trouble, I think, if you smart one."

He smiled again and threw Willoughby hard against the stairwell door. Willoughby slid slowly down, gasping for air. The big man barely gave him a second to catch his breath before his boot kicked out. Willoughby was barely able to dodge it. "I'm going," Willoughby spat as he pushed to his feet. "You don't have to kick." He threw a quick glance behind him before heading down the stairs. The big man lumbered just behind him.

"Good for you, I no hungry," he grinned. "I think you be a nice, tasty treat."

He followed the comment with a deep, rumbling laugh. "Yes, tasty I do believe." He kicked out again, but Willoughby was ready, lunging to the side. The boot still grazed him, causing him to stumble down the last few stairs. Gates gave another laugh and then barked into a headset. "Wolfer, I just kick the boy to you. You be ready. He be wanting a nice sleep. This one, we give to the Big Man. Watch for Belzar's wild brat, the one with the red dot. Let me know if there be trouble."

"Who is the Big Man?" Willoughby managed as he struggled back onto his feet; "Who is Diablos?" The huge, black man stepped down onto the final stair and flung out his hand without warning. The back of his plate-sized hand hit Willoughby in the cheek like a slab of concrete. It slammed him into the wall. His face stung and his ear was ringing, but before he could push back away from the man, the brute had grabbed him by the jacket collar and jerked him into the air again. He shoved him against the door for a moment while he reached down with his free hand and flung open the door to a small equipment room. He flicked a light on, and then swung Willoughby inside the room and sent him careening against a wall of instrument dials. He laughed again. "Who be the smart one now?" The big man slammed the door shut.

Willoughby barely had time to push again to his feet before the door flew back open and a short, stocky man in black fatigues stepped into the room. He was pouring a milky liquid onto a filthy rag, a breathing mask over his face.

"Don't worry," the man's muffled voice said, "this don't hurt. It just takes a few minutes and then all the pain goes away."

Willoughby desperately searched the room for some place to run. His nose was bleeding from the blows of the big black man. This man was smaller, but still considerably larger and bulkier than himself. A direct attack with nothing but bare fists did not seem a very wise course of action. He tried to think of some other way to defend himself, but there were no windows or doors, and nothing visible in the room to use as a weapon. He shot forward, trying to dodge under the man's stubby arms. At the same time, he slapped out at the cloth the man was holding and tried to knock the container of milky liquid to the floor. Neither attempt worked. He did not knock the rag or container away, nor did he escape. The man was exceptionally fast and unbelievably strong. He grabbed Willoughby with one arm, and slapped the rag over his mouth and nose. Willoughby fought and struggled, determined not to breathe in the fumes from the rag, but the stocky man would not budge and he had to breathe. He fought the urge, but eventually, he had no choice—*he had to breathe!* Trying to jerk away from the rag, he sucked in a great gasp of air. The rag's noxious fumes burned his throat and lungs. He coughed, kicking and punching, but he could feel his strength ebbing, ebbing...

The stocky man (Wolfer, was it?) yelled out the door to the black man, Gates. "Hey, you know Reese is storming mad, right? All this killing and still no treasure…"

Willoughby had to suck in breath again. *All this killing? Reese?* His mind screamed, trying to hold consciousness just a minute longer. *Reese—the man with the tattoos; the man who had been photographing Antonio's shop—wasn't he the one in charge?* What were these men after? *A treasure… A treasure of what?*

He was losing the fight. Like sand leaking through his fingers, his thoughts eroded. A booming voice echoed through the void. "Reese? He don't scare me, with hiscrawling tattoos and black-ops training. He ain't much unless Belzar is there holding his leash." He couldn't make sense of the words. They floated about like pieces of an incomprehensible puzzle. A laugh sounded, followed by a metallic click, like the sound of a machine rifle being cocked. "When the time is right," someone said, "I'll handle it." The words seemed to echo: "*I'll handle it, I'll handle it, I'll handle it…*" Willoughby tried to turn his head, to think of who spoke, but all sound was slowly fading as he sank into a place beyond words—a cold place, a dark place, where an infinite abyss opened before him, and he was falling, falling, falling.

20

The Shaft

James Arthur had a throbbing headache and an awful taste in his mouth. *Where was he?* He sat still, breathing, trying to remember. *Strange*, he thought, *why is breathing such an effort?* He felt something tight around his ribs. He glanced down: *thick ropes*. He could feel cold steel beneath him and at his back. They had propped him into a sitting position, his hands tied to some sort of metal pipe. *They?* He tried to focus his left eye. *Who were they? What had happened?* He tried to think.

The room was dark. He raised his head slowly, feeling a wave of dizziness and nausea. His slight moan triggered another sound in the room.

"*Amigo*," a voice whispered. "Are you awake?"

Dr. J focused on the voice. He knew it. "Antonio!" he managed to croak through a strained voice and raspy, irregular breath. His head was throbbing and his neck felt swollen. "Where are we?"

He tried again to remember what had happened. He had been on deck, talking with Willoughby. They had to end their conversation because someone was watching them—a crew member, one he had never seen before—a huge, black man. Willoughby had headed down the stairs.

He had turned back toward the basketball court, a ball tucked under his arm. He passed the huge man. He heard a sound. He turned, and... That's all he could remember clearly. There was a feeling of choking, and then he remembered seeing a face. The black, scarred face had a half-moon smile. It burned in his mind, seeming to loom at him out of the haze.

"I cannot say for sure," Antonio's voice came back, weak and gravelly. "I think we are... in a ventilation chamber... below the engine room."

"How long," James Arthur started, then stopped to remoisten his lips. "How long have I been out?"

Antonio seemed to consider this for a long moment. "Many hours—perhaps even as much as a day." He coughed, speaking slowly, in a whisper. Each sentence seemed a struggle, causing him to slur at least a third of the words.

"You sound bad," Dr. J said, trying to glance behind him. "How long have you been here?"

Antonio coughed again. "I came upon them the night of the music performance. I noticed unusual crew...I would see them only briefly...always below decks. I think they boarded that night, one or two at a time. I argued with the captain, telling him we had to turn back. He did not believe me. He did agree to trigger a silent alert. I...I left the performance to come down the stairs to the barbershop. H.S. prepared an emergency communications console for me there. I was going to contact him directly, but I was attacked before I could reach the shop..."

"You think the captain sent the silent alarm?"

"I...don't know, but I wonder how much it matters now. I saw many of the crew, piled in heaps in this room when they first brought me here. They were all dead. I think they threw them over the rail. I heard them joking…about the night. They called it a 'midnight feast for the beast,' referring to the sharks, I think.'"

James Arthur tried to focus his eyes on the heavy bands of hemp that held him to the cold steel pipe. His hands were angled sharply toward his back and lashed tight. He struggled, but could not even wiggle them.

"You were lucky to be unconscious," Antonio continued. "They tortured me, wanting to know of our mission, something about a, a shining pendant. They wanted to know about H.S…" His voice trailed off. "They beat me," he coughed, his voice cracking. "They beat me badly, James Arthur." He panted, as if the very act of speaking were draining what little energy he had. "I am dizzy and sick. I do not know how much longer I can stay conscious."

"Did they say anything to you—anything that could lead us to who's behind this? Did you see any tattoos?" Dr. J felt as if his tongue were swollen.

Antonio took a long time answering. "I, I did not have a chance to look in the sunlight and it is dark down here…but who else?" He was silent for a moment. "Why the interest in the mission?" he finally hissed. "Not interest in the technology, but interest in the *mission*…What has H.S. not told us?"

James Arthur pulled again against the tight cords holding him fast. "I don't know, but Hathaway Simon seems to be really big on things hidden. He has to know something is wrong here by now. I find it hard to believe that, with all our safeguards, we could have been caught so blind. It shouldn't be possible. Does this whole thing seem a little fishy to you?"

Antonio grunted. "Yes, it feels as though we are pawns...in some elaborate game of chess."

"Hey," James Arthur said, still breathing heavily, "have you heard anything about Willoughby? Do they have him yet? What about Sydney or Dr. O'Grady?"

Antonio sucked in a deep breath and was about to speak again when another voice, much younger, hissed out of the darkness.

"They have about everyone—everyone but me. Not many are still breathing."

Dr. J. strained to pull his head around to see who had spoken. There was a slight ping of metal, a short jolt, and then the sound of something heavy clinking quietly to the floor. A moment later, he felt the friction of something sharp cutting at his bonds.

"Who are you?"

"They call me T.K." It was a girl's voice that whispered back. The voice carried an accent...Australian, or possibly New Zealand. He had heard it before. Suddenly, it came to him—*it was the voice of the cabin girl!*

"Last I saw, they were holding Willoughby, Sydney, and O'Grady in a cabin on deck four," she said, cutting faster. "I can guess why the girl is being held there, and they seem to have a special interest in Willoughby, but I don't understand why O'Grady is there. Why isn't he down here with you two?"

She paused a moment, but neither Antonio or Dr. J had an answer. She continued; "The big black guy said Willoughby is a prize for some guy called the Big Man. There's another guy they keep talking about—someone called Belzar. He seems to be looking for some kind of special pendant or something. It's all pretty confusing. The big black guy seems to be ordering around most of the crew, but he doesn't dare order around the Belzar guy for some reason. That's all I've been able to get so far."

"That's a lot," Dr. J said as his bonds finally fell away. He jerked his arms around with a grimace and then peered toward the girl's voice, into the shadows behind another wide pipe. She had already moved to the pipe where Antonio was tied and had begun working on the ropes.

"I've a way out, but we've got to move fast. Can you both walk?" The cabin girl kept working as she spoke. James Arthur began to untie his feet hurriedly.

"How have you picked up so much and still avoided getting caught?"

When there was no answer, he scanned the room. About four yards away, there was a hole in the wall. A metal grate leaned against the wall to the side of it. He moved quietly to it, back in the shadows behind more piping.

"You've been hiding in the ventilation ducts," he observed. "That's how you've been able to eavesdrop on them."

T.K. helped Antonio untie his feet, and then helped him stand. She led him silently toward the open shaft and helped him climb in, motioning for Dr. J to get in. James Arthur tried to force a smile but it came off as more of a wince. He motioned for her to go first. "My mama always taught me to be a gentleman."

T.K. hesitated, motioning Antonio to enter the shaft first. Antonio seemed too dazed to argue. He pushed in, wincing slightly as he wedged himself into the narrow space and pulled himself forward. T.K. slid gracefully in after him. She whispered back to him; "Go in feet first so you can pull the grate up. There's a "T" junction about 8 yards up. You can turn yourself around there."

James Arthur followed the instructions, cramming himself in feet first. He grabbed the grate and carefully pulled it back into place over the end of the shaft. Luckily, there were no bolts holding it in—only the friction of a tight fit. Once it was pulled securely into place, he began carefully sliding backward, hoping that at some point, the shaft would widen a little so he could get himself turned around. He had backed about five feet into the shaft, angling around a sharp bend when T.K. grabbed his foot, pinning it down with a sense of urgency. He froze.

The darkness was suffocating but he could still see out the grate. He had not slid completely around the sharp bend in the shaft yet, but footsteps and voices were only a few yards away. He didn't dare chance making a noise as he pushed himself the rest of the way around the bend and out of sight of the grate. *Was he far enough into the shaft that he could not be seen?* He barely breathed as the door to the small room burst open. Heavy footfalls rushed to the cut ropes in the room just outside the shaft. A short, stocky man came into view. The man was barely visible in the dim light, but almost every inch of his skin was covered in tattoos. The tattoos writhed as his muscles tensed and flexed. The man shot to his feet and did what appeared to be a quick search of the room. There was a sound of cabinet doors being opened and slammed. A huge foot loomed out of the dimness to kick at the metal grate. The stocky man bent down and peered through, into the shaft. James Arthur had flattened himself and shut his eyes tight when the boot had kicked the grate. He could hear his heart pounding. *His clothes were dark, his skin was dark— would that be enough?* After what seemed an eternity, the man stood again and James Arthur heard him move away.

Venturing a quick peek, he watched the man walk back to the cut ropes. Dr. J silently observed as the man bent and picked up a scrap of rope from the floor. The man lashed out viciously at the metal pipe in front of him.

"*Tight!*" he screamed to someone evidently just beyond the door. "I said *tight*, Braiden! Belzar will not be pleased!" The man dug nervously at the snake tattoos running up his arms.

A robust, curly-headed man waddled into the room. He, too, bent to look at the ropes. "I tied them tight!" he spat, picking up a bit of discarded rope. "Somebody's been in here. See for yourself, Reese! The rope's been *cut!*"

Reese grabbed the man by his collar, yanking him upright. "Save your excuses for Belzar. *You're* the one who's going to tell him!"

"Tell him what?" a voice hissed from the shadows. Two more figures stepped quietly into view, keeping a step or two back from Reese and the heavy-set man. One was an older man of slighter build. He walked with a noticeable limp and what looked to be a metal cane. The other was even smaller—a girl with brown skin and a mane of wavy black hair. Reese let go of the heavy-set man, pointing down to the cut ropes.

"So," the man said, slowly circling the discarded ropes. Reese stepped back out of sight, as did the girl. The heavy-set man, the one Reese called Braiden, began to perspire. He stammered, "I, I did tie them tight. I, they—"

The man with the cane stopped, sniffing at the air. "Bats in the belfry, have we? Skeletons in the closet, secrets in the stairwell…Really outdone themselves this time, have they? Skipped away to another time? You better hope not, Braiden."

Braiden opened his mouth to speak, but with lightning quickness, the thin man's cane swung hard, catching him in his ample midriff. Braiden fell to his knees, grunting from the pain. He spat out blood. The thin man swung the cane again, this time missing the man's head by only inches. The cane slammed into the piping, leaving a two-inch dent.

Braiden glared up. He spat out another mouthful of blood. "This ain't the end to it, Belzar! I'd say my prayers if I were you, 'cause your days are numbered!"

"Possibly," the man called Belzar agreed, "but that's not your problem at the moment, is it?" He slammed another dent into the metal pipe. "Incompetence disturbs me, Mr. Braiden. You were left in charge of the prisoners, and yet, where are they? I wonder how your superior will react when he knows you allowed your quarry to escape. I hear he's…a bit less than forgiving." A series of ship pumps shuddered to life, as if startled by Belzar's harsh blows. "Now," Belzar continued over the sound of the pumps. "I'd say you haven't much time… I'd say you should tear this ship apart if you have to, but *find those hostages!*"

The man called Braiden pushed back to his feet. There was a mixture of anger and fear in his eyes. The fear seemed to win out and the man stumbled toward the door. Dr. J caught a glimpse of a dark tattoo just under the man's left ear. When he was gone, Reese turned back to Belzar. The man breathed in sharply and then pursed his lips. "Watch your back," he said simply. Reese nodded, then without a word, followed Braiden out the door.

Belzar watched him go, and then turned slightly so that the light caught his face. It was hard and chiseled, anchored by fierce blue eyes—blue like nothing James

Arthur had ever seen; blue, with the chilling bite of ice. He began to pace the room, banging his cane randomly at pipes or at the wall. Just as he banged the grate and started to bend down to peer through into the shaft, the girl with wavy black hair jerked toward him. Her arms tensed as her words spewed out like venom. It was obvious that she had waited just long enough to be sure that they would not be overheard.

"No blood, you said! No mess! No one would get hurt!" Despite her anger, the hiss of the words was only faintly audible above the sound of the pumps. "You said the crew would be put in rowboats! They were supposed to be put overboard to slow the rescue effort. You never said anything about a bleedin' *massacre!*"

"I know. I'm sorry—" Belzar began, but the girl cut him off. She was almost sobbing now, her arms trembling.

"I've been up there on deck, Belzar! There's not a single rowboat missing and Gates isn't even trying to hide the blood. You said Reese could control the brute—that's a joke! There's blood everywhere—pools and pools of it!"

Belzar put an arm around her. "It's awful, I know. Gates is a maniac. He likes killing. He's soon to be one of those, what does Mr. B. call them?"

"Fly boys," the girl mumbled.

"Yes…fly-boys. Gates follows his own rules."

"But you said you had a plan! You said *you* would be the one in control! Are you telling me now that *Reese* was the extent of your plan? How could you not have known that something like this would happen? *I trusted you!* Is finding that pendant really worth allying us with that, that *cult?* Is it worth getting ourselves killed?"

Belzar patted the girl's head. "You don't understand what the pendant means. It can manipulate space and time. It's a power beyond anything you can imagine." He tapped softly on the floor with his cane.

"And that's what it's all about to you, isn't it?" the girl said softly. "*Power...* What happened to just finding our way back home?"

"Power is how we'll get there, Hautti. But the game has changed now. It's not just about you and me anymore. It's not even about settling my score with Hathaway Simon—that will have to wait. If this, this cult as you describe it, is able to get their hands on that pendant before we do, I fear there won't be a home for us to go back to."

The girl was quiet for a long moment. "So, tell me about your plan. You said you had it meticulously worked out. You said you would tell me when the time was right. I think the time is right."

"I know that this cult wants the same thing we do, so I calculated that the mysterious Mr. B. would help us make it onto the ship and give us time to search. I knew it was a risk—we don't know if the device is here—but we do know that Hathaway Simon built this vessel with a doorway. We know that he has hidden a secret access to that door somewhere. I believed that, with your talent, and with Reese's muscle, we could hold the brutes off long enough to snatch the pendant, and then flee the ship through the time door once our search was done. But you haven't been able to find the secret access to the door." He spoke so quietly now that James Arthur had to strain to hear him.

"That's the whole plan?" the girl asked.

"Yes."

"That's a stupid plan, Belzar! They would have killed the boy if I hadn't stepped in and jerked the rag away.

That Wolfer guy is almost as bad as Gates. The idiot poured at least a triple dose into the rag! So, now he's barely conscious. I don't believe the girl is the key to finding the doorway at all. I think the key will be the boy—Willoughby. You haven't watched him like I have. There's something about him—not just his uncanny ability with numbers."

"Did you have time to speak to the violinist?"

"I had a few minutes."

Belzar raised his eyebrows. "What did she say?"

"She doesn't seem to know anything about the pendant, and she thought I was crazy for suggesting there's a doorway and hidden entrance on the ship."

"You believe her?"

"I do. I watched her closely. She wasn't lying." There was a short pause, then the girl continued. "So what do we do now?" Her voice had lost some of its edge.

"We follow the plan," Belzar sighed. "Is the tracking device installed and broadcasting?"

"I installed two of them; one on Willoughby, and one on the girl. I've turned them on, but the two are being guarded so closely that I haven't been able to break them free."

Belzar thought for a moment. "Tell the guard that I want to see him. I'll be in the stairway. That's close enough that he'll probably be willing to step away for long enough to see what I want. That will give you a few minutes to help the boy and the violinist escape."

"Okay. One question: Why did Gates put that old doctor—O'Grady I think—up there? Why didn't he bring him down here with the other two?"

"I haven't the faintest idea. That wasn't my instructions."

"He's a problem."

"I don't care about him. Let him escape first. I'll tell the guard about the two that escaped down here. That will give you time to send the Professor off and initiate a plan with the other two. After five minutes, you shout and point in the direction that the professor ran. In the excitement, you step out of the room and the two kids escape. It will be perfect."

"I hope it works. You know it's only a matter of time before Gates makes a move on us. What is he waiting for?"

Belzar stared down at his cane. "For me to find the pendant, I suppose. I've given the brute very sketchy information, using Reese as a go-between as often as possible. Until they know the item isn't on the ship, I think they'll leave us alone. Even then, they may want to keep me searching. I know more than any of them how to find the pendant and who we're up against."

"Have you turned off the cloak?"

"Just before I came down here."

"It won't take Hathaway Simon long to figure things out. How long do you think we have before he sinks the ship?"

"It depends. As soon as his team has escaped, or he's convinced they're dead, he'll want to sink the ship. He'll wait until he's sure she'll sink where no-one can get at her. We need to let his team lead us to the doorway and learn how to use it before that happens. It's our only safe escape. I would begin to worry in another three hours or so. By then, we need to be off this ship."

The girl sighed. "One way or another, I want off this ship. I have to say, taking this ship was too easy. It feels like some kind of a trap. You really believe that Simon, with all his technology and brilliance, didn't see something like this coming? Yet, why would he let this massacre take place? I can't get past the feeling that there's a hidden agenda here."

"With Hathaway Simon, there's always a hidden agenda," Belzar said coolly.

"Any clue?"

Belzar took in a sharp breath. "No. Not yet. But I tell you, Hathaway Simon always has a reason for what he does. He hides his agendas just like he hides his technology. They're hard to see, even when in plain sight. I find it hard to believe he would consciously allow a massacre on this scale, which would mean something is distracting him."

"Agreed, but what?" The girl turned away and gave a deep sigh. "Well, I better get back so I can help Willoughby and his violinist friend get away so we can start tracking them. I hope this works."

"It will," Belzar said, draping a bony hand over the girl's shoulder. "We'll find that entrance, Hautti. We have no choice. I have no intention of letting this ship become our grave."

The girl started toward the door and then turned back. "Are you taking Reese?" she asked. "Does he even know what this is all about?"

"Do any of us?" Belzar mused. "Reese knows enough. He comes with us for now. We may lose him at some point, but he's good to have around in the tight spots. I can imagine he'd do quite well for himself back where we're going. He's a good fighting man. Of course, there's the issue of his tattoos. It's hard to think of who would appreciate those. Maybe a pirate king?" Belzar grinned. He walked over to the pipe beam where the cut ropes lay littered on the floor. "Neat trick cutting those ropes and disappearing. How do you suppose they did it?"

The girl didn't say anything. She continued toward the door.

"Remember, we have no more than three hours," Belzar called after her. "If we've no success by the two-hour mark, we'll have to find another way off the Absconditus. I know how you feel about the boy."

The girl stopped in the doorway and turned back. "Belzar, I doubt you know how I feel about anything. But I do want to get home, back to my people." Without another word, she strode soundlessly away.

21

Cedar Chest

It was a waking nightmare. His vision was blurred and distorted. Everything around him was dimly lit. Willoughby heard voices, muffled and indistinct. His body ached. He felt tangled and bent. He tried to move. "Shh!" a voice hissed in his ear. "Be still!" The whisper was barely audible, but he felt the hairs on his neck quiver. *Sydney?* He fought to focus his eyes, but could see only blackness. His head was still swimming and his body felt twisted, curved like a pretzel. A second body was curled over his back. He could feel the body's heat and sense arms and legs wrapped tightly around his middle. There was a scent too—a not altogether unpleasant scent. *Where was he? Was he dreaming?*

He had, of course, imagined what it would be like to be cuddled close to Sydney, but he had imagined more his arm being tight around her, not having her draped over his back while they bent down in some—where were they? A cupboard? A container of some kind? He breathed in. He could still taste and smell the acrid fumes of the rag, but they mingled with another scent. He concentrated on the scent. It was a strong scent. An image of freshly cut wood came to mind and then he knew. *It was cedar. The smell was cedar!*

He tried to breathe in again, but the weight of the girl against his back made it hard. He felt dizzy and thought for a moment that he might be sick, but fought the nausea down. Why were they crammed into this dark space that smelled of cedar? What was the space? *Was it a closet?* No. If it was a closet, they could stand up. *Was it a trunk?* The muffled voices suddenly moved closer and became much clearer. They stopped almost directly overhead.

"Where's the key to it?"

This voice was deep and gruff.

"I don't know. Why would I want to look through some sailor's stinking clothes?"

The last voice was higher-pitched and soft, a girl's voice. Willoughby's eyes focused on a crack where a miniscule line of light leaked in. He noted that the crack was actually a thin line that etched the darkness with a rim all the way around—*a lid!* It was a chest! He and Sydney were stuffed into some kind of cedar chest and someone was trying to cover for them.

"Listen," the girl's voice whined. "You were the one who was supposed to put the boy out. Did you even know what you were doing with that stuff? You could have killed him! Luckily, he just held his breath until he passed out, so the dose did little damage—except allowing him to escape. Didn't you think to watch him for a few minutes to make sure he stayed out? Didn't you think to check back on him to make sure the dose was adequate? I'm sure Gates—"

"Gates ain't gonna hear nothin' about this," the deeper voice hissed menacingly, "because you're gonna help me find them kids, and you're gonna do it now."

"*Me?* I've got other assignments, in case you've forgotten. You still have the professor next door. You haven't managed to lose him yet, have you? Maybe he knows something."

"*Shut up!*" There was a loud slap and a whimper. "Now, search this room from top to bottom. FIND ME THAT KEY!"

"I don't take orders from you!"

There was another whimper and then low, menacing words; "You're testing my good nature!"

The girl's voice hissed out, as if through clenched teeth; "The only good thing about your nature is that you're down-wind from me! Now let go! If there's something of value in that trunk, do you really think the key would be in this room? It's probably on the sailor who bunked here—one of the unfortunate souls you threw overboard to the sharks!"

The menacing voice grunted an obscenity, but seemed to see logic in the girl's words. He leaned down and lifted one end of the chest, dropping it to the floor. "That ain't clothes in there," he spat. Willoughby heard feet shuffle. The man seemed to be moving away from the chest. There was a muffled gasp and then a short burst of gunfire. Bullets ripped through the corner of the chest. There was a sound of breaking glass. Then something heavy thudded to the floor. Everything had happened so fast. Sydney flinched, pulling taut. At the same time, Willoughby felt a white-hot burning across his shoulder. Sydney squeezed harder. Willoughby gasped and then bit his lip. *It hurt!* The shoulder stung so intensely that it brought tears to his eyes. He felt suddenly faint and noted a wetness trickling down his back. The chest lock rattled and the lid flew up. The bright light blinded him. Then, it

250

was as if everything were in slow motion. Willoughby winced, pushing forward. He knew suddenly, inescapably, that he was going to vomit. Sydney's legs still held him. They were in the way. He tried to push them apart, but the bile was coming too fast. He retched all over the side of the chest, his lap, and Sydney's leg. He heard Sydney's voice again, much louder this time as she jerked away from him.

"Ahh! Yuck!"

He tried to grab at the side of the chest, but missed, swaying dangerously.

"Yuck!" Sydney repeated, pushing to her feet behind him. She quickly stepped from the trunk. Willoughby tried to push up again, but the world was spinning hard, his ears were ringing, and his shoulder burned with unimaginable pain. Everything seemed a blur.

"You were hit! You're hurt!" a girl's voice said. Willoughby tried to look over and focus. It was the voice he had heard while inside the chest—the girl who had been covering for them. She had wavy, dark hair and bronze skin. As she loomed into view, he could see that her lip was bleeding. She grabbed him around the waist and pulled him to his feet. She didn't seem worried about the vomit. She had strong arms, though she appeared thin and a bit wiry. She turned her head and shouted instructions at Sydney, careful to keep her hands away from the soiled areas on his shirt and trousers. "Get a wet rag from the bathroom. We need to clean him up first as best we can, and then get him out of this chest and check that wound. I don't think it's too deep. It looks like the bullet only grazed him, but he's losing a fair amount of blood. We'll need to bandage it somehow. Hurry! We need to get him to the bed."

Willoughby swayed as Sydney returned with the rags and the two girls worked to clean him up. Sydney was obviously *not* having a good time. When the job was done, the bronze-skinned girl tried to steady him as he stepped feebly out of the chest. He noticed that she had a red dot in the middle of her forehead. For a moment, he was sure he knew the girl, but he couldn't seem to place her. He had barely gained his footing on the floor when another wave of nausea washed over him. He turned back quickly, breaking away from the girls just in time to bend down and grab the edge of the chest. He retched in it a second time. The two girls were talking animatedly behind him, and then someone wiped his face and mouth with a cool towel. They let the back of the towel cool his brow. "There," the girl with the dot said. "That should make you feel better...Now—I need to get you over to the bed, Willoughby. Do you think you can make it?"

Willoughby gave a short nod. He allowed himself to be led to one of the two single berths in the cabin. *How did this girl know his name? How had they gotten him into the trunk? Had this girl been trying to hide them—to help them? Why? He had not seen her in the crew before, yet he HAD seen her...somewhere.* He glanced over again at the cascade of wild, dark hair and the brown, delicate face, and most importantly, the red dot. He knew he had seen her before, *but where?* An image flashed suddenly into his mind. He was in a class at Worhington Hills. As he looked over the sea of classmates around him, his eyes fell on an exotic girl, seated a few desks over. She had a red dot in the middle of her forehead. She smiled at him, pointing first to him, and then to the red dot. The image skipped to the girl with army boots in the library. *This was the same girl!*

Words came to Willoughby's mind. *"Watch for Belzar's brat, the one with the red dot,"* the big, black man had shouted only moments before the foul rag had been clamped over his face. Willoughby shuddered, remembering the sour taste of the poison or whatever they had put in the rag. He tried to block the burning sensation he still felt in his throat and nose. *Who was this Belzar? Was he a good guy? Why was his "brat" trying to help them?* He tried to remember what they had called the big, black brute. He saw in his mind the looming, pock-marked face. *Had they called him Gates?*

The girl with wavy hair helped Willoughby onto the bed. "I don't know if you remember me, but we've met before—long story, no time to review it. My name is Hautti."

Hottie? He did not remember that name. Why had she been at his school? He tried to remember the name he called her at school. *Had he ever even learned her name?* Sydney sat down beside him. She wasn't exactly cool, calm, and collected, but she was considerably better off than he was.

"Hautti, with an 'au', as in, 'She's a real—"

Willoughby tuned out her voice. He concentrated on her appearance. The only visible side-effects she showed from her confinement were slightly rumpled clothes, tangled hair, and a few wet marks on her jeans where she had washed off his vomit. Her eyes were a different story, though. Even though she tried to put across the idea that she was in control, he could tell she was worried—maybe even a little scared. She glanced around the room, seeming to want to look anywhere except directly at him. He looked back to the other girl. She was trying to clean his wound. *What was her name again? Hottie with an 'au'?* He tried to push through the fog in his brain, but he couldn't.

He started to ask her why she was helping them when a poker of hot pain shot through his shoulder. "Ahhh!" he gasped, feeling he might pass out at any second. "Sorry," the girl said. "Brandy is the best I could do for a disinfectant right now." She slapped a clean washrag over the wound and taped it down with duct tape. "Luckily, this buffoon had a roll with him," she said, pointing to the tape.

Sydney helped Willoughby slide his arm back into his shirt. Her grip was light on his arm, as if she were afraid she would break him. The wavy-haired girl stood and started to kick broken shards of glass under the beds and behind one of the small desks. Willoughby looked around the cabin. He noted that it was smaller and less ornate than his cabin. He also noted a huge man with an AK-40 machine gun sprawled on the floor just beyond the wooden chest. Blood trickled from a wound on his head. The girl must have hit him over the head with a glass object that had shattered. As she cleared the floor on one side of him, she rolled him onto his side and started on the other, making sure to mop up the spilt blood.

Willoughby looked away from her to Sydney, who was carefully eyeing the room as she pulled the shirt closed around him. She seemed to be taking stock of the situation. He glanced down, trying to do the same. He noted with relief that his sneakers were securely on his feet and seemed to have escaped the splatter of vomit. He could smell the wet spots on his shirt and jeans where the girl had tried wipe the vomit off. He felt another stab of pain as Sydney buttoned his shirt. There was another wave of nausea, but he was able to control it this time. He still couldn't make sense of things. *Why had this girl been in his school? How was she involved? Why was she helping them?*

The room flickered in and out of focus. The girl with the red dot on her forehead seemed to float away, and then float back. He felt unnatural, like he had stepped outside his body and was viewing everything from a spectator's viewpoint.

"Sydney," he managed, as she continued to work on his shirt. He felt stupid and embarrassed. "I'm uh, I'm sorry...I'm sorry," he began, his words slurred. "I was so cramped in there, you know, in there, together, and your...your chest—I mean, *the* chest—*the* chest—I mean, we were slammed together, and that chest—well, it was hot in there, and cramped...and I felt it—I felt it touching me, you know, touching, that chest—I mean, I mean, *the* chest—and..." He fought desperately to clear his fogged head, wondering who this babbling idiot on the bed was.

The girl named Hottie (with an 'au') gave a short laugh.

Willoughby felt himself flush. "I mean," he tried again, fighting to frame his words, but Sydney stopped him with her hand to his lips.

"Just...just leave it, okay? I know you didn't mean to throw up on me, and I, I don't think you should be talking right now."

"You think?" The girl with wavy hair offered, still chuckling to herself.

Willoughby barely heard them. His head had chosen that very moment to spin wildly again. He felt himself falling and gripped at the bedclothes. Sydney pulled him back up, steadying him. She placed the cool rag back on his forehead. The pain and dizziness eased. Willoughby looked back over to the man on the floor. He pointed with a shaking hand.

"You...hit him," he said to the red dot girl.

The girl nodded. "Yes, I did."

"Is he…dead?" Willoughby gulped.

"No, but he deserves to be. He wouldn't have thought a thing about killing you, and did his share of killing others. But I'm not like that."

The girl looked up at him with a pained expression. Willoughby had a sudden flash of memory. He had bumped into the girl in the hall once. She had knocked the books from his arms. He had expected her to hurry on as if nothing had happened like most of the kids at his school would do, but she hadn't. She had stopped and helped him pick the books up. "Thanks for not hurrying off," he had said. She had smiled at him with this same pained expression. "You don't even know my name, do you? I'm not like that," she had said. He had just nodded and gone on.

Who was this girl? Who was she working for? Was she connected with the tattooed man, Reese?

The girl looked at Sydney. "Others will be here soon. We don't have long. I've told you what you need to do. I'll give you as good a head start as I can. Tie my hands up. Your professor friend is two doors down."

Sydney looked over, blankly; "Why are you helping us?"

The girl looked up, fire in her eyes. "I'm a scientist, *not* a butcher! I was promised no one would get hurt. None of this was supposed to happen."

"What *was* supposed to happen?" Sydney asked.

"We were supposed to find a particular artifact—a pendant. That's all. We were supposed to locate it and take it, hopefully without anyone even knowing, and leave. That was it."

"Pendant?" Willoughby mumbled, but the girl ignored him.

"So why didn't you?" Sydney asked. "Where was this…this pendant thing?"

"It was supposed to be in H.S.'s cabin. We knew he wasn't here. The plan was to sneak in there at night."

"How did you know he wasn't here?"

Hottie with an 'au' gave Sydney a critical stare. "It's not important. What is important is that the pendant isn't there, and unless you know where it is and can help us find it, the operation defaults to big, bad Gates's plan—which seems to be to kill everyone first, then take the ship apart, bolt by bolt."

"This 'Gates' guy doesn't work for you?"

"No. My, uh, my *dad* needed financing and muscle. He got mixed up with the wrong people, and now he's in trouble, I'm in trouble—we're all in trouble. This, this cult that's under Gates has its own agenda. Killing people is like drinking water to them. We're only alive because they *need* the knowledge my dad has about the artifact. As soon as they get that, they'll probably kill us, too. My dad is trying right now to secure us a way off this floating morgue. He told me to stay put, but when I heard that slime, Wolfer, had put Willoughby down, I knew I needed to get here fast. We don't have time for more talking, though. If you want to escape, you need to get up and help me."

"*Escape?*" Sydney pointed to the man on the floor. "There are two dozen armed brutes out there like him—with guns! You may be able to walk among them, but Willoughby and I can't."

The girl sighed. "I know that. I've got a plan, but we've got to hurry!" She had walked quickly to the man sprawled unconscious on the floor and grabbed him under the arms. "For now, *help me!* We've got to get this one and his gun safely locked in the trunk."

Sydney sprang from the bed and helped the girl drag the man to the chest.

"I know a lot about Hathaway Simon. For one thing, he's famous for building himself a backdoor. We know it's hidden somewhere on the ship because we found the markings for a gateway below-decks. Any idea where he might have hidden an entrance?"

"*Gateway?*" Sydney frowned. "How do you know all this?"

The girl motioned for Sydney to heave. The two girls managed to drape the man over the lip of the chest and roll him in. He thudded down into the vomit. "Yuck!" Sydney said again. The wiry girl manipulated his legs around, threw in the gun, and then closed the lid. She locked it with a satisfying click and pocketed the key. "Just where he belongs!" she said with a note of finality. "Okay," she added, panting. "It's not important how I know—my dad was…an acquaintance of Dr. Simon, and they did work on gateways together. I've been raised on time travel theory. Of course, we never had the money to bring anything to fruition like good old H.S. When my dad tried—well, we got Gates. Then, we heard about the pendant and thought that would be our ticket to the big-time. Gather the bits of rope you were tied with. I think they got shoved under the pillows. I'll go get the professor. When I get back, you two need to go! Think where H.S. would have hidden that door. I can detain whoever comes for maybe 20 or 30 minutes—maybe send them in the wrong direction—but that probably won't give you more than 45 to 50 minutes at the most." The strange girl seemed frank and decisive. She disappeared out of the cabin door.

"What do you think?" Sydney said in a low whisper as she turned to walk back to the bed. "Is this girl a complete nutter or what? Do you think it's a trap? Or could H.S. really have a gateway on the ship?"

"He does have one…here," Willoughby mumbled. "It's built into…the, the ship…Antonio found it." An image flashed suddenly in his mind. Sydney had just pirouetted into her cabin and shut the door. H.S.'s cabin was only one door over. While turning away, toward his own cabin, he thought he had seen out of the corner of his eye a bluish glimmer—a short number string, very faint, floating in the air. *Where had it come from?* He studied the memory. *It had seemed to float out from H.S.'s door…*

"Sydney," he said, fighting another wave of nausea and dizziness. "I think I know…I think it's…it's in his cabin—hidden in H.S.'s cabin."

"How do you know?" Sydney stared at him, trying to determine if he was coherent.

"Trust—" Willoughby started. He tried to open his mouth again to whisper, but the wild dizziness spun the room. His wound burned, oozing blood. He grabbed at the bed sheets, teetering dangerously.

"How would you know that?" Sydney repeated.

Willoughby could no longer hear her. He felt himself spinning backward. The floor rose up to hit him. He struggled to push back up, but he was spinning again, off into darkness.

22

Navigating the Vents

Antonio had pushed barely 20 yards further into the shaft when he had to stop, breathing heavily. Sweat poured down his face.

"Why are you stopping?" T.K. whispered, her voice barely audible above the hum of air pushing through the vent.

"Can we speak?" Antonio managed in a weak whisper.

"You can whisper. We're over a group of storage rooms. I've been checking the grates. They're all dark."

Antonio nodded, even though he knew T.K. could not see. "I am not good with tight spaces. How much further have we to go?"

Dr. J had caught up with them. He was panting heavily as well. The act of turning himself around in the vent had taken more energy than he had imagined.

"Can we slip out into one of the dark rooms? I need some fresh air as well. I also need to look at Antonio's wounds. I don't have any medical supplies with me, but I might be able to help him lose some of the pain."

"Okay," T.K. whispered. "The kitchen storeroom is coming up. I know the chef kept it locked and kept the key on a chain around his neck. I doubt any of these murderers would have known that, so they would probably have to shoot the door open. We need to stay close to the grate and we can't risk any light, though, understood?"

"Yes," Antonio whispered.

"Antonio, I need you to go about ten yards further. When I tap you on the leg, stop. I'll go out the grate first. There will be a short side pipe, about four or five feet long. When you hear me push the grate out, slowly back up until you can turn into the short pipe. James Arthur will hold back until you're out. You got that Dr. J?"

"Got it," Dr. J whispered.

Antonio led them forward another ten yards or so until T.K. tapped his foot. He stopped, hearing her arch into the shorter pipe and push something metallic clear with a slight grunt of effort. Moments later, he had backed up and made his way into the darkened room. T.K.'s hands helped guide him until he sat against a cool wall, breathing heavily and grateful to be out from the confined space. James Arthur came next. Antonio heard him work his way over to sit within whispering distance. He took in a deep breath and seemed to steady himself before leaning over.

"I'm going to place my hands lightly just below your ears," Dr. J whispered softly. "I can't see good enough to have a good look at the wound, but I'm going to help you with the pain." Antonio felt the tips of James Arthur's fingers press slightly into his neck. "Concentrate on these points of pressure," Dr. J continued. "Imagine that all the energy of your mind is focused at these two points." Antonio tried to focus as he was directed. "Now," James Arthur said, "imagine all that energy beginning to seep outward through your body." James Arthur's voice was low and soothing. Antonio felt the pressure points ease and new points form at his temples, then on his shoulders, and then under his arms. He noted suddenly that he was breathing easier. His heart rate had slowed. The pain had eased. James Arthur sat back.

"That was…amazing," Antonio said softly. Dr. J pushed up beside him on the wall. He was silent for a moment, seeming to focus his own energy, and then he spoke in a calm whisper.

"Did you hear the conversation back there?"

"I couldn't make most of it out," T.K. answered. "I thought I heard a name—Bel-something."

"Belzar," James Arthur offered. "He's one of the leaders. From the conversation, it seems there may be two of them, and they don't get along."

"I heard something about a, a gateway," T.K. added.

"Yes," James Arthur sighed. "I think that may be our way off the ship if we can find it. The Belzar guy was talking to a girl—I couldn't get a good look at her. They seemed to know about the time gateways. They say there's one on the ship, but they haven't been able to find the entrance. They think Willoughby and Sydney might lead them to it. That's why they didn't put them with us. They're letting them escape. O'Grady is there too, I don't know why."

"There is a gateway on the lowest level. Willoughby was going to try to find its entrance," Antonio croaked. "It's some kind of experimental gateway. H.S. held tight control on the design of the ship. He would not even let me see the blueprints. That is why I was so interested in doing my own exploration of the vessel when we arrived. I found ingeniously-hidden symbols for the gateway. I believe the whole hull is a part of this gateway's structure. I have no idea where the other end of the hole might be connected, but anywhere would be better than here. We cannot hide in these ducts forever. H.S. will have to sink the ship before long to keep its technology from falling into the wrong hands."

T.K. piped up, "What are you guys talking about? What's this '*gateway*' thing? Even if we find a way off the ship, we're in the middle of the Atlantic Ocean. There aren't many cell towers around here."

"A gateway," James Arthur began, "is a sort of transport device. Kind of like a, a…what do they call it on *Star Trek*?"

"A transporter," Antonio offered breathlessly. "Only this device works with both space and time."

T.K. raised her eyebrows, peering at the two through the dark. "Come on—*beam me up, Scotty?* You can do better than that."

All three sat quietly for a moment, sucking in ragged breaths as the sweat trickled down them. Finally, Dr. J spoke. "Where would he put it? It would be hidden somewhere in plain sight, in a place secluded enough from traffic to make it accessible most of the time."

"H.S., my friend, is never predictable. It could be anywhere."

"You guys aren't going to tell me, are you?" T.K. whispered.

"We already did. A gateway," Antonio mumbled, "is a door that can transport people to different times or spaces."

"You're serious?"

"Yes," Antonio sighed.

"*A time door?*" T.K. whispered back, trying to get her mind around the idea. "You're telling me H.S. put a functional time door on this ship?"

"Something like that," Antonio continued. "Although it could be only a feeder gateway that transports in space to the time gateway, or it could be both."

"Both?" James Arthur asked, his whisper coming out louder than he had meant it to. T.K. immediately jumped in to hush him. They lay there panting and quiet for a moment. When it was clear that no one had heard them, Antonio continued in a barely audible whisper.

"It is something new H.S. has introduced—an ability to use the physical hole to transport across space to other holes in linear time, as well as to transport through time to an anchor facility. It's an extension of the feeder network, allowing a person to travel to any of the anchor facilities from a single gateway."

"And that was supposed to make sense to me?"

"No, but it made sense to me," Dr. J whispered back, "which brings us back to, where would he have hidden the door? We need to get moving or I'm going to melt clean through here."

T.K. gave an irritated sigh. Antonio turned toward her. "We can discuss the technical complexities later. James Arthur is right. We need to be moving, and we need a plan. Think back; in your duties, did you ever come across unexplained symbols?"

T.K. thought for a moment. "No."

"Did you pick up anything else from the conversation you heard, James Arthur?"

Dr. J took in another deep breath. "They mentioned something about a cloak. The girl asked this Belzar if he had turned off the cloak."

Antonio gave a low moan. "They were cloaking the ship—probably sending false feedback to the monitors. Unless H.S. tried to contact us, there would be no cause for alarm. That explains much. You heard nothing more about the gateway?"

"No... Wait—there's one more thing I remember. They mentioned some guy called Mr. B. Not sure what his involvement is."

"While I've been hiding in the vents, I've heard a lot about a guy named Gates. I saw him once. He's a big black guy. I heard him mention reporting to Mr. B. I think he may be the one in charge of the whole thing." They all went silent, leaving only the soft hiss of air from the vent to cover the sound of their breathing. T.K. broke the silence.

"Wait...I could swear H.S. went into his cabin the last time he visited us and never came out. Could that mean something?"

"His cabin," James Arthur mused.

Antonio leaned back. "Yes. H.S. would have wanted to control access. His cabin is a good guess, I think."

"I understand very little of this conversation, but am I right in assuming we head for H.S.'s cabin?"

"Yes," Antonio grunted quietly. "Can you lead the way and get us there without being heard?"

T.K. paused. She seemed to be thinking through the route in her head. "It's doable," she said. "We're on the right side of the ship and most of the cabins on this floor were unoccupied. It'll take a good hour to cover the distance at the rate we're going, though. Can you make it Antonio?"

"I'll make it," Antonio said. "Don't worry about me."

"Dr. J, you go first, Antonio, you can be second, and I'll bring up the rear."

"How will I know where to go?"

"Keep straight the same way we were going until about mid ship where you'll feel airflow going up. You'll also feel a rope. I bolted one in at the vertical vent before anyone came on board. The Captain sometimes asks me to keep an eye on things. That's part of the reason I wasn't captured like the rest of you. You'll climb up two floors, and then turn left. We need to go very slow so that we minimize the noise. There is a maintenance closet two grates over after we re-enter the horizontal vents. We can stop there for another brief rest, and I'll give the rest of the directions. I have the key to the closet, so it will also be locked. Ready?"

"Does it matter?" Antonio grinned weakly.

"No," T.K. admitted. "It just seemed civil to ask."

"Civility is high on my list at the moment," Dr. J chimed in with an equally weak grin. He then sighed, rose to his knees, and climbed back into the narrow vent.

23

Numbers on Air

Willoughby tossed and turned in a fitful dream. He was a child no more than three. A man towered over him—a thin, angular man, rubbing a sparse, black goatee. A woman's voice called out: "Gustav, it's for you! Some guy calling long distance from England. He has a British accent. Any idea who would be calling you from Cambridge?" The man seemed deep in concentration, looking out over a chessboard with eight pieces on it. His face clouded over. "Yes, I do. Tell him I'll call him back." The man rearranged the pieces on the board, seeming to brood, and then he looked over, noticing Willoughby for the first time. He smiled.

"So, what do you think of my chessboard?"

Willoughby looked at the chessboard. Something was wrong. The pieces were all wrong, but he didn't know why. He didn't answer.

"You don't know what to think of it, do you?" his father continued. "It's not chess that I'm playing here. I'm working on a famous puzzle. That's why there are eight different kinds of queens on the board and nothing else. See, to solve the puzzle, you have to find all the ways that the eight queens can be placed on the chess board so that no queens are able to attack each other. That means that no two queens can share

267

the same row, column, or diagonal. It's not as easy as it sounds. This is a row, this is a column, and this is a diagonal. Now, this is the last queen I have to place. Can you see where I can place it where no other queen is on that row, column, or diagonal?" He turned the board so that Willoughby could see it better. After a long moment studying the board, Willoughby pointed to a square. Gustav's face beamed.

"Good," he said, "very good. You see patterns and potentials in the world around you. That's a gift, Willoughby. Don't take it for granted. This ability may come naturally to you but it doesn't to many others. Some work their whole lives and never develop an ability to see with the clarity and understanding that you do. These words may not mean a lot to you now, but try to repeat them in your mind. Try to remember them."

Willoughby felt himself slowly becoming conscious. Why had this dream come to him now? It was one of the last memories Willoughby had of his father—his father asking him to try to remember. Even at his young age, he had tried to listen, to understand, to remember the words his father said. Were they really the same as they had been in the dream? Who could say? He only knew that this dream had come to him several times, and the words didn't change. The dream had come frequently before he turned eight, and then less frequently. This was the first time he had thought of those words since his twelfth birthday.

Willoughby became vaguely aware that he was shaking. He sucked in a deep breath and tried to focus his mind. He was done with the dream now. Why couldn't he wake? He took another breath and remembered the nausea and searing pain in his shoulder. He turned his mind back to the dream in order to force himself to think.

When had it been that he finally began looking for the puzzle his father was working on in the dream? He forced his mind back. He had started looking for it toward the end of second grade, but it wasn't until third grade that he had found it. The Eight Queens Puzzle soon became a favorite pastime. He had worked out scores of solutions. He read about the puzzle's history. Proposed in 1848 by a chess player named Max Bezzel, the puzzle had attracted many mathematicians over the years, including Gauss, Cantor, Nauck, Gunter, and even James Glaisher. It was primarily his interest in this puzzle that had drawn him toward higher-level mathematics and especially unsolved mathematical puzzles. In a way, this had been the beginning of his road to uncovering the solution to the Riemann Hypothesis.

His mind finally focused and his shivering stopped. He cracked open his eyes. He was flat on his back in a dark room. *Was it the room where he had been locked in the chest with Sydney?* It felt different. He could hear Sydney speaking in low tones with someone nearby. The answering voice had an Irish accent. *Dr. O'Grady!* He tried to sit up, but felt an immediate wave of dizziness. He made out piles of broken furniture and scattered belongings all around him in the dim light. He eased himself back down. They must have dragged him or carried him somehow to this place. *Where was he?* He tried to remember details from before he passed out. He vividly recalled the cramped cedar chest and the searing pain in his shoulder. He remembered the other girl—the one with wavy black hair—who had helped them. He remembered being helped out of the chest and a strange conversation while sitting on the bed. The other girl had wanted them to find something. *What was it?* He remembered Sydney asking him if he thought the girl was crazy. *Why?* Because she thought there was a gateway onboard! He had told Sydney it was in H.S.'s cabin. He had tried to tell her to just trust him. Could this be where they were?

He let his eyes trail around the room again. For as far as he could see, the room had been reduced to rubble; drawers had been dumped onto the floor; shelves hastily emptied; bedding torn off beds and mattresses split open. All the wreckage had been piled into heaps several feet high on the floor. *Had Sydney and O'Grady done this?* Of course they hadn't. Those men—the hijackers—they must have ransacked the room earlier. He thought again of the girl from his school. Why had she helped them?

O'Grady burst out in a frustrated whisper. "I don't see any gateway, Miss Sydney. Surely, had there been one, it would have been found when they tore the room apart. Are ya sure the lad was in his right mind? We've been over every inch of the room, and those murderous brutes seem to have been quite thorough."

"He said it's here," Sydney snapped, keeping her voice low. "Besides, it's logical. Where else would H.S. put it so he could slip on and off the ship as he pleased? It's got to be here."

Willoughby opened his mouth to let them know he was conscious, but stopped himself. Where was the gateway? He had glimpsed the numbers floating in air, but what did that really mean? True, he had seen the numbers near the gateway at the Certus Grove and at Antonio's shop, but how close did that mean the gateway was? It could be one floor up, or one floor down, or somewhere else in one of the nearby cabins. Still, what Sydney said was true; if H.S. wanted to slip on and off the ship without being noticed, his cabin was the most logical place for him to hide it. He stared around at the walls...*nothing*. Had he gotten them to drag him all this way without being caught only to tell them now that he wasn't sure where the gateway actually was? *He had to think!* He had to clear his mind.

The voice of Gustav came back to his mind. "*You see patterns and potentials in the world around you.*" Patterns and potentials... As the words faded in his mind, he eyed the room once again.

"Do you remember exactly what the boy said?" Dr. O'Grady asked, breaking the silence.

"Well," Sydney whispered, "he, he said something about numbers floating in the air and then he was out again."

"Ah," Dr. O'Grady sighed, "and did he happen to mention Bigfoot?"

Willoughby ignored the conversation, turning his head slowly. He focused on any faint traces of light that seemed to burn against his eyelids. Suddenly, out of the corner of his eye, he noted a brief glare. He turned to look at it straight on. It was near the front of the room, coming from a slice of chilling blackness. He stared at it, concentrating, coming to realize that it was one of the cabin's closets. The closet door was partly ajar. He studied the door inch by inch in the dimness, forcing his mind to fill in details he couldn't see. The bulbous handle on the door emitted a soft, momentary glow. Spirals of ghostly numbers curled and flexed around the glow, seeming to float in the air. He pointed feebly.

"There," he said in a hoarse whisper.

Sydney spun. "You're conscious!"

"There—where does it go?"

"Where does what go?"

"That slice of darkness."

Sydney bent down to help him to a sitting position. She looked where he was pointing. "Uh, that's a closet."

"It's also the gateway. Help me over there. Any idea where it connects?"

"No. I only heard about it when your, uh, your girlfriend told us about it."

"She's not my girlfriend."

"Huh. I don't think she knows that." Sydney said as she and Dr. O'Grady heaved him to his feet. "She was certainly protective of you, thankfully."

Willoughby didn't have the energy to reply. Already, he was feeling nauseated and dizzy. "Just get me to the closet," he hissed in a low whisper.

"Do ya think you can figure it out, lad?"

"I don't know," Willoughby said. "I'll try."

As Sydney and Dr. O'Grady helped him navigate the wrecked room, they heard something else further down the hallway. It was a voice, and then footsteps, coming closer. They picked up the pace. The voices were only two cabins away. They skirted around the last pile of rubble. Footsteps were only one cabin away. They stepped into the closet.

"Quick—shut the door," Sydney whispered to Dr. O'Grady in a voice that was barely audible. The closet went pitch black and silent. Willoughby breathed heavily. His heart was so fast he wondered if the others could hear it. They were breathing hard as well. He put a hand against the wall, hoping to stop his head from spinning. With his other hand, he reached out and touched the knob to the closet door. It felt incredibly cool to the touch and spun in his hand like the lock to a safe.

They listened, perfectly still. There were loud voices in the doorway to the cabin, and then the voices seemed to move away. When the room again was silent, Willoughby spoke. "I think this knob is directional—like some sort of tuning mechanism."

He turned the knob carefully, noting each time the number strings around it spiked in intensity. Each time this happened, he changed the knob's direction. On the fifth number, something happened. There was a clicking sound from the door and then the sound of bolts shooting into place. From outside the closet, someone yelled something that was inaudible. *Someone was still there!*

Willoughby paused for a long moment. The knob now physically glowed so that all in the closet were illuminated in its eerie light. *Was the glow visible from the outside the closet?*

"Is this what ya have been seein', my lad?" O'Grady asked, leaning over to whisper in his ear. "Are we moving? Where will it be taking us?"

Willoughby shook his head. *It didn't make sense!* The door had locked. The numbers were there. Why hadn't they entered the time gateway? He clutched at the walls of the closet, determined not to faint again. There was another shout from outside, then a thundering bang as something heavy hit against the outside wall.

"They know we're here," Sydney hissed. "They're trying to break in. What do we do, Willoughby?" There was panic in her voice. She, too, groped at the closet wall. Willoughby turned his attention back to the device. The knob was still glowing bright orange. He moved toward the door just as a second *bang* sounded. He pushed his hand against the inside of the door. It was cool and when his hand touched it, he felt a slight suction. On impulse, he threw himself against the door. He felt an immediate tug that sent him spinning, falling through open space. It was like a dream. Numbers blazed past in blistering streaks of light, whirling around his appendages like water around a bubble. He could barely open his eyes for the brightness. He noted strands of differing sizes as they occasionally slowed just long enough for him to catch hints of their equations. Within seconds, they had sped back into solid streaks of light. He felt a tug of g-force, like riding a killer rollercoaster, but did not feel the sensation of being pulled apart and slammed together again that had marked his first visit with H.S. Suddenly, all number streaks slowed. When they stopped completely, he felt himself slam onto a soft, springy floor. His head pounded and his eyes did not seem to want to focus.

He tried to right himself, to push himself up. There was an odd smell—a smell of sweat, dust, and something else—*was it fish?* The light was dim. He barely had time to move when someone slammed into him from behind. He was knocked flat again. Seconds later, another body fell on top of them. The three bodies struggled to get up and out of the tangled heap they had become. Willoughby felt smothered, like he couldn't breathe. He choked, struggling to pull himself free, even as he felt consciousness once again ebbing away. He crawled slowly forward a few paces and began to retch.

24

Snake in a Basket

The three made relatively good time, Antonio thought. He concentrated on slow, steady movements that made little sound. Whenever they heard voices, or footsteps, they froze until the sounds went away. Once, they had been forced to lie motionless for what seemed twenty minutes while two foul-mouthed men searched a cabin. The men seemed to be searching every cabin, but luckily, they had been moving in the opposite direction down the row of crew berths.

When they reached the knotted rope T.K. had hung in the vertical shaft, however, stealth was more difficult. They had to move more quickly and it was almost more than Antonio could manage to pull himself up. In the end, James Arthur had turned onto his back and dangled his legs down, instructing him to grab hold of his legs. He then slowly pulled Antonio up the rest of the way, while T.K. pushed from below. The three lay panting in the vent once all of them had cleared the bend in the pipe and could rest horizontally. Finally, T.K. tapped Antonio's ankle, signaling for him to continue, and Antonio had passed the word on to Dr. J. A few minutes later, James Arthur found the grate to the maintenance closet. It took him a few minutes to quietly remove it and make enough room for the three of them to huddle together.

"So, are you a spy?" Antonio at last asked after they had sat in silence for a moment, their backs leaning against boxed equipment. He directed the question at T.K.

"So, are you a secret paramilitary organization beaming people around in time and space?" T.K. countered.

James Arthur gave a slight grin. "You hear that, ASEC? We look paramilitary."

Antonio moaned. "We are in no way military. We are dedicated only to science and history."

"And that's why this ship has a hidden nuclear reactor, a titanium hull, and laser cannons?"

Antonio was quiet for a moment. "So," he finally said. "You know your ship."

"Of course I know my ship," T.K. whispered back, a hint of irritation in her voice.

"A titanium hull and lasers could be for Arctic exploration."

"Or they could be for some sort of covert military operations."

James Arthur raised an eyebrow. Antonio noted the look with irritation. "You could jump in you know, Mr. JAWs."

Dr. J forced a wider grin. "Oh, but you're doing so well!"

Antonio turned back to T.K. "We are on a mission to learn more about the seer, Nostradamus. Do you know of him?"

"Of course," T.K. shrugged. "He's the guy that predicted the terrorist attack on the Twin Towers."

Antonio tried to roll his eyes, though with the swelling, it looked more like he was suffering from an eye tic. "I see you peruse the internet."

T.K. nodded. "Of course, but that doesn't mean I believe it." She looked away. "The Captain taught me to be curious and keep an open mind. He found me when I was, when I was little and alone. He became like a father to me."

"Are they holding the Captain?" Antonio asked softly.

Dropping her head, T.K, drew a hand across her eyes. "No. The Captain was among the first to be killed. I saw them throw the body overboard. I was hiding behind the anchor chains." There was a long silence. Finally, in a shaky voice, she continued. "He was shot through the head and thrown to the sharks like all the rest. Only H.S.'s *team* was allowed to live. They killed indiscriminately— everyone. They would have killed me too if they could've found me." Her voice had become scarcely discernible.

Antonio watched her wipe a tear from her cheek.

"I'm sorry." he said, placing a hand on her shoulder.

"Save it," T.K. said bitterly, shrugging the hand off.

No one spoke for a long moment. Finally, T.K. wiped her cheek again and pointed. "It's time for us to go. James Arthur, stay in the main shaft heading that direction. Turn left at the next junction and stay to your right. I scratched an 'X' on the right side of the grate that we want. Feel the side of the vent and you'll find it." Antonio cocked his head slightly as if curious about why she had marked H.S.'s cabin. T.K. shrugged. "That's a cabin that was of interest to me long before this mutiny."

James Arthur sucked in a long breath, gave T.K. a soft pat on the shoulder, and started toward the ventilation shaft.

"Wait," T.K. said. She pressed a small knife into his hand. "Just in case you need it," she said. Dr. J took the knife, staring at it as if it were a foreign object. He hadn't been in a fight since schoolyard days, and did not consider himself a violent man. Still, T.K. was right. He might need it. He gripped the knife handle tight and disappeared into the vent. T.K. motioned for Antonio to follow. Antonio shook his head.

"No. Please, you go next. I would like just a few more moments to focus my energy as James Arthur showed me. I will catch up and tap you on the ankle before you exit into the cabin."

T.K. peered at him, hesitant, and then turned toward the vent. "I'll wait for you at the grate. Don't take too long."

Antonio gave a quick nod and watched her disappear into the ventilation shaft. He took a deep breath. How had Dr. J worked his magic? He placed fingers behind his ears at the base of his neck and began to apply slow pressure. At the same time, he tried to focus and concentrate on the pressure points. He was somewhat familiar with the ancient Chinese healing arts, but something James Arthur did was different. He had felt energized after just a few minutes of Dr. J's touch. Of course, he wouldn't admit that to the good Doctor. Nor would he confess that his own attempts to repeat the exercise were not nearly so effective. Finally, with a sigh, he rolled over onto his knees and pushed into the vent.

Even in the short distance they had to H.S.'s cabin, James Arthur had to stop the group twice. Once, he heard yelling from somewhere up ahead. The second time, he heard a sharp smack—like the sound of steel hitting against steel.

After long pauses, Dr. J moved quietly and cautiously forward. It was not long before he found the "X" T.K. had spoken of. He slowly, carefully removed the vent grate and pushed it to one side. He then slid out into the darkened room.

Barely any visible light streamed in from the hallway. Seeing no movement in the shadows, he closed his eyes and concentrated on listening. He heard nothing. The room seemed quiet and dead. A slight stream of reflected light came into the cabin through the open hall door. He surveyed the room. He could tell that the cabin had been thoroughly plundered. Every piece of furniture had been slashed, broken, or mutilated in some way. Contents of every drawer were dumped onto the floor. A mountain of shattered glass and splintered wood had been shoved toward the center of the cabin.

He allowed his eyes to sweep every inch of the room before he rose slowly to his feet and began to make his way toward the sliver of light shining in from the hall. He stepped carefully, running one hand along the wall while holding the knife with the other. If the hallway was clear, he could sneak back to his own cabin and grab his penlight. He kept it in an old gym bag. They could use it to more thoroughly search the room. He felt the far edge of H.S.'s walk-in closet and noted a different texture to the wall. It was smoother, and felt somehow colder. His eyes narrowed. This was definitely an area he would have to scrutinize more carefully. He pushed on to the closet door. It seemed heavy and thicker than a normal door. One tap told him why—the door was metal.

Before he had a chance to move any further, he heard a sound from the hallway. He froze, listening intently. From a couple of doors down, he heard loud curses and harsh laugher echo as two men closed a door and hurried away in the opposite direction. James Arthur waited until their voices had completely faded, then began to inch forward again. As he cleared the closet opening, he heard the metal door creak further open behind him. He spun around, brandishing the knife. A dark shape, barely visible in the dimness, sprang out of the closet. The shape was holding something pointed at Dr. J.

"*How does it work?*" the form's raspy voice croaked.

James Arthur took a step back, eyeing what he guessed to be a gun. "What are you talking about?" he whispered, breathlessly. The shape took another step forward, confirming his fear. It was a man, the man with the steel cane, and he had a large gun, aimed expertly at Dr. J's heart. "I don't like repeating myself," the man said. Strangely, he also seemed to be attempting to keep his voice low. "Move—this way, so I can see your face." The man slowly circled around. James Arthur turned, but did not lower the knife.

"I'll give you one last chance," the man whispered. "Show me how the gateway works, and I may let you live. You have 30 seconds."

James Arthur's mind was racing. He felt sweat dripping down his face and from his hand. *What was the man's name? Belzar, or something like that? Was he a killer?*" At that very moment, there was a slight rustle of sound at the ducting near the back of the cabin. "*James Arthur?*" T.K. whispered with concern in her voice. The noise was just enough to distract Belzar for a split second. Dr. J pounced, knocking the man's steel cane away and pushing him backward over a low pile of rubble. The man fell, firing his gun wildly. One bullet barely missed Dr. J's ear before he ducked quickly behind the metal of the closet door. Another bullet pinged off of the metal.

"*Get back!*" Dr. J hissed toward the back of the dark room. The man named Belzar was swearing now, already climbing to his feet.

"You know it's a losing battle," the man croaked breathlessly. "You can't escape. I've got men all over these halls. You hurt me, and you're dead." The man paused, seeming to rummage for his cane. Dr. J couldn't hear anything else from the back of the cabin. Hopefully, T.K. had figured out that there was trouble and slipped away, back into the ventilation shaft. The man seemed to find what he was looking for and moved closer. "Your one chance—the one chance for you and your friends—is to trust—"

James Arthur did the only thing he could think to do. He slammed the closet door shut. He immediately heard a cry of rage as the man outside pounded his steel cane against the walls of the closet. From the metallic ring of steel hitting steel, he knew the walls were metal as well as the door. He recalled the sound of steel hitting steel that he had heard earlier. *Could it have been Willoughby and the others escaping?* If this was the doorway, how did it work?

He gripped the knob of the metal door tight. There was a clicking and whirring sound that came from the *inside* of the door itself. Bolts locked into place. He stared down and saw that the doorknob in his hand was glowing. He turned the knob cautiously. It spun easily. *This was it, then! This was the gateway!* But where would it take him? The knob must be the key. It probably had coded destinations. He heard a click. The man called Belzar screamed again in anger, lashing out at the wall in his fury. *With all the banging, could this man damage the door?* James

Arthur thought. The knob glowed brighter. The interior of the closet began to feel cold, like the inside of a refrigerator.

Panic rose in James Arthur's mind. He wasn't sure what to do. The cold seemed to be flowing out from the metal door. He reached his hand up to touch the door's humming surface. It pulled softly at his fingertips. The inside walls vibrated quietly around him. What started as a slow pull became a sudden jerk, and the pressure of the tug ripped him off his feet with such force that it felt as if he had been shattered into a million pieces. The sensation was much different from his first trip through a time hole. He felt disconnected, numb—as if he were an immense, floating shape, spread across eons of time. A cracking pain yanked his body back together. It winded him. He fell, gasping. Eventually, he crashed into what appeared to be a stack of woven furniture or containers of some kind. He sucked in a desperate breath. His brain fought to orient itself. Finally, he could sit up, breathing heavily. He looked toward a soft, flickering light. *Was it a candle? Where was he?* He felt around, getting a sudden bad feeling in the pit of his stomach. The containers he had crashed onto were large and putrid smelling. They appeared to be baskets, woven out of a stiff, prickly reed. They had cushioned his fall, for which he was grateful, but the smell they unleashed made his eyes water. He rolled off the baskets and pushed to his knees, realizing that he still had the knife clutched tightly in his hand. *Well, that was one good thing—he had, at least, some protection.*

As soon as his chest stopped heaving and the dizziness subsided, he crawled away from the pile of baskets. When he was several yards away, he turned back to a sitting position to dust himself off. He checked to make sure he was not injured.

Glancing around, he found that he was in some kind of low chamber. He could see the baskets where he had fallen, smashed now in front of a low wall that was carved into the shape of something. He couldn't quite make out the shape because the candlelight was too dim and was low, along the foot of the back wall behind the baskets. *Weird entrance to an observation facility*, he thought to himself. He again thought of the blue-eyed maniac, Belzar, banging on the walls of the gateway. He thought of how he had spun the doorknob. His gut tightened. *Maybe this wasn't an observation facility at all! Maybe he had free-fallen through time!* He scanned the rest of the chamber. There was a small, rounded opening opposite the wall with the baskets. The ground beneath was cool, covered in fine sand. He heard voices approaching, and a flicker of torchlight played upon one of the sides of the rounded opening. James Arthur quickly pushed back into a corner, out of sight of the opening. He eased tightly against the wall and tried to slow his breathing. There were two voices—men shouting at each other in a language he did not recognize. It sounded like Arabic.

He wondered, briefly, if he would have been better off hiding behind the smashed baskets when a reptilian hiss issued from behind one of the taller baskets that he did not smash. He froze, glimpsing something dark slither up over the lid of the basket. He pushed even further back into the corner, his hand brushed against a pile of decaying rags. The light from the torch had become brighter as the voices stopped outside the chamber. Something hard was sticking into his back, but he dared not move. He shifted his weight very slowly and very carefully. He glanced down at what he had pushed up against. The light from outside the chamber added a little more illumination, enough for him to at least get an idea of his dim corner. To his horror, he discovered that the decaying rags he had brushed against hung limply from a crusted skeleton. Feeling with his hand, he found that the frame's broken forearm was poking him in the back—*the room was a tomb of some sort!*

Shadowy forms bent down and a man holding a torch stuck his head through the door to the chamber, just far enough that Dr. J could see the folds of his turban. He tensed, as stiff as the skeleton to his side. He felt his hand tighten around the knife in his fist.

Light from the torch spilled across the room, illuminating it clearly. The room was rectangular, carved with smooth, exacting angles and lines. Painted across the walls and ceiling were what looked like mathematic equations. Just over the stacks of reed baskets, the image of an enormous king cobra was chiseled into the wall, its hood flaring. From the general disarray of the clay pots and baskets, it was obvious that James Arthur wasn't the first person to disturb the tomb. Footprints and drag marks led out through the opening, as if someone had already dragged out a share of the room's contents.

Closer to the entrance, arranged on either side of the narrow chamber, were heaps of bones, dressed in scraps of armor and tattered clothes, with swords and shields beside them, half buried in the sand. Possibly half a dozen complete skeletons lay on their backs or leaned up against the rock wall. *Was he in a pirates den?* James Arthur slowed his breathing as the man looking in pointed excitedly at the hiss from atop the tall basket near the back wall. A huge black cobra bobbed its head up again, its hood flaring, its eyes glowing in the torch light. There was a nervous laugh as the turbaned head pulled back and the men hurried away quickly.

Odd reaction, James Arthur thought. Then he heard the hiss again, and thought that the two grave robbers, or pirates, or whatever, had the right idea. Dr. J waited a moment, until he could no longer hear the voices moving away, and then slipped quietly out after them. He had no desire to stay in a narrow chamber with cobras and dead men.

What he saw when he exited the chamber, however, took his breath away. The narrow chamber led out into an enormous cavern of some kind. He stared in amazement, looking down onto the remains of a massive underground arena. The narrow chamber he had just exited was not alone. In the fading glow of a dozen or so torches spread throughout the arena, he glimpsed dozens, maybe even hundreds of other low, rectangular doorways, identical to the one he had just exited. The arena terraced down in wide increments, each slab roughly ten feet high and about twenty feet wide, curving around the sides of the arena in a semi-circle. It reminded him of the tiers of a Roman amphitheater. The stage at the very bottom of the arena was in the shape of a perfect circle. It was lit by twelve carved cobra statues, each burning with an odd blue flame. In the center of the circle, a checkered floor sparkled like glass. Inlaid across the checkered glass was a symbol, etched in pure gold. James Arthur made out the lines of a symbol—*it was the same symbol H.S. had shown them when they had met in the chart room!*

He backed slowly away from the edge of the top tier. *He had to get out of here!* This was no observation facility, or ingenious escape route. *He had jumped out of a frying pan and landed smack-dab into the middle of a fire!* A faint swish echoed from the shadows behind and above him. He spun, thinking he heard a sudden footfall, when a raised shovel floated down out of the darkness above his head. It slammed into the side of his skull and the world went black.

25

The Cave of Horrors

T.K. had waited until she was sure that Antonio was okay and able to follow before she cautiously set out down the narrower shaft after James Arthur. When they turned the corner and caught sight of the still-open grate to H.S.'s cabin, they heard scuffling. T.K. motioned Antonio back. She called out to Dr. J. Someone fell. A shot rang out and James Arthur yelled something unintelligible. A door slammed. A raspy voice snarled angrily. *"Come out of there!"* Something solid slammed against a far wall. A sound of heavy breathing punctuated short grunts of anger and disgust. T.K. eased to the edge of the open vent. She could barely make out a dark form on the far side of the room, inspecting what appeared to be a closet door. It was the man with the cane. He had his back to her as he tapped his cane on the door and walls around it. She pulled swiftly and quietly out of the shaft, crouching behind a stack of broken furniture.

"Well, well..." the raspy voice mumbled. "Pray tell, for what purpose would one build a metal closet?" The voice was quiet for a moment and then the figure turned. "If you don't want to play, I guess I'll just have to find your friend!" The stooped silhouette peered toward the back of the room. T.K. had already begun to work her way quietly around the heaps of furniture, pulling a long knife from a sheath just under her ankle-length dungarees. The man started to edge toward the back of the room. He stopped suddenly, cocking his head and listening as a metallic whirr sounded and the closet door clicked open. He chuckled to himself, turning back to the closet. He approached it cautiously.

"So, you do want to play," he said.

There was no answer. He reached the closet. "Come out!" he yelled. No answer. He pulled the door slowly open, running his fingers over its inside and twisting the knob. This was the chance T.K. had waited for. She crept closer, seeing that the man had taken a short step into the closet, his cane at the ready. He banked it against the walls.

"Hello," the man rasped. "Why, there's no-one here."

He stepped back out of the closet, again inspecting the knob.

T.K. had quietly risen to her feet and closed the distance. The man spun just as she sprang at him, swinging his cane wildly. Ducking under the swing, T.K. pivoted to his blind side, grabbing a fist-full of hair and pointing her knife at his throat in one fluid movement.

"To the light," she hissed, kneeing the man forward.

The man called Belzar let himself be pushed toward the open cabin door. He spit out a retort through gritted teeth. "Our missing 'cabin girl' I presume? So that's how the others got free. You're not a simple crewman. Who are you—a trained bodyguard?" T.K. didn't answer, just continued to push. "Don't want to speak? I don't know what you think you can accomplish. All I have to do is bark one order, and there will be twenty men here with machine guns to cut you down before you get five yards away."

"It's hard to call out through a slit your throat," T.K. whispered just as harshly. "Shut up, or I'll stop showing patience." She pushed him into the dim light from the corridor, yanking his hair so that his face twisted. She could now see his eyes. They were deep, vibrant blue. She jerked him back into the shadows, the knife pinching his skin. "*It is you!*" she spat. "*Why would Habus' spineless stooge be attacking his ship?*"

Belzar grew suddenly very still. "Where did you hear that name?" he managed to rasp. T.K. kept the pressure on the blade. "I heard it from you, Belzarac—and from Hannuktu. Yes, it's taken a long time for me to find you, but find you I did. You were stupid and careless to use your real name."

"Those are names long dead," Belzar managed in a hoarse grunt, blood trickling down his neck.

"You murdered my father. You are responsible for my brother's death. Now, your henchmen have murdered the only other father I've ever had. Tell me one good reason why I shouldn't slit your throat!"

"Ah!" Belzarac coughed. "*Tainken Keilhar!* The child princess that *didn't* die."

"No. She didn't—and you're running out of time. One good reason, Belzarac!"

"First, I didn't murder your father," the man spat, barely able to speak. "Second, those aren't my men."

"What do you mean?"

The man was silent. T.K. eased up ever so slightly on the knife. "I was...hired to rob your father, not kill him. He never took the pendant off. I tried to bluff him and snatch it. He had a hidden dagger. We scuffled. It, it was an accident. Habus saw. He..." Belzar was barely able to get the last word out. He gasped for breath. T.K. realized that she had unintentionally increased the pressure on the knife again.

"Finish!" she demanded, barely slackening the knife's pressure. Belzar coughed.

"He, he was the brains. He ran. I followed. Your brother...followed. You...You must have followed. Thought I saw...in the shadows. You must know the rest—about my leg."

Belzar feigned a collapse on the side of his bad leg. Using the temporary distraction to perfect effect, he twisted away from T.K.'s knife arm, swatting the arm with his cane so that the knife sliced superficially at his neck. He spun back around, delivering a roundhouse kick to T.K.'s gut, followed by a slam onto her shoulder with his cane. The blow drove T.K. to the floor. Belzar rocked on his legs, fighting for breath and wiping blood from his neck. He towered over the crumpled form on the floor, his cane poised, watching for movement. When it was clear that T.K. was in no shape to counter-attack, at least not immediately, he slipped his free hand into his coat pocket. There was a click and he withdrew his automatic pistol. He aimed it at T.K. as she rolled onto her back, one arm guarding her face. Belzar forced a crooked smile.

"As for your other father," he croaked, "If you're talking about the Captain of this cursed ship, you can thank Gates and his mysterious boss for that—a tall man, always wears a trench-coat. He calls himself 'Belzy,' or 'Beelzebub,' or some such rot. I wouldn't let Gates know you're alive if I were you. He seems to like to see things die."

"Why are you here?" T.K. managed.

"I came to get something Habus took from me—something that's rightfully mine!"

"That you stole from my father?"

"Perhaps. Anyway, the artifact doesn't seem to be here and that idiot and his *muscle* have killed or lost anyone who could have helped us find it." The man stared down, breathing heavily. "If you weren't such a risk, I might want to keep you around. You've filled in rather nicely. Perhaps your father taught you how to use the pendant?"

"I wouldn't help you even if I did know what that pendant is. I only know you killed for it."

"I'll kill for it again," Belzar confirmed. He looked down, his eyes blazing. "Will you die today for it, Tankien Kielhart, Princess of the people who never were?"

"What is Habus doing with it?" T.K. calculated that this may make Belzar hesitate, and she was right. He raised an eyebrow.

"Well, that's the million dollar question, isn't it? I can't say. I only know he took it from me and left me high and dry—left me in that stinking cave all alone. Well, not alone. I was there with the beast, now wasn't I?"

"We're both after Habus."

The man's fierce eyes studied T.K.

"Yes, which means we're probably both after the pendant. Now, it looks like it's slipped through my fingers again. I'll find it, though, and when I do, I'm going home. Sorry, there's only room for me and mine on my return journey. A Princess would mean complication. I will, though, have revenge for both of us before I go." He took a rattling breath. "Now, my not-so-young princess, I have to kill you." Extending his gun arm slightly, he pointed the barrel at T.K.'s head. "Believe me, it's better this way. If Gates were to find you…"

The sentence was never completed. A sudden arc of movement ended in a rain of shattered glass. Liquid slapped to the floor smelling of alcohol. Belzar dropped the gun, falling limply forward. Antonio shuffled into the light, swaying slightly on his feet, holding the neck of a shattered whisky bottle. The pungent odor of the liquor filled the room. He forced a weak smile.

"Trouble with the boys, *senorita*?"

T.K. nudged Belzarac. The man was out cold. She scrambled away from him, finding her knife and pausing long enough to return it to the sheath at her ankle. "Thanks," she said, pushing slowly to her feet, nursing her bruised shoulder. "Where'd you get the bottle?"

Antonio shrugged. "It was hidden in the springs of his bed. H.S. once told me he always hides something in the springs of his bed." He tossed the jagged neck to the floor. "I did not expect a bottle, though. H.S. doesn't drink. Perhaps the alcohol was poisoned—a double weapon, no?"

T.K. started to respond, but paused, holding up a hand for silence. Muffled voices came from far down the corridor. "Belzar? *Belzar?* Mouse says he thought he heard gunfire." Feet shuffled in their direction. The voice called out again. There was a tense silence.

"*Quick,*" T.K. motioned toward the closet. "He was inspecting the closet when I jumped him. Its walls are made of metal of some kind." She kept her voice to barely above a whisper. They pushed quickly to the closet and quietly closed the door. "Is there a lock?" Antonio whispered as T.K. let go of the knob. There was a sound of bolts locking into place. The knob began to glow a bright orange. "Look," T.K. said, "the knob spins like the dial of a safe." She had moved the knob slightly to a point where it had seemed to click.

Voices and footsteps grew louder from outside the closet. They couldn't be more than a few yards away. The knob began to turn on its own. T.K. stepped away from it.

"I, I didn't do that."

"No, but you seem to have triggered some sort of automated program."

The knob stopped and changed direction, then stopped again. The door became quiet. Antonio moved forward. "It's the entrance," he said. "We've found the entrance to the gateway. That's why James Arthur is no longer here. " Outside in the room, excited shouts erupted. Debris was being flung about in an apparent attempt to search the room. "The ventilation shaft!" someone cried.

T.K. gripped Antonio's arm "How does it work?" she whispered. "Where will it take us?"

"I don't know," Antonio croaked. "If we triggered some automated function, perhaps to one of our facilities? But the door has been dented. There is even damage to the doorknob. It could be dangerous." He was studying the doorknob, which still glowed. Something slammed against the outside of the door. Bullets pinged off the metal walls.

"Antonio," T.K. said, hearing the chaos outside the closed door growing. "You must know how to work this thing! We need to get out of here!"

"This is...a new design," Antonio croaked, exasperated. The door became suddenly cold, as if it had turned to ice. Antonio touched it and felt at first a sluggish pull. He grabbed T.K.'s arm and opened his mouth to warn her, but before he could, an intense jerk yanked them both forward, exploding outward. Antonio felt an odd disconnectedness, as if his soul were spread across a smothering blackness. Then, with a crack, he was yanked together again. He was falling. He glanced around and caught a momentary glimpse of T.K. splashing beside him into a pool of briny, odorous water. The water stung his eyes and throat as he plunged below the surface. He struggled back up, rocketing out of the water with his arms flailing, gasping for breath. The water seemed to glow with strange phosphorescence. T.K. burst up a few yards away. He tried to clear his vision.

"*Where*—" he started, dazed and wild-eyed. T.K. cut him off.

"No! *NO!*" She wiped her eyes and turned in the water. A faint glow filtered down from the black, slimy walls as well. "*Not here!*" she shrieked, an edge of panic in her voice. "Quick—*follow!* We've got to get out of this water fast!" She took off swimming, slicing crisply through the dim pool. Antonio had finally gotten his eyes dried and focused. They seemed to be in a cave of sorts. He could see a narrow rock shelf a few yards ahead. T.K. was frantically swimming toward it. She called to him over her shoulder. "Swim, Antonio! No time to explain. Just *swim!* Swim as if your life depended on it, because it probably does!"

Antonio couldn't make out what was going on. "You know this place?"

"*Listen to me!*" T.K. screamed. "Something comes into this cave, something—"

Her eyes grew large as Antonio heard a faint splash behind him. "*Swim!*" she screamed.

Antonio felt a shiver run down his spine as something large and rubbery slapped against his leg. He tore at the water, fighting to close the gap between himself and T.K. Out of the corner of his eye, he glimpsed an enormous dark coil slice up out of the water. He kicked harder.

"*Hurry!*" T.K. screamed. "*Faster!*" She had already dragged herself onto the ledge and stood, knife in hand.

Another black coil rippled the water barely ten yards away. Antonio lunged for the shelf and felt a hand grab his shoulder. T.K. bent low, helping him onto the rocky ledge just as an ugly, angular head burst up to tower over them. It was at least five feet across. Antonio rolled onto his back and tried to push further onto the ledge. The beast rose up higher, hissing and dripping water. A foul stench washed over them as it pulled its fangs wide in a trumpeting roar. T.K. screamed back. Her eyes burned with an animal intensity. She brandished her knife with speed and skill. The yellow slits of the beast's eyes narrowed as it jerked its head back and struck.

26

Pink Shores

Willoughby felt hands lifting him. His limbs were weak and his head was spinning mercilessly. His throat burned. They put him on some sort of stretcher and wheeled him out. *Out where?* The air was cool. There was a breeze that smelled…that smelled of ocean. Voices were shouting. Willoughby leaned suddenly over the side of the stretcher to retch again. His throat began to throb. He wanted to look around, to figure out where he was and who was with him, but his eyes could not focus beyond one or two feet away. There were men with yellow jackets and a woman with a white frock and short hair. He thought he saw Sydney once, trailing behind, also escorted by someone in a white frock. He was loaded onto a vehicle. He noted a neat, black "O" on the pocket of one of the yellow jackets and relaxed. Wherever they were, Observations, Inc. was aware of it. *They were safe!* The release of tension in his body allowed him to drift again, his consciousness ebbing away and the cold, dark of oblivion returning…

He was again falling through the void of light. Numbers streamed by, various strings slowing into visibility. A particular string interested him. It was slightly darker than the rest. He reached out to touch it. The numbers were all prime numbers, repeated in a mirror loop. As soon as he touched the string, the numbers disappeared. He was in free fall in deep space. A long, rectangular plane fell in front of him, mirroring his fall as if it were connected to him in some way. It had a reflective surface made of crystal or glass. He stared into the surface and saw himself staring back, but the reflection felt wrong—alien in some way. He noted tiny strands of number strings sparking to existence around the edges of the reflection. They began to climb in circular spirals around the image's fingers and hands and arms. The number strings climbed up the images' legs and encircled its chest. The features of the face began to age and change. The frame of the reflection grew taller and leaner. The eyes became swirling threads of number with jet-black pupils in the center. The number strings melted into the image's skin.

Willoughby stared in horror. He was looking directly into the face of the man he had seen at Antonio's—the tall man with the trench-coat. The face smirked. "Even now, you are changing. You can't run from what will be. Already, Willoughby, you begin to see we are connected!"

"No!" Willoughby cried, kicking out at the crystal. It pivoted, its top, right corner slamming into his injured shoulder. Willoughby cried out in pain...

"There," a soothing voice cooed in his ear. "It's over."

Willoughby felt sweat on his forehead. A gentle hand wiped it with a wet rag. He was breathing heavily, lying on his side. His clothes had been removed and he was covered by some sort of pajamas that left his injured shoulder bare. He saw a white-clad nurse taking a silver basin out, making a face that told him that whatever was in the basin was nasty. He saw a few blood-soaked cotton swabs sticking over the edge of the basin. A young, dark-skinned man in a scrub suit stood just on the edge of his line of sight. The man seemed to be pulling at something.

"He's awake, doctor," the soothing voice from behind him said. The voice was female—obviously another nurse. "Good...Just a few more stitches and you'll be good as new," the doctor said in a low mumble. His voice carried a sort of colonial British accent. "Are you in pain?"

"Yes," Willoughby managed. The blinding pain he had felt in his dream had been steadily subsiding, but it was still there. He felt another wash of cool liquid over the wound. The pain deadened further. The doctor, still holding the suture, watched as the nurse dabbed the shoulder with what felt like a sponge. "Is that better?" he asked. Willoughby croaked something that sounded like "uh-huh."

"Good," the doctor said, then went on with his sewing. Ten minutes later, he sighed. "Forty-eight stitches." He tied the final stitch with a pinch and snipped off the excess thread. He then began to bandage the wound. "That was a sizeable bullet. You're lucky. It could have been much worse. You had enough Sevoflurane in your system to put down a baby elephant. That alone could have killed you. You were lucky to have smart friends. I'm not sure how they knew to force water down you, but it allowed you to clear some of the nasty stuff out of your system. Funny thing is, though—the Sevoflurane may have actually helped to slow internal bleeding from the bullet. It may have kept you from acute shock."

"Sevoflurane? What is it? They put something on the rag." Willoughby managed groggily. He was trying to remember who had forced water down him.

"Yes. It can be crudely administered with a rag, which, as I understand it, is how they gave it to you. It's a common analgesic, but can be deadly enough when administered poorly or in overpowering doses." The doctor gave him a curt smile. "I'm Doctor Kensington, by the way. I'm the corporate physician, so I get the best of all worlds—the past, the present, and of course, anything I can get my hands on from the future. Nothing surprises me, but I will say I rarely get to work on one so young, and this is the first time I've dealt with Sevoflurane poisoning. But you're out of the woods now, and I have other patients to see. I'll be back early tomorrow to check in on you and change that bandage." Offering a slight pat on Willoughby's good arm, the doctor turned to leave.

"Wait," Willoughby said. He tried to sit up further, but dull pain shot through his shoulder when he tried to move it. He could tell that the place where he had been shot was heavily bandaged. "Where am I? Is this a hospital? How is my shoulder?"

The doctor turned back. "You are in Bermuda, and don't worry—you did not travel in time, only space. This is not really a hospital. It's more like a maintained villa. Your shoulder is torn and we had to dig out residual matter from the bullet, but it should heal nicely now. I would take it easy with that arm until the stitches come out."

Willoughby let his eyes flick around the room. "Where am I? What time—what day is it?" He had a vague recollection of throwing up a lot into a basin. It seemed that Sydney had been there. He couldn't see any basin now, though. In fact, the room looked almost like the President's Suite in some high-brow resort. The furnishings followed an early colonial theme with island-inspired art covering the walls. A sheer crimson curtain fluttered at an open window a few feet from his bed, and a single French door stood open just beyond it. The door seemed to lead out onto a balcony or veranda. Outside, Willoughby heard the sound of waves breaking onto the sand. The doctor smiled at him.

"It's late afternoon. You've been with us about a day and a half. You were brought straight here after your escape from the Absconditus. You've been very sick, Willoughby, hovering in and out of consciousness."

"Sydney? Dr. O'Grady?" Willoughby croaked.

"Sydney, I believe, is right outside the room. She's pestered me for an update on your progress about every fifteen minutes. Dr. O'Grady is in his suite next door."

"What about Antonio, James Arthur, the Captain, T.K…"

The young doctor frowned. "I'll tell H.S. you're up and asking questions next time he calls. He's due for a visit, I believe, sometime tomorrow. He told me he would be here two or three days this time." The man gave a nod, turned, and exited the room. The nurse, a young, dark-skinned woman with her hair pinned down behind a crisp white nurse's cap, came back into the room. She walked straight to him, fluffed the pillows at his back, and helped him get another drink of water. "You can easily lean back now. Are you comfortable? Is there anything I can get for you?"

"No," Willoughby said, seeing Sydney enter the room. He looked down, noticing for the first time that the pajamas he was dressed in were flamboyantly colored in a wild jungle print. He looked like an advertisement for the Rainforest Café, and his shirt only covered one arm, bandages taped down across his exposed shoulder and the other pajama sleeve hanging limp down his back. He felt a bit awkward and embarrassed, trying to puff out his chest a little, until the pain in the shoulder threatened to make him faint and he decided to abandon the idea.

"Hey," Sydney said as the nurse exited. "Nice to see you again—well, when you're not throwing up, that is."

"Nice to be seen again—when I'm not throwing up," Willoughby mumbled wryly. "Except..." He stared down at his pajamas. Sydney couldn't hold in a snicker as he looked back up. "So, I suppose you're to blame for the Amazon neon ensemble?"

She leaned over onto the foot of the bed. Her outfit was, as usual, impeccable. She wore faded jeans with strategic holes in the knees, a tie-dyed shirt, and a loose-fitting sweater.

"I could have been really cruel and gotten you teddy bears, or smiley faces. They had a Hot Wheels set I considered..."

Willoughby shrugged. "Hot Wheels are cool. I was thinking more like Avengers, but please tell me that you did *not* dress me."

"I did *not* dress you," Sydney repeated with a wily smile. "Well, mostly not—I did help here and there."

"Uh!" Willoughby groaned. He didn't have the energy to be properly embarrassed, but he did make an attempt. He'd probably turn beet red when he thought of it later. Sydney brushed a strand of silky hair out of her eyes. Her eyes still sparkled, even though they looked different today—slightly pained and very tired. She raised her wrist to straighten one of her half-dozen bracelets.

"So...that was a nasty couple of days. How are you feeling?"

"Sore... Exhausted... Weak... Confused—is this a multiple choice question?"

Sydney smiled. "Sarcasm and wit in the face of, of danger… We carry on—brave, smart, and debonair to the end! That's us, isn't it?"

Willoughby looked down at his pajamas. "Debonair?"

Sydney didn't laugh. She just looked at him. She had made her pronouncement as if she were pointing out the tip of an iceberg and inviting Willoughby to jump on. Willoughby felt too tired to explore icebergs just now. He stared blankly at her, noting that the well of bubbly energy that was her trademark seemed, for the moment, to have run dry.

"Well," she said finally, "*you're* only debonair when you're not throwing up on me, or my chest, or the floor, or the sidewalk, or the nurse—"

"I threw up on your chest?"

"On *the* chest, thank you very much. Let's not start that again!"

Willoughby didn't feel much like sparring at the moment. Just two days ago, they had both come mere inches from death. He was still trying to get his head around that. He turned away, looking toward the window where the breeze rippled the sheer crimson curtains. "How did this happen, Sydney? A guy tried to poison me. Another guy shot at us. A girl I barely know put her life on the line to help us. Did they get out okay?"

Sydney looked down, fiddling with the hole in her jeans. "Who? Your girlfriend—what was her name? Bambi? Bimbo? Ah, yes—hottie!"

Willoughby rolled his eyes. "Spelled with an 'au.'"

"Yes," Sydney admitted, "spelled with 'au.' Why did she risk her neck for us? She was with *them*. I don't know if she got out."

Willoughby rubbed at his eyes. "None of it makes sense. How could it have happened? Is everyone safe? Did everyone get out okay? Where are James Arthur and Antonio? Did T.K. and the Captain get out?"

Sydney looked away. She didn't answer Willoughby for a long moment, and when she did finally speak, she kept her eyes staring down at the floor. "Almost nobody got out Willoughby. You, I, and Dr. O'Grady are the only ones we know got out. H.S. thinks James Arthur and Antonio tried to use the same doorway we did, but may have ended up in some other time. Otherwise, they would have contacted us by now. I spoke with him a little bit ago. He isn't here now, but should arrive late tonight."

Willoughby barely heard her discussion of H.S. He was trying to make sense of what she just said. "What do you mean that 'almost nobody' got out?"

Sydney was still staring at her shoes. A single tear made tracks down her cheek. "They killed them," she said softly. She looked up, pain in her face. "They killed them all, Willoughby. They threw dozens of bodies into the sea. I got a glimpse of the deck when we were getting you to H.S.'s cabin. There was blood everywhere."

Willoughby stared at her, stunned. "They, they couldn't have gotten everybody. T.K. was going to hide out in the kitchen area. Did they search?"

Again, Sydney was silent.

"Sydney?"

Sydney looked up, tears running freely now. "H.S. didn't have a chance to search the ship. When the board determined that none of the team was still on-board, they had no choice but to sink her. They couldn't let the technology fall into hostile hands."

"Sink her? Without even checking to see if anyone had escaped capture?"

Sydney sucked in a breath. "They counted bodies, Willoughby. All the crew, with the exception of T.K., are accounted for."

"James Arthur and Antonio are where?"

"That's the thing; we don't know where they went, because they didn't show up here. It's possible that somehow the mechanism got damaged, or that they managed to change the mechanism setting or trigger one of the memorized addresses. They could be anywhere, Willoughby, and the cabin-girl could be with them. I heard one of the—one of *them* say something about needing to find the girl. They already had me, and what other girls were there on the ship?"

"But H.S. would know where the gateway was linked, right?"

Sydney shook her head. "He knows they went somewhere. They were monitoring the vital signs of the team as a precaution. H.S. immediately set in motion a rescue attempt when there was evidence of trauma and no communications could get through. Then, our vital signs showed up in Bermuda. James Arthur was on the ship for about fifteen minutes longer than we were, but then his vital signs disappeared from our present time altogether. About ten minutes later, Antonio's vital signs disappeared. There was no ebb in the signs—no hint that they died. They were just there, then gone."

Willoughby gulped. "I'm, I'm not understanding. What observation points could they have gone to? Surely, H.S. can have each of them checked."

Sydney waited a while to answer. She bit her lip. "H.S. says that the Absconditus gateway is like no other. It isn't tied to a specific tunnel through time, just as the ship itself isn't tied to a stationary structure. This allows it to scan for various holes, the way a radio tuner scans for stations. The doorknob on the inside of the closet was the tuning device. Luckily for us, we had you. Your talent allowed you to find the right combination to bring us here—still in our time. H.S. still doesn't know how you did it. He wonders if we came here because this was the last place he came when he left the Absconditus. He usually anchors his yacht here. He thinks there may have been a residual imprint still in the time-field buffer, or some such—you'll have to talk to him for more details. The others, they didn't have any way to select proper coordinates. If they turned the knob just a little bit, or if the gateway mechanism was damaged in any way, they could have been flung almost anywhere, Willoughby."

Willoughby remembered how easily the knob had spun in his hand. "But H.S. said all observation posts are set up at the earth's strongest holes. If this is true, isn't it likely that they were directed toward one of those? Has H.S. checked all the observation posts? They might be at one. They might need help."

"H.S. agrees with you. We've been checking and monitoring all the posts. He believes the strongest possibility is that they would show up somewhere near one of the larger holes. But as hours tick by with no word, it becomes equally likely that they went through some smaller or uncharted hole. H.S. is putting together a search plan."

Willoughby sank back into his pillow. He stared over toward the window. "I, I can't believe it. How could the Captain, the crew—how could they all be dead?

Sydney seemed stricken. She looked down, started to speak, and then stopped herself. She brushed another tear from her eye, and then stood and walked slowly over to the window. "They just killed them. They killed them all. They didn't ask for anything. They knew everyone on the team, and everyone else…" Her voice went silent as she brushed away another tear. She sniffed. "So far, we've fished 23 bodies out of the ocean. The crew was only 24. Some were partially eaten by sharks. The Captain's body, at least, was intact. We haven't found T.K."

Willoughby felt a knot in his chest. His throat went dry. "*Why?*"

Sydney looked over. She wiped a quick hand across her face. "I don't know. Why does anyone do horrible things?"

Willoughby stared at her. He felt numb. "What good is H.S.'s technology if he can't secure his assets?" He felt blind rage inside. "How could they have taken over the whole ship with no-one knowing? How did they do that right under H.S.'s nose?"

"H.S. feels responsible," Sydney said, walking slowly back to the bed.

"Yeah, he should!" Willoughby barked back. "A lot of people died—for what? What's this really all about?"

Sydney opened her mouth to reply, but stopped. What was there to say?

Willoughby looked away. He was tired. His whole body ached. This certainly wasn't what he had imagined when he joined Observations, Inc. For the first time, he began to see a darker side to a quest for adventure. He pulled his knees up under the covers and looked back at Sydney as she sat again near the foot of the bed. She adjusted herself, aware that his eyes were on her. Her mascara had made little tracks down her cheek.

"None of us ever imagined this could happen."

Willoughby sighed. Sydney wasn't to blame for any of this. He decided to try to change the subject. "When did you say H.S. would be here?"

"I don't know," Sydney replied. She looked toward the window. "They have odd beaches here. Have you ever been to Bermuda? The sand is actually pink." She bit her lip, tears starting up again. "You've really got a spectacular view from your room. I think you'll enjoy it once you're up and around."

"Sydney," Willoughby gulped. He slowly, carefully pulled the covers off and scooted to the side of the bed. He put his feet over the edge, and then tried to move sideways. He winced, the pain intense. "Could you come over and sit on this side of me? If you bumped my bad shoulder, I think I might put a hole in the roof."

Sydney forced a grin as she sniffed. She slowly stood and made her way to his other side. He draped a shaky arm around her shoulders. She crumpled in, sobbing. *Okay, what was he supposed to do now?*

"Hey," he said, patting her gently. "This last two days have been, uh, horrible. If it helps to cry, then, cry." After a long moment, she looked up, determined to regain control. "H.S. never seems to be around at the critical times."

"Yeah, I have a few things to say to our dear Director," Willoughby said, feeling the anger flare again inside him.

Sydney looked over. "I don't know if I can live like this, Willoughby. I keep seeing the images of those dead crewmen floating in the water. I keep thinking of James

Arthur and Antonio. This isn't what I thought it would be." She sighed. "Why are we really here? Why did we jump at this?"

They were questions Willoughby had asked as well. He hadn't wanted to search for an answer too hard. He was too afraid of what the answer might be. He had a nagging feeling that these events could have more to do with him than anyone would ever guess. He looked away for a moment.

"So, what's H.S.'s search plan?"

"You mean for Antonio and Dr. J?" Sydney sniffed. "He said that if they didn't end up around the big holes, they should have landed somewhere around the fifteenth to eighteenth century, based on the position of the Absconditus, star charts, and current magnetic readings. He's working with a team to create a search perimeter. That's all I know."

Willoughby shook his head. "Three centuries of time and the full geography of earth. How could anybody find them?"

Sydney pulled away slightly. "We've got to give H.S. a chance. Besides, there are things you don't know. H.S. doesn't want me to tell you—he wants to brief you himself—but I will say the story gets even more complicated. He said that this time, he'll tell you everything."

"This mission can get more complicated?"

Sydney frowned and nodded. "I'm sorry, Willoughby. I wish I could tell you, but I made a promise. He says that it's critical he talk to you himself."

Willoughby nodded. He slowly moved away, pulling his feet back under the covers. Sydney helped him ease back onto the pillows.

"Did any of the hijackers get away?"

Sydney studied him a moment. Her eyes were swollen, but still beautiful. She shook her head. "We don't know about that girl who helped us and her dad. There was an unexplained discharge from the gateway door. They have escaped just like Antonio and Dr. J. The rest—H.S. blew the bulkheads. The ship sank in less than seven minutes. It rests almost a mile under water. I don't see how anyone else could have made it out."

Willoughby closed his eyes. *Did he want the brutes on the ship brought to justice?* Yes. *Could he see that H.S. had little other choice besides sinking the ship?* Yes. But drowning was a horrible way to die. It was also hard to imagine that the proud, beautiful ship that had filled him with such wonder, such a sense of adventure, was suddenly *gone*. Sadness and a sense of heaviness settled over him. He eased back onto the pillows feeling suddenly too tired to think.

"Sydney," he said softly, "I think I need some quiet now."

"Yeah," she said. "I'm sorry to hit you with all this...all this emotion." She started toward the door, stopping in the door frame. She turned back forcing a smile. "You were, uhm, you were good to talk to."

It was Willoughby's turn to nod.

"Get better," she said. She left the room, partially closing the door behind her. Willoughby felt a strong breeze from the window. He heard the crashing boom of the surf outside. It made him think of Sydney's concert. He remembered floating in the air, looking down at the sea and seeing the ghosts of past mariners, of Sydney's people, answering the call of her song. He imagined seeing the crew of the Absconditus now in the ghostly mix. So much had happened so fast. Would James Arthur, Antonio, and

T.K. all become ghosts in the memory? He tried to shut out the melody of Sydney's music in his head, but couldn't. It lulled him into a restless sleep as new, hot tears ran down his cheeks and wet his pillow.

27

Nomad's Land

James Arthur woke to a harsh moaning. He tried to focus. There was pain in his head. His mouth was dry. He tried to force his senses past the pain; *what was that pitiful sound?* With a start, he realized it was *him!* His breathing came in labored, jagged spurts, and he winced with each intake. The sound echoed around him. Feeling out with his arms, he found himself in a narrow rock tunnel. Rough-hewn walls hemmed him in on both sides and a rough ceiling loomed maybe three feet from where he lay. His feet were partially covered with rubble and when he shook them free, he discovered that he was all but naked. Only his torn briefs still clung to him. He felt the end of the tunnel with his feet. It was blocked with rock and dirt. *He had been buried alive in a rock-walled shaft!*

Fighting the urge to panic, he closed his eyes and forced himself to focus energy. He focused on the pain at the back of his skull. Finally, as the pain became less debilitating, he re-opened his eyes. As they adjusted to the dark, he noted the faintest hint of light from further up the tunnel. He slowly rolled onto his stomach. A sharp pain and dizziness washed over him as he lifted his head. He touched where the shovel had hit him and again concentrated, focusing all his energy. Sweat dripped from his brow. He could tell the wound on the back of his head was a bloody mess. He started to crawl, slowly at first. Every part of his body ached and the air was stale and dusty. He coughed, wondering if Antonio felt this way after his brutal treatment on the Absconditus. The thought of his friends gave him renewed energy. He had to find his way back to them. He quickened his pace toward the dim light.

When he reached it, he found that the small sliver of illumination was, in fact, a thin crack that snaked up through maybe 25 feet of rock. The light finding its way to him was sunlight. *He wasn't buried as deeply as he first feared!* If he kept pushing his way up the slight incline of the shaft, maybe he could find a way out.

Pausing a moment to catch his breath, he felt a tickle on his foot. He was about to kick whatever creature was pestering him away, when he glimpsed an armored tail— *scorpions!* He gritted his teeth and remained still until the tickle moved away. Fighting panic, he began to move slowly, pushing forward again. He worked to silence his breath as he moved so that he could hear the scurrying of viscous arthropods. Two other times he was forced to steel himself as one or more of the creatures crawled over his body, one even climbing over his shoulders and down his face. "It could be worse," he whispered to himself. "There could be snakes." As if to mock him, he heard a hiss from somewhere up ahead. "It's worse," he grunted. Mustering every ounce of courage, he pushed on.

After what seemed like hours, he came, exhausted, to a larger crack in the side of the wall. This one was about three inches wide and the light seemed to have cleared the area of vermin. He basked in the shaft of sunlight, glimpsing through the crack an expanse of barren scrub-brush. He could just make out what appeared to be a narrow desert ridge on the other side of the crack. Low hills of red and brown sandstone stretched into the distance for as far as he could see. He squeezed his fingers and then hand through the crack just enough to grab the edge of the rock about six to eight inches out. He gave a pull with all his might. The rock budged a little. He pushed and pulled alternately. Eventually, he worked a thin, flat piece of rock free. It allowed him to fit his whole arm through the hole. He began to work on another rock, dislodging the crusted sand and mud that had been used to mortar the rocks together. It was slow, tedious work, but the hole began to grow. Sweat poured down his face, stinging the wound on his head. His hands and arms became raw and bled. Eventually, however, the hole was large enough to give him the hope of squeezing through.

It took him almost as much time and effort to get through the hole as it had to dig it. Gaping scrapes on his shoulders, arms, and thighs dripped bright blood as he finally pulled free of the stone shaft. He rolled over and propped himself against a small boulder, panting with exhaustion as he tied the elastic of his briefs back together. The sun had started to set in the distance. He could see no signs of civilization. His back ached and his head throbbed. He lay back against the boulder and closed his eyes. After dozing for a moment, a sound of rustling jolted him back to attention. He heard voices. He pushed to his feet. In the distance, he could see what looked like a camel caravan, winding slowly through the hills, heading away from him. He waved his arms, crying out, and then stopped abruptly. He had realized two things—first, he didn't know who these people were, and second, he was mostly naked. True, he was covered in chalky white dust and blood, but that left him looking more like a ghost or zombie than like a human being.

He stared frantically around, searching for a place to hide should the desert travelers prove hostile. The high sand ridge was practically barren, offering no good cover. He scrunched down as low as he could behind a flat boulder and watched.

The caravan had indeed stopped, and a few of the camel riders had dismounted. He heard strains of heated argument and tried to place the language, but could not. After a few moments, the riders mounted their camels and the caravan continued. One lone camel turned back to head in his direction.

"Okay," James Arthur whispered aloud. "One camel is good."

He heard a sudden rustle from an outcrop of rock barely 30 feet away. As he turned, a figure, dressed like a Bedouin, came around the edge of a low boulder. The figure had long, flowing robes and a headdress that covered the face, head, and neck—everything except the eyes. It was a woman. When she saw him, she screamed and fell to her knees. James Arthur jumped back, glancing hurriedly behind him. *What was the woman screaming about?* Then he remembered he was mostly naked. He hurriedly snatched up one of the flat rocks he had wrenched free from the shaft wall and tried to use it to cover his nakedness, still looking around to see why the woman seemed so horrified. Then the thought struck him— perhaps the woman was terrified of him? Looking down, he saw how sickly he looked, caked with dust and blood, and he *had* just crawled out of a tomb.

"Hey!" he cried in a scratchy tone. "Hey, no—this isn't my tomb! You don't think that—listen, I, I was *robbed!* Seriously, I'm not dead! This isn't my tomb!" The woman had now risen from her knees and was inching forward, pleading look in her eyes. He backed away, holding one hand up to stop her while still holding the rock with the other hand. Suddenly, he had an idea.

"*Halt!*" he cried, puffing out his chest. "*I am, at last, come! I have crossed the great divide and, uh, conquered the banks of that dark, most foul river—that torrent of damned souls!*"

The woman stopped, seeming unsure, her arms outstretched. She called out a name, over and over. The name sounded like *Crorrose.* She seemed to plead with him. He had no idea what she was saying, but she certainly seemed to be in considerable emotional distress. She was close enough now that he could make out that her skin was old and shriveled, even though her voice was velvety soft. He stepped back again, sucking in breath.

"Weep not, good woman! I will set at naught the ills of thy good labor, but thou must *halt!*" James Arthur squared his shoulders and tried to find a more natural, purposeful way to hold his rock. He was still backing away, swaying slightly from side to side, when the woman threw her hands up in a sudden exclamation, reaching out to him and calling the name again. She poked forward and touched him. Her eyes suddenly widened with wonder and she held out her arms as if to rush forward and embrace him.

Two things happened at that moment. First, James Arthur jumped back and saw too late that he had landed on the very edge of the sand ridge. One more inch would have sent him careening off into a chasm maybe fifteen feet deep. He tried to right himself, flinging out his arms, but then the second thing happened. The sand at the edge of the chasm began to crumble, sending him tumbling backward off the ledge. The rock he had been holding to cover himself flew up from his hand. It was flung straight up, twisting end-over-end as he plummeted backwards. He slammed hard against the sand floor of the chasm, the blow severe enough to knock the wind from him. Seconds later, the rock, still tumbling end over end, nailed him square in the groin. He felt his eyes bulge as he pushed it away and tried to groan. A wave of nausea swept over him and bile rose in his throat. He wheezed and gasped as the world spun around him.

His wild eyes lit momentarily on the top of the ridge, where he saw the old woman peering down, still reaching out her arms to him. As he struggled to breathe, he thought he heard a crunching sound and felt the ground shudder. The dimming sky faded in and out of view. He forced himself onto his side and saw a pair of leather boots the size of trash bins approaching him. The boots were attached to baggy pantaloons, which were attached to a buttoned jacket, crisscrossed by gun belts that rested heavily on monstrous bulges. James Arthur gasped. This was no man. *It was a woman!*

The giantess shook her ragged mop of hair back and grinned. She said something to a smaller, skinny man behind her. James Arthur squinted. The man stepped closer, carrying a shovel. *There were hints of blood on its blade!* The skinny man cocked his head and said something back. The two laughed, the giantess filling the air with her booming guffaw. James Arthur couldn't tell if the giant woman planned to eat him, or just leave him there in the desert to die. Her huge boots disappeared a moment, and then she was back. Dr. J struggled to his knees, determined to somehow stand up. The huge woman threw a coarse blanket over him. She wrapped it tight, then bending slightly, snatched him up with a single sweep of her huge arm. She hefted him onto her shoulder like a sack of flour or a roll of carpet. He tried to protest, to break free, but the woman's laughter boomed even louder as she pinned him easily with an arm whose muscles tightened under the skin like coils of an anaconda.

28

Bones of the Alchemist

Despite a state of deep exhaustion, Willoughby did not sleep soundly. He woke several times, noting how the room dimmed by slow degrees as the afternoon waned and the evening came. A nurse came in around dinner time, but he sent her away. No, he didn't want anything to eat. No, he didn't want to listen to music or watch TV. He only wanted to be left alone. As the night fell, he chose to leave the room lights off. He spent his restless moments searching the shadows as they slowly lengthened and crept across the room. Finally, when the room was pitch-black, he allowed himself to fall into a deep sleep. If he dreamed at all, he wasn't aware of it.

He woke to the curtains being yanked back and bright sunlight streaming into the room. "Good morning," a cheery voice said above the rattling sound of a breakfast trolley. Willoughby recognized the voice. "H.S.," he said, sitting up and rubbing his eyes. He saw that the nurse had opened the curtains, and H.S. was pushing the trolley. "Careful," H.S. said, reaching the side of the bed. Willoughby had risen too suddenly and the room suddenly seemed to be spinning. He eased himself back down against the pillows. H.S. held a small cup up to his lips, allowing him to sip a little cool juice. He took the cup.

"I can hold a cup just fine," he said. He held it in his lap, waiting for the room to settle down. He pushed up further on his bed—slowly this time—and took another sip. The cobwebs cleared. He began to feel more coherent. He breathed in the smell of the hot breakfast. He found that he was ravenously hungry.

"That's all for me?" He asked, shakily, pointing at several dishes arranged across the top of the trolley.

"Piping hot, and prepared by a consummate chef, namely, myself," H.S. smiled. Willoughby reached out and took a steaming croissant. "I'm, uh," he managed apologetically, his mouth partially full; "I'm really hungry."

H.S.'s smile tightened. "I know you're angry with me, Willoughby. I don't blame you. I'm angry with myself. The Captain and his crew were mostly hand-picked—by me. Losing them all in such a, a senseless, horrible event is inexcusable."

Willoughby looked over at the man, taking a moment to swallow. "What's really going on, H.S.? Nothing makes sense to me. What have you not told us?"

"I told you some of it," H.S. said. "We had no idea they had infiltrated us so deeply."

"Who? The, the dark brotherhood or whatever you called them?"

"Yes. They reprogrammed our security net, which should have been impossible. Evidently, they have some kind of technology we are completely unaware of. They hoodwinked us into believing that all was well on the ship. They were able to cloak the entire Absconditus and feed us false status reports and data. The only thing that saved us was they didn't seem to know that we monitored life signs of all the team. When we began to see erratic readings, we tried to contact the ship and the ruse was over.

"We tried to mount a rescue, but there was no time. You, Sydney, and Dr. O'Grady arrived within the hour. Our satellites soon confirmed a trail of corpses floating at various depths in the wake of the ship, and then James Arthur and Antonio disappeared from our scanners. At that point, there was nothing more to do but collect and identify the bodies and sink the ship."

Willoughby had stopped chewing. "Who are these guys really, H.S.? What are they after? I want the truth this time."

H.S. stared toward the open French door. "It's a nice morning. If you take it very slowly, do you think we could move our discussion to the veranda? There's a table there and you do have a beautiful view."

Willoughby took a deep breath. He did want to get out of the room, if only for a little while, and the thought of sunshine, fresh air, and a beautiful view lifted his spirits. He also sensed that H.S. wanted to be well clear of any potentially prying ears. He nodded. H.S. smiled and moved the breakfast out. He then came back in to help Willoughby, who had pushed to the edge of the bed by then. H.S. helped him put on a pair of slippers and stand. They slowly threaded his arm through the loose-fitting sleeve of his pajama shirt, being careful of the bandages. He could only button two buttons and looked a little like the hunchback of Notre Dame, but as H.S. helped him slowly to the wrought iron table outside, he decided it was well worth the few moments of pain and discomfort. The view *was* beautiful.

Blinking from the bright sun, H.S. crossed the veranda. Standing at the rail looking out, he inhaled. Willoughby followed his gaze. They were three stories up in a white stucco complex at the top of a low cliff. Below the cliff, black rock jutted up out of pink sand, framed at the edges by tufts of thick green bushes and grass and swaying palm trees. The water was a vibrant turquoise-blue. He found the warm, yellow sunshine and the rhythmic crash of the waves intoxicating. For as far as he could see, brightly-colored houses, condos, and hotels dotted the cliff greenery with a variety of pastel hues. The white sails of schooners plied lazily in and out of the coves, and boats sat at anchor in the heart of a wide bay far to the left. He breathed in deeply, trying to memorize the smell and taste and feel of the fresh morning breeze.

H.S. turned back toward him. "See? Better I think."

Willoughby had to work hard to tear himself away from the view. His shoulder was still unbearably tender, but he otherwise felt suddenly improved. H.S. had placed a pillow on the table for him to rest his arm on. The man wandered back to the table and inspected the polished silverware. He then moved the tray of food, cup of juice, and small saucer with one croissant left over to the table. Willoughby watched.

"You say you cooked this yourself?"

H.S. raised an eyebrow. "Eggs Benedict, dry toast, local fruit, and a special recipe oatmeal you'll find nowhere else!"

Willoughby picked up a spoon. He took a bite of the thick oatmeal concoction. His eyes widened with surprise. "It is good."

H.S. smiled. He placed his hands behind his back and stepped back over to the rail. Sounds of crashing surf seemed to rejuvenate him. He turned suddenly. "I am going to give you a string of numbers, Willoughby. I want you to tell me the first thing that comes to your mind: 92.12 (4,5,6,7,8,9) 7-G." He waited a moment. "Does this number string mean anything to you?"

Willoughby thought for a moment. The number sequence had an odd familiarity. It took several moments, but at last an answer popped to his consciousness. It came in the way of his father's voice, spoken slowly and carefully as he showed Willoughby a new configuration of queens on the chessboard. He had been studying the *Eight Queens Puzzle* again. "Why are you moving them again?" Willoughby had asked. "It's another solution," his father had said. "Listen carefully—I want you to remember this: there are 92 'distinct' solutions to the Eight Queens puzzle and 12 'fundamental' ones." The words had been repeated again to Willoughby on several other occasions. One night, several years after his father had disappeared, while he plotted Eight Queen solutions on his laptop, the words came suddenly back to him. He wrote them down in his math journal, and now H.S. was asking about them. Willoughby looked up, cocking his head with interest.

"I have no idea what the numbers in parentheses could be, but 7G might designate a chessboard location. My father loved to work on a math exercise called the Eight Queens Puzzle. He would put eight different queens on a chessboard and try to place them so that no queen was able to take another. He told me there were 92 distinct solutions to the puzzle, and 12 fundamental ones. Put together... I don't know, but he seemed adamant that I remember these numbers—92 distinct solutions and 12 fundamental ones. I'm sorry. Does that help?"

"Yes," H.S. said. "I guessed you would have an answer for me."

Willoughby waited for him to go on. He finished his oatmeal and buttered a piece of toast. Still, H.S. did not speak. "Why did you throw those numbers at me?" Willoughby finally asked, the slight breeze rustling his hair. A gull flew by, kiting on the breeze. "What are your suspicions? You still haven't answered my first question. What does a number string have to do with two dozen people being brutally murdered? Why did the Absconditus have a titanium hull, lasers, and a nuclear generator? What kind of group could infiltrate your security technology so completely? Your technology is supposed to be light-years ahead of anybody else in this time. Who are these people? Are they even *people?* What were they after? Why weren't we told about the gateway on the Absconditus? What kind of gateway is it?"

H.S. raised a hand. "Do you plan to let me answer any of these questions, or will you keep throwing out questions until the sun sets?" He gave Willoughby a crooked smile. "Take a breath. Eat your oatmeal. I shall endeavor to dissect your barrage of questions." The man pursed his lips and studied his shoes for a moment, as if trying to decide where to begin. When he looked up, his face was gravely serious.

"The nuclear generator you refer to is inactive. You can rest assured that it is still intact, and though disabled, is safely contained. There will be no negative effect on the ocean and we will retrieve the ship as soon as possible. The salvage team is already on its way. We will reclaim the Absconditus soon after the ship is officially proclaimed *lost* by the authorities.

"There is a gateway of sorts on the Absconditus. It's different from the ones that lead to our observation decks. It is to be used by those with specific skill in navigating the time grid. I had planned to use it specifically to train you. You see, there is no attached destination deck to guide your path with this gateway. I told you in the orientation meeting that you would not be using a tethered hole on this mission. You weren't told about the special gateway on the Absconditus because I wanted to keep your focus on Nostradamus first. If you remember, *he* was to be the focus of our trip to France. There is good reason for you to know all you can about this supposed seer, as I'm sure you gathered from the orientation, but yes, there is more that you don't know."

H.S. paused for a moment, watching a young woman walk her dog on the pink sand. He turned back to Willoughby. "How soon did you know about the lasers, the generator, and the titanium? Did you discover this on your own, or was it Antonio or one of the others that brought it to your attention? I thought we had hidden our toys quite cleverly."

"Not cleverly enough to get past Antonio. He told me about them. How did a gateway on the lowest deck of the ship operate a doorway in your closet? That was my contribution—I helped Sydney and Dr. O'Grady find the closet doorway."

"How?"

"I saw numbers hovering for a moment on the air when Sydney first gave me a tour of the ship. They were equations like the ones I saw in the Certus Grove building."

H.S. narrowed his eyes. He seemed to want to pursue the numbers issue, but decided against it. He returned to the questions Willoughby had asked. "The closet in my room was designed to be at the exact apex of the power arc generated in the gateway. We used the titanium ribs of the ship to multiply and focus the effect. The gateway is not tied to a single hole, but was designed to continually tune itself in to the closest, strongest hole available from any given point where the ship may be. When close to a big hole, it can facilitate both the transfer across space only—a process we call '*skimming*'—as well as the transfer through time that you are already familiar with.

"Our doorway here in Bermuda, for example is built on a small, stationary hole, which allows it to bridge to an enormous, stable hole in ocean depths not far from this island. The Absconditus may well have been tuned to that same large hole."

"What is *skimming?*"

"We haven't time today to go into detail. Suffice it to say that we have almost a hundred doorways worldwide, and they are all connected. The gateway at the top of the Certus Grove building alone is tied to a dozen different doorways. It will eventually be tied by way of a small, stable hole, to a doorway at Antonio's Corner Barber. A very simplistic explanation is that we use the magnetic charge of stable holes to slingshot matter around. I know that is not a completely satisfactory explanation, but it will have to do."

Willoughby had finished the oatmeal. He tasted and then devoured the cup of fruit on his tray. "You still haven't explained the construction of the Absconditus. Why was it built more like a war ship than an exploration vessel?"

"It wasn't. Your error is in misunderstanding the true mission of the Absconditus. The ship was built for arctic excavation. The lasers are to cut a path through the ice. The titanium hull is to keep ice from closing in and crushing the ship. The nuclear generator is to power the ship when arctic winds are too harsh for sails."

"Why arctic exploration?"

"Willoughby, we are a clandestine organization. We disseminate information to the members of the organization on a need-to-know only basis."

Willoughby narrowed his eyes. "I just survived two attempts on my life. At least 24 people have died and I have friends who are still unaccounted for. I would say that makes me 'need to know.'"

H.S. turned, his shrewd gaze bearing down on Willoughby. "Okay. Hidden under the ice less than thirty miles from the pole, is one of the largest and most unusual stationary holes we've ever uncovered. Your mission to France was, in an indirect way, designed to prepare you for the much larger mission of accessing this hole. We call it a *prime hole*."

"A *prime hole?*"

"Yes. We believe that it's one of the world's core holes—a hole tied to the heart of mother earth. We have long theorized that prime holes anchor a planet's timeline. Due to their strength and constancy, we also believe that these holes can connect us to holes in the distant reaches of our galaxy, possibly even our universe. We believe it might be possible to use this hole to skim through the galaxy in much the same way as we skim between spaces here on earth."

"Why is this hole so important?"

"We are operating somewhat in the dark right now. Our predecessors long planned for the day when we would find the theoretical hole. They collected data for centuries to help us locate, contain, and learn to control such an extraordinary resource. But the data has been lost, which brings us to our second challenge, and to the number string I asked you about."

Willoughby took a nibble of his toast, listening intently.

H.S. pursed his lips. "To fully understand what I am going to tell you, Willoughby, we need to go back about twelve years." He paused, looking back over the railing. A pair of gulls had seemed to notice him eating and swooped over to investigate. They lighted several feet away from the table. H.S. shooed them away, and then walked over and seated himself at the table. He leaned forward, clasping his hands together.

"When I became Managing Director of Observations, Inc., I was entrusted with the data we had collected on the prime hole. The information was deemed so sensitive that I was compelled to wear it on my physical person at all times. It was my job to see that it didn't fall into the wrong hands. The data was encoded into a unique molecular computer, one that is completely flat. I wore it around my neck, beneath my shirt. Shortly after you turned three years old, this computer was stolen from me. Time as we know it now stands at risk. What happened on the Absconditus is only a shadow of what may happen if someone is able to learn how to use that hole before we can properly safeguard it."

"There was a girl on the ship who helped us escape. I knew her from school. I think she was sent there to spy on me. She said they were looking for a pendant, or something."

"Yes. That is what the computer was disguised to look like—an ordinary pendant. It appears, however, that someone is quite aware that the pendant is more than it seems."

"You say someone. I thought it was that group with the mark."

H.S. sucked in a deep breath. "We thought the Cult of the Mark was all we were dealing with. Now, I don't know. They may be working with or for someone else. Nothing we know of them would indicate an ability to skirt our defenses as easily as they did. I don't know how much they understand. Do they know of the prime hole? Have they already found it and just need the pendant to learn how to control it? Only one thing is perfectly clear to me—we *must* find that pendant before they do."

"Wait, if this cult didn't steal the pendant, who did?"

H.S. sighed. He looked down for a moment, and then unclasped his hands. "The man who stole my pendant, Willoughby, was your father, Gustav."

Willoughby stared at H.S., stunned. A bite of toast lay half chewed in his mouth. When he finally recovered enough to chew again and swallow, the bite felt like lead going down. "*My father?*"

"Yes," H.S. nodded. He reached beneath his shirt and pulled out a gold chain. "He also stole this gold chain." The chain had blemishes and pock marks on it and looked very old. "I want you to read something for me, Willoughby. It's a clipping from the *London Times*. I was very angry at Sydney when they published it. She was careless." He handed over the newspaper clipping. Willoughby scanned the article. It was the same article he had snatched from Antonio's shop, with that haunting picture of Sydney in medieval dress.

"I've, uh, I've read this…Were the chain and the staff found with the skeleton?"

H.S. nodded. "We have been watching all artifacts that turned up from earlier centuries. As I explained to you earlier, time works to return things to their rightful place. We were confident your father's remains would turn up."

"*Remains?*" Willoughby felt as if someone had punched him in the gut. H.S. looked over, his face drawn.

"Your father died in another time, Willoughby. It has happened. We can't change that. The fact that his remains were returned means time *meant* for it to happen this way." He looked down at the tips of his shoes. "It's one of the reasons that I moved up the recruitment age for you so you could go on this mission." Willoughby opened his mouth to speak, but H.S. stopped him. "Let me explain. It's important for you to understand how everything relates. A hidden piece of parchment was found in the staff. I shared parts of what was written on the parchment with you at the orientation meeting. Do you recall?"

Willoughby blinked. "Yeah... 'Mathematician, beware of the Beelzebub.' It was a letter from Nostradamus to his son, wasn't it?"

H.S. leaned against the rail. "Yes, Willoughby—a letter signed by Nostradamus, hidden in a staff found next to human remains that, according to the dental records, belonged to your father."

The words washed over Willoughby. For a long moment, only the sound of the waves crashing against the shore and the lonely cry of the gulls overhead penetrated the silence. He looked at his unfinished eggs-Benedict and pushed the tray away. "You're saying that you think my father *was* Nostradamus, aren't you?" he managed to croak.

H.S. considered the question. "For a time, yes... I think he may have been the Nostradamus who was a seer.

Perhaps the Michel de Nostradame who was a physician, the man who disappeared when he was unable to save his own wife and child from the plague—perhaps that was the true 16th century man."

Time seemed to slow to a crawl. Willoughby was having a hard time getting his mind around the revelation. He gulped and looked away. "I need to hear the whole story."

H.S. breathed in. He slowly stood and walked back to the rail. He turned back toward the table, rocked forward on his feet, and clasped his hands behind his back. He had the air of a man ready to share a painful memory.

"We hired Gustav to work on a platform for us in Peru. He lived a very erratic life back then, never long in one place. He was a secretive man, haunted by demons he would not discuss. He rarely spoke of his family, and never gave an explanation for his elusive lifestyle, but all in all, he *was* brilliant. While he was deemed too unstable to invite into the organization, we did use his services. We tried to keep the purpose of his work unclear, but he saw through us. He guessed what we were really building.

"About a week before the project was finished, your father broke through security and headed straight for the unsecured time hole. Luckily, I happened to be there that day. One of the security guards tried to stop him. They thought they could talk to him, reason with him. But he was wild, out of his mind. He said they had found him, and he had to go."

"Who had found him?"

"We don't know Willoughby. Perhaps the same people who attacked the Absconditus? I got to the platform just as he was about to jump into the raw hole. I called to him. He let me come up. We spoke. He knew about my pendant somehow and wanted me to give it to him. I couldn't do that. He grabbed for it. In the scuffle, the chain broke and it, along with the pendant, fell from my neck. Gustav snatched them just as a piece of unfinished platform gave way. He tumbled down, into the unsecured hole.

H.S. paused. When he spoke again, his voice was lower. "The pendant was always running, charging itself from my own magnetic aura much like an automatic watch charges itself by the movement of the arm wearing it. The computer was programmed to locate and map new time-hole possibilities around me, and to help me gauge the strength of these holes. It was not a passive, but an active piece of technology. It would have called attention to itself for someone able to read the ripples of time."

H.S. peered at Willoughby as if to emphasize the possible implications of the statement.

"And?" Willoughby said, unwilling to let the man know that he well understood the implications.

H.S. shrugged. "We searched for your father, but to no avail. Our best estimations, judging from star map calculations that Dr. O'Grady helped us uncover, put his whereabouts somewhere in the 16th century. When his remains were discovered in the cave in Oban, Scotland, we meticulously searched the cave. We found the staff and the chain, but we're certain that the molecular computer was never there. It has a residual signature we should have been able to detect. We have to find it, Willoughby."

Biting back a hot surge of anger, Willoughby glared. "You knew I might meet my father in France. Were you planning to tell me, or just wait and see what happened?"

H.S. stared back at him, unblinking. "I don't know. I hadn't decided what I would do. I wasn't even sure I would let you go through with the assignment. I wasn't sure how this knowledge would affect you. Would it put you in more or less danger?"

Willoughby scoffed. "So, instead, you put me on a ship full of murdering cut-throats who kill everyone in sight. What a great plan! You might have told the rest of team. Of course, two of them are who knows where—lost somewhere in the corridors of time. I want out, H.S. I no longer want any part of this."

H.S. bowed his head. He had the look of a wounded bird—a guilty, wounded bird. He looked up again, holding Willoughby's gaze. "I did tell the team, Willoughby. They knew."

The words hit Willoughby like a dagger. He fought to keep hot tears from coming. "Antonio, James Arthur, Sydney—they all knew?"

H.S. nodded.

Willoughby pushed away from the table. Despite the pain in his shoulder and his dizziness, he stumbled away from H.S. toward the other end of the veranda. He stood at the railing and looked out over the view that had, moments ago, seemed so warm and magical and inviting. Now, everything around him seemed suddenly plastic and cold. He brushed at his eyes. *Why was he crying? Why couldn't he better control his emotions?*

Despite the fact that his father had been gone for over twelve years, he had always hoped that he would someday find him, that he would bring him back. What kind of true friend would keep something so personal from him? He knew he was reeling from his ordeal on the Absconditus and possibly still in shock, yet there was something else—a fear that maybe his friends had been right in not telling him. *What if his father did masquerade as the seer Nostradamus? What if he was somehow connected with the ones that took the Absconditus?* At last, he wiped an arm across his eyes and looked back toward H.S.

"Does anything besides the staff and chain connect my father with Nostradamus?"

H.S. hadn't moved from where he leaned against the rail. "There are certainly a number of curiosities. If the seer Nostradamus was actually from 21st century America, it would explain the accuracy of his predictions."

Willoughby sniffed, looking back. "I…I find it hard to believe. What about Nostradamus' letters to his son? The people of that time were convinced that the seer was Michel de Nostradame."

"Yes," H.S. nodded. "It is possible that your father was merely befriended by the real man—that they became friends or partners somehow. It is also possible that when Michel disappeared after being unable to save his family, he disappeared for good. It was a couple of years before a man, *claiming* to be Michel de Nostradame, came back, and references from the period suggest he had changed in many ways during his absence."

"So you're saying my dad stole your computer and chain, and then traveled back in time so he could knock off a man called Nostradamus and become an infamous seer? *Why?*"

H.S. sighed. "I didn't say he knocked off anyone. I do not think your father was a bad person, Willoughby. I think he was being pursued by someone. I think he found himself in a strange land and had to improvise. Perhaps he tried to nurse Michel back to health, but failed. Maybe, in an effort to communicate through the ages, he assumed the identity of Michel and began to write his predictions, his quatrains. That's why I asked you to study the quatrains.

Perhaps they were an attempt to get a message to us, a message to *you*. Scrawled across the back of the parchment from Nostradamus to his son was the number sequence I told you earlier. Who would know what that sequence meant but you? Perhaps the real son that letter was meant for was you."

Willoughby considered the words. "Why did you lie to me? You told me you didn't know where my father was, or if he was alive."

"That's not completely accurate. From a certain perspective, I told you the truth. The remains found in the cave are that of a man in his late seventies. Traveling in time, we might be able to find your father in his forties or fifties. If we can find him, he will be alive, just not in this time period."

Willoughby wiped at his eyes. "Will we be able to bring him back?"

H.S. looked away. "I don't know Willoughby. It would depend on what your father wants, on what time will allow." H.S. moved slowly back to one of the metal table chairs and seated himself. "There's something I need to say to you, Willoughby, but I don't want to say it when we're 30 feet apart."

Willoughby looked up, tears still streaked across his cheek. H.S. motioned for him to come back to the table. After a moment's hesitation, he did. He sat, leaning back in the wrought iron chair feeling miserable. H.S. clasped his hands again on the table.

"I made a mistake—a terrible mistake. Antonio and Sydney begged me to let them tell you, but I thought it was best to wait. I didn't then, nor do I now, know if any of what happened with the Absconditus is related to our search for your father. Please don't blame the others. Not even James Arthur was keen on the plan once he came to know you. But they trust me. This time, I let everyone down."

Willoughby was trying to hide the crop of fresh tears leaking from his eyes. He found it hard to meet H.S.'s gaze. He, too, had held back information that could have been valuable to the team. He had meant to tell Antonio sooner, but he wasn't sure what he had really seen, and with all that was happening as he was recruited into Observations, Inc., it didn't seem as important. When he heard about the Petersburg break-in and realized it was important, he told Antonio, but it was too late by then. Could it have made a difference in the capture of the Absconditus? Could it have saved any of the lives lost? He found it hard to think.

"How do you know Gustav didn't just destroy the pendant?"

"We don't," H.S. admitted. "But I know how the machine was built. He would have had a hard time destroying it. Besides, I think the loss of the crystal computer, and the tragedy of the Absconditus, are somehow related. Gustav clutched the chain even in death. My suspicion is that he knew it linked him to his true life, his true identity. Maybe he believed someone would figure things out someday. Maybe he thought it might be you and that you would come for him." His words trailed off.

Willoughby sat there, staring blankly at the ocean. "So, what now? We have dangerous information at large. We have a seer who may or may not be my father, and may or may not have the computer that holds this dangerous information. We suspect that there are others after this computer, or '*pendant*.' These others seem to have technology equal to or greater than our own." He sat suddenly forward in the chair. "I have information, H.S., which you're not aware of."

H.S. gave him a curious stare. Willoughby adjusted his arm on the pillow before continuing.

"I did tell Antonio on the ship, but I don't think he had a chance to relay the information. I think I may have seen the man who is pulling the strings. I think he's the head of this cult who has been watching us—who was responsible for the attack on the Absconditus."

It was H.S.'s turn to lean back in his chair. Willoughby carefully explained about the time freeze, about seeing the face staring at him out of the light and not knowing where it came from, and about the conversation he overheard between the man who owned that face and the tattooed man who had been photographing Antonio's shop. H.S. listened carefully, not interrupting. When Willoughby was done, he tapped a finger on the tabletop, seeming to be lost in thought.

"You say the tattooed man referred to this man as Mr. B?"

"Yeah," Willoughby said. "The ones that took over the ship referred to someone they called 'BL' or the 'Big Man.' They called me a special prize for him. Do you think it could be the same guy?"

"Hmm...Mr. B, Big Man, BL...Could this be the same entity associated earlier with the cult? Could this be Beelzebub?" H.S. shook his head. "I don't know, Willoughby."

Willoughby gulped, looking down at his empty plate. "Uh, do you think...Do you think I messed up by not telling you earlier? Could I have helped prevent all this?"

"I think we're all asking ourselves could we have helped prevent this. Perhaps if we had each done things differently, the outcome could have been affected. Perhaps it would have made no difference at all. I do know one thing," H.S. forced a smile. "I know that you, Willoughby, *are* a prize." He pointed down at Willoughby's plate. "For now, eat. We need to get you better."

Willoughby reluctantly picked up his fork and began eating the eggs. H.S. watched him for a moment, his mind far away in thought. At last, he spoke.

"Those who attacked us a few days ago, Willoughby, spent months in planning this attack. They had already infiltrated our defenses long before you were recruited. If there is any blame here, it is on me for being too convinced of our technological superiority. I should have been more careful. Had you told me this earlier, I don't think it would have changed anything. The plans of our attackers were too far along."

Willoughby breathed in, a sense of relief flooding over him. A seagull swooped low, making a loud cry. H.S. stood, giving Willoughby another tight smile.

"Now, I suggest you eat quickly. If you choose to take lunch on the veranda as well, you may want to do the same. These gulls mean business." He pushed his wrought iron chair back and stood. "Get some rest today. We leave on my yacht tomorrow evening. You have a whole day to regain your strength. Dr. Kensington will be around in the early afternoon. I have things to attend to, but I'll be back in the morning. I've given Sydney and Dr. O'Grady an assignment on the other side of the island. I thought you might like a day to yourself. Sydney may sneak in for a moment when she's back, but it should be late. You can always pretend to be asleep if you're not in the mood for a chat."

Willoughby puffed out his cheeks. "Thanks."

With that, H.S. was gone. Willoughby breathed in deeply. This was no longer only about Observations, Inc., or mathematics, or adventure, or even saving or impressing his friends. He had been meant to find H.S. For whatever reason, he was already a part of this, even before he knew. Now that he did know, there was nothing for it but to accept his quest, whatever that quest might be. There was no running away. There was no turning back.

For the rest of the day and until the sun sank to touch the water in a blaze of color before him, Willoughby alternated between resting, reading the few books H.S. had left him on Nostradamus, and standing for long moments at the rail of the veranda, staring out over the pink sand, the turquoise ocean, and the blue, blue sky. Sydney did sneak in just after it got dark. Willoughby followed H.S.'s suggestion and pretended to be asleep.

"Hey," Sydney whispered. He didn't respond, his eyes shut tight. She stood there a long moment. "Well, I just wanted you to know that, uh, that I did want to tell you about your father. I had a big fight with H.S. about it, but…H.S. has been like a second father. I'm sorry."

Willoughby still didn't respond, though a tear may have escaped his eye. He tried to push his face toward the pillow so she wouldn't see. Finally, she left. When he was sure that she was gone for good, he opened his eyes and stared at the ceiling.

The last thing he thought of before drifting off to sleep for real was his earlier talk with Sydney. Things felt different when he thought of Sydney now. The trials they had been through together made them more, well, more sensitive around each other. Everything she said seemed to hurt, or to send his heart into dancing cartwheels. How weird was that?

He thought about sitting on the veranda with her, not saying a word, just watching the sun set over the ocean. *Well, okay,* Willoughby had to admit to himself; *this is Sydney—maybe the part about not saying a word is too much of a stretch.*

29

The Blind Eye

Antonio drifted back from the verge of unconsciousness. He was being dragged. The terrain under him was hard and uneven. His leg burned with every movement as if it were on fire. *Who was dragging him?* He tried to focus his eyes. Pain shot through his whole body and he gasped. He tried to raise his head but could not seem to make the muscles work. There was too much pain. The black head of the fanged beast had snapped down on him. *Was it dragging him?* A shiver of terror racked him. *How many times had the beast bitten him? Was his leg even there anymore?*

"Keep still," a panting voice commanded. "You need to listen—listen carefully Antonio!"

Antonio felt a flood of relief. Whoever was dragging him, it was *not* the monster.

"We're not out of this yet. You're heavy. I'll have trouble moving you myself. Can you hear me? We need to get away from the water—somewhere under the rock."

Antonio recognized the voice. It was T.K., the cabin girl, or…His mind was drifting. What had that brutal man called her? He tried to think. *Princess*…He had called her *child* princess. In fact, his exact words had been "*the child princess who didn't die.*" The man's name had been Belzar. They were on a ship—the Absconditus. Belzar had aimed a gun at her. He had saved her. He remembered the closet, the glowing knob. Then they had been falling into the dark waters of a cave, and a black beast had risen up from the water. It had attacked. He saw in his mind the cabin girl, T.K., slicing at the beast with a fury and intensity he could never have imagined of one so attractive and petite. She had struck the beast at least three or four times, forcing the massive head to finally let go.

Antonio tried to pull up, but a wave of pain washed over him and the world went suddenly black. He drifted in and out after that, through what seemed to be hours of pain and nausea. He vaguely remembered T.K. bending over him, staring in his eyes, and then cutting his pant leg open. Finally, he managed to move his head.

"What happened?" he croaked in a harsh whisper. He noted that T.K. had a blood-soaked rag tied around her forehead and a line of drying blood on her cheek. She turned toward him.

"Good, you've regained consciousness. We need to get you up under that ledge. If you're asking why we're both still alive—why the beast didn't kill us—I got a lucky slice across its nose. It sank away, but you've been out for hours. It will be back soon…can you move?"

Antonio was distracted from the pain for a moment. *How was he able to see?* They were in a cave with no visible opening, yet there was light. He studied the cave ceiling. It was alive and glowing.

"The light…the ceiling…"

T.K. followed his gaze. She wiped sweat from her brow. It was hot and humid in the cave. "It's glowing algae. It reacts to vapors from the water. Smell that metallic scent? Kind of like a cross between rust and sulfur? That triggers it. Sometimes it's brighter, sometimes it's almost dark. When the waters are being agitated, more vapors are released and the algae glows bright." T.K. stepped toward a jagged wall of rock only partially covered by the glow. She pointed at a dark crevice.

"In there is where I need to move you. I need you to go in first, so I couldn't really drag you."

Antonio took a pained breath and forced a look at his leg. The pain was barely tolerable when he tried to move it. He dropped his head back, relaxing the leg. "How bad is it?"

"I'm no doctor, but I don't think it's broken. The fangs didn't hit an artery. Once the poison works its way out of your system, I think you'll live."

"Poison?" Antonio moaned.

"It's mild," T.K. answered. "I'm not sure if it actually injects venom or if it just infects you with nasty bacteria from its teeth. Either way, I've lived through it before. Your chances are at least passable."

"Thank you for that," Antonio mumbled. T.K. turned from him and started to carefully scale the wall. Antonio watched, his eyes narrowing.

"Where are you going?"

T.K. climbed higher—as if she hadn't heard the question. Finally, as she began to carefully pull herself onto a thin ledge, possibly twenty feet up the rock face, she spoke. "I told you before—the beast will be back. He's been gone too long already. If we don't stop him somehow, we both die."

Antonio watched, spellbound, as the girl pirouetted ever so slowly until her back was to the rock and her face peered out over the dark waters. She eased her hand down and pulled her knife.

"You have a plan then?" Antonio asked.

"No. I just like the view," T.K. snapped. "Of course I have a plan!"

Antonio waited a long moment. "Well?"

"Well what?"

"Are you…going to tell me?"

"No."

"Am I part of this plan?"

"Absolutely," T.K. flashed him a tight smile. "You're the bait… I suggest it's in your best interest to push yourself into that crevice beneath the overhang." She pointed again to the dark space near the base of the rock wall.

"*The bait?*" Antonio tried to move, pushing himself up from the cold cave floor, but he fell back, wincing from intense pain. "I…do not think…this is such a good plan."

"That's why I didn't want to tell you about it." T.K. watched the dark waters, adding in a barely audible mumble, "I should have known. It's what comes of getting mixed up with H.S."

It took Antonio a moment to get the pain completely under control. When he finally spoke it was through gritted teeth. "You speak…as if you know something about him."

"I told the Captain not to work for him. He shouldn't have ignored me." There was bitterness in the girl's voice. Antonio thought he saw her wipe at a tear. He decided to change the subject.

"How do you know this place? How did you know that—Belzar?"

"That *Belzar* is a thief and a murderer. A long time ago, he worked for H.S."

"H.S. never mentioned—"

"Yeah, well, I'm sure there are a lot of things H.S. never mentioned to you. Unfortunately, now isn't the time to discuss them."

Antonio was feeling dizzy from trying to talk, but it kept his mind off the idea of being bait. "If I am to attract... the beast, I deserve to know my chances."

T.K. bent her knees slightly, her knife at the ready. She sighed. "Better if you can make it to that crevice... When the beast surfaces, you don't need to do anything. It will smell you. It knows that you're hurt, that you're weakened. You are frightened, aren't you? It needs to sense your fear."

"Oh, I think I can play that part well." Antonio tried to force a smile.

"It will strike at you without hesitation, then, I'll drop on its head and slash out its eyes."

Antonio thought for a moment. "What if you miss or are thrown off?"

T.K. shrugged. "Well... then we both die horribly."

Antonio couldn't help it. The plan was so hopeless that all he could do was offer a weak laugh. He breathed out a sigh. "Die horribly you say, as if it is a stroll down the boulevard..."

"Life is a stroll down the boulevard. What do you want me to say? Every street eventually ends."

"What are we facing? Is it a giant sea snake?"

T.K. wiped at her forehead again. "No. You didn't see its whole body—only its neck. It has the body of a giant seal."

Antonio thought for a moment. He almost stopped breathing. "A plesiosaurus? All the way back to the Jurassic...? No. We couldn't have traveled so far back. Not without a connecting bridge."

"Tell that to the plesiosaurus..."

T.K. looked up, suddenly tensing. "Push to the crevice, Antonio—NOW! *It's here!*"

Antonio heard the water ripple. He tried to rise onto his elbows, fighting to push toward the crevice, glancing around for anything he could use as a weapon. He grabbed at a medium-sized rock and slid it over. The beast burst out of the water, splashing a wave of warm stink over him. Its eyes glowed deep amber in the dim light. It pushed its head higher until it was a good twenty feet out of the water. The head was hideous, flat and pointed, and at least five to six feet wide. Antonio was afraid it would see T.K. on her ledge of rock, but she had frozen, becoming absolutely still. The beast spun its head, as if looking for her, and then turned back to Antonio. It trumpeted in a deafening roar, spraying spittle and seaweed all around. Antonio pulled his hands to his ears and roared back. The beast coiled its head to attack. It shot forward, sharp rows of fangs bared in an angry hiss. Antonio rolled sideways, pulling his rock to block the fangs. At the edge of his vision, a blur of motion collided with the darting head. T.K. was only able to hold on for a matter of seconds and was then thrown sideways, back into the pool of odorous water. She had made her few seconds count, though. The beast coiled and screamed, protecting a badly bleeding left eye.

It plunged back into the pool, coiling and uncoiling its neck. Its cries literally shook the cave. As it writhed in the water, it pushed back, slamming against the far wall.

Then it was gone, plummeting back to the depths from which it came. The cave grew silent. Antonio heard the sound of his heart beating and his gasps of ragged breath. He heard T.K. struggling back toward the rock ledge where she began to pull herself up. Moments later, the beast shot out of the water again. T.K. rolled up onto the ledge. The writhing beast turned its good eye on her. It trumpeted again, slamming once again against the far wall before shooting out in a beeline for the girl. Its head reared into a striking pose. Fangs bared, the beast coiled, trumpeting wildly, then its open jaws shot down in a lightning strike. T.K. screamed.

30

Time Fusion

Samuel Allan Wasser carefully polished a stretch of mahogany rail that curved along the upper sideboard of H.S.'s forty-foot yacht. The morning was still soft gray as a slight mist was rising up from the gently lapping waters of the expansive marina. He liked the tart tang of the salt-water air in the early morning and the bite of the cool sea breeze. For too long, he had allowed himself to be pinned to his duties on land, stuck in empty board rooms and dark limousines. He should be celebrating his escape from duty and deliberation. Why couldn't he enjoy his return to the sea? He looked over a spit of pink sands toward a ridge of low hills, dark-green pools of shadow looming out of the morning fog. The boy was somewhere there, in their private facility along the ridge. He had almost died H.S. said. Yet he did not. He lived while others were now lost. Sam considered this, pushing hard at the railing.

Willoughby knew him as simply *Sam, the chauffeur.* And so he had been to the boy. He had observed the boy twice a day, Monday to Friday and occasionally on weekends. He had ferried him to and from that appalling snobbish school he was forced to attend, and occasionally, to and from other events. He had been observing the boy for almost two years now. Antonio's opinions were valued, but were not enough. He had wanted to get to know the boy for himself. He applauded Willoughby's disgust for pompous academia, his mathematic brilliance, his brooding sarcasm, his penchant for bravado and longing for adventure. Most of all, he admired the boy's unspoiled good nature. It had been a hard decision to make, to bring the boy into the fold. Had it been the right decision?

Sam smiled to himself. Willoughby never suspected he was more than a chauffeur. Of all the hidden things within his secretive organization, perhaps *he* was the best-kept secret of all. Born to money, he had soon tired of it. As a young college prep student, he had been determined to seek out something extraordinary to do with his sizeable fortune. So it was that when, during a brief college stint at Princeton, he crossed paths with a minor Cambridge professor named Hathaway Simon, peddling wild tales of the origins and nature of time, he had lent a listening ear. Most of his contemporaries thought the man mad, but he didn't speak like a madman. He spoke with an authority that hinted at something stranger than wild theories. He spoke as if he had real experience channeling time.

Thirty-seven years later, here they were—he looking every bit of fifty and H.S. having seemed to barely age a decade. The man did have experience in time, extensive experience as it turned out. The evolution of Observations, Inc. had been bizarre, but exhilarating.

Looking over the gleaming wood rail, his mind brushed on H.S. He had confronted him about his ability to defy aging. The stout man had claimed it was the result of his frequent travels outside of time. Sam had begun to suspect there was more to it than that. He had traveled outside of time too—a considerable amount of time—yet he looked merely young for his actual age of fifty-nine. Now, with the events of the past week, coupled with the disaster the previous year in St. Petersburg, Hathaway had begun to hint at a far more complicated tale. He was, he confessed, a survivor of an ancient organization, one that had been wiped out by a calamity of epic scale. He claimed to be one of a kind.

Sam wasn't sure he believed the man. Still, H.S. had delivered on the time travel technology. He *was* brilliant, and there were few like him around. Yet, what, exactly, was his "*kind?*"

Sam's head came up with a quick snap. H.S. was approaching from a far corner of the pier. He held two steaming cups in his hands. Most likely, it was fresh brewed coffee from his private store of exotic beans. The man would probably sip from both cups before climbing aboard and offer the one he least favored to Sam. He walked with the air of an earl, ready to graciously bestow a fiefdom on some unsuspecting courtier. When they first met, Sam had sensed nobility in the man. His theories had seemed pure madness, and the amount of funding he asked for was enough to run a fair-sized country, but if even a fraction of the technology actually worked...

He could never have guessed how successful his collaboration with H.S. would become. After a demonstration of the first observation site, he knew. He had stumbled upon secrets that any group in the world would fight to control. If he chose, the wealth of the world could be at his feet. People would lie for their secrets, steal for them, and yes, unrepentantly kill for them. He had no illusions about their precarious position. So, he had been careful, ever so careful. He helped the professor drop out of sight, his papers and theories conveniently disappearing. As for himself, the billionaire socialite became a haunted and tormented hermit. He kept himself apart from the world of men, allowing Sam, the chauffeur, to be born. Of course, that was only the beginning. He set up an obscure umbrella corporation. All the new company's dealings were funneled through a labyrinth of foreign shell companies. He set up a pseudo headquarters in Japan. His Asian Board of Directors had never actually met him. All company business was conducted by conference call or email. Every plan was laid down in layers, with considerable smoke and mirrors and never a smoking gun.

Not even Sydney suspected that *Sam, the chauffeur*, was her father's senior partner. How could a mere chauffeur control one of the shrewdest men in all of Asia— a legend among the Tokyo elite? True, the Tokyo faction had wanted to see quick financial results from their relatively sizeable contributions, but that had been easy enough. Observations, Inc. yielded prestigious and financially lucrative finds from all over the globe by cleverly mining the pages of time.

As the company grew, however, Sam had made it clear that money was not what he was about. He had grown to want something more. His dreams were of spreading a footprint across *all* time, not just a decade or a century. He wanted to touch the future as well as the past. He wanted to know what it felt like to see God's perspective.

Was everything they had done, everything they had built over the past forty years now falling apart? *How could someone have learned their secrets?* Fewer than twenty people knew what the company was really about. Each had been meticulously reviewed before being brought into confidence, and even then, he had his inner circle watched every second of the day. Their houses and phones were bugged. Even H.S. fell under his scrutiny. Only one in the circle had escaped his full scrutiny. The boy... Willoughby had seemed so, so innocent. He had been unable to suspect the boy of any guile or foolishness. *Had he been mistaken?*

H.S. stepped aboard the gently rocking boat. Sam straightened as the robust man handed him a cup of steaming coffee, then stood, sipping his own like a king who has deigned to share a moment with the stable boys. Sam ignored the arrogance. He was used to Hathaway by now. He took a sip from his coffee, suspicious that he was not the first to sip from it. He looked out toward the hills, giving H.S. a quick nod of thanks. Truth be told, he had enjoyed watching Willoughby. With no family of his own, it had been nice to feel, at times, like the boy was some favored nephew, or perhaps, a long estranged son. He turned, leaning against the rail, and studied H.S.

"You didn't report to me of your discussion with the boy."

H.S. stared into his coffee with a smile. "Come now, Sam. We both know you were monitoring the entire conversation."

Sam didn't argue. "Anything new to report this morning?"

H.S. wrinkled his nose. "Since 10 pm last night? No, I think not." He let out a heavy sigh. "We must let time and our people probe through this latest mess. I expect we will have answers soon."

Sam pursed his lips. "Why do I feel, my friend, that after thirty-seven years, and billions of dollars of my money, I scarcely know what our little ventures are truly about?"

H.S. smiled. He patted Sam on the arm. "Because, my dear fellow, you are smarter than you look."

Sam gave the wood rail a final half-hearted wipe, and then tucked his rag away. "When are you going to tell me who these people are? What was this mission really about?"

"I deal in time, Sam. I've told you what I know in the present. The past and the future are subjects of speculation."

"You've told me everything, have you? Like where you were when all this started unfolding? You may smooth-talk your way past the others, but not me."

"How can I talk to you about things I don't even fully understand myself? I have shared everything at this present moment that I can. When I know more, I shall tell you more."

With a flourish, H.S. turned and strode toward the control room. Technically, he did own the yacht, and Sam had tasked him to act like he did so as to protect his cover. H.S. didn't have to relish in the job, but then, that was H.S. Sam scanned the hatch while sipping again at his steaming brew. He had been involved with every phase of this beautiful vessel's construction, from the earliest sketches to the final plans, to the completed vessel's launch. No expense had been spared. He considered the sleek craft. It was a masterpiece of elegance and style, much like his beloved Absconditus, which now lay at the bottom of the ocean. Acting as "Captain" of the ship allowed him to take pride in making the polished wood shine, the brass fittings sparkle, and the tinted windows gleam. In truth, Sam liked pretending to be a working man, albeit an upper-crust working man. Funny how it seems that the very thing you are not is the thing you long to be.

He looked nervously toward the row of white condos just coming visible along the top of the ridge.

H.S. called out to him before ducking below. "I'll check in with the care facility and central ops to see if there's anything new. Anything you want me to ask them?"

Sam gave a distracted shake of his head. How could he explain his feeling that this boy, that Willoughby, was already a part of something that even H.S., even Observations Inc., with all its impressive technology, couldn't fathom?

H.S. lingered in the doorway a moment, studying him. When he finally ducked below and disappeared toward the front control room, he wasn't gone for long. Sam barely had time to get down half his coffee before Hathaway was stumbling back onto the deck, his eyes wide.

"How long have the control lights been flashing?"

Sam turned toward the man, somewhat annoyed by the accusation in his tone. A flashing glow reflected red from somewhere below. His brows knit in an expression of surprise. H.S. was moving quickly toward the gang plank.

"The magnetic detectors are going crazy. A full funnel collapse is in progress—guess where?"

Throwing his coffee into the bay, Sam crushed the cup, jamming it into his pocket.

"What does it mean?"

H.S. had almost reached him. "I don't know. I think it's safe to say, though, that Willoughby may have been more the focus of the mutiny on the Absconditus than we initially believed."

"What are they doing? Can we stop them?"

H.S. frowned. "I have no idea what this means or what they're up to."

"Do they have him?" Sam said more forcefully.

H.S. pulled up short, shaking his head. "Not yet. I'm still reading full vital signs."

Sam snapped into action, flinging himself over the rail onto the pier. "I'll bring up the car."

As he sprinted ahead toward the parking structure, he stole a glance back. H.S. had made it down the gang-plank and was already huffing as he fell into a trot behind him. Sam had rarely seen the man this agitated. Clearly, something more was happening than he knew. He wanted answers. He'd been patient long enough. He imagined the shape of a full magnetic collapse on the screen. It would look like a digital tornado. He had seen them before, when the time technology had amplified the gravity between branes to widen tunnels in time large enough to suck solid matter through, even living matter. *Were they trying to take the boy?*

With a sense of foreboding, he had to face facts. This was no terrorist organization or organized crime syndicate they were facing. No one had leaked their secrets to powers in this world. This was, well, this was from somewhere else. He felt the rush of adrenalin. *What had they unleashed?* Hair pricked up on the back of his neck.

If he was right, rushing to Willoughby's side may not be nearly enough.

31

Foresight

The squeaking of a cart wheel woke Willoughby. It took him a moment to place the sound. It was the little cart that the hospital, or convalescence center, or whatever this place was, used for wheeling in his meals. They called it a '*Tea Trolley.*' He cringed slightly as the squeak grew louder. *Couldn't they oil that wheel?* He pushed the covers up and rolled over, noting through cracked eyelids a dim, gray light from outside. A wafting smell of bacon hit his nose and he felt his stomach rumble. He rubbed at his eyes and slowly pushed up to a sitting position. "Hey," he said, still trying to clear his vision. He shook his head. "It's morning already? What time is it?"

He turned to look at the digital clock beside the bed. The numbers read 6:16. "A little early for breakfast isn't it?" He mumbled, turning to arrange the pillows behind him. He was about to lean back against the metal of the bed frame when another smell assaulted him. His head jerked back. This was a nasty, putrid smell. His eyes shot up, filled with alarm. It was the man pushing the cart to his bed. The man was black as pitch. He wore a white smock, pulled hap-hazardly over a bulging frame. His head was down and turned slightly away. He had not responded to any of the comments Willoughby had made.

Willoughby fought to focus his eyes better, rubbing the sleep out of them and wrinkling his nose. The closer the man got, the worse the smell became. It overpowered the smells of the breakfast. The man stopped pushing the trolley. Willoughby shrank back against the steel frame of his bed as a tingle ran down his neck. Something was wrong. The man pushing the cart didn't exactly walk, but rather, shuffled, like someone with palsy. In a quick glance, he noted that the grayish light bleeding from the edges of the curtains did not have the clarity of sunlight. It seemed more like a glow—a fuzzy light that shifted and fluttered. Here and there, he saw glimpses of spinning number strings.

The man had picked up the breakfast tray, almost gingerly, and turned to place it on Willoughby's night stand. His smock was obviously too small for him, gaping hideously at each button. Tattered jeans stuck out from the bottom of the smock, barely containing thick legs that led to enormous dilapidated sneakers. The sneakers and jeans were sopping wet. Bits of seaweed clung limply to the frayed cuff of the jeans, and trailed the laces of the shoes. The man had left a visible trail of water and seaweed along the tile floor. Willoughby studied the man. His frame seemed vaguely familiar. His putrid smell wafted over again. Willoughby felt his eyes sting. It was all he could do not to ask the man to get back, or go away, but something told him this would be a bad idea. *Where had he seen this man before?* He still couldn't see the man's face clearly.

Forearms rippling in tight curves, the man pointed to the breakfast tray on the low table beside the bed. He finally looked up. His face was scared and covered with open sores, as if something had been nibbling at him. He peered out with eyeballs that seemed to have been bleached of all color. Willoughby gasped. *He knew this man!* Protruding black lips split into a white-toothed grin. *This was Gates—the black man who had orchestrated the bloodbath on the Absconditus!* How had he gotten off the ship? What had happened to his face and eyes?

Gates seemed happy with Willoughby's look of shock and disbelief. He grinned even broader. "How be …our mathematical genius… this day?" he said in a rank, hoarse whisper. "He be…one to put two and two together, I think."

Willoughby recoiled anew from the smell. The air seemed forced from the man's mouth in a series of constricted spasms as the man did not seem to breathe. He would gulp air like a fish—just enough to force his words out. The man picked up a steak knife from the breakfast tray.

"This time, I think… we make sure he be armed."

He tried to hand Willoughby the knife, but Willoughby refused to take it. The man smiled a sick, crooked smile. He took the knife and jabbed it forcefully through the palm of his hand. Still grinning, he closed the hand into a fist and twisted his arm so that Willoughby could see the point of the knife poking out of the back of his fist. The man's skin had a sickly pallor and there was no blood at all from the knife wound.

"I think you be liking my trick?" the man hissed. He forced out a grunt of air in something like a laugh.

"Enough Gates," a voice called out of the shadows. The voice had a faintly familiar European accent. "Your fun is over for the time being."

The huge black man opened his fist, jerked the knife out of his hand, and placed it carefully back onto the breakfast tray. His sneer grew more intense as he slowly backed away from the bed. He stopped a few steps back, his white, bleached eyeballs still staring at Willoughby, unblinking.

"You must forgive his appearance," the voice continued, moving closer. With effort, Willoughby tore his eyes away from the spectacle of the white eyes glaring at him. He searched the room and located the source of the other voice. A tall figure stepped slowly into the light. The man had thin, bony features and wore a trench coat, buttoned to the neck. Willoughby knew him in an instant. *It was the same man he had seen when time froze near Antonio's shop, the same one he heard speaking afterward to the tattooed man.*

"I'm afraid our friend here has been in stasis at the bottom of the sea. I let him…sit there for a year or so before I called." The man came to a stop toward the center of the room.

"But," Willoughby mumbled. "He was on the ship."

"Yes," the tall man agreed. He strode forward again, seeming already bored with the conversation. "He was on the ship in *your* timeline. He sunk with the ship in *your* timeline. I don't operate in your timeline. I don't operate in any timeline—or, perhaps more accurately, I operate in all timelines. I sent Gates back to his own time, but kept him in the same space when I saved him at the last second. I put him in stasis there at the bottom of the ocean, a reminder of his pathetic failure. It has been a long, cold year for him, waiting for me to call." He stopped beside the huge black man. "You may have noticed he's not in the best of moods." Gates tensed. The tall man smiled, turning back to Willoughby.

"When I created this junction—a junction, by the way, is an intersection of timelines that creates a point slightly outside of time—I called him here. Time bleeds out very, very slowly from a junction. Do you understand what I'm telling you, what Gates is?" He stared down at Willoughby quizzically.

Willoughby probed the words in his mind. He didn't understand what the man was getting at. One thing was crystal clear, though. He returned the huge black man's piercing gaze, trying to see behind the glaring white eyes. "I know you're trying to frighten me. You purposely *aged* him, giving him the eaten face and the hideous eyes, and the foul smell, because you wanted," he pointed at the hulking form, forcing himself to swallow hard and complete the sentence. "You wanted him to intimidate me."

The tall man smiled, clapping softly. He had small, pointed teeth. "Bravo, but," he held up one long, bony finger, "intimidation is not the right word. Had I merely wanted to frighten you, I could have found much better means than this. No, the better phrase to use is, *warn you.*" He gave a slow sigh and stepped toward the bed. "I think it only fair that you know who you are dealing with." He glanced again at the white-eyed horror that stood as still as a statue, dripping on the floor.

"He does have a singular effect, though, don't you think?" Turning back to Willoughby, he licked his lips. "As I began to explain, he's not exactly dead. Your friend, Mr. Gates, has perhaps a thousand heartbeats left of life. He's just mostly dead. I control how quickly those final heartbeats tick away." His smile returned. "If he plays his cards right, those final beats could stretch to infinity."

"He's not my friend," Willoughby choked. This made the big man grin. Despite his revulsion and fear, Willoughby couldn't help but be fascinated. "How do you keep the final heartbeats at bay? Time slows during time travel, but it doesn't stop, at least not in my calculations."

"Yes, your calculations…That's the trouble. Your training is woefully incomplete." The man's smile had no warmth. "I could help you, Willoughby. I live the numbers of time. At present, you can merely observe them." He paused, his cold, blue eyes seeming to bore right through Willoughby's skin. "You do see them, don't you? You see layers of the complex mathematics of time, I know you do." The man was fishing. Seeing no response from Willoughby, he changed tack.

"Have you ever wondered why you see what you see? There is a reason, you know. I could tell you. I could teach you a mathematics that opens the universe to your call." He spoke softly, moving slowly to the foot of the bed. Watching Willoughby, he tapped his bony finger along the metal frame.

Willoughby blew out a breath. "Yeah, right. You'd make me like him." He pointed at the black man.

"No." The tall man continued to tap his finger, his eyes narrowing. "No, you could *never* be like him, Willoughby. You are something else entirely. Something special—more special than you know."

Willoughby didn't like the way the man said "*something special.*" He bit his lip.

"Anyway," the man continued, turning from the foot of the bed. "Gates is not my only…*pet*. I have created stasis-fields around hundreds of choices. I pull them just enough out of time to keep them from being seen. I keep them seconds away from total death until I need them. A rather unique army, wouldn't you say? At any particular moment, I could create a zombie scene more horrifying than the best Hollywood director could imagine." He barked a short laugh.

Willoughby pointed at the hulking shape of Gates. "That's why he doesn't bleed—his heart isn't beating, or it's beating too slowly to give him a pulse. But gravity—"

The man raised an eyebrow. "You are curious." He tilted his head slightly, studying Willoughby. "You have to be of the bloodline. Even though your hands betray that you are absolutely terrified, your brain refuses to shut down. There's curiosity in your eyes. That's good." He looked down, running his long thin finger along the cold metal of the bed frame. "Outside of time, the heart doesn't need to beat. There is no need for blood. Final heartbeats are more muscle spasms than anything else. They occur as the brain dies. I root my pets in their own time. I call them when I need them, allowing them to step out of their time for brief periods, functioning almost normally due to the stunting of time travel itself. Like a top set spinning, the soul has certain inertia. It continues to spin for a while. In stasis, however, seconds away from physical death, there are things lost. My pets eventually lose the ability to talk. Their reasoning is affected. They become somewhat, well, *volatile*."

The tall man stepped around the end of the bed frame, grinning. He sat down on the foot of the bed. "Mr. Gates may actually bleed a little at some point. But not today."

"Zombies are real?"

The man laughed. "I'm sorry, but I find it unbelievably comical how many myths my work has spawned." He pointed to the black man. "You see the reality there. Magnificent, isn't he? Did you know there are even cults created around the concept of the zombie? From time to time, I find human gullibility unimaginably useful."

Willoughby's eyes narrowed. "Wh—what are you? Do you control the Cult of the Mark?"

"Cult of the Mark?" The man returned a cold smile. "My, but you do your homework. Yes, I control the feeble cult—for what good it does me. It's so hard to find good help these days. I'm afraid that I have no answer that would make sense to you on the first question. It would take more time than I have today to help you understand who, or as you put it, *what* I am. Just say I am one of the hungry ones."

"You're a vampire?"

The man laughed again. "Did I suck Gate's blood? Heavens no! Next thing I know, you'll have me in some love triangle with a precocious female and a testosterone-laden werewolf. No." He bent his head down. "But I do feed. Power is the sustenance I crave. The *will* has a power I feast on. It is a power that holds time, that organizes space, that controls infinity, universe by universe."

Willoughby could barely speak. "That's why they call you Beelzebub, Prince of the Devils. You steal people's will."

"That is only one of my names. I have others—Azazel, Belial, Iblis, Keeper of the Underworld, the Dark Lord, Black Lazarus. I've had more names than you can count. I even have names that come from my hosts. Most recently, they called me *Doctor Death*."

"From the Third Reich?" Willoughby recalled that Dr. Death was the name of one of the few German war criminals who had never been caught.

"Beelzebub," the man mused, ignoring the question. "Because we are many…" He snapped his eyes up. "Yes. That is one of the favorites among my friends." He gave a sigh, brushing at the hem of his coat. "Speaking of friends," he rose to his feet, "your H.S. was certainly thorough. A cruise missile sent to sink the submersible meant to rescue Gates and his boys. Simultaneous charges on the bulkheads of the Absconditus so that she sank in minutes. It went down like a stone."

The man had a distinctive European accent. Thinking on the man's claim of being Dr. Death, Willoughby recognized it as German. The man moved closer. He was close enough that Willoughby could study the impeccably clean and pressed trench coat, buttoned tight from his knees all the way up to his collar. The man turned quickly and waved Gates away.

"Leave us," he commanded. The big fellow reacted slowly. His head came up with a growl, but seemed unable to do anything but heed the command. He gave a slow nod, whispering in a low growl, "I be seeing you later." He smiled his hideous grin, then turned and shuffled toward the small French door connecting the room with the veranda. A trail of dirty seaweed puddles marked his jerky gait. When the muscled arms yanked open the door, Willoughby caught a glimpse of a fully lighted veranda that seemed to be crawling with number strings. The light appeared to be a mix of several different shades of sunlight. It streamed in many directions at once, while trees swayed and didn't sway at the same time. There was a blinding flash. Willoughby saw shards of numbers whirling around its edges as if being sucked into a whirlpool. Then Gates was gone.

The tall man turned back to Willoughby. "So, we are alone."

Willoughby felt a pang of terror. The smooth, cool voice of this man was even more frightening with the white-eyed zombie, Gates, gone. Did this man, or demon, really have power over death—could he keep beings like Gates on the edge of dying indefinitely? What kind of technology would give him an ability to control space and time with such ease? He spoke of "hungry ones." Did that mean he wasn't alone, that there were others like him? What did he mean, "*Because we are many?*"

"Questions, questions," the man said, shaking his head. "You might as well speak them aloud. It makes the conversation go easier. No, I don't have ultimate power over death—not yet. I can play on the will of weak men, using them across time as I see fit for a time. I do use a form of technology for those who can understand it. To the brainless mass, my work is described by words such as 'witchcraft,' and 'dark magic.' "

The man was only a few feet away now. He seemed taller than Willoughby first thought. *Could he be growing, changing form here in this room?* He dismissed the thought, deciding it was a trick of the light. He thought back to the night when he had glimpsed him, first sticking his head through the rip in time, and then talking to the man covered in tattoos. What had that man's name been? Reese?

"How's Reese?" Willoughby said in barely more than a whisper. He was hoping that the question would throw the man off, but the tall man scarcely even blinked.

"Ah, yes. About that…I knew, of course, that you were listening." The man removed a pair of black, leather gloves slowly from his pocket and began to pull them on. "He is quite well, actually. I saw to it that he, Belzar, and that silly Indian girl managed to escape the ship after they fulfilled their purpose."

"Which was?" There was a slight quiver to Willoughby's voice.

"To help you and Sydney escape, of course." The man appeared irritated with the question. "Your other friends managed to wound Belzar before escaping themselves, but not seriously. He still has a part to play in this."

"Antonio and James Arthur escaped alive?"

"Yes, I believe that's what you called them. They are alive, but facing…challenges." The man placed a black, gloved hand on Willoughby's headboard. He was unnaturally thin and gaunt up close. Wispy white hair hung over his balding head. He had pulled it into a short ponytail which ran down his back. His eyes seemed to grow darker, as if they were drinking in all the shadows of the room. He raised an eyebrow.

"The one you call James Arthur has an appointment with a colleague of mine. I check in on him from time to time. He might be a candidate for my menagerie. For the time being, he's found himself quite a woman. *Oh, the tales he will tell*…She seems rather taken with him, which hopefully means she won't eat him." The man seated himself again on the edge of the bed. "He might make a good fly-boy."

Willoughby narrowed his eyes. "*Fly-boy?*" he managed, his voice barely a whisper.

"Of course," the man said with a matter-of-fact tone. "Beelzebub—Lord of the flies. You didn't think that referred to the pesky insect, did you?"

"You're insane. You're a nutca—" Willoughby never finished the word. He was suddenly aware of the man's unblinking, cold eyes. Pain shot through his arm.

"Yes. Reese spoke of the fly-boys. I thought you would have put that and Beelzebub together by now. You do remember the mention don't you? It's one of the few things that can scare the tattooed man. Didn't you notice? I brought one as my driver that night. I even parked where you could get a good look at him. I thought you might find him *interesting*."

Willoughby pushed back against the metal frame of the headboard. "What do you want of me?"

"Many things, but first, I want you to find the seer stone that H.S. calls the '*pendant*.' We will need that to complete your," he rose his eyebrows, "*education*."

"Why?" Willoughby hissed, feeling the pain in his shoulder again. "It's not a seer stone. It's a computer, and I have no idea where it is. Even if I did, why would I do anything for you? Because of you, lots of innocent people are dead. I was almost killed. My friends are missing, and that's only what I know about."

"That's the point, isn't it, Willoughby? Your friends *are* missing and there are lots of things you *don't* know about." He paused for a moment letting this sink in. "You'd be surprised at what you might want to do given the right circumstances. You see, it's easy to be brave when you have no concept of what there is to lose. I could help you find your friends if you really want to find them. I know things about the girl, too. Sydney is her name? Her future is…interesting, particularly for you. You would like that, wouldn't you, Willoughby? You would like to see the future more clearly?"

Willoughby said nothing. The man's voice was so silky, so soft, but the cold still ached in his shoulder. His mind raced. *Did this demon speaking to him really know about his friends, about Sydney?*

The man smiled.

"Fear is an art, Willoughby. Real fear doesn't happen as a sudden jolt. It is carefully cultivated, built one brick at a time. You have to really know your opponent. You have to give him a glimpse of the darkness in you. I must say, Willoughby, I don't find you very frightening."

Willoughby wanted to get away, to somehow escape the blistering gaze of this sick being, but the pain in his shoulder spread and held him pinned. The man's eyes bore into him.

"You can kill me," Willoughby gasped, "but I won't join your cult."

The man barked a laugh. "*Kill you?* Join my cult? I wouldn't dream of either. I'm not trying to recruit you. You are smart. You are gifted. I have a far *greater* proposition in mind for you." Curling his black gloved fingers, the man lowered his hand. The pain gripping Willoughby eased.

"People live, people die, Willoughby. You aren't a normal person."

"What do you mean?" Willoughby whispered.

"You are one of the bloodline. You show signs of the gift."

"Bloodline? Gift? What are you talking about?"

Stepping away from the bed, the man looked toward the outside veranda.

"You sensed my movement through time. You pulled me into a junction, effectively pulling yourself out of time and freezing the world around you. That's how I first became visible to you. You called *me*, Willoughby. I didn't call you. You have to be part of the bloodline to call through time."

"What?" Willoughby's thoughts were spinning. "*I* froze time?"

"Tell me, how detailed were the equations flashing across your mind? Did you see numbers crawling over reflective surfaces, or did the equations hover as geometric shapes?"

Willoughby was caught off guard by the sudden turn in the conversation. He didn't want to disclose anything, but his need for answers pushed him to reply.

"I saw them as number strings. I saw floating number strings, moving in wavy lines through the air. They glowed, and they floated."

The man walked over to look out the window. "In the past, the gift was called *foresight*. Men known as prophets or *seers* were blessed with an ability to read the on-going equations of time. They could predict outcomes. They could see things that were hidden. The ability is most rare, but once in a while, one is born with the gift. Most haven't the mathematical skill to understand it, to see these flashes of equation for what they are. They stab in the dark and make a few lucky predictions.

"Then there are those who are special. Born of a special blood, they have the ability to see patterns, to read the weaves of time. These are the ones whose *will* can unravel time. You are more special than the others in your group could ever understand. You are in this time for a reason, Willoughby. I mean to help you come to understand what that is."

Questions churned in Willoughby's mind. *What was this demon trying to say? What did he really want? What need could he have for the pendant? His technology was obviously far above anything H.S. could have.*

"So, we've talked." The man pulled at his gloves. Willoughby once again felt the icy grip on his chest. "I will give you time to think. I never force my hand. It's just that I'm quite good at opening minds to a different point of view, one way or another."

Willoughby felt a sudden lump in his throat. *What had he done?* Who was he placing in danger now? How could he stop this monster from orchestrating more death on his account?

The man stood and walked over to where Willoughby had shoved his breakfast cart. He tipped the cart back up and carefully arranged the food back on the plate. He pushed the cart back to the bed. "Eat your breakfast, Willoughby. You and I have unfinished business. We have a history you are just waking up to."

Willoughby tried to follow the words but it was no good. He wanted this conversation to be over. He looked frantically around the room. No curtains moved. No clock hands ticked. There were no ambient sounds at all. Strange patterns of light playing across the floor as if from a dozen suns were the only hints of movement. *What would happen if he ran for it?* Could he break out of this—what had the man called it? Could he break out of *this junction?* What if he came out in some different time? How would he get back, how could he find H.S. and Sydney again? The shadow of a bird flitted across one of the streams of light.

"H.S.!" he shouted as loud as he could muster. "Dr. O'Grady? ...*Anyone?*"

"What about Sydney?" the man smiled. "You wouldn't want to forget her pretty face. After all, she's the one who sings only for you, right? Or are you still angry with her? She did betray you, you know. You trusted her, and she betrayed you. They all did."

Willoughby stared at the man with sudden resolve. "You're messing with me." He shook his head. "I don't have to buy it."

The man licked his lips. "Yes, brave to the last..." He pushed the plate of food to the edge of the cart and stepped over to sit at the foot of the bed. "Go on! Eat up. It's still piping hot. No heat can escape in a junction out of time. While you eat, I'll tell you a story."

Willoughby didn't move.

Seeing that Willoughby had no intentions of eating, the man sighed. He folded his hands in his lap. "Suit yourself. The story goes like this: once upon a time, there was a man who had a gift. His was different from your gift. He had a way of looking at science with a cold, clever rationale devoid of emotion. He became particularly skilled in genetics. He surmised that, with the proper testing, mankind could be better, how should I say, *engineered*. When he stumbled upon a chance to pursue this testing, he took it. One day, he was smitten by the beauty of one of his *patients*. She died, of course, but not before giving birth to a son. As the son grew, sadly, he was not able to know of his parentage. But in time, this boy began to exhibit a powerful gift with numbers and equations. This brought the boy to the attention of certain, uh, acquaintances of his father. His father invited the son to join him in the bold, new world that he was creating. But, the son did not share his father's dream. He ran away from his father, and from his gift. He hid himself far away. He tried to hide the fact that he, too, had fallen in love and had a son…

"I did not tell Reese everything that I suspected about you that night months ago, Willoughby. I did not tell him that I thought you might be a grandson."

The man looked down at his black gloves. "So, you see Willoughby, there is much you don't know."

Willoughby felt as if someone had just slammed his face into a brick wall. "*No!*" he shouted, shoving the cart away so hard this time that the plate clattered to the floor. "I have no connection with you! I'm not part of any bloodline—just *get away!*"

"Unfinished business does get resolved." The man flexed his gloves and glanced around the room. "For now, you have much to think about." He leveled his cold, dark gaze on Willoughby and dipped his chin. "Until next time…"

Willoughby sensed untold cruelty in the man's eyes, but forced himself to return the stare. "The power of will," he said, his voice wavering slightly, "is something a person gives up. It's not something someone else can take."

"Oh, but you are giving it up." The man flashed a tight smile. "Pity you so seldom realize it."

A flash of light erupted from the foot of the bed and the hulking form of Gates tumbled out of it. He straightened, his shoulders hunched and his muscles rippling. He had thrown off the white smock revealing a massive chest that writhed as if snakes were hidden just under the skin.

"*He be mine?*" he hissed, barely holding the massive frame in check.

"No." The tall man looked back toward Willoughby. "Not just yet." He motioned Gates forward, heading in the direction of the hallway door. "Oh," he said, stopping and turning at the door. "As the junction collapses, you may hear echoes from your friends. Listen carefully. You could hear clues that help you find where they're hiding. Of course, I would warn you to keep a close eye on the pretty one. Sydney, too, interests me. But then, you want nothing to do with me." He held out his arms in mock disappointment. "Goodbye, Willoughby." The man turned and stepped through the door.

Willoughby was engulfed by a blinding heat as the junction collapsed. As his vision started to clear, he thought he saw for a moment a pool of dark water beyond the foot of the bed. Something massive hit against the inside wall of the room causing plaster to fall and a huge crack to appear. He heard Antonio scream. There was another voice—*it was T.K!*

"Get back! You're in no shape to fight!"

"*I won't let you face it alone!*" Antonio's voice was weak, but firm.

Willoughby searched the fading light. "Antonio? T.K.!"

There was no response. A second later, the room was still. Light in the room returned to that of normal early morning sunshine. It was strangely quiet, though. Willoughby noted the tipped over coffee pot on the floor, steaming. The steam seemed thicker and more plentiful than it should have been. It seemed to be taking on a shape. He heard a hissing voice.

"You come before me, Queen of the Desert, alone, James Arthur?" a high, female voice cackled.

The steam suddenly solidified. It twisted to look at Willoughby as the fully formed head of a cobra. Pulling dark coils from the dark coffee seeping out onto the floor, the head reared back, opened its fanged mouth, and it struck. Willoughby screamed, throwing a pillow up to protect his face. The apparition vanished. Sydney ran up the hall.

"*Willoughby, what's wrong?*"

"Stay out!" Willoughby screamed, not sure if the junction had completely faded. "Get away from here, Sydney! I only want H.S.!"

A nurse hurried up behind Sydney.

"Get the director!" Willoughby shouted at her.

The nurse stared a moment, bewildered, then hurried off. Sydney stared, stunned and a little hurt. She took another step into the room. "Willoughby, I—"

"*Get out, Sydney!*" Willoughby shouted. "Don't give me your attitude—just listen to me for once! Is that so hard? I don't have time right now to spell it out for you—*get H.S.!*"

Sydney's face clouded. She whirled, biting her lip, and left. Willoughby caught a glance of Dr. O'Grady, who had ambled up behind her, probably attracted by the screaming. She grabbed him by the arm and herded him before her. When the two were gone, Willoughby noted that the sound in the room had also returned to normal. He pushed to the edge of his bed, reaching with shaking feet for his slippers. He could barely get the feet in once his toes found them. He was trembling almost uncontrollably. He didn't want to spend one more minute in this room than he had to. Pulling a pair of jeans and a t-shirt on, he heard heavy footsteps on the stairs. H.S. stormed into the room.

"What the devil, Willoughby?" the panting man said, peering around the room.

"Yeah," Willoughby said, pulling the shirt gingerly down over his bandages. "The devil." He motioned toward the veranda and led H.S. out of the room.

32

The Requiem

The story tumbled out of him in torrents, his voice rising and falling, words crashing against each other like waves breaking on a rocky coast. He had to get it out—not analyze or emotionalize it—just *get it out.* It was as if the mere act of telling what he had seen, what he felt, what he heard, might somehow free him of its implications. Perhaps he thought that by telling H.S., he would see how ridiculous it was. *Zombies? Eyes that could freeze you in place?* How could anyone believe such rubbish? But the telling only made it that much more real.

He had seen with his own eyes a man appear out of nowhere and disappear to nowhere, without any doorway or technical aid visible. He had watched this same man command a white-eyed zombie beast that he had once known as the man Gates. Could these have been mere tricks of the light? Had they been delusions? When the torrent ended, he leaned on the rail, biting his lip, trying not to cry. H.S. would probably think it was all a dream— a horrible, bad dream. Only he knew it wasn't. He knew what he saw, what he sensed. He couldn't run away from it. He shivered, despite the growing warmth of the sun.

H.S. watched him closely. He had listened with rapt attention. He had stood rigid by the rail, and now looked away, peering intently at the sea. When he looked back, he raised a hand and put it gently onto Willoughby's good shoulder.

"You're right. This, this visit was meant to rattle you, Willoughby."

"Do you think the guy's for real? What about his claim to be my, my *grandfather?*"

H.S. squinted into the rising sun. A dozen yachts and sailboats were bobbing in the turquoise bay. "Something has latched onto you. It's trying to manipulate you. I wouldn't trust anything he said. This was bound to happen with your, your gifts. I hadn't expected it so soon, but the man, or demon, or whatever we want to call him, understands the significance of your abilities. If you're asking do I believe in the existence of a single devil, and do I believe this being could be the focus of all evil worship, not just the head of a stray cult, I would answer, '*no.*' Don't get me wrong; I believe there are many shades of dark hearts, and this, uh, *creature* certainly wants to frighten us. I simply believe that these kinds of creatures thrive on misinformation. Their powers, as considerable as they may be, are easily magnified by the imagination. They become greater, or more fearsome—even invincible—with the telling, until myth, and the fear myth brings, becomes their greatest weapon. Fear plays into a bully's hand.

"Let me tell you what I believe is more important for you to hear. I believe, Willoughby, that good always triumphs in the end. I believe order is more powerful than chaos—that light will trump darkness every time. This doesn't mean we'll never face moments that frighten us, that bring pain and hardship. What it means is that we find balance in the journey, that our good moments transcend those that are horrible and sad. Thus, we learn to see *behind* the darkness. Does that make sense to you?"

H.S. pulled his arm away with an affectionate pat. He stepped back to the rail, leaning out over it. Willoughby gave a short nod. He waited a moment and then spoke.

"So, what now?"

H.S. turned back to face him. He folded his arms.

"Willoughby, I'm not your father, but I do know a thing or two about bullies. You never beat a bully by playing his game. I would say, as hard as this may be, that you should swallow your fear for now. Don't spend your time dwelling on what this meant, or what he meant by that. He wants you to be confused. Forget about this conversation until you can think back on it with a clear, calculating eye. In the meantime, work with me to learn more about your gift and help me find the team. Each good thing you do can only frustrate someone who wishes to use you for ill. In time, I suppose he'll show up again. The best thing for you is to be ready."

Willoughby looked up fiercely. "This guy travels in time without any visible technology. He claims to be hundreds of years old and has an army of zombies at his beck and call. He's watching me and maybe Sydney. How can I be '*ready?*'"

"Prepare to go on the offense."

"This is no ordinary bully."

"So? The good you do doesn't have to be ordinary either."

Willoughby looked out over the bay, considering. He had to admit that talking to H.S. had calmed him considerably. "That's easy to say, but how do you just let something like this go?"

"You fill your mind with other things—other thoughts, other projects, other duties. The mind cannot live in a void. So, fill it. You'll know you're ready to look back on this incident when you start to question the mechanics of *why?* Then, you'll move on to *how?* The Bible says, *'Ask and ye shall receive.'* Engage your mind in analysis and discovery. As layers of mystery are stripped away, you uncover knowledge and opportunity. An active mind is the enemy of manipulation. The more you understand, the less you fear. Let's try it; why would this man want to frighten you?"

"So I'd join him?"

"Perhaps…but why the interest in the pendant? Why the talk of your 'bloodline?'"

Willoughby shrugged. "I don't know. I asked the same question, but couldn't get an answer."

"Ah! There we are! Avoidance of the question tells us what?"

"That he didn't want me to know the answer," Willoughby said, "or," he added, warming to the process, "that he didn't completely know the answer?"

"Whoever, or whatever this man is," H.S. said, turning to face him again, "he has a technology far beyond what we possess. But it does not appear that he is omnipotent, hence his desire for the pendant. He has limitations—rules he must abide by. What if we discover them?"

"Then we learn how to defeat him."

"Possibly," H.S. said smiling; "very possibly."

Already, Willoughby was starting to feel like himself again. His mind was engaged. His muscles had stopped shaking.

"I need to learn more about this guy. Then I can stand up to him. Then I can face him."

"That's the spirit! Face him down! Only then will you be able to face yourself, which is the more important thing." H.S. grinned, patting Willoughby again on the shoulder. "You're not alone in this battle, Willoughby. You have a team, and, if I may say so, a good one." He breathed in the crisp morning air before continuing.

"You and Sydney will move to my personal yacht tonight. From there, we will begin to explore this unusual gift of yours. I think you know, Willoughby, that your visitor spoke the truth when he noted how rare your gift is. Of course he has an interest in you. When you better understand your gift, you'll know why. You need to better understand yourself, too. If you don't understand yourself—what you believe, who you are, what you want to do with your gift—just understanding the gift may not help you. You could be tricked into using it in ways you never intended. Knowledge is freedom, but freedom is only the beginning of wisdom. It can just as easily lead to chaos as to peace." He pointed to Willoughby's chest. "Here is where you will find what really matters. Not out there." He motioned to the wide expanse of the world. "Everything out there is simply tool or distraction."

Willoughby pointed back to the room with a good-natured grimace. "That was a powerful distraction," he mumbled. H.S. gave him a broad smile.

"Yes, and many of them are. Now," he clapped his hands together. "Did you have any breakfast? I saw the remains of your plate scattered across the floor. How about I have a piping hot breakfast brought out to us on the veranda?"

"Thanks, but I'm not really hungry right now." Willoughby sighed, looking out over the bay. H.S. watched him.

"Well," he mused. "You may be interested to know that, while I was being alerted to your needs, a certain young lady, wielding her violin like a machine gun, about trampled me to death while storming out the door. She did not seem to be a happy camper."

"She was pretty mad?"

"Well, let's just say I don't think she'll be playing Schubert. You know this hasn't been easy for her either, Willoughby. I think she needs you—more, even, than she may know. For some reason, you two seem to need each other."

"Any idea where she went?"

"Oh, yes," H.S. said conspiratorially. "She seems to be spending a good deal of her time in a little cove just over that ridge." He gave Willoughby a light pat on the back. "Now, I'll be downstairs having a decadent feast of hot cakes and omelet and you go try to fetch her. When the two of you are packed, we'll leave straight for the yacht together. Agreed?"

Willoughby nodded. "Sure," he said softly.

H.S. gave him another light pat on the arm before leaving. Willoughby stood at the rail, peering over the capping waves, thinking of the things H.S. had said. After several long moments, he turned, eyeing the far side of the veranda. A series of narrow, protected steps led down to the ground level. He made his way to them and started down, hugging the side of the white stucco building, until the steps spilled out onto a patch of green grass. He continued along a rolling sidewalk which bordered the grass over a hill. As the hill dipped down between two rows of apartments, he saw a sliver of pinkish sand. When he reached the sand, he took off his shoes and walked around the edge of a shallow dune to the beachfront. Following the narrow stretch of beach around a gentle rise, he came to the cove. It was nestled between the apartment buildings on one side, and a curving series of cliffs on the other. The sandstone cliffs were at least 100 feet high at the crest. They fell off sharply, dipping down to the row of beachfront apartments where the sliver of beach began.

Willoughby looked out over the sparkling water. The cove was punctuated by a half-dozen jutting rock structures. The sandy crescent of beach was maybe 60 feet long.

He searched the sand carefully. It was deserted. He turned to note a sailboat anchored at an arched rock about 90 or so yards out to sea. He did not see Sydney. He scanned the cove again. It had taken him almost a half hour to make his way to this spot, and rivulets of sweat were pouring down his cheeks. The sand was starting to feel hot, and the water looked inviting. He waded a few feet in. That's when he heard the sad, lilting melody of violin music. It was played in perfect sync with the crash of the waves. He squinted, shading his eyes.

Sydney had waded about fifteen yards out and was standing by an outcropping of black volcanic rock. The water came all the way to her waist when waves came in, but sank to about her knees when they went out. She appeared to have her eyes closed, completely engrossed in her music. Willoughby stood for a long moment, listening to the spiraling tune. It seemed to crescendo as each larger wave crashed over the rock, sending bursts of spray into the air. Finally, as the music peaked, he began to wade quietly through the water toward her. He could see that

Sydney was wearing jeans and a strange midnight-blue blouse that had long sleeves. He hadn't noticed what she was wearing up in the room. He had been too concerned with getting her out—away from the danger. The sleeves flared at the ends so that they actually touched the water. Her hair was whipping in the breeze, and he could hear her bangles and bracelets jangling as she played long before he could see them. At least half a dozen necklaces were draped around her neck and he knew without asking that she wore at least one or two ankle bracelets. She held her violin high and still as the final notes of her composition echoed off of the cliff face. He had stopped about a yard or two behind her. She slowly folded her arms, hugging the violin to her chest to protect it from the waves.

Though his jeans felt like they weighed twenty-pounds, and he was beginning to feel the exertion of the hike, Willoughby moved as quietly as he could until he came up beside her. She opened her eyes, a sad, far-off look focused on the sea's horizon. He did not look at her, but focused his own eyes in the same direction.

"That sounded really…final," he said.

"Yeah," she answered. "It's my requiem. Now I wait for a huge wave to come, crash over this rock, and bury me, engulfing my form and sweeping me under. I will disappear below the waves and be swept out to the heart of the lonely sea. In the fading dusk, they'll find my violin, battered and washed up on the sand."

"What about you?" Willoughby said, still staring forward.

"They will never find me. I will be consumed by my sisters of the sea."

"Is that…necessary?"

"Of course. It's a requiem. Don't ask stupid questions."

"Well," Willoughby squinted forward. "I'll give you this. It's dramatic."

Sydney cracked just the hint of a smile, though she did not change her gaze. "Yeah."

"Kind of depressing, though," Willoughby added.

"Yeah."

"I think a good swig of kava could do you some good about now."

Sydney's stare finally broke. She lowered her head, trying not to snort as she let go a snicker. She quickly recovered. "So, you're here to apologize?"

"Uh, sort of," Willoughby said. He looked over at her. "But can I do it back on the beach where my clothes can dry off, or do we need to stand out here all day? This water is *cold*."

"I was hoping you would say that," Sydney admitted, breaking into a smile and turning back toward the beach. Once they reached the shore, they found a small outcrop of rock to sit on. They squeezed what water they could out of their jeans and shirts.

"What's that blouse?" Willoughby asked, watching Sydney carefully squeeze out the sleeves.

"It's a gypsy blouse—the kind wild pirates wear."

"Wild pirates?"

"Well, women pirates."

"So, you're a wild woman pirate now? With a violin?"

Sydney didn't answer. She only smiled. Willoughby got the sense that she was waiting for him to begin his apology. "That whole requiem thing was kind of dumb, you know."

"Oh, really?" Sydney responded. "Stupid like, '*With your chest—I mean, in your chest—I mean, the chest all around, touching?*'" She had intoned his slurred voice perfectly.

"I said that?"

Sydney looked at him, her eyebrows raised and her eyes sparkling. Willoughby blushed. "Well, you do remember I was sick, right?"

"Are you saying you don't like my chest?"

"No," Willoughby looked away. "Uhm, not at all. Your chest is, uhm, fine—really good." He couldn't fight the grin on his face. "Really full and—"

"Shhh…" she said, putting a finger to his lips. "Maybe you shouldn't be talking right now…"

He looked over at her. Her eyes were still sparkling. Her lips were spread in a slight smile. *Did she want him to kiss her?* For a moment, he panicked. He stared at his feet. Luckily, the moment passed. The wind tousled Sydney's hair. "Uh," he started. "I, I didn't mean to yell at you. There was a reason I told you to get out of the room."

He told her the whole story—about the encounter with the tall man who called himself Beelzebub, the encounter with Gates, and the discussion with H.S. He told her everything. She listened quietly, not saying a word. When he was through, she stared at him, and then out over the choppy blue of the sea.

"So you don't hate me for not telling you about your father."

"No," Willoughby said, and he realized that he meant it. "I didn't tell anybody about seeing floating numbers in the air initially, or about seeing the tall man."

"Who do you think he is? *What* do you think he is?"

Willoughby leaned back. "I don't know. But he seems to have interest in us both, so, maybe we should stick together."

Sydney smiled, sneaking a glance over at him again. "Okay." After a moment, the smile faded. She looked away. "This has all come upon us so fast. Everything has changed."

It was Willoughby's turn to scour the cove. For some reason, he felt a stinging in his eyes. "It's like I woke up in the middle of a nightmare, only it's *real!* It's my life! And the stakes aren't just life or death, they're like, you're the hero, here—go save the world." He rubbed his eyes. "I may be good at math, but how is that going to stop this guy? How is that going to help me find out about my Dad, help us find our friends? I feel like suddenly, everybody is looking at me, and that's," he sniffed, "that's a lot worse than just facing death."

Sydney was watching him. She slipped her arm into his, looking away as she softly took his hand. "You ever heard of the great stage director, Vsevelod Meyerhold?"

Willoughby sniffed. "Uh, no."

"He was perhaps the greatest stage director of the 20th century. As a contemporary of Stanislavski, Tolstoy, and Chekov, and teacher of Sergei Eisenstein, he changed the face of modern theater."

"I'm familiar with Tolstoy and Chekov. Wasn't Eisenstein a famous film director?"

"Yeah," Sydney looked over at Willoughby with a quick smile. The wind was toying with her hair and the sun shone golden on her face.

"So, what happened to this Meyerhold guy? Why haven't I ever heard of him?"

Sydney frowned. "His wife was brutally murdered—a woman he loved more than life itself—and then he was arrested and accused of being a spy. He was shot by a firing squad and all of his works and papers were ordered to be burned. What we know about him is only because Eisenstein and a few other friends secreted his works away, hiding them in the walls of their houses."

Willoughby looked over. "And this story helps because…?"

"Well, it's a fascinating story, set against the backdrop of the Russian revolution, but my point is that, in a letter to his wife, Meyerhold spoke symbolically about the storms that used to swoop down on him when he was a little boy. He never forgot them, and saw in them some of what one experiences in life. He described them as terrible and yet beautiful at the same time. What he was saying is that real life often has two faces, both staring at us at the same time. We have to choose which face we see."

Willoughby smiled. "So, no more requiems?"

Sydney tapped his arm. "Promise—not for a while, anyway."

"There *are* good things about this trip. I got to meet you. I know more about Russian theater. I, I know what it feels like to be crammed into your chest."

Sydney punched him.

"Come on," he yelled, standing up. He turned and shouted at the waves. "YOU DON'T SCARE US, BEELZEBUB! We WILL find our friends—so there!"

Sydney jumped to her feet. "Yeah, and we're not afraid of you, you old bully, whoever you are!" she shouted at the top of her lungs. "We've got sunsets to see, and beautiful music to write, and problems to solve, and a lot of dramatic stuff that still needs to happen—*with* musical accompaniment!"

"Yeah, and good, very *dramatic* musical accompaniment!"

"And we have family we need to find, and family members we need to learn to talk to!" Sydney added. "So…"

"So," Willoughby added, "bring it on!"

"Yeah! Give us your best shot!" Sydney yelled.

People in the white apartment buildings that lined the ridge and the top of the cliffs were probably searching the waters to see who these young people were yelling at—or what. The two of them screamed for a good five minutes, brandishing taunts and throwing rocks. Then, arm in arm, hand in hand, they turned and headed back along the beach, following the footprints they had earlier made, their feet somehow lighter on the sand.

CPSIA information can be obtained at www.ICGtesting.com
Printed in the USA
BVOW041730120613

323069BV00001B/1/P

9 781600 478642